ALIEN SEX

OFF LIMITS

TALES OF ALIEN SEX

EDITED BY
ELLEN DATLOW

ACE BOOKS, NEW YORK

This Ace Book contains the complete text of the original hardcover edition. It has been completely reset in a typeface designed for easy reading, and was printed from new film.

OFF LIMITS: TALES OF ALIEN SEX

An Ace Book / published by arrangement with
St. Martin's Press, Inc.

PRINTING HISTORY
St. Martin's Press hardcover edition / February 1996
Ace mass-market edition / April 1997

The Putnam Berkley World Wide Web site address is
http://www.berkley.com/berkley

ISBN: 0-441-00436-9

ACE®
Ace Books are published by The Berkley Publishing Group,
200 Madison Avenue, New York, NY 10016.
ACE and the "A" design are trademarks
belonging to Charter Communications, Inc.

PRINTED IN THE UNITED STATES OF AMERICA

10 9 8 7 6 5 4 3 2 1

FOR MERRILEE HEIFETZ

CONTENTS

FOREWORD

ROBERT SILVERBERG

THE ESSENTIAL THING TO KEEP IN MIND ABOUT SEX IS THAT
its inherent purpose is to bring two alien beings together to
create a third being different from them both.

I'm talking strict biology here, of course, taking things right
down to the teleological nitty-gritty. Whatever sex may happen
to mean to you or you or you or me, the inarguable fact remains that the whole sexual thing was programmed into most
living organisms above the level of viruses and bacteria for
the primary sake of bringing about an exchange of genetic
material between two individuals who belong to the same species but otherwise may have very little in common—who resemble each other physically in a certain superficial way, but
who have different identities and perceptual equipment, a
whole array of different secondary physiological characteris-
tics, and even, to some extent, different kinds of internal organs. (Some different external ones, too!)

That's really at the bottom of it all, you know: moving
those gametes around, getting sperm and egg together, bringing about fertilization, calling into being a single-celled zygote
that carries one set of chromosomes from its male parent and

another from its female one. If all goes well, cells divide, the zygote expands to become an embryo, and in time a new individual comes forth, carrying a mix of chromosomes that will cause it to resemble its parents in most major respects but to be, nonetheless, something new and unique.

This procedure, this business of sexual reproduction, is high-priority stuff indeed in the evolutionary scale of values. Without it, without the constant shuffling of genetic information that the meeting of gametes creates, species would never vary from one generation to the next. The newborn organisms would be exact replicas of their progenitors—carbon copies, xeroxes, backup disks, whatever metaphor you want to use. Exact replicas, that is, except for the inevitable entropic degradation that eventually would set in, comparable to the blurriness that occurs when you photocopy something that is already a tenth generation copy of the original document. There would be no evolution, no recombination of genetic matter to bring new and perhaps improved models of the organism into existence. There would only be the slow, steady slide for generation after generation toward looking like something that has been passed through the photocopy machine of ten different offices.

Nature takes the concept of sexual reproduction so seriously that it has programmed all these interesting pleasure-syndromata into us to make sure that we keep on doing it. No matter how we think about the need to have gametes meet and shuffle their chromosomes together, we tend to keep on engaging in sexual acts because doing so is, for most of us, an extremely enjoyable thing. (And, because we are highly evolved beings as a result of thousands of generations of combination and recombination of chromosomes, we have in relatively recent times cleverly figured out ways of receiving the pleasure without following through with the biological consequences. The childless but sexually active heterosexuals of the world, the homosexuals of various sorts, and many purely solitary folk as well, have all separated themselves from the business of gametes and zygotes but most assuredly are still paying attention to those hardwired pleasure impulses that were installed in them at the moment of conception to keep those moments of conception coming along.)

You see, I hope, where this line of reasoning is heading. Sex is an innate drive, put there for significant biological reasons; it impels each organism in a centrifugal fashion, outward from the center of its own biological boundaries to seek physical union with an organism that is fundamentally different from itself in many ways—that is, in fact, an alien being with its own identity, behavior patterns, and physical form; and human beings, although they are driven by this innate need just as much as nematodes and fruit flies and salamanders are, are such complex and ornery creatures that they have extended the definition of what is an acceptable sexual partner far beyond the innately prescribed one of same-species-other-sex. As the stories in this book demonstrate, we are capable of reaching quite far afield indeed.

But always—whether the love object is the girl or boy next door or some sleek aquatic being native to Betelgeuse XII—the process involves opening the boundaries of one's being to something alien, something that is not-oneself, something that differs from oneself in a fundamental way. The chromosomes tell the tale. There is only one of me on this planet, and only one of you, because nobody else has my particular mix of genes, and nobody else has yours, and therefore we are really alien beings in respect to each other. Yet we each have something that the other wants; and so we come together, in trepidation and hope, attempting to transcend the boundaries that separate us from each other. Sometimes the effort is successful, sometimes not. In any case, it remains fundamentally true that *all* sexual encounters are meetings between aliens who must transcend the barriers of their alienness if they are going to attain any kind of union—whether they be those kids holding hands outside the movie theater or Mrs. Tompkins getting it on with the thing from the Aldebaran system during the interstellar cruise. As the stories you are about to read will demonstrate.

INTRODUCTION

ALIEN SEX, PUBLISHED IN 1990, WAS NOT SO MUCH ABOUT aliens and sex but rather about human sexuality in all its strange forms and how men and women interact. It included about half reprints—classics from between 1968 and 1985, and half original stories written around 1989. Science fiction has traditionally been a bit hesitant about dealing with sexual and gender themes. There have always been notable exceptions—Philip José Farmer's "The Lovers" (1952), Theodore Sturgeon's *Venus Plus X*, and the writings of James Tiptree, Jr., Ursula K. Le Guin, Samuel R. Delany, Gardner Dozois, Joanna Russ, Brian W. Aldiss, and John Varley. But in the past ten years, science fiction seems to have become a hothouse of speculation on sexuality and gender. This may be a result of the AIDS crisis or the extraordinary breakthroughs in bioengineering; for whatever reason, there are more writers than ever before exploring and questioning sexuality in their work. Nicola Griffith, Michael Blumlein, Eleanor Arnason, Geoff Ryman, and Richard Calder are just a few of the newer ones.

In contrast to *Alien Sex*, more of the stories in *Off Limits* deal with the physical dangers of sex. There appears to me a more *overt* awareness of the AIDS crisis and how it affects our relations to one another. At least four stories in *Off Limits* take place in societies beset by sexual plagues and focus on the personal and political ramifications of these plagues for individuals and society at large. Paranoia looms large, it brings out the worst in people, and generally, those in power have not made what most of us would consider the right decisions dealing with the crises. Instead of finding cures they blame the victims (sound familiar?). Brian Stableford, Elizabeth Hand, and Mike O'Driscoll have all imagined worlds in which the worst future has happened and adjustments have been made—usually to the detriment of females.

One thread running through the stories in *Off Limits* is the "prostitute as protagonist"—the outsider, as independent woman, as whore; prostitution as a means to avoid entanglements. Who has the power in these relationships and why? Is prostitution honorable? Why do men (and occasionally women) feel they need to pay for sex? No matter one's views, the oldest profession is inextricably tied to gender politics and is here to stay—although some writers see future prostitutes biologically enhanced with special pheromones or as living dolls. Another common thread is the third world serving as fodder for the more "civilized" world, with individuals using the beautiful and alien in unclean ways.

The four reprints run the gamut from the innocence and experimentation of the sixties and seventies (Silverberg's "The Reality Trip" and Delany's "Aye, and Gomorrah . . .") to radical feminism as a political force (Ings's "Grand Prix") to right-wing fanatics who long to, and who have the power to, turn back the clock on sexual freedom (Hand's "In the Month of Athyr").

In general, I have found that most of the material submitted to both anthologies was tinged with a paranoid view of male-female relations. What's especially interesting is that both men and women are looking at the issue with jaundiced eyes. As for the stories that actually have aliens in them (by Susan Wade and Roberta Lannes), the question arises: how can we know what aliens want when we can't even agree on what humans want from each other in a relationship? There are some lighter-hearted stories here, but again, as in *Alien Sex*, most share a dim view of the present and near future as we fumble toward an answer to the question ''what do women/men want?'' Martha Soukup's, Gwyneth Jones's, and Lisa Tuttle's stories seem to indicate that women want just what men think they want—power as symbolized by the penis and the beard. Or perhaps women don't know what they want. The stories are disturbing and seem to ask whether men and women can ever communicate? Or will we all remain alien to each other? Let's hope that this fictional analysis of the problems confronting male-female relations leads to reconciliation in real life.

THE REALITY TRIP

ROBERT SILVERBERG

I AM A RECLAMATION PROJECT FOR HER. SHE LIVES ON MY floor of the hotel, a dozen rooms down the hall: a lady poet, private income. No, that makes her sound too old, a middle-aged eccentric. Actually she is no more than thirty. Taller than I am, with long kinky brown hair and a sharp, bony nose that has a bump on the bridge. Eyes are very glossy. A studied raggedness about her dress; carefully chosen shabby clothes. I am in no position really to judge the sexual attractiveness of Earthfolk but I gather from remarks made by men living here that she is not considered good-looking. I pass her often on my way to my room. She smiles fiercely at me. Saying to herself, no doubt, You poor lonely man. Let me help you bear the burden of your unhappy life. Let me show you the meaning of love, for I too know what it is like to be alone.

Or words to that effect. She's never actually said any such thing. But her intentions are transparent. When she sees me, a kind of hunger comes into her eyes, part maternal, part (I

1

guess) sexual, and her face takes on a wild crazy intensity. Burning with emotion. Her name is Elizabeth Cooke. "Are you fond of poetry, Mr. Knecht?" she asked me this morning, as we creaked upward together in the ancient elevator. And an hour later she knocked at my door. "Something for you to read," she said. "I wrote them." A sheaf of large yellow sheets, stapled at the top; poems printed in smeary blue mimeography. *The Reality Trip,* the collection was headed. *Limited Edition: 125 Copies.* "You can keep it if you like," she explained. "I've got lots more." She was wearing bright corduroy slacks and a flimsy pink shawl through which her breasts plainly showed. Small tapering breasts, not very functional-looking. When she saw me studying them her nostrils flared momentarily and she blinked her eyes three times swiftly. Tokens of lust?

I read the poems. Is it fair for me to offer judgment on them? Even though I've lived on this planet eleven of its years, even though my command of colloquial English is quite good, do I really comprehend the inner life of poetry? I thought they were all quite bad. Earnest, plodding poems, capturing what they call slices of life. The world around her, the cruel, brutal, unloving city. Lamenting the failure of the people to open to one another. The title poem began this way:

> *He was on the reality trip. Big black man,*
> *bloodshot eyes, bad teeth. Eisenhower jacket,*
> *frayed. Smell of cheap wine. I guess a knife in*
> *his pocket. Looked at me mean. Criminal*
> *record. Rape, child-beating, possession of drugs.*
> *In his head saying, slavemistress bitch, and me*
> *in my head saying, black brother, let's freak in*
> *together, let's trip on love—*

And so forth. Warm, direct emotion; but is the urge to love all wounded things a sufficient center for poetry? I don't know. I did put her poems through the scanner and transmit them to Homeworld, although I doubt they'll learn much from them about Earth. It would flatter Elizabeth to know that while she has few readers here, she has acquired some ninety light-years away. But of course I can't tell her that.

She came back a short while ago. "Did you like them?" she asked.

"Very much. You have such sympathy for those who suffer."

I think she expected me to invite her in. I was careful not to look at her breasts this time.

The hotel is on West 23rd Street. It must be over a hundred years old; the façade is practically baroque and the interior shows a kind of genteel decay. The place has a bohemian tradition. Most of its guests are permanent residents and many of them are artists, novelists, playwrights, and such. I have lived here nine years. I know a number of the residents by name, and they me, but I have discouraged any real intimacy, naturally, and everyone has respected that choice. I do not invite others into my room. Sometimes I let myself be invited to visit theirs, since one of my responsibilities on this world is to get to know something of the way Earthfolk live and think. Elizabeth is the first to attempt to cross the invisible barrier of privacy I surround myself with. I'm not sure how I'll handle that. She moved in about three years ago; her attentions became noticeable perhaps ten months back, and for the last five or six weeks she's been a great nuisance. Some kind of confrontation is inevitable: either I must tell her to leave me alone, or I will find myself drawn into a situation impossible to tolerate. Perhaps she'll find someone else to feel even sorrier for, before it comes to that.

My daily routine rarely varies. I rise at seven. First Feeding. Then I clean my skin (my outer one, the Earthskin, I mean) and dress. From eight to ten I transmit data to Homeworld. Then I go out for the morning field trip: talking to people, buying newspapers, often some library research. At one I return to my room. Second Feeding. I transmit data from two to five. Out again, perhaps to the theater, to a motion picture, to a political meeting. I must soak up the flavor of this planet. Often to saloons; I am equipped for ingesting alcohol, though of course I must get rid of it before it has been in my body very long, and I drink and listen and sometimes argue. At midnight back to my room. Third Feeding. Transmit data from one to four in the morning. Then three hours of sleep, and at

seven the cycle begins anew. It is a comforting schedule. I
don't know how many agents Homeworld has on Earth, but I
like to think that I'm one of the most diligent and useful. I
miss very little. I've done good service, and, as they say here,
hard work is its own reward. I won't deny that I hate the
physical discomfort of it and frequently give way to real despair over my isolation from my own kind. Sometimes I even
think of asking for a transfer to Homeworld. But what would
become of me there? What services could I perform? I have
shaped my life to one end: that of dwelling among the Earthfolk and reporting on their ways. If I give that up, I am nothing.

Of course there is the physical pain. Which is considerable.
   The gravitational pull of Earth is almost twice that of Homeworld. It makes for a leaden life for me. My inner organs
always sagging against the lower rim of my carapace. My
muscles cracking with strain. Every movement a willed effort.
My heart in constant protest. In my eleven years I have, as
one might expect, adapted somewhat to the conditions; I have
toughened, I have thickened. I suspect that if I were trans-
ported instantly to Homeworld now I would be quite giddy,
baffled by the lightness of everything. I would leap and soar
and stumble, and might even miss this crushing pull of Earth.
Yet I doubt that. I suffer here; at all times the weight oppresses
me. Not to sound too self-pitying about it, I knew the conditions in advance. I was placed in simulated Earth gravity when
I volunteered, and was given a chance to withdraw, and I
decided to go anyway. Not realizing that a week under double
gravity is not the same thing as a lifetime. I could always have
stepped out of the simulation chamber. Not here. The eternal
drag on every molecule of me. The pressure. My flesh is always in mourning.
   And the outer body I must wear. This cunning disguise.
Forever to be swaddled in thick masses of synthetic flesh,
smothering me, engulfing me. The soft slippery slap of it
against the self within. The elaborate framework that holds it
erect, by which I make it move: a forest of struts and braces
and servoactuators and cables, in the midst of which I must
unendingly huddle, atop my little platform in the gut. Adopt-

ing one or another of various uncomfortable positions, constantly shifting and squirming, now jabbing myself on some awkwardly placed projection, now trying to make my inflexible body flexibly to bend. Seeing the world by periscope through mechanical eyes. Enwombed in this mountain of meat. It is a clever thing; it must look convincingly human, since no one has ever doubted me, and it ages ever so slightly from year to year, greying a bit at the temples, thickening a bit at the paunch. It walks. It talks. It takes in food and drink, when it has to. (And deposits them in a removable pouch near my leftmost arm.) And I within it. The hidden chess player; the invisible rider. If I dared, I would periodically strip myself of this cloak of flesh and crawl around my room in my own guise. But it is forbidden. Eleven years now and I have not been outside my protoplasmic housing. I feel sometimes that it has come to adhere to me, that it is no longer merely around me but by now a part of me.

In order to eat I must unseal it at the middle, a process that takes many minutes. Three times a day I unbutton myself so that I can stuff the food concentrates into my true gullet. Faulty design, I call that. They could just as easily have arranged it so I could pop the food into my Earthmouth and have it land in my own digestive tract. I suppose the newer models have that. Excretion is just as troublesome for me; I unseal, reach in, remove the cubes of waste, seal my skin again. Down the toilet with them. A nuisance.

And the loneliness! To look at the stars and know Homeworld is out there somewhere! To think of all the others, mating, chanting, dividing, abstracting, while I live out my days in this crumbling hotel on an alien planet, tugged down by gravity and locked within a cramped counterfeit body—always alone, always pretending that I am not what I am and that I am what I am not, spying, questioning, recording, reporting, coping with the misery of solitude, hunting for the comforts of philosophy—

In all of this there is only one real consolation, aside, that is, from the pleasure of knowing that I am of service to Homeworld. The atmosphere of New York City grows grimier every year. The streets are full of crude vehicles belching undigested hydrocarbons. To the Earthfolk, this stuff is pollution, and they mutter worriedly about it. To me it is joy. It is the only touch of Homeworld here: that sweet soup of organic compounds adrift in the air. It intoxicates me. I walk down the street breathing deeply, sucking the good molecules through my false nostrils to my authentic lungs. The natives must think I'm insane. Tripping on auto exhaust! Can I get arrested for overenthusiastic public breathing? Will they pull me in for a mental checkup?

Elizabeth Cooke continues to waft wistful attentions at me. Smiles in the hallway. Hopeful gleam of the eyes. "Perhaps we can have dinner together some night soon, Mr. Knecht. I know we'd have so much to talk about. And maybe you'd like to see the new poems I've been doing." She is trembling. Eyelids flickering tensely; head held rigid on long neck. I know she sometimes has men in her room, so it can't be out of loneliness or frustration that she's cultivating me. And I doubt that she's sexually attracted to my outer self. I believe I'm being accurate when I say that women don't consider me sexually magnetic. No, she loves me because she pities me. The sad shy bachelor at the end of the hall, dear unhappy Mr. Knecht; can I bring some brightness into his dreary life? And so forth. I think that's how it is. Will I be able to go on avoiding her? Perhaps I should move to another part of the city. But I've lived here so long; I've grown accustomed to this hotel. Its easy ways do much to compensate for the hardships of my post. And my familiar room. The huge many-paned window; the cracked green floor tiles in the bathroom; the lumpy patterns of replastering on the wall above my bed. The high ceiling; the funny chandelier. Things that I love. But of course I can't let her try to start an affair with me. We are supposed to observe Earthfolk, not to get involved with them. Our disguise is not that difficult to penetrate at close range. I must keep her away somehow. Or flee.

Incredible! There is another of us in this very hotel!

As I learned through accident. At one this afternoon, returning from my morning travels: Elizabeth in the lobby, as though lying in wait for me, chatting with the manager. Rides up with me in the elevator. Her eyes looking into mine.

"Sometimes I think you're afraid of me," she begins. "You mustn't be. That's the great tragedy of human life, that people shut themselves up behind walls of fear and never let anyone through, anyone who might care about them and be warm to them. You've got no reason to be afraid of me." I do, but how to explain that to her? To sidestep prolonged conversation and possible entanglement I get off the elevator one floor below the right one. Let her think I'm visiting a friend. Or a mistress. I walk slowly down the hall to the stairs, using up time, waiting so she will be in her room before I go up. A maid bustles by me. She thrusts her key into a door on the left: a rare *faux pas* for the usually competent help here, she forgets to knock before going in to make up the room. The door opens and the occupant, inside, stands revealed. A stocky, muscular man, naked to the waist. "Oh, excuse me," the maid gasps, and backs out, shutting the door. But I have seen. My eyes are quick. The hairy chest is split, a dark gash three inches wide and some eleven inches long, beginning between the nipples and going past the navel. Visible within is the black shiny surface of a Homeworld carapace. My countryman, opening up for Second Feeding. Dazed, numbed, I stagger to the stairs and pull myself step by leaden step to my floor. No sign of Elizabeth. I stumble into my room and throw the bolt. Another of us here? Well, why not? I'm not the only one. There may be hundreds in New York alone. But in the same hotel? I remember, now, I've seen him occasionally: a silent, dour man, tense, hunted-looking, unsociable. No doubt I appear the same way to others. Keep the world at a distance. I don't know his name or what he is supposed to do for a living.

We are forbidden to make contact with fellow Homeworlders except in case of extreme emergency. Isolation is a necessary condition of our employment. I may not introduce myself to him; I may not seek his friendship. It is worse now for me, knowing that he is here, than when I was entirely alone. The things we could reminisce about! The friends we might have in common! We could reinforce one another's endurance of the gravity, the discomfort of our disguises, the vile climate. But no. I must pretend I know nothing. The rules. The harsh, unbending rules. I to go about my business, he his;

if we meet, no hint of my knowledge must pass.

So be it. I will honor my vows. But it may be difficult.

He goes by the name of Swanson. Been living in the hotel eighteen months; a musician of some sort, according to the manager. "A very peculiar man. Keeps to himself; no small talk, never smiles. Defends his privacy. The other day a maid barged into his room without knocking and I thought he'd sue. Well, we get all sorts here." The manager thinks he may actually be a member of one of the old European royal families, living in exile, or something similarly romantic. The manager would be surprised.

I defend my privacy too. From Elizabeth, another assault on it.

In the hall outside my room. "My new poems," she said. "In case you're interested." And then: "Can I come in? I'd read them to you. I love reading out loud." And: "Please don't always seem so terribly afraid of me. I don't bite, David. Really I don't. I'm quite gentle."

"I'm sorry."

"So am I." Anger, now, lurking in her shiny eyes, her thin taut lips. "If you want me to leave you alone, say so, I will. But I want you to know how cruel you're being. I don't *demand* anything from you. I'm just offering some friendship. And you're refusing. Do I have a bad smell? Am I so ugly? Is it my poems you hate and you're afraid to tell me?"

"Elizabeth—"

"We're only on this world such a short time. Why can't we be kinder to each other while we are? To love, to share, to open up. The reality trip. Communication, soul to soul." Her tone changed. An artful shading. "For all I know, women turn you off. I wouldn't put anybody down for that. We've all got our ways. But it doesn't have to be a sexual thing, you and me. Just talk. Like, opening the channels. Please? Say no and I'll never bother you again, but don't say no, please. That's like shutting a door on life, David. And when you do that, you start to die a little."

Persistent. I should tell her to go to hell. But there is the loneliness. There is her obvious sincerity. Her warmth, her eagerness to pull me from my lunar isolation. Can there be harm in it? Knowing that Swanson is nearby, so close yet sealed from me by iron commandments, has intensified my sense of being alone. I can risk letting Elizabeth get closer to me. It will make her happy; it may make me happy; it could even yield information valuable to Homeworld. Of course I must still maintain certain barriers.

"I don't mean to be unfriendly. I think you've misunderstood, Elizabeth. I haven't really been rejecting you. Come in. Do come in." Stunned, she enters my room. The first guest ever. My few books; my modest furnishings; the ultrawave transmitter, impenetrably disguised as a piece of sculpture. She sits. Skirt far above the knees. Good legs, if I understand the criteria of quality correctly. I am determined to allow no sexual overtures. If she tries anything, I'll resort to—I don't know—hysteria. "Read me your new poems," I say. She opens her portfolio. Reads.

> In the midst of the hipster night of doubt and
> Emptiness, when the bad-trip god came to me with
> Cold hands, I looked up and shouted yes at the
> Stars. And yes and yes again. I groove on yes;
> The devil grooves on no. And I waited for you to
> Say yes, and at last you did. And the world said
> The stars said the trees said the grass said the
> Sky said the streets said yes and yes and yes—

She is ecstatic. Her face is flushed; her eyes are joyous. She has broken through to me. After two hours, when it becomes obvious that I am not going to ask her to go to bed with me, she leaves. Not to wear out her welcome. "I'm so glad I was wrong about you, David," she whispers. "I couldn't believe you were really a life-denier. And you're not." Ecstatic.

I am getting into very deep water.

We spend an hour or two together every night. Sometimes in my room, sometimes in hers. Usually she comes to me, but now and then, to be polite, I seek her out after Third Feeding. By now I've read all her poetry; we talk instead of the arts in general, politics, racial problems. She has a lively, well-stocked, disorderly mind. Though she probes constantly for information about me, she realizes how sensitive I am, and quickly withdraws when I parry her. Asking about my work: I reply vaguely that I'm doing research for a book, and when I don't amplify she drops it, though she tries again, gently, a few nights later. She drinks a lot of wine, and offers it to me. I nurse one glass through a whole visit. Often she suggests we go out together for dinner; I explain that I have digestive problems and prefer to eat alone, and she takes this in good grace but immediately resolves to help me overcome those problems, for soon she is asking me to eat with her again. There is an excellent Spanish restaurant right in the hotel, she says. She drops troublesome questions. Where was I born? Did I go to college? Do I have family somewhere? Have I ever been married? Have I published any of my writings? I improvise evasions. Nothing difficult about that, except that never before have I allowed anyone on Earth such sustained contact with me, so prolonged an opportunity to find inconsistencies in my pretended identity. What if she sees through?

And sex. Her invitations grow less subtle. She seems to think that we ought to be having a sexual relationship, simply because we've become such good friends. Not a matter of passion so much as one of communication: we talk, sometimes we take walks together, we should do that together too. But of course it's impossible. I have the external organs but not the capacity to use them. Wouldn't want her touching my false skin in any case. How to deflect her? If I declare myself impotent she'll demand a chance to try to cure me. If I pretend homosexuality she'll start some kind of straightening therapy. If I simply say she doesn't turn me on physically she'll be hurt. The sexual thing is a challenge to her, the way merely getting me to talk with her once was. She often wears the transparent pink shawl that reveals her breasts. Her skirts are hip-high. She doses herself with aphrodisiac perfumes. She grazes my body with hers whenever opportunity arises. The tension mounts; she is determined to have me.

I have said nothing about her in my reports to Homeworld. Though I do transmit some of the psychological data I have gathered by observing her.

"Could you ever admit you were in love with me?" she asked tonight.

And she asked, "Doesn't it hurt you to repress your feelings all the time? To sit there locked up inside yourself like a prisoner?"

And, "There's a physical side of life too, David. I don't mind so much the damage you're doing to me by ignoring it. But I worry about the damage you're doing to you."

Crossing her legs. Hiking her skirt even higher.

We are heading toward a crisis. I should never have let this begin. A torrid summer has descended on the city, and in hot weather my nervous system is always at the edge of eruption. She may push me too far. I might ruin everything. I should apply for transfer to Homeworld before I cause trouble. Maybe I should confer with Swanson. I think what is happening now qualifies as an emergency.

Elizabeth stayed past midnight tonight. I had to ask her finally to leave: work to do. An hour later she pushed an envelope under my door. Newest poems. Love poems. In a shaky hand: *"David you mean so much to me. You mean the stars and nebulas. Can't you let me show my love? Can't you accept happiness? Think about it. I adore you."*

What have I started?

One hundred three degrees fahrenheit, today. The fourth successive day of intolerable heat. Met Swanson in the elevator at lunch time; nearly blurted the truth about myself to him. I must be more careful. But my control is slipping. Last night, in the worst of the heat, I was tempted to strip off my disguise. I could no longer stand being locked in here, pivoting and ducking to avoid all the machinery festooned about me. Resisted the temptation; just barely. Somehow I am more sensitive to the gravity too. I have the illusion that my carapace is developing cracks. Almost collapsed in the street this afternoon. All I need: heat exhaustion, whisked off to the hospital, routine fluroscope exam. "You have a very odd skeletal structure, Mr. Knecht." Indeed. Dissecting me, next, with three thousand medical students looking on. And then the United Nations called in. Menace from outer space. Yes. I must be more careful. I must be more careful. I must be more—

• • •

Now I've done it. Eleven years of faithful service destroyed in a single wild moment. Violation of the Fundamental Rule. I hardly believe it. How was it possible that I—that I—with my respect for my responsibilities—that I could have—even considered, let alone actually done—

But the weather was terribly hot. The third week of the heat wave. I was stifling inside my false body. And the gravity: was New York having a gravity wave too? That terrible pull, worse than ever. Bending my internal organs out of shape. Elizabeth a tremendous annoyance: passionate, emotional, teary, poetic, giving me no rest, pleading for me to burn with a brighter flame. Declaring her love in sonnets, in rambling hip epics, in haiku. Spending two hours in my room, crouched at my feet, murmuring about the hidden beauty of my soul. "Open yourself and let love come in," she whispered. "It's like giving yourself to God. Making a commitment; breaking down all walls. Why not? For love's sake, David, why not?" I couldn't tell her why not, and she went away, but about midnight she was back knocking at my door. I let her in. She wore an ankle-length silk housecoat, gleaming, threadbare. "I'm stoned," she said hoarsely, voice an octave too deep. "I had to bust three joints to get up the nerve. But here I am. David, I'm sick of making the turnoff trip. We've been so wonderfully close, and then you won't go the last stretch of the way." A cascade of giggles. "Tonight you will. Don't fail me, darling." Drops the housecoat. Naked underneath it; narrow waist, bony hips, long legs, thin thighs, blue veins crossing her breasts. Her hair wild and kinky. A sorceress. A seeress. Berserk. Approaching me, eyes slit-wide, mouth open, tongue flickering snakily. How fleshless she is! Beads of sweat glistening on her flat chest. Seizes my wrists; tugs me roughly toward the bed. We tussle a little. Within my false body I throw switches, nudge levers. I am stronger than she is. I pull free, breaking her hold with an effort. She stands flat-footed in front of me, glaring, eyes fiery. So vulnerable, so sad in her nudity. And yet so fierce. "David! David! David!" Sobbing. Breathless. Pleading with her eyes and the tips of her breasts. Gathering her strength; now she makes the next lunge, but I see it coming and let her topple past me. She lands on the bed, burying her face in the pillow, clawing at the sheet. "Why? Why why why WHY?" she screams.

In a minute we will have the manager in here. With the police.

"Am I so hideous? I love you, David, do you know what that word means? Love. Love." She sits up. Turns to me. Imploring. "Don't reject me," she whispers. "I couldn't take that. You know, I just wanted to make you happy, I figured I could be the one, only I didn't realize how unhappy you'd make me. And you just stand there. And you don't say anything. What are you, some kind of machine?"

"I'll tell you what I am," I said.

That was when I went sliding into the abyss. All control lost; all prudence gone. My mind so slathered with raw emotion that survival itself means nothing. I must make things clear to her, is all. I must show her. At whatever expense. I strip off my shirt. She glows, no doubt thinking I will let myself be seduced. My hands slide up and down my bare chest, seeking the catches and snaps. I go through the intricate, cumbersome process of opening my body. Deep within myself something is shouting NO NO NO NO NO, but I pay no attention. The heart has its reasons.

Hoarsely: "Look, Elizabeth. Look at me. This is what I am. Look at me and freak out. The reality trip."

My chest opens wide.

I push myself forward, stepping between the levers and struts, emerging halfway from the human shell I wear. I have not been this far out of it since the day they sealed me in, on Homeworld. I let her see my gleaming carapace. I wave my eyestalks around. I allow some of my claws to show. "See? See? Big black crab from outer space. That's what you love, Elizabeth. That's what I am. David Knecht's just a costume, and this is what's inside it." I have gone insane. "You want reality? Here's reality, Elizabeth. What good is the Knecht body to you? It's a fraud. It's a machine. Come on, come closer. Do you want to kiss me? Should I get on you and make love?"

During this episode her face has displayed an amazing range of reactions. Openmouthed disbelief at first, of course. And frozen horror: gagging sounds in throat, jaws agape, eyes wide and rigid. Hands fanned across breasts. Suddenly modesty in front of the alien monster? But then, as the familiar Knecht-voice, now bitter and impassioned, continues to flow from the black thing within the sundered chest, a softening of her response. Curiosity. The poetic sensibility taking over. Nothing human is alien to me: Terence, quoted by Cicero. Nothing alien is alien to me. Eh? She will accept the evidence of her eyes. "What are you? Where did you come from?" And I say, "I've violated the Fundamental Rule. I deserve to be plucked and thinned. We're not supposed to reveal ourselves. If we get into some kind of accident that might lead to exposure, we're supposed to blow ourselves up. The switch is right here." She comes close and peers around me, into the cavern of David Knecht's chest. "From some other planet? Living here in disguise?" She understands the picture. Her shock is fading. She even laughs. "I've seen worse than you on acid," she says. "You don't frightened me now, David. David? Shall I go on calling you David?"

This is unreal and dreamlike to me. I have revealed myself, thinking to drive her away in terror; she is no longer aghast, and smiles at my strangeness. She kneels to get a better look. I move back a short way. Eyestalks fluttering: I am uneasy, I have somehow lost the upper hand in this encounter.

She says, "I knew you were unusual, but not like this. But it's all right. I can cope. I mean, the essential personality, that's what I fell in love with. Who cares that you're a crab-man from the Green Galaxy? Who cares that we can't ever be real lovers? I can make that sacrifice. It's your soul I dig, David. Go on. Close yourself up again. You don't look comfortable this way." The triumph of love. She will not abandon me, even now. Disaster. I crawl back into Knecht and lift his arms to his chest to seal it. Shock is glazing my consciousness: the enormity, the audacity. What have I done? Elizabeth watches, awed, even delighted. At last I am together again. She nods. "Listen," she tells me, "you can trust me. I mean, if you're some kind of spy, checking out the Earth, I don't care. *I don't care.* I won't tell anybody. Pour it all out, David. Tell me about yourself. Don't you see, this is the biggest thing that ever happened to me. A chance to show that love isn't just physical, isn't just chemistry, that it's a soul trip, that it crosses not just racial lines but the lines of the whole damned species, the planet itself—''

It took several hours to get rid of her. A soaring, intense conversation, Elizabeth doing most of the talking. She putting forth theories of why I had come to Earth, me nodding, denying, amplifying, mostly lost in horror at my own perfidy and barely listening to her monologue. And the humidity turning me into rotting rags. Finally: "I'm down from the pot, David. And all wound up. I'm going out for a walk. Then back to my room to write for a while. To put this night into poem before I lose the power of it. But I'll come to you again by dawn, all right? That's maybe five hours from now. You'll be here? You won't do anything foolish? Oh, I love you so much, David! Do you believe me? Do you?''

When she was gone I stood a long while by the window, trying to reassemble myself. Shattered. Drained. Remembering her kisses, her lips running along the ridge marking the place where my chest opens. The fascination of the abomination. She will love me even if I am crustaceous beneath.

I had to have help.

I went to Swanson's room. He was slow to respond to my knock; busy transmitting, no doubt. I could hear him within, but he didn't answer. "Swanson?" I called. "Swanson?" Then I added the distress signal in the Homeworld tongue. He rushed to the door. Blinking, suspicious. "It's all right," I said. "Look, let me in. I'm in big trouble." Speaking English, but I gave him the distress signal again.

"How did you know about me?" he asked.

"The day the maid blundered into your room while you were eating, I was going by. I saw."

"But you aren't supposed to—"

"Except in emergencies. This is an emergency." He shut off his ultrawave and listened intently to my story. Scowling. He didn't approve. But he wouldn't spurn me. I had been criminally foolish, but I was of his kind, prey to the same pains, the same lonelinesses, and he would help me.

"What do you plan to do now?" he asked. "You can't harm her. It isn't allowed."

"I don't want to harm her. Just to get free of her. To make her fall out of love with me."

"How? If showing yourself to her didn't—"

"Infidelity," I said. "Making her see that I love someone else. No room in my life for her. That'll drive her away. Afterwards it won't matter that she knows: who'd believe her story? The FBI would laugh and tell her to lay off the LSD. But if I don't break her attachment to me I'm finished."

"Love someone else? Who?"

"When she comes back to my room at dawn," I said, "she'll find the two of us together, dividing and abstracting. I think that'll do it; don't you?"

So I deceived Elizabeth with Swanson.

The fact that we both wore male human identities was irrelevant, of course. We went to my room and stepped out of our disguises—a bold, dizzying sensation!—and suddenly we were just two Homeworlders again, receptive to one another's needs. I left the door unlocked. Swanson and I crawled up on my bed and began the chanting. How strange it was, after these years of solitude, to feel those vibrations again! And how beautiful. Swanson's vibrissae touching mine. The interplay of harmonies. An underlying sternness to his technique—he was contemptuous of me for my idiocy, and rightly so—but once we passed from the chanting to the dividing all was forgiven, and as we moved into the abstracting it was truly sublime. We climbed through an infinity of climactic emptyings. Dawn crept upon us and found us unwilling to halt even for rest.

A knock at the door. Elizabeth.

"Come in," I said.

A dreamy, ecstatic look on her face. Fading instantly when she saw the two of us entangled on the bed. A questioning frown. "We've been mating," I explained. "Did you think I was a complete hermit?" She looked from Swanson to me, from me to Swanson. Hand over her mouth. Eyes anguished. I turned the screw a little tighter. "I couldn't stop you from falling in love with me, Elizabeth. But I really do prefer my own kind. As should have been obvious."

"To have her here now, though—when you knew I was coming back—"

"Not *her,* exactly. Not *him* exactly either, though."

"—so cruel, David! To ruin such a beautiful experience." Holding forth sheets of paper with shaking hands. "A whole sonnet cycle," she said. "About tonight. How beautiful it was, and all. And now—and now—" Crumpling the pages. Hurling them across the room. Turning. Running out, sobbing furiously. Hell hath no fury like. "*David!*" A smothered cry. And slamming the door.

She was back in ten minutes. Swanson and I hadn't quite finished donning our bodies yet; we were both still unsealed. As we worked, we discussed further steps to take: he felt honor demanded that I request a transfer back to Homeworld, having terminated my usefulness here through tonight's indiscreet revelation. I agreed with him to some degree but was reluctant to leave. Despite the bodily torment of life on Earth I had come to feel I belonged here. Then Elizabeth entered, radiant.

"I mustn't be so possessive," she announced. "So bourgeois. So conventional. I'm willing to share my love." Embracing Swanson. Embracing me. "A *ménage à trois,*" she said. "I won't mind that you two are having a physical relationship. As long as you don't shut me out of your lives completely. I mean, David, we could never have been physical anyway, right, but we can have the other aspects of love, and we'll open ourselves to your friend also. Yes? Yes? Yes?"

Swanson and I both put in applications for transfer, he to Africa, me to Homeworld. It would be some time before we received a reply. Until then we were at her mercy. He was blazingly angry with me for involving him in this, but what choice had I had? Nor could either of us avoid Elizabeth. We were at her mercy. She bathed both of us in shimmering waves of tender emotion; wherever we turned, there she was, incandescent with love. Lighting up the darkness of our lives. You poor lonely creatures. Do you suffer much in our gravity? What about the heat? And the winters. Is there a custom of marriage on your planet? Do you have poetry?

A happy threesome. We went to the theatre together. To concerts. Even to parties in Greenwich Village. "My friends,"

Elizabeth said, leaving no doubt in anyone's mind that she was living with both of us. Faintly scandalous doings; she loved to seem daring. Swanson was sullenly obliging, putting up with her antics but privately haranguing me for subjecting him to all this. Elizabeth got out another mimeographed booklet of poems, dedicated to both of us. *Triple Tripping,* she called it. Flagrantly erotic. I quoted a few of the poems in one of my reports to Homeworld, then lost heart and hid the booklet in the closet. "Have you heard about your transfer yet?" I asked Swanson at least twice a week. He hadn't. Neither had I.

Autumn came. Elizabeth, burning her candle at both ends, looked gaunt and feverish. "I have never known such happiness," she announced frequently, one hand clasping Swanson, the other me. "I never think about the strangeness of you anymore. I think of you only as people. Sweet, wonderful, lonely people. Here in the darkness of this horrid city." And she once said, "What if everybody here is like you, and I'm the only one who's really human? But that's silly. You must be the only ones of your kind here. The advance scouts. Will your planet invade ours? I do hope so! Set everything to rights. The reign of love and reason at last!"

"How long will this go on?" Swanson muttered.

At the end of October his transfer came through. He left without saying goodbye to either of us and without leaving a forwarding address. Nairobi? Addis Ababa? Kinshasa?

I had grown accustomed to having him around to share the burden of Elizabeth. Now the full brunt of her affection fell on me. My work was suffering; I had no time to file my reports properly. And I lived in fear of her gossiping. What was she telling her Village friends? ("You know David? He's not really a man, you know. Actually inside him there's a kind of crab-thing from another solar system. But what does that matter? Love's a universal phenomenon. The truly loving person doesn't draw limits around the planet.") I longed for my release. To go home; to accept my punishment; to shed my false skin. To empty my mind of Elizabeth.

My reply came through the ultrawave on November 13.

Application denied. I was to remain on Earth and continue my work as before. Transfers to Homeworld were granted only for reasons of health.

I debated sending a full account of my treason to Homeworld and thus bringing about my certain recall. But I hesitated, overwhelmed with despair. Dark brooding seized me. "Why so sad?" Elizabeth asked. What could I say? That my attempt at escaping from her had failed? "I love you," she said. "I've never felt so *real* before." Nuzzling against my cheek. Fingers knotted in my hair. A seductive whisper. "David, open yourself up again. Your chest, I mean. I want to see the inner you. To make sure I'm not frightened of it. Please? You've only let me see you once." And then, when I had: "May I kiss you, David?" I was appalled. But I let her. She was unafraid. Transfigured by happiness. She is a cosmic nuisance, but I fear I'm getting to like her.

Can I leave her? I wish Swanson had not vanished. I need advice.

Either I break with Elizabeth or I break with Homeworld. This is absurd. I find new chasms of despondency every day. I am unable to do my work. I have requested a transfer once again, without giving details. The first snow of the winter today.

Application denied.

"When I found you with Swanson," she said, "it was a terrible shock. An even bigger blow than when you first came out of your chest. I mean, it was startling to find out you weren't human, but it didn't hit me in any emotional way, it didn't threaten me. But then, to come back a few hours later and find you with one of your own kind, to know that you wanted to shut me out, that I had no place in your life—Only we worked it out, didn't we?" Kissing me. Tears of joy in her eyes. How did this happen? Where did it all begin? Existence was once so simple. I have tried to trace the chain of events that brought me from there to here, and I cannot. I was outside of my false body for eight hours today. The longest spell so far. Elizabeth is talking of going to the islands with me for the winter. A secluded cottage that her friends will make available. Of course, I must not leave my post without permission. And it takes months simply to get a reply.

Let me admit the truth: I love her.

January 1. The new year begins. I have sent my resignation to Homeworld and have destroyed my ultrawave equipment. The links are broken. Tomorrow, when the city offices are open, Elizabeth and I will go to get the marriage license.

THE REALITY TRIP
Robert Silverberg

The month is January, 1970. It's the era of *Hair,* the psychedelic revolution, the Nixon presidency, and a lot of other extraordinary cultural phenomena. I live in a grand mansion in one of the most secluded and conservative sections of New York City, but I've been letting my hair grow long, have started wearing sandals, vividly striped trousers, and startling polyester shirts. I don't know it yet, but I've already embarked on the course that will sweep me, in another year or two, into a strange new life in California. And this story is by way of being a preliminary report on some of my research into the burgeoning counterculture of the moment.

The hotel where it takes place is a recognizable version of the Chelsea, that weird old nineteenth century monstrosity in lower Manhattan where marginal avant-garde artists of all sorts long had liked to hang out, and for all I know still do. (I got to know the place because Arthur C. Clarke customarily used it as his pied-à-terre when visiting New York. Arthur might not seem like anybody's idea of a marginal avant-garde artist, but he was, please remember, the man who provided the basic conception for Stanley Kubrick's quintessentially sixties film *2001,* and he was utterly at home in the place.)

An alien, living unnoticed in the Chelsea for nine years? Why not? And— in one of those torrid New York summers—getting entangled sexually with a goofy poetess who lives down the hall? Why not? Why not? And falling in love, and getting married? Far, as we said, out. Why not? It seemed like a funny idea for a story. And that was the motto of the times, anyway: *Why not?* Why not? Why not?

Susan Wade's short fiction has appeared in *Amazing Stories, Fantasy & Science Fiction, First For Women, Snow White, Blood Red, Black Thorn, White Rose,* and *Ruby Slippers, Golden Tears.* Her first novel, *Walking Rain,* a magical realist/ thriller hybrid, was recently published. Her second novel is tentatively called *Northern Lights.* She lives in Austin, Texas.

"The Tattooist" is about another alien/human encounter, this one with darker consequences for the human.

THE TATTOOIST

SUSAN WADE

THE MAN WALKED INTO HER SHOP ONE TUESDAY AFTERNOON in early fall and said, "Missus? I want you to tattoo my penis."

Claren was tucking needles into their sterilization envelopes and didn't even flick him a glance. She'd been in the business long enough to learn.

"I don't do penises," she said.

He didn't say anything, just kept standing there with his bulk blocking her light.

"Try Kevin Klardey down on Eighth," she said after a moment, still not looking up. "He does 'em sometimes. When he's in the mood."

The late afternoon sun slanted through the windows of the old frame house she'd converted to a shop, pooling mellow and golden on the dark wooden floors. A beautiful day; she didn't want it ruined by this pervert.

He leaned down and carefully positioned a thousand-dollar bill on the table in front of the autoclave. "I don't explain well, Missus," he said. "I want *you* to tattoo my penis."

21

• • •

Terry was setting the table when she got home around six-fifteen, and their unrestored Hyde Park bungalow smelled delectably of ginger and garlic. He was wearing bicycle shorts and nothing else.

Claren came up behind him, slid her arms around his wiry cyclist's body, and squeezed. "Miss me? Whatever you've been cooking smells wonderful."

He set down the plates and turned around to give her his full attention. "You know it. I'm winging it, sort of a Szechuan stir-fry. Now that you're home, I'll start the rice." His dark hair was beginning to thin a little on top, but there wasn't a single strand of grey in it. She already had a thick streak of silver over one eye, which he said was elegant. They had been together for twelve years.

"I doubt I'll make it that long—I'm starved." She rubbed her face across the dark fur of his chest, inhaling deeply. Terry's bare skin always made her imagine how she could decorate it. "God, I love your pheromones. Have I told you that lately?"

"Not since this morning, darlin'. Did you skip lunch again? I made pasta salad for you to take." He gave her a final squeeze and turned back to fold the red bandannas they used for napkins.

"I didn't think about it till I was already at the shop," she said, heading for the fridge. Its frosty breath gave her a delightful shiver as she examined the contents. She poured herself a glass of orange juice, then found some Havarti cheese. A slice would hold her. "Had a weirdo come into the shop today. Offered me a thousand bucks to tattoo his prick."

Terry came into the kitchen and ran water into the rice steamer. "He give you any trouble? Hey, go easy on that cheese. Don't want to spoil your appetite."

"Nah. I broke it to him gently that true artists are unmoved by the lure of filthy lucre."

"What'd he do?" Terry had added salt to the water and was adjusting the flame of the gas burner.

Claren paused, then downed the rest of her juice. "It was funny, I got the impression he was pleased. He said that was why he wanted me to do it—because I'm a real artist. Then somebody else came into the shop and he left."

"Did he at least leave you a tip?"

"Ha," Claren said. "Gonna grab a shower."

"Ten minutes till showtime," Terry warned.

"Wouldn't miss it for the world." She gave him a wink and whipped open the snaps on her shirt. Then she treated him to a little bump-and-grind as she backed across the living room toward the hall.

He followed her, whistling and clapping, until she tossed her bra onto the sofa. Then he said, "The hell with dinner," and came after her.

The big man returned to the shop two days later.

Claren was by herself again, which wasn't all that common—she had a robust clientele and lots of walk-in business. But she had blocked off some time that afternoon to work on new designs for an upcoming convention. Having the man turn up just then made her uneasy; she wondered if he had kept watch and waited until she was alone. But he held his big body so awkwardly as he came toward her—his head hunched forward and his big hands fidgeting with a manila folder—that he seemed more deferential than threatening.

She looked up and waited. No point in encouraging him.

This time, he didn't speak. He opened the folder and laid it in front of her on the drafting table.

Claren glanced down, expecting a nude picture of him. The folder did contain a stack of photographs, but they were cut from a magazine. Probably *Skin Art*. The one on top was of a woman's legs in fishnet stockings—a back view, showing garters and seams. Claren recognized those legs—and the stockings—instantly. The tattoo had taken four months to complete, and was precise in every detail. Most people probably never realized that Lindy's trademark fishnets weren't real.

The man turned the picture over, revealing the one underneath. This one was of a man's upper arm, twined with four strands of barbed wire. The top three strands had broken, their barbs scattering and transforming into crows that rose in a spiral toward the top of his shoulder.

Even after six years, she was still proud of the design. Some of her first custom work. For Manuelito, who had escaped from a Salvadoran prison camp and come north to establish a relocation center for other refugees. Claren was pleased to see that the tat remained dark, its lines still distinct against Manny's gorgeous bronze skin.

The man turned to the next clipped-out photograph. This was of the chiropractor who had asked her to tattoo his back with the bones and muscles of the spine. Claren examined the work critically. It could have come straight from Gray's, the illusion so powerful, the *trompe l'oeil* effect so real, that it looked as if the man had been expertly flayed.

Which, in a sense, he had been. One of the reasons Claren preferred this medium was that her work went beneath the surface. Most visual artists worked flat, but her canvases were impregnated with the images she created.

The man began to turn the picture over. She tapped him lightly on the wrist and moved away.

"You've made the point," she said. "You know my work." She propped her butt on the sill of the window next to the drafting table and crossed her arms.

"Your work," he said, then paused.

Though he spoke with no discernible accent, Claren had the impression that he was translating his words into English.

"Is special," he said.

"Thank you."

His oversize hands rose from the folder for the first time and grappled with the air, as if they would wrestle words from it. "You twist the real, Missus. Make us see what is not. Give the person a mask that instead of concealing . . . reveals him."

"Yes," she said. A hot spot was forming in her chest. Nothing felt better than having someone grasp the point of her work. Nothing.

"I have need of your skill," he said. "Will you look, please?" He brushed through the pictures in the folder and offered the last one to her.

This one was a Polaroid snapshot. She took it, knowing before she saw it that it would be of his prick.

At first, she thought the photo was overexposed, but then she realized that his prick actually was that pallid and featureless. He had almost no pubic hair, and his balls looked pale too.

His prick was normal size, maybe even a little bigger than average. But the shape was undifferentiated—no mushroom shape to the head, no foreskin, no visible glans—not so much as a vein showing. And the skin had no texture at all. It looked like one of those plastic vibrators that pretend to be for something other than masturbation. No, it looked . . . embryonic.

"Inside, I am human, Missus," he said. "I am like other men. Will you give me a mask that shows this?"

Claren hadn't smoked in eight years, but she had a sudden longing for a cigarette—a sense-memory that blurred her vision: the hot-sulfur snap of the match, that first sharp curl of smoke reaching her lungs as the tobacco caught. Reflexively, she groped for the pack that always used to lie handy on the corner of her table. Nothing there, of course.

She inhaled sharply. Could she? Her heart was racing. It had been a while since she'd had a real challenge. A real test of her mastery of *trompe l'oeil* technique.

But was it safe? She looked him over slowly, then relaxed. He had come to her for her skill, not because he was kinky.

"It will take a long time," she told him, "probably at least twelve weeks. Four sessions, three weeks apart." She did not insult him by mentioning the pain. She could tell he understood that. "And it will cost . . . a lot."

He nodded, a humble quality to the gesture. She stared at the skin on his face and arms, but it seemed normal—faintly tanned, without much hair.

Claren was suddenly ashamed, for no reason she could have named. "Come back tomorrow at six," she said.

She fidgeted at the dinner table, needing to talk about the new commission, but reluctant to bring it up. Terry would be irritated with her for taking on an evening client, especially one who might be a pervert.

He was always annoyed when she worked late, because it cut into their time together.

"What's on your mind, darlin'?" he said. "You seem jittery."

"Took on a long-term job today. After-hours gig. Twelve weeks, off and on."

Terry's mouth compressed. "Why nights?"

She shrugged. "Not enough time free in my day schedule."
Taking the easy way out—you should be ashamed of yourself.

He was shaping his mashed potatoes with the tines of his
fork, making furrows down the sides. The gravy spilled onto
his plate like hot wax from a guttering candle. "Which nights?
How late do you think you'll be?"

"Tomorrow night's the first session. After that, I'll have a
better idea of how long it'll take. We'll probably do Fridays
three weeks apart to let the skin heal." She noticed how careful she had been not to say "his skin," much less, "his
prick," and that added to her uneasiness. She didn't usually
keep things from Terry. "So how was your day?"

"Same old, same old. Tests on that new ceramic stuff. No
big bangs for a while."

Terry was an engineering assistant at one of the university's
research facilities. They did a lot of defense work, developing
materials and weapons with high-energy electrical pulses. He
loved the huge daisy wheel generator they used for their gi-
gavolt experiments, the "big bangs."

Once Terry got started on his job, she was off the hook. He
wasn't the type to pester her about a decision she'd already
made; she wouldn't have to talk about her new customer again
unless she felt like it.

Claren asked him a question about the materials experiment
and took a bite of her salad.

As he answered, she watched the supple movement of the
skin of his face, deeply tanned from all his cycling.

He has such beautiful skin, she thought. She daydreamed
designs for it, lulled by the rhythm of his voice as they finished
dinner.

She was restless all the next day, waiting for six o'clock, and
wondering if the man would actually show up. She had come
in early that morning to have some uninterrupted time to work
on the design she would use to make his penis seem ordinary.

Ordinary. Why did he want to look like everyone else? Most
of her customers came to her because they wanted to look
special.

But she was pleased with her drawing. Plenty of texture.
She would fool the eye into seeing shape where there was

none; add definition and color—she'd even included a throbbing vein in the design.

He arrived two minutes before six. She flipped the "Open" sign to "Closed" and locked the door behind him before walking around the two front rooms of the shop to draw the shades. For this job, they needed privacy. The light inside the shop seemed brighter once the outside world was shut out.

The muscles in her calves were tight. *Routine,* she thought, *stick with the routine.* She handed him a clipboard and said, "Fill out these forms, please," then went to get a large white bath towel and a plastic squeeze bottle of liquid antiseptic soap.

He was still writing his name on the release form when she came back, and Claren had to resist the temptation to tell him to finish it later. *Routine,* she reminded herself.

Her tattoo equipment was already laid out on her worktable, but she sat down on the tall stool in front of it and rearranged everything. She would be using small clusters of needles, for a very subtle effect. Too much intensity of color would be a mistake; it would only look artificial. She was going to make this poor guy's prick look more normal than Norman Rockwell's. *Lifelike, instead of like some freak,* she thought. The prospect was satisfying.

The man brought her the clipboard and said softly, "I have finished it, Missus."

"Fine," she said, and pointed at the soap. "There's a bathroom through that door and to the left. Strip and scrub—and make sure you wash behind your ears, hear?"

He hesitated for a moment, seeming confused by the wisecrack. Then he gave her a tentative smile. "Yes, Missus."

As she watched him shamble toward the bathroom, Claren had another sharp craving for a cigarette. After he closed the door, she called, "Hey—leave your shirt on so you won't get cold."

He was pleased with her drawing, and climbed eagerly into the reclining chair.

The texture of his flesh was stranger than she'd expected. After she folded the towel back from his massive thighs, Claren wondered if he was human.

The skin of his prick was fine-grained and very smooth, like a baby's. Maybe he was a burn victim? But she'd tattooed people disfigured by burns before; his flesh didn't have the shiny ruined look of a scar.

Awkwardly, Claren reached over and touched him. His skin was hot and more taut than she'd thought it would be—but it was still skin. *Completely human,* she assured herself. And then, looking at the pale swollen-cigar shape of him, the unnatural symmetry, she corrected herself. *Well, maybe not completely.*

About eighteen square inches of skin to be tattooed, she estimated. Though none of it was actually square, of course. Artists who needed a flat canvas to work were pikers. With four sessions, that was about four and a half square inches each time. She hoped he was as tough as he was big.

She swabbed him down with alcohol, applied a topical anesthetic, and sprayed him with green soap and water. Then she picked up the duplicating paper she'd traced the design on and positioned it carefully on his prick. She rubbed a deodorant stick across the paper to transfer the design, then pulled the stencil away. The drawing had transferred clean.

Claren dabbed a glob of petroleum jelly at the base of the shaft—the area she'd be starting on—and smoothed the gel out. It would help the needles run smoother over the skin and make the excess dye easier to wipe off.

For once, she was reluctant to use surgical gloves; she liked the sensation of touching his skin. But it wasn't safe to work without them.

She selected a three-needle cluster soldered onto a bar, picked a tube, and loaded both into the tattoo machine. She would work in a soft pinkish brown pigment first, outlining the design in a very fine line.

She was used to touching flesh. Very accustomed to it, but this was different; when she touched him, it was as if an electrical connection had been closed. She was no longer herself.

Or, rather, not only herself. Now she was feeling things with his big shaggy body as well: his enormous heart thubbing-dubbing in her chest, the slabs of his heavy flesh enfolding her organs, odd layers of muscle rippling as she moved her arm.

Claren applied the cluster of needles as if in a trance, carefully stretching out their textureless skin to ensure the proper application of color. She felt the pressure of the needles entering their flesh, a burning cut in the penis she didn't have.

In spite of the local, it was excruciating.

Without asking him about the pain, she applied more anesthetic and waited a couple of minutes to let it take effect. She continued the work, but before long a chain of sweat was forming along the line of her upper lip and across her cheekbones. Feeling it from both sides—jabbing the bar and taking the needle—was a strain.

After she had the defining lines laid in, she switched to another bar with a broader cluster of needles soldered at a shallow angle. She used a tawny tint for background shading, then went back over the same area with a pale rosy apricot.

Claren paused and swabbed the sweat off her face. Then she wiped the blood and excess dye from his prick. The tat looked too distinct and dark now, but she knew it would fade to the right tone once the skin healed. Blood welled up on the shaft, and she blotted it off again. He flinched, and moved his thigh against her forearm.

Not a freak. The thought came from nowhere, but carried a note of utter authenticity. It was followed by another, even more startling: *—genuine mutation—our kind breed true—*

She jerked her arm away. For the first time, she noticed that his eyes weren't brown. They were an intense dark grey.

The narrow web of skin between her fingers was itching furiously.

"That's enough for now," she said. Her voice rang strangely in her ears. Her fingers had a fine tremor as she positioned the bandage on his prick. "You can get dressed."

Obedient as always, he lifted himself down from the chair, drew the towel around him, and shambled toward the back. She rummaged through the drawer of the desk to find a copy of the "Caring for Your New Tattoo" instructions for him.

When he returned, he asked her, "Again in three weeks, Missus?" as if uncertain of her answer.

● ● ●

Claren nodded, but could not speak.

"You seem tired, darlin'," Terry said later.

"Long day," she said. She was lying flat on the sofa, staring at the ceiling. The water stain near the corner was shaped like a human heart, ventricles and all.

Terry came over, stripped off her sandals, and started rubbing her feet. He was good at it; firm pressure in the right spots, no tickling. Eventually, the strangeness inside her began to break up and flow away.

Terry sensed it too. He worked his way up her calves, kneading the tight muscles like taffy. When he reached her thighs, Claren pulled him down on the sofa and climbed on top of him. He grinned, but let her lead.

She lay against him, both of them fully clothed, and breathed in his smell. Now and then she moved a little, rubbing her breasts against him, cupping herself around him as he got hard.

She felt like she did in the bathtub sometimes, as if she were drinking the water through her skin. Except this time, it was Terry she was absorbing. Everything she loved about him was soaking into her as she touched him: his strength, his playfulness, his warmth. His familiarity.

They lay nearly still together for so long that when she finally peeled his shorts off and took him inside her, they came on the third stroke.

The next morning at the shop, she studied the man's data sheet and release form. He had given his name as Hadrian Franklin, his mailing address as a post office box in Tracker's Point, Montana, and had left the line for a phone number blank.

She tattooed twenty-three other people that week. The college student who wanted a permanent gold chain around her ankle was the most interesting of the new clients. None of the others was interested in a *trompe l'oeil* effect. And Brad the Birdman came for his sixteenth appointment; the glorious blue-and-yellow macaw plumage on his back and shoulders was two-thirds done now.

None of it was as absorbing as the work on Hadrian Franklin. Claren spent every spare moment soldering new combinations of needles together in preparation for their next session.

Hadrian had healed well, and now that the skin had peeled, the coloration of the tattoo was precisely the right intensity. Because only the base of his prick was tattooed, it looked like a wax model that was starting to melt.

Claren was unsettled by the half-formed look of it. For the first time ever, she felt remorseful that her design was altering this smooth expanse of skin.

He remained silent, his huge body quiescent under her hands. Claren found herself wishing she hadn't told him to keep his shirt on last time; she was curious about how the rest of him looked. Was he really a mutant?

She knew the answer at once. He was.

Confused enough by the thoughts she had while tattooing him, she didn't try to talk as she worked. Normally she kept up a conversation with her clients to distract them from the discomfort. But with Hadrian, she felt the pain too. It was as if she were tattooing herself, only stranger.

The pain intensified as she moved closer to the tip, cradling his prick in her left hand as she tattooed. She'd gotten the knack of using her left thumb to stretch the skin out as she worked, to keep the detail of the tat clear enough.

Claren wiped off the blood and dye and switched needle bars. As she applied the new cluster, she wondered where he was really from, where he really lived.

The answer formed—not an image that built up one element at a time, but a complete picture that seemed to bloom instantly in the center of her brain. She was in a large log building, like a refectory, filled with people. Big bulky men and women, all with pale golden skin and dark grey eyes.

"Is that your home?" she blurted out. "In Montana?"

He looked at her sadly. "Yes, Missus."

"How—" Claren set down the tattoo machine and swiped the sweat from her face. "*Why* do I see it?"

He looked down at the blood that was welling from his penis. "Apologies, Missus. The pain—and you are touching me. My containment is not so strong when I hurt. And touching, skin closeness—" He stopped.

She waited for a moment, then realized he was stumped. He simply didn't have the words to explain more. But why did he look so guilty?

"It's okay," she said. "I don't mind seeing things—feeling—the things you—"

Her reassurances didn't seem to convince Hadrian. He looked guiltier than ever, like an overgrown child caught tormenting his sister.

She blotted the blood away and picked up the needle again. The duality of sensation was like a drug. Painful pleasure.

"Actually," she whispered, "I like it."

She tattooed six inches of skin in that one session.

She was very late getting home. Terry was waiting up for her, which irritated her. She had wanted to lie on the sofa by herself, undisturbed, and mull over what she had learned about Hadrian. Think about the sensation of pushing the needle bar and taking it inside her flesh at the same time.

She had wanted to think about him and masturbate.

But Terry was all over her, wouldn't leave her alone until she yelled at him. Hurt, he retreated.

They each went to sleep unsatisfied that night.

The next morning, he asked her to close the shop at noon so she could come to his cycle race. Feeling guilty about her snappishness yesterday, she agreed.

The races were usually colorful, if a little boring—Terry mostly went in for track racing. But that day she found the lean, defined muscles of the cyclists' legs and backs disturbing. Claren tried to watch the racers, but kept averting her eyes in distaste.

She managed to pay attention to Terry's race, and she cheered for him when he won. His was the second to the last match. Afterward, the cyclists all went to the Tavern for beer and nachos, and Claren went along dutifully. Animated from the victory and the congratulations of his friends, Terry didn't seem to notice her uneasiness. She was glad. How would she explain it? That the way their muscles were shaped looked wrong to her?

Watching Terry's flushed face across the table, she knew he would want sex later. And she didn't.

On the way home, still feeling expansive, Terry sped up North Lamar, weaving the Toyota nimbly around the barriers construction crews had left all down the center lane.

"*This* isn't a race," Claren said.

"Sure it is! A race to see who gets home soonest." He reached over and slid his hand up her thigh.

"The way you're driving," she said, pumping acid into the words, "it'll be a miracle if we get home at all. If you're going to speed, at least keep your hands on the wheel."

The preemptive fight she had started escalated quickly. Within minutes, it spread from Terry's driving to her irresponsible attitudes and finally to money.

He slept in the spare room that night.

Hadrian was three minutes late for his appointment. Claren was a nervous wreck by the time he arrived. The weather had turned cold the night before, giving them a crisp bright day on the line between autumn and winter. As he entered the shop, he swept air that smelled of woodsmoke inside with him.

"Missus," he said, and picked up the towel she had ready for him.

As he turned toward the back, she said, "Hadrian."

She had never called him by name before.

He looked at her, his dark eyes like pewter in the fading evening light. "Yes, Missus?"

"I've been thinking—your shape. The way you really are— it's beautiful. Why did you want to change it? Have me cover it up?"

There was a long pause before he answered. Why had she asked him this aloud, instead of waiting until they were touching? She could find out anything she wanted to know when she touched him.

Maybe I'm afraid to know, she thought.

"I am in love, Missus," Hadrian said, and went into the back.

Her heart pounding, Claren rearranged her needles. He was in love. Who with?

He came all the way from Montana to have me tattoo him. But that doesn't mean—

She thought of daisies. *He loves me, he loves me not.*

Claren wasn't certain she was ready to find out. But she could hardly wait to touch him again.

She ended up tattooing the entire underside of his penis in that session.

When she came in at midnight, Terry was still up. She could tell by the way he was looking at her that he was going to insist on making love. He watched her hungrily, and with a certain bitterness.

Claren's jaw clenched. *Don't even bother, Terry,* she thought. *It's not going to happen.*

But later, as he labored over her breasts and laved her with his tongue, doing everything he could to stimulate her, she thought of Hadrian. As she summoned the memory of his resilient, smooth skin, his strangeness, her thighs started to quiver.

What is happening to me? she wondered. *Is this the seven year itch, starting five years late?*

But the tremble in her inner thighs didn't dissipate, and as Terry entered her, she fantasized about touching Hadrian, the silky different feel of him under her fingers. She imagined it was *his* penis pushing into her; she pictured him penetrating her from behind. But in her fantasy, his penis looked as it had when she first saw it, before she ever touched it with a needle.

For the first time in weeks, she came. She came spectacularly, with a spasm that arched her against Terry's hips hard enough to leave bruises along the inside of her thighs.

The next session with Hadrian was the last they had scheduled. It was set for early December, the checkup on the finished design, to make sure Hadrian's skin had healed properly and do any touch-ups needed.

Claren waited until he was in the chair, then told him she needed to see him with an erection to make sure the tat's coverage was complete.

She expected him to touch himself and turned away to afford him a little privacy, but watched from the corner of her eye. His big hands didn't move.

His penis flowered instantly, like a time-lapsed photograph, a big satiny movement of muscle that made her nipples tighten.

"You must examine me, I understand," he said.

So she had his permission.

She looked at his prick without touching him. The design showed excellent detail. She had stretched the skin carefully as she did the work, and very few places needed touching up. Her mouth was dry and her skin was damp as she reached for him. No gloves this time. She was anticipating the erotic image that would form in her brain at the contact. When they touched, she would discover what excited him.

And, she realized, *he will know how much he excites me. Daisy chain, he loves me—*

His skin was hot, and even silkier than she remembered. The second she touched him, the image leaped across the gap between their minds like a high-voltage spark—instant and whole before her.

A woman. Human. Of course, what had she expected? One of his own kind would not have been disturbed by his shape, his differences. But the *woman*—

Her face was angular, a sculpted narrow pixie face. She had skin like milk and hair the color of maple leaves in the fall. *The color of burning,* Claren thought as she burned. She was nude, slim-bodied; with flame at the crown and between her legs, and all that smooth moon white skin.

—shivering allure—forbidden fruit—an outsider—

Claren pulled her hand away from Hadrian only with great difficulty. It was as if her muscles had convulsed from an electric shock. But it was an orgasm convulsing her, and she was breathing in gasps as the spasms pulsed through her belly. She thought of the woman's skin and hair, and licked her lips. Instantly, she came again, a climax so powerful that she couldn't help groaning aloud.

She leaned against the cabinet, legs trembling. Her hand was wet. She stared at it stupidly. A silvery gel was thick on her fingers.

Claren looked at him.

He seemed unembarrassed.

Of course, she thought, *I'm the one who was so horny I came. I came first.*

He clambered down from the chair, looped the big towel around his waist, and went to the bathroom.

Claren grabbed a paper towel and wiped off her hand. She was still trembling, and her crotch felt pulpy.

When he came out later—dressed again—she said, "One session of touch-ups should do it. Tomorrow evening, same time, okay?"

He gave her a nod before he went to the door.

But the connection was still open between them—a faint and static-y afterimage, already fading—and she knew she would never see him again.

He was ready for his lover—his human lover—now.

When she got home, Terry was setting the table. He was wearing cutoffs and nothing else, in spite of the early winter chill. The hardwood floors were cold and drafts flowed from the warped window frames. Gooseflesh pricked his arms.

"Aren't you cold?" she said.

He looked up, then away from her.

What was he thinking?

"Nah. Might as well enjoy going bare as long as I can. It's almost winter." He brought two bowls of stew to the table.

She could see him shivering. *I don't even know him,* she thought. *Look at all that hair on his chest—it even makes him smell funny.*

She averted her gaze. Her mouth was dry. She licked her lips, and was struck by a flash-image of the woman—Hadrian's *lover*—pure white skin and flaming hair—

Claren sat down at the table and unfolded her bandanna napkin with fingers that shook.

Terry pulled out his chair and started to join her. His nipples were pale brown bare spots in the forest of dark hair on his chest. It was nauseating.

"For Christ's sake," she said. "Put on a shirt, will you? We're at the dinner table."

•   •   •

[Author's note: The barbed wire and flying crows tattoo described in this story is the work of tattooist, Henri, of Electric Expressions in New Orleans.]

THE TATTOOIST
Susan Wade

There's something inherently fascinating about tattoos. And I've always been interested in *trompe l'oeil* effects. When I got the idea for this story, combining the two seemed natural.

After I did the first draft, there was a lot of discussion among my writing friends about what Hadrian's unretouched penis should look like. *Lots* of discussion, but no consensus. Then one morning, I got phone calls from two friends—one of them from Oklahoma City, because my friend was traveling—who said the same thing: "Susan, I think I've solved your penis problem!"

I'm still hoping the agency I work for doesn't record my incoming phone calls.

John Kaiine is the author of the novels *Fossil Circus* and *Clay (gone to hell)*.
He is a professional photographer, artist, and ex-gravedigger. He lives in a house
by the sea with his author wife, Tanith Lee, and a black-and-white cat.

In Kaiine's tale of a john and a prostitute, the need of the man to seek control
over at least one aspect of his life takes precedence over everything else.

DOLLY SODOM

JOHN KAIINE

IT IS NOT RAINING, BUT THAT DOES NOT MATTER. SMITH
leaves the tram and crosses the street. He wears a white trench
coat, carries a suitcase. He has no hat. Night has started, the
lights have been lit. Detail is bleached out: His shadow lacks
substance. He turns a corner, and there before him is *The Years
Hotel*.

The door is ajar, always open. He climbs the iron steps and
enters.

In the lobby there are cards on a platter on a tall wooden
stand. Vellum cards, white, edged in black, bearing the legend
CALL AGAIN. CALL AGAIN.

"Yes?" There is a man's voice behind him. Smith turns.
The Man with the voice wears an old boater; pallid strip of
ribbon around the brim.

"Yes?" says the Man.

His mouth flaps, he shifts the suitcase from one hand to the
other. Grey folded eyes, dull as dreams. He speaks, wiping
fingers to his mouth: "I've a . . . I've a hankering for regret."

The Man says nothing. Stands there, looking. A bug skits
about the light.

Smith cannot swallow. He should turn and walk away,
should never have had those old thoughts. And then he re-

members. He must ask. Request. "Hair," he says, "I like hair."

"Room eight. Top floor," says the Man.

Smith, toward the stairs.

Somewhere, someone breathes.

When he has his foot firm on the bottom step, he throws a fleeting glance round at the Man: Eyes in the shadow of the brim of his hat. Smith tells him, "I'm not proud of what I do."

The Man would laugh, but has forgotten how.

Smith climbs the stairs. The decorative dead haunt the walls: Faded red roses on withered wallpaper. He reaches the first floor, turns down a corridor, passing a door behind which he hears a rustling sound, a voice whispering, confetti in the mouth, repeating the word, "*sorry,*" over and over. He hurries on.

On the second floor there is a room in which all that hangs in its wardrobe are flypapers.

He lingers outside a room, hearing the stroking of sepia photographs. The pornography of nostalgia. The passion for shadows. On the fourth floor he can smell burnt blossoms.

It is rumored that there is a room up on the seventh, full of moths, where one can spend frail moments wrapped in a silk shroud awaiting the delicate mouths of moths, nibbling ... devoured by hours.

The top floor is webby. Dust has shattered mirrors. Clocks have drowned in the dampness. Room 8 stands before him.

Smith pulls the door open, steps in. It is a little room of dry plaster walls, there is a bunk, a wireless, a candle on a table, and in one corner there stands the Doll. The door flaps shut behind him. A burnt-out light bulb hangs from the ceiling. He lights a match, and soon there is candlelight burning in an old tin cup.

He hears movement in a room below, pipes rattling, water running. Someone weeps, prays, washing away life with soap.

He takes from the suitcase a stoppered vase full of rain. A stolen puddle. He produces other things also.

He approaches the Doll, crouches before it, will not let himself touch the porcelain smooth face or fragile white hands. It was an early model, almost antique, but then he liked the past, the old thoughts of rain and hair and . . .

The Doll is four feet in height, the usual perfect face of lips and lashes. The modest pigtail of coarse grey hair. She wears a blue dress, blue as eyes. And beneath, he lifts the hem, the garment of grey. Smith strips her, touching only clothing.

The Doll is naked now in her whiteness, with just the hint of shade in the rounds of her contours, and there, behind, between her legs is the simple apperture, the slot for the coin. Stamped above it, the ancient logo of RAMPION INC., and beneath, the word or command, "ENJOY."

He rummages through his pockets, pulls out a fist of copper pennies. Careful then, behind the Doll, dropping loose change into the slot. The coins clatter, collect internally. Little machineries grind softly, cogs whir and *twitter,* her hair begins to grow, coiling out from the hole in her head. The more money installed the more hair grows. He will not look, cannot. His hand shakes, he turns away, unknowingly brushing by her, nudging her into motion. She topples light, from foot to foot. Side to side. Unseen Forward.

He switches the wireless on. There is the hum of old electricity. A machine warmth and cadmium yellow glow fill the room. He reads at names on the wireless tuner, remembering. "*Brussels, Helsinki, Luxembourg . . .*" A soft trumpet breaks in through static, and then a piano with crooner crooning, blending a melody. He removes things from the suitcase: Bible pages, torn, stained. A dried daisy chain.

He cannot hear the Doll as she teeters toward the door, coins rattling heavy inside her, buying the growth of harsh grey silk from her white hollow head.

Smith wants to look, to see her standing there, her hair about her, tumbling to the floor, but he will wait and concentrate on the music until he can wait no more and then he will turn and read from the fragments of Isaiah and Deuteronomy and he will drape the dead daisies over her eyes and . . .

The Doll has tottered into the door, nudged it open, continued out. A draft of air snuffing the candle's flame. *She has taken the light with her.* There is only the dim orange glow of the wireless now. Wax smoke shifting in the gloom.

Turning quickly, Smith sees her hair vanish from view beyond the swinging door—

She has walked out on him.

"No, not again."

He hears his own voice in darkness. The wireless band plays on. He rushes after her.

She has teeter-tottered along the hall to the stairway, and tumbles now, from side to side, weighted with coin, pulled back by sprouting mass of rough grey pigtail. Tumbling down the stairs, foot to foot on the narrow treads.

And here is Smith chasing after—

Her hair is getting longer, he can *see it growing, pouring* from her head. Racing down the stairs now, he's reaching out for her, but she's always thirteen or so steps ahead.

The carpet underfoot is crumbling; damp as candy cotton, the banisters rusting away, the walls seem to sweat. He cannot hear the wireless playing anymore, just coins clattering *inside*. Funny, he can't remember climbing up all *these* stairs. There are no hallways, no landings, just a staircase stretching down into darkness, as if it has no end.

She does not slow in her tottery descent, but goes faster, an impossible speed. Her hair *skkrittching* out, thin strands of grey like old comic book speedlines. But Smith can't reach her—

thirteen or so steps ahead—

He tumbles, headlong, reaching out, deaf to rattle of coin and his own screaming.

No longer *running down,* merely falling down.

Down to a darker silence.

Down.

DOLLY SODOM
John Kaiine

Dolly Sodom came scene for scene and almost word for word in a dream. It was written in an afternoon whilst listening to the *Tubeway Army* album.

Sherry Coldsmith has been writing and selling stories since 1989. Born and raised in West Texas, she studied computer science, then worked as a software designer and computer systems manager for several large corporations in Great Britain. Now living in central Texas, she spends her time writing fiction, working on a master's in film studies, and watching old movies. Other stories by her can be found in *Dark Voices*, *Other Edens*, *Skin of the Soul*, and *When the Music's Over*.

The title comes from a poem by Federico Garc'a Lorca and the story is one of the few historical fantasies in this volume. "The Lucifer of Blue" especially interested me because of the colorful backdrop—very few writers have used the Spanish Civil War as the impetus for their fiction. And relatively few have made prostitutes their protagonists (although at least three have in this anthology).

THE LUCIFER OF BLUE

SHERRY COLDSMITH

> *". . . I recognized it immediately as a*
> *state of affairs worth fighting for."*
> —GEORGE ORWELL, HOMAGE TO CATALONIA

THE *LONDON TIMES*, THE *NEW YORK TIMES*, BAD TIMES: IN Barcelona in 1937, I had expected to see the stigmata of all three. I'd certainly noticed the reporters; randy and cocktail-loaded, they roamed the Hotel Continentál freely. But they had been the only blemish on my visit. The perfect round of fresh linens, good meals, and hot baths had made me wonder if there really was a civil war on. My only acquaintance with the war was through the Spanish newspapers I translated for Dickie. The fact that I knew Spanish was a sign of Dickie's good old English pragmatism. If he'd wanted a woman whose skills were limited to the boudoir, he would have brought his wife along. Yes, Dickie did everything quick and on the cheap. Even dying. He'd had his heart attack in the time it takes to lose at cards. And now I was packing. The bad times were here.

I was tying the ribbon on my hatbox when I heard the porter's knock. I reminded myself of Loyalist etiquette—don't tip, call him *camarada* and not *señor,* and if you think he's a Fascist and you want to expose him, insult the Virgin.

"It's unlocked."

The door swung open, revealing the youthful face of one of the New York reporters. "Dangerous, Miss Dade. You never know who might be in the corridor."

The sight of Gary Bartow put me off my stride a little. He'd been rather cold to me lately. "Would you be a dear and go fetch the porter?"

He smiled, a narrow opening at best. "Where are you really headed, Miss Dade? Poor old Sam Boywold thinks you're off to Toulouse, but I know for a fact you can't afford the fare— unless you've snagged a little work since the funeral?"

Bartow wasn't looking me in the eye. I could just imagine how the truth about me was revealed: Dickie's pudgy fingers are choking a glass stem. Bartow is drawling about the horrors of prostitution. Then Dickie says, "It just so happens that I have some *personal* experience of the trade . . ."

I turned to the mirror and blotted my lipstick. I said to Bartow's reflection: "Do you wish to procure my services?"

"As a translator or a whore?"

Bartow folded his arms, evidently pleased with himself now that he'd insulted me, thereby saluting Motherhood and all that is decent. Some men are so easy to read. You'd think a girl as perceptive as me would be busy in bed, cajoling some journalist into filling Dickie's shoes. But I had pretended to be an ordinary career girl; now, I wanted nothing more than to sneak away quietly, before more people found out I was a liar.

I pulled on my coat, picked up my portmanteau and my hatbox, all without help. I said as sincerely as I could, "I hope your stay in Barcelona turns out better than mine."

I was halfway down the hall when I heard him come running after me.

· · ·

Bartow actually insisted on riding in the taxi with me, though he kept very quiet. The taxi pushed its way past cyclists and donkey carts in the Plaza de Cataluña, keeping a pace that a crawling baby could rival. The buildings were tall and narrow, with iron balconies and triplets of arched windows. A moldy winter distemper had crept up the sallow walls. I wondered at the dearth of motorcars, then remembered reading that the Loyalists had commandeered nearly everything that burned petrol.

The taxi swerved, skirting a water-filled crater in the road. "Did mortar fire do that?" I asked, incredulous.

"Dickie didn't show you the town? There're craters all over. And plenty of bullet holes if you look. When the Fascists seized the army, the unions and the Anarchists twisted the government's arm into giving everyone a gun or two. Though they didn't have to twist very hard. The government had to make up for the army it had lost to Franco. In Barcelona it was mainly the Anarchists who drove the Fascists out last summer. And while they were at it, they seized the city government."

"Sheer opportunism."

"Maybe. But if Uncle Sam ever calls me up to fight for the sake of the future, he'd better ask me what kind of future I want."

"And he'd better not call collect," I said, quoting Mr. Durante. I studied our surroundings more closely. The red-and-black flag of the Anarchists and the tricolor of the Spanish government hung from many shop windows. Signs boasting the establishment of a collectiva were everywhere, even on the bootblacks' boxes. Political posters smothered the walls. What bare masonry you could see was scarred and pitted. Had gunfire really done that?

The taxi pulled up outside a terraced house, a sliver of Gothic architecture that soared skyward. As I got out, Bartow said, "Why don't you work at the hotel? I'm sure—"

"Wives," I answered simply. "Some men travel with theirs."

He looked down at his big, scarred hands. He hadn't always been a reporter. "Then come and work for me, for heaven's sake. I don't trust my translator—"

I tried to smile graciously. "You wouldn't tell a barber to hang up his towel just because his razor's been stolen."

He gave me an embarrassed smile. Before he could say more, I went to join my luggage inside the deep alcove of the house's entrance. Wrought iron like a skein of black lace protected the door's window and made it impossible to see inside. I pressed the bell stud. I considered that I'd come to the wrong place, that this was not Saint Mary's Infirmary. But then I noticed the sign. In handwritten letters, it read, "Patrons are reminded that the women inside are comrades." I laughed out loud. What did the girls here think a rigid pecker was? Some form of revolutionary salute?

I was still laughing when the bolt clicked back. A young woman appeared and burbled something in Catalan. She wore a tight skirt and an old-fashioned tulle fichu that sculpted her bosom into buoyancy. "Are you in trouble, *camarada?* We know someone who can help you."

I was sure that she did, but it wasn't an abortionist I needed right now. "I telephoned yesterday. I'm Miss Dade."

Her smile gave way to a gaze of bold appraisal. Everyone in Loyalist Spain stared at you like that, even the bellboys and lift attendants. I knew what she was thinking. Though I had my coat on, it was easy to tell I was too thin for Spanish tastes.

"May I speak to the proprietor please?"

The woman looked as though she might spit at me. "If you can ask that, you are no comrade."

At first, I had trouble understanding her meaning. Then the word *collectiva* hit me with full force. It seemed even the whores had lost their senses. A knocking shop without a madame would be like a war without a general. Who mollified a patron when he couldn't have the girl he wanted? Who threw the girl out for shamming an illness? And what was to keep the girls from stealing from me?

I pulled myself up straight. If I didn't find work soon, I wouldn't have any money to steal. "Make me a comrade, then. Swear me in. I'll take an oath in blood if I have to."

She gave a little satisfied grunt. "Come back later. We're busy right now."

I didn't buy it. "I have two grams of Salvaran and the

means to dispense it, comrade." She looked at me quizzically.
"Medicine, darling. It's good for the clap."

Now I did have her attention. Without a complaint, she
helped me get my luggage inside the foyer. It was a dark,
stark place, with a mahogany table and a single brass lamp
with a fringed, box shade. A long flight of stairs led upward,
then curled back on itself, vanishing into the murk. I followed
her down a corridor past the staircase. I glanced into the salon.
Though the shutters were closed, I could make out satin pil-
lows and brocatelle sofas. Everything was excruciatingly
clean. Carlisle Street had been just the same, as if to reassure
the gents that syphilis was like ptomaine and could therefore
be warred against with brush and bucket.

We went through another door. The light was blinding after
the hall. Seven or maybe eight women sat in a room that was
half dayroom and half glassed-in loggia, like a greenhouse.
Ferns, geraniums and bloodred hyacinths sprouted from every
shelf and alcove. There was a child in the middle of the group,
seated on a hassock in a cloud of white lace flounces, her face
buried in her handkerchief. The sobs were mixed with little
gasps of Catalan. Her voice was decidedly unchildlike.

She lifted her face from the hankie. I saw from her bulging
forehead that she was a dwarf, with deep-set eyes imprisoned
in a whorl of blue paint. She was an improbable schoolgirl in
her lace and pigtails. The other women, all in shifts and night-
dresses, were clustered around her, trying to get her to drink
from a *porrón,* a beaker that shoots a stream of wine directly
into the mouth, bypassing germ-ridden lips. The *porrón* is
ideal for passing around.

One woman, round and rosy in the flesh, looked up and
said, "The English girl?" The gaiety in her voice cheered me.
She got up, leaving the other women to comfort the dwarf.

"*Salud!*" she said, kissing me on both cheeks. Though still
in her nightdress, she was painted up like an actress who
works on a stage a thousand miles from the audience. "I have
been praying for a girl to make the Americans happy. They
like them skinny."

"We shouldn't let her join," the one who'd brought me in
said. "She doesn't know what comradeship is."

"Alma, give her a chance," said the woman in front of me.

"This is Alma Almirall, Miss Dade. I am Jacinta." She gestured that she would introduce me to the others later. The two of them led me upstairs.

Alma and Jacinta were lounging on the cot next to mine in the house's stuffy attic dormitory. They eyed my things while I put them away, making me wish I had a lockable case for my silks.

"What's wrong with the girl downstairs?" I asked.

Alma snorted. "We'd all like to know that. We took her in because we felt sorry for her and now she cries all the time."

"Don't listen to Alma," Jacinta said. "Gabriella has plenty reason to be upset. You might have heard about—"

Alma interrupted with a groan. "The wilder the story, the more Jacinta repeats it. But tell her the Fascists are a kilometer from Madrid and she forgets it before dinner. You know the priest who carved his own throat?"

"Father Abelardo?" I asked. He had bled all over the steps of the Sagrada Familia church—a locked church—I had read. Loyalist Spain had little love for clerics.

Jacinta nodded excitedly. "He bade his followers to water his grave with the blood of whores, to win the Evil One's assistance. And you know, those three girls did disappear—"

"And my auntie's parakeet got sick that week, too," Alma said, with an impatient clink of her bracelets.

"Is that why Gabriella was crying?" I asked. "Did she know the girls?"

"No, I don't think so. I think she knew the priest." Jacinta's voice had dropped to a whisper. "She knows he can do it."

"Do what?"

"Get Lucifer to bring a new army to Franco."

I couldn't help laughing. She'd obviously been reading one of the thrill-mongering pro-Fascist rags known to prey on the superstitious. "So you don't know why Gabriella is crying at all, do you?"

Jacinta sat up, lifting her chin very primly. "Why would she keep the newspaper clipping about him in her drawer?"

Alma pinched Jacinta's plump thigh. "Why would you know what's in her drawer?"

"While I carefully folded the last of my silks," Jacinta said, "a friend of mine saw a vapor at the Sagrada cemetery—"

"Steaming horseshit," Alma declared.

I wished the girls would leave me to my Penguin. And my plans. In six weeks, I should have enough to take me to France on a holiday and then on to England. The Continent could keep its extremes, its Hitlers and bead mumblers. I'd had enough.

Alma got up from her sagging bed. She took my hat from the stand and tried it on, admiring herself in the mirror. "How did *you* run out of money?"

The hat, an indigo tricorne, looked lovely on her. Too lovely. "The man who brought me here liked to gamble."

"You *gave* him your money?" Jacinta asked.

"No, he stole it from my hiding place. Then he lost it, to another newspaperman. Eddie Mercel? He has a famous by-line." But of course they hadn't heard of him. "Anyway, Dickie had the good grace to die of a heart attack right on the card table."

This made even Alma laugh. She was responsible for the financial scheme around here, I'd been told. Soldiers from the Loyalist militias were charged a normal fee. Men who had mistreated or knocked up their girlfriends were charged double. Suspected Fascist sympathizers were reported to a militia man. I can't say I liked the world I was finding myself in, but my curiosity was piqued. And where would I be without curiosity? I'd be in a café on Brighton's promenade, wiping down tables and accepting the first spotty youth's offer of six brats and a crumbling terraced house.

"Why didn't you get it back from this Mercel?" Alma asked.

"He won it fairly. I did ask Eddie for it," I hastened to add. "Demanded it in fact but—"

"You didn't get it back," Alma said sneeringly. She repositioned the hat and posed as if for a photograph. "Vida," she said, rolling my name around on her tongue. "You should live up to a name like that."

In Spanish, it meant "life" but for my mother it had meant "visionary." At the time of my birth, she had still believed that England's green and reasonable land was everything her

English soldier had promised, a paradise where a Russian Jewess could know a life of peace and tolerance.

"Jacinta, I'm going out," Alma said.

"You haven't got time to go anywhere!"

"My monthly came early," she said breezily, then she sauntered out the door, my hat on her head.

I suppose that many brothels are started in times of war but I wonder if it wouldn't be wiser to invest in a Turkish bath, like the one we had in Finsbury back home. Many of the militiamen who came to us were staying in evil little boardinghouses that did not offer the means of a good wash. These men would come to our door with no higher ambition than a bath. They shuffled in, their new boots already on their feet, their parcels of new clothes in their arms. Fortunately, the girls had purchased several tin tubs. Filling bucket and tub was up to the gentlemen themselves.

I should admit I did not become aware of this straight away. On that first evening, I seldom stepped into the salon, or into the hall for that matter. Instead, I stayed in the Blue Suite, one of the six bedrooms on the middle floors (though if the room had any color scheme at all, I was unable to detect it). There I waited for my tick-and-turns. I had thought the girls simpleminded when they said men would come to me without seeing the goods first. But the first militiaman came along soon enough, though "man" is an overstatement. He was barely sixteen, a Spaniard, in fact. He spent himself in my hands while I examined him. He stuttered something, then disappeared like a fawn.

After he'd left, it struck me that here, unlike Carlisle Street, I wouldn't be relying on regulars. I wouldn't have to feign pleasure in the hope of persuading some East India banker that I gave better value than the competition. The war, I imagined, would always send along another soldier.

My mind humming pleasantly with this thought, I cracked the door a little, to signal I was ready for the next man. He came along before I had time to touch my book (Mr. Forster's *A Passage to India*). It seemed that the militiamen did trust the *camaradas* to deliver up one red-haired, English-speaking girl. This lad, like the last one, wore a red-and-black scarf, the closest the Anarchist militiamen came to a uniform. His new trousers were excruciatingly stiff. He was scarcely inside the door when he said, in English, "Can you really—"

"It's my mother tongue, too," I said.

I was not at all prepared for what happened next. He plopped down on the threadbare chaise, planted his face in his hands, and cried.

"Wh-wh-what's wrong?" I asked.

It took some minutes—too many minutes—to get him calm again. It seemed that he hadn't heard a woman speak his own language since he'd left Chicago. He declared me beautiful. To my horror, I contradicted him. He served in the Abraham Lincoln Brigade—*La Quincé Brigada*—he told me proudly. The Quince Brigade I told him and he laughed heartily at my lame joke. I told myself that the next time I saw him, I would have better jokes to tell.

A little after 3:00 A.M., I went to the loggia, a watery cocoa in my hand. As I entered, I caught a glimpse of Gabriella as she slammed the door to the patio behind her.

"Gabriella, come back!" Jacinta called.

Jacinta was sitting on a dusty wicker sofa, a frown on her face, her maquillage thoroughly wilted at this hour. "Vida, maybe you can figure out why she's mad at me."

I had an urge to march upstairs to bed, but I took a seat beside her. No doubt, she had been grilling Gabriella about the deranged Father Abelardo.

"A Captain Hidalgo came to her this evening," Jacinta said, sighing. "Not for the usual, though. I was passing in the hall and I couldn't help overhearing his voice."

"I see."

"He was calling her a traitor. I listened only because I wanted to find out why all the girls in Gabriella's old infirmary all quit at the same time. Hidalgo said that all the other girls had the decency to go back to their families. Well, just now I asked Gabriella what Hidalgo thought he was doing, talking to her like that. I was very polite, you see, and—"

The door to the house swung open. Alma walked in, flinging her coat off and clicking her hands as if she wore castañets. She still had my tricorne. Two more girls came in behind her, wearing warm, sturdy robes. They, too, had cocoas.

"I did it, Vida!" Alma said. She plunged a hand into the frothy fichu of her blouse and brought out a roll of *pesetas*. Licking her fingers, she began counting off the notes.

"My money!" I carefully put my cup down. Then I lunged toward her.

"Not so fast," she said in English. Apparently, the Yanks had taught her something. "Half for the house, half for you."

I didn't like this idea but then she had done the work. "And what about you?"

"De nada."

I had encountered this in Spain before. Ask a Spaniard for a lift to the station and she'll take you all the way to France. Though it broke my heart to do it, I offered her half of my half.

Alma shook her head. "You will stay here and teach me English. Reading and writing. *Okay?*"

I smiled to hide my nervousness. "One doesn't learn the language of Shakespeare in just a few lessons."

Her hands had found their way to her hips. "So? How long did it take you to learn the language of Cervantes?"

"I was an unusually quick study."

"Close the door!" Jacinta said, interrupting us. "You're letting all the heat out." One of the girls had stepped out onto the patio.

"I think there's a swan out here," the girl called back.

"You need spectacles," Alma said.

But we all followed her outside, curious to see this renegade swan. The air was crisp for once. All trace of the cold mist we'd had during the day had vanished. There was indeed a flash of white in the poplar's branches. We all realized, at the same time, that we were looking at a lacy skirt, fluttering in the faint breeze. Gabriella had hung herself.

To me, Gabriella's suicide was a sign of loss of nerve during wartime. I didn't let it prevent me from honoring my obligation to Alma or from settling into a routine. Oh, I was homesick at times. To drink a strong cup of tea, to get the newspaper off the steps in the morning, to buy a Penguin in Charing Cross Road, would have been heaven. The only thing

I didn't miss was my old customers at Carlisle Street: junior ministers who railed about racial hygiene; Harley Street doctors who scrutinized your female parts as if they'd like to see them pickled in a pathological museum. Still, there was worse employment. I had once been a typist at three pounds, two shillings a week. In that profession, having a good education means that, as well as typing a young man's dissertation, you help him write it. If you're lucky, he'll buy you a nosegay.

Telling Alma about my old customers helped to usher them into distant memory. Alma and I, the only speakers of English in the house, were like children with a secret code. Alma was a surprise in both languages, however. She loved the revolution and Buster Keaton one-reelers. She yearned for Anarchist brotherhood yet planned to desert to England, and then to America if the Fascists got too close.

"When I get to England," she said one day, "I'm giving up the life."

"You'd rather scrub floors? Would this be some penance for leaving Barcelona?"

"I couldn't do this work anywhere else," she insisted. "To work this life in England would always remind me of here, where I was happy. Aren't you happy here? The priests may not think so, but we're like a tonic for our boys."

To hear Alma talk, being a prostitute during wartime was like working for the Red Cross. You'd think the war depended on us. I suspected that Alma's reassurances were for her own benefit; they made her feel less of a coward for not joining her sister at the front.

There was something about Barcelona's atmosphere of revolutionary hope that put courage into everyone. Even Gary Bartow had joined the militias. His letters were fascinating. The *brigadistas* had a passion for equality and brotherhood that may have played well in America, for all I knew, but would have gotten them laughed out of London. Mr. Bartow wrote that neither side had enough ammunition to do anything more than hold the line and carry out a raid or two. Lice were a bigger worry than the enemy. Still, hearing of the war, even in its current stalemate, reminded me of how easily I had slept back home.

I told myself that I was sleeping just as easily here. Business was getting brisker all the time. The custom was steady and the competition peculiarly feeble, for Gabriella's brothel was not the only one to close. Two more followed suit because the girls inside suddenly swore off the trade. If this kept up, I would have a large pot to take back to Britain, where a good many people thought Mussolini was the name of an opera singer.

One spring evening, some of us sat in the salon, the phonograph idle because my friend back home had yet to send us the needle that could not be had in Barcelona for love or money (we had tried both). It was a quiet night. No militia transports had come in that day and the train from Barbastro was keeping to a Spanish timetable. It was due in today but not expected until tomorrow. I was reading a letter from Gary Bartow. He hoped to be on the Barbastro train.

The front door's buzzer went off. I was having my monthly so it was my turn to officiate. I hauled myself out of the deeply puckered chair.

The man I admitted into the foyer was so peculiar it was hard not to stare. His skin was so pale and taut it looked like it had been glued directly to his bones, with no intervening tissue. His tongue worked in his mouth for a moment, then he said, "Bring me a girl." The voice was more powerful than I had expected. He held out a roll of *pesetas*.

"*Camarada,* wouldn't you be better off getting a doctor?"

His eyes brightened for a moment, as if blazing with rage. The words, "I got the money," rattled across his lips.

I walked back into the salon. "This one looks like he's been put through a wringer," I whispered, loud enough for them all to hear.

Jacinta put down the penny dreadful she'd been reading, and said, "Last week, *I* had to take the one with no nose!"

There followed a clamor of excuses from Esmeralda and the other girls. Finally, Alma stood up and left the parlor.

I sat down and picked up the Lorca poem she'd been translating, a likening of the sea to Lucifer. Not content to placidly reflect the sky's blue depths, the sea desired Heaven's azure light for itself, and was thus condemned to the endless spasms of waves. Finding the verse an inauspicious omen, I didn't read the rest of the poem but took to staring at the Chinese clock on the mantelpiece. Its gold orbs seemed not to spin at all. Above it, there hung a painting of two nude women embracing. I looked from the painting to the clock, back to the painting, back to the clock. A dried husk like Alma's customer could take hours. Some clever inventor, I thought, needs to build a machine that will dangle your book from the ceiling, so you can read while the gent pumps away.

After forty minutes, I decided he'd gotten his money's worth. I marched up the stairs, then knocked on the door of the Green Suite, the room Alma preferred. "Can I bring you anything?" I asked.

There was no answer. Perhaps she'd decided on another room. Plenty were available on such a slow night. I turned the knob and found to my horror that it was locked. I put my eye to the keyhole but saw only a chair. "Alma! Alma!" I cried. There was no answer. "Jacinta! Esmeralda! Where is the key?"

Pandemonium followed: doors swinging open, nerves jangling, Jacinta shouting that no one had keys to the rooms. No one had ever had them. She ran upstairs, the house's front and back door keys in her hands.

"Hurry!"

Neither key fitted the lock. She reinserted the first one, jiggled and twisted and worked at it until the latch popped.

Jacinta flung the door open. Before I could see the bed, I saw Jacinta cross herself, the first time anyone in Spain had done this in my presence. Then I looked at the bed.

Alma was straining at the ribbons that bound her hands and feet to the bed. A rag separated her jaws. Her skin—I had always admired its fine, caramel cast—was smothered in a pale, viscous sap. It had soaked the rag in her mouth and glued her eyes shut. I mention her condition first because it was the most important thing to me and because the object on top of her was not comprehensible. My senses denied it. But like a nightmare that begins slowly, the thing gathered detail. The long bones of his feet and legs, lying between her whitened legs, reminded me of scraps tossed out after a feast. Its white hipbones lay caught between her thighs and its rib cage had engulfed her breasts completely, as if the skeleton had not possessed a sternum. The evil grin of its skull lay close to her slippery cheek.

Alma struggled to say something. It sounded like, "my eyes."

Constantina rushed over to rub Alma's eyes with the corner of the sheet. "Keep them closed, just for a second," I said.

I stood over the bed and tried to yank the skeleton away by its feet. The bones snapped off in my hands. I moved around the bed, gripped the hipbone and the rib cage and gently pulled. There was a hideous, sucking sound as the thing came away. I wrapped the bones in a sheet while Constantina finished wiping Alma's eyelids. "Take that thing downstairs and burn it. Get her a robe, someone!" Esmeralda found a nightgown. It seemed that Jacinta had fled.

Alma opened her eyes. "Vida," she said plaintively. I helped her put her arms in the gown. She was as limp as warm candle wax.

We scrubbed her with pumice stones until her flesh glowed and the rich, rotting smell of semen was gone. The filling of the bath and the rattle of the boiler were the only sounds we made. Alma did not say a word. Perhaps somewhere there is a language that provides the means to explain what we had seen. But none of us could speak it, so we said nothing at all.

Sometime in the night, I'd heard Jacinta creep back into her bed. I had gone to her for comfort but had found myself comforting her. It seemed that she had never forgotten Gabriella's hoarded newspaper clipping. In her tormented imagination, the skeleton was the advance guard of Satan's army, called down by Father Abelardo and his blood-nourished grave. Gabriella, Jacinta insisted, had been bedded by one. Having no better explanation of what we'd seen, I kept watch over Alma throughout the night, lest she wake and become another swan in our trees.

The next morning, Alma's smile upon waking was bracing. It seemed possible, even likely, that she remembered nothing.

"When does the train from Barbastro come in?" she asked. A sigh came from Jacinta's bed. She was waking up.

"I imagine it's already in," I said.

"Then why are we all sleeping?"

I looked up at the attic windows. Bright morning sunlight rimmed the black shades. "It's hours until we open, Alma."

She sat up and glanced at the slumbering figures of the other girls with disapproval. "We should open now."

"Steady on," I said. "A girl's got to have some time off."

She swung her legs down and pushed up from the cot over my protests. "I will call Santiago," she said, referring to the stationmaster. "He'll pass on the word we're open."

I laughed aloud, which was the wrong thing to do, I know, but I'm never at my best when sleep runs short. "You'll never get the others to vote for that!"

Jacinta was now sitting up, her face long with worry. Alma was at her mirror, washing herself at the basin on the floor and rubbing her feet with perfumed oil. Esmeralda, confused, went to the window and tugged the cord, flooding the attic with light. Everyone was staring at Alma.

"I don't think it's good for you to work today," I said.

She whirled around, eyes blazing. "You dare to say that when you know how they risk their lives for us! How could you refuse a single one of them?"

"I only refuse the ones who can't pay." She seemed to flinch away from this. "You aren't suggesting we give it away, surely."

Jacinta got up and came to Alma's side. "Alma, you must rest. Remember Gabriella."

Alma pushed her away. "She was an hysteric. Why would she have anything to do with what happened to me?"

Everyone was holding her breath and praying that Alma would say what had happened. She dragged her brush through her hair and said, "Who crossed herself last night, I want to know? Who prayed while I was sleeping?" The other girls all lowered their eyes. "You pathetic, ignorant whores. He gave me chloroform. I passed out. Who knows what happened? He had an accomplice. The skeleton was brought in through the window, maybe. Or up the stairs while you sat on your fat behinds. The Fascists torment us to destroy our will! They know we give our men the will to fight!"

Everyone looked relieved beyond measure. Constantina, the youngest of us, stood up from her bed, her shawl about her shoulders. "We could work free. For a day. To boost morale."

"I would do it for a day," Jacinta said.

"Listen to yourselves," I said, furious. "You're just whores! The Fascists don't waste a single thought on you. The lack of a nail in a horseshoe will make more difference to the war than all the whores in the world."

"Get out," Alma said.

I struggled to remain charitable. "Well, I *have* got my monthly," I said evenly. No one spoke to me as I dressed.

I had spent the day languishing in cafés and dress shops. Finally, desperate for someone to talk to, I remembered Mr. Bartow's letter. I found him in the Hotel Continentál savoring his first cocktail in months. Now we were on the Ramblas, strolling beneath the poplars and the curved necks of the streetlamps, dimmed because of worries about air raids.

"I can't get over how much has changed here," he said. "Would you look at that storefront!" We were walking beside the window of an exclusive boutique. Rows of bonbon boxes gleamed like gold teeth. "He was selling supplies to militiamen just a few months ago. And have you noticed all the tailored suits in town? It looks like the upper crust are back from whatever country home they retired to when the Anarchists took over."

"I *like* the boutiques."

He shook his head. "It used to be that the people couldn't do enough for a militiaman, now they duck across the street when they see him coming."

"You are a dirty lot before you've cleaned yourselves up."

"Then they should offer us baths, not contempt. I'm afraid it's all going to come apart, Miss Dade."

"You journalists are all alarmists."

"Maybe so. But the Loyalists aren't getting the help of the British or the French and without that they're doomed. Moscow won't help as long as it has an alliance with Paris. The Bolsheviks are telling the Communist brigades to forget about Franco and concentrate on keeping Spanish Morocco from falling to the Loyalists. Because if Spanish North Africans obtain self-rule, then all of the Arabs—in the French holdings as well as in the British Near East—will rebel. Don't you believe it when the British press blathers on about how the

Spanish government can't be supported as long as it harbors 'extremists.' English moderation must be music to Hitler's ears.''

"You're a lot of fun."

"So are you," he said, without my sarcasm. "Are all London working girls as nice as you? No painted nails? No tight skirts?"

I decided to ignore that. "When I was growing up during the Great War, my mother said that a cloud of evil had descended on Europe. Do you think—"

"That's happening here? What an odd way to put it."

I relayed every detail of what I'd seen the night before, including Alma's explanation. "She's right, of course. I wouldn't be so concerned if she hadn't woken up this morning an even more fanatical revolutionary. Out of pure zeal, she's giving it away today."

"So much more sensible to do it for money."

"If the transaction is a fair one."

"Spoken like a true Englishwoman—all moderation and sweet reason." He lit another cigarette. "I'll worry about Hitler devouring your country some other night. Tonight, I'd like to take you back to my room."

"I'm indisposed."

He took my hand. "In my room is one of those huge Victorian showers. You know the kind? Like a big monkey bars with steam blasting you from every direction. We could put it to good use."

"All right," I said. "If you promise to stay off politics."

I was surprised to find myself alone in the bed. He was an early riser, I told myself. I got up, made a toga with the sheet, then found my way into the enormous bathroom. He was at the mirror, his back to me. He'd cleared a patch on the steamy glass and was briskly shaving himself. A towel protected his stiff collar.

"You're up early."

"Got things to do," he said. He didn't even look at me.

Nostalgically, I glanced at the shower, remembering last night. "When do you go back to the front?"

"I'm not going back," he said. The razor slipped along his

cheek. He was bleeding but seemed not to notice.

"You're *deserting?*"

He grinned at his cut. "I'm not a coward. I'm going to fight for Franco."

I stood there, my jaw dangling, I'm sure. He watched his blood turn the shaving lather pink. "Go on, now," he said. "Get back on the job and stay there."

I certainly wasn't going to let him see how disturbed I was. I stepped back into the room and started getting dressed. I could attend to my morning functions in the lady's room of the hotel lobby.

Instead of taking a cab, I walked to St. Mary's, my mind filled with all the things I wished I had said. The more I walked, the more bewildered I became. I thought I knew Gary's type: a recently baptized militiaman so on fire with brotherhood and justice, he'd die smiling for the cause. What could have changed him in a night? In one, single night?

I rounded the last corner and saw the house there as always, the shudders and blinds tight against the morning sun. The sheer familiarity made my skin prickle. I ran to the door.

I knew that something was wrong as soon as I heard the silence inside. I looked in the parlor but found no one there. I walked down the hall, then opened the door to the loggia, just a crack. The little woodstove was dead. I opened the door the rest of the way and found Jacinta on the wicker sofa. She was staring fearfully into the middle distance. Upon seeing me, she burst into tears.

It was some time before Jacinta could win her breath back from her sobs. But eventually the story came out. Dozens of militiamen had queued up outside once the word of free services had gotten out. All of them were dirty. Many were syphilitic. A citizens' committee came and tried to shut down the infirmary for the day. The girls went out into the street, to jeer at the committee for being bad comrades. Eight or ten men were loitering at the corner.

Jacinta stared at the floor as if a shell were lying there, waiting to explode. "Those boys shot the committee members, one after another. I tell you, Vida, not one comrade survived."

"Is Alma alive?"

Her expression was full of pity—pity for me, I realized.

"After they shot the comrades, they told Alma to get back to work, to make sure Constantina and Esmeralda worked hard, too. If the whores told anyone about their sickness, the men would come back to kill them."

"We're not diseased!"

Jacinta shook her head. "You still don't understand. Alma and the women who touched her spread disloyalty, just like a fever. It turns good militiamen into the murderers of their comrades. I told you the skeletons were just the beginning."

My mouth was as dry as sand. "You're talking rubbish, Jacinta."

"No one can find his bones," she said hollowly. "Constantina put them in here by the stove, but they could not be found."

"So? Someone—"

"I think he is back in his grave, growing the flesh to walk the earth again."

I thought of Gary's change, of how complete it had been. Would the same thing happen to the next man, and the next? I couldn't work anywhere. Beneath my skin, I could feel the busy soldiering of bacteria. I suddenly understood why Gabriella had killed herself and why that irate militia captain had called her a traitor. With no hope of a husband and no belief in other work, she had simply chosen a quick death over a slow one.

"Where is Alma?"

Jacinta almost smiled. "She is spitting back at the Fascists. They think they have given her a sickness, but they have given her a weapon, to turn back on the Fascists." She added something in Catalan, but I had no trouble with her meaning. Alma had gone to the front.

I was sitting on a gun crate in a trench, the notebook and pencil in my hand part of my ruse. I was posing as a lady correspondent in pursuit of a story and a friend. We were a hundred yards as the crow flies from the line of Fascist redoubts. I had learned that Alma, when she had stopped here, had claimed a sister was working in a brothel in Huesca, a town three miles inside the Fascist lines. She had convinced them to let her pass, so she could find her sister and bring her back.

One of the soldiers fed a dried rosemary branch to the fire in the middle of the trench. Overhead, between the planks supporting the trench, the dark indigo sky was thickening to black. I watched three men climb out of the trench, to go dig for potatoes in no-man's-land. I waited fifteen more minutes and then told a comrade who was laboring over a cookfire that I was crawling to the next trench, to continue "my story." She gave me two ovoid objects, a little larger than goose eggs, which turned out to be bombs. She showed me how they had two pins, a stiff one to be removed shortly before the approach of danger and a loose one to be removed seven seconds before detonation. She advised me to crawl all the way.

I shouldered my rucksack, then clambered up the ladder and slithered over the sandbags of the parapet, onto the ground. Even in the dark, I could sense that the valley between me and the Fascist lines was a wasteland: bullet-chipped stones, forlorn weeds, a few dwarfed and withered oaks. I could just make out the flag of the Fascist redoubt. The road to Huesca was off to the right of that, I'd been told. I started crawling.

I had gone only a few yards when I noticed an awful, fecal smell. I was burrowing into soil little cleaner than a latrine.

In no-man's-land, I found my special, private fear, a dread of nightsoil and festerment. There was no reason to be here, I told myself. I could take the train to Toulouse and then down into Fascist Spain. I lay there without motion and actually considered doing this. My fear that Alma was demented got me moving again. She needed me. She'd better need me. I would keep her from staying too long in one place. We would work one village and then another, moving on just before the Fascists realized that we were turning their men into traitors.

I had covered ten more yards, perhaps, when I realized how cold the night was. The chill seemed to be falling from the sky and rising from the ground. I glanced up and saw the stars wink out: clouds. I could see a dry Spanish oak, low and spreading, maybe ten paces from me, but beyond that, I could see nothing. Somewhere in the direction I was tending, a gun fired. I saw the distant greenish bloom of what I presumed was a rifle flash. Then blackness. The memory of the rifle flash was all I had to fix my position on. I stood up. Crawling had been a noisy business anyway. Surely it was only sound I had to worry about now. I took a step, then listened. I could feel the bombs in my jacket pocket, not as a physical presence, but as my personal angel of death.

I had covered another forty yards or so when I heard a low grunt of laughter. I dropped to my face, too terrified at first to even worry if I'd somehow disturbed the bombs. Every muscle in my back spasmed, bunching against the bullet I was sure was on its way. But then I heard the sound of digging and remembered about the expedition to recover what potatoes remained from the prewar crop. In my mind, I could hear the song the men had gone out singing:

There were rats, rats, rats that swallow cats,
in the stores, in the stores!

Heaven only knew what they'd make of me. They'd probably shoot me for a spy. I scrambled away from them, heading for an outcropping of boulders. In the murky night, the stones looked like a fist, thrust up from the earth.

. . . rats that swallow cats,
in the quartermaster's stores!

I decided to stay where I was for the moment. They couldn't dig potatoes all night. I estimated that I was not more than seventy-five yards from the Fascists. If I continued tending toward the east of where I'd seen the rifle flash, then that should take me to the ridge. From there I might be able to see the lights of Huesca.

Over the next few minutes, the clouds seemed to thin slightly. I could make out a large stand of reeds some thirty yards away. A little stupid from my exertions, I found it too easy to let my mind wander, to imagine that the grasses were sugar cane and that I was on a tropical holiday. It seemed entirely natural that the grasses should be swaying, even though there was not a whisper of wind. The night was as silent as a jewel.

. . . in the quartermaster's stores!

The grasses were dividing, separating. The shadows within merged into a single, many-limbed juggernaut, pointing a forest of spikes at the sky. They were men, I realized, with rifles and bayonets. I buried my face into the soil but found I could not keep my gaze away from them. I almost fainted with relief when I saw that the phalanx was not advancing toward me but to the other side of the outcropping in which I cowered.

But the potato diggers would still be there. Infinitely slowly, I dragged myself to a gap in the stones. I could see the men, still stabbing at the ground with their crude sticks. I wanted to scream but could not make myself do it. I saw the three men at the front of the phalanx lower their rifles, pointing them at the Loyalists. But they did not fire.

Before the men could scream, the juggernaut was upon them. Bayonets sliced across throats. With a strength that could not be human, the enemy swarmed over the men, tearing heads from bodies as if they were snapping wings off a chicken. Not a bullet was wasted, not a sound made. The men gathered themselves into a juggernaut again, into a unitary, martial force, a single spearhead aimed at the Loyalist line.

I lay there, motionless, protesting against my inner voice before I even realized what it was telling me. I'm not a soldier, I pleaded. *You have to warn them,* it said. I got up and took the bombs out of my pockets. I pulled the stiff pin out of each one, twisting them out as the *camarada* had shown me. I whirled around, panicked because I could not see the knot of men. Then I did see them near the oak I had noticed earlier. I made myself walk forward. The beast did not look back, but moved forward, relentless as a machine. If I could warn the Loyalists at the right time, I thought, then the Fascists would be in range of their machine gun. But what was a machine gun's range? I had no idea.

When it seemed that I was two-thirds of the way back up the slope on the Loyalist side, I took out the bombs and held them both in one hand, my fingers aching as they splayed to grasp the weapons. I pulled one pin out and lobbed the bomb at the nest of men. It exploded near the group, provoking an instant burst of machine-gun fire, so immediate it sounded spontaneous. I did not wait to be sprayed as well. I ran back down the hill, barely having the presence of mind to disarm the other bomb.

I didn't want merely to run, I wanted to take wing, to get to Huesca and Alma and have it all over with. I plunged through squalls of mist that swallowed then disgorged me. The enemy may have been following me, or maybe not. I didn't care. Death would almost be a mercy, I thought; for then it would be over.

Suddenly I was falling, my feet knocked out from under me. I landed hard on my sternum and realized, after considerable kicking and flailing, that I'd tripped over a wire. Then I saw the parapet of a Fascist redoubt. I leapt to my feet, ready to run as fast as my legs could carry me.

"Alto."

My knees were trembling so hard, I nearly fell again when I saw the soldier's silhouette, the talon of his bayonet. He was framed by the wash of light from the trench.

"I am lost, *señor*" I said. "I have to get to Huesca. I have a friend who has gone there. Have you seen her?"

His laugh had a bitter note I didn't like. "Yes, I've *seen* a woman . . ." He shifted his rifle and brought out a match, striking it against his boot. He held it up to my face and studied me in the match's brief flare. I could feel its heat.

I took a deep breath and let my good sense rescue me from the horror I'd seen but a few minutes before. This boy was hardly a child. Surely I could persuade him to let me pass.

"I'm alone," he said tonelessly.

"We are all alone, *señor*."

"I mean, I'm alone in the trench," he said.

The leer in his voice had been unmistakable. "All right. But you can't have it for free, soldier."

I could see him fumbling in his pocket. He threw a few wadded notes at me. "It's all I've got, bitch." He sounded oddly relieved, as if he hadn't wanted to force me. I picked up the notes. He stood aside and gestured to the ladder.

I swung a leg over the parapet. At first it seemed that the trench, stretching away for about ten yards, was empty, just as he'd said. Then I stepped onto the ladder and saw the sleeping figure almost directly beneath me. She was curled up on her side, a blanket covering her to the chin, her black hair tangled and stringy. Her skin was chalk white.

"Alma!" She did not turn her head.

I dropped to the ground as soon as I could. Alma seemed to stare at nothing, but she did blink. She was alive.

I rushed to her cot and put a hand on her forehead. She was as cold as a stone. Numbly, I petted her hair. "It's me. I'm here."

She looked confused for a moment. I think she tried to smile. She said something but her voice was too soft for me to hear. I put my ear to her mouth. "It takes sides," she whispered.

I heard the sentry come down the ladder and come to stand behind me. "We can't use this cot," he said stupidly.

"What's wrong with her?"

"Our lieutenant, he goes crazy when he finds out she makes him and his men stronger. He says maybe she makes the machine gun a cannon!" He cocked his jaw toward the end of the trench, where a machine gun tripod stood on scaffolding. The boy said, "They ruined her before I could take my turn."

I lifted the blanket. Blood had completely soaked her torn skirt and the cot underneath was stiff with dried blood. No, I thought, the soldier wouldn't want to use this bed. I pulled the blanket back up to her chin.

"They put other guns down there, too," he said petulantly.

Alma was whispering again, her dry lips scarcely parting for the words. "It takes sides."

"What does, sweetheart?"

"Evil."

"We can talk later," I said. It was a stupid, stupid thing to say, but I kept on repeating it, even as her eyes fluttered open and stayed open.

"I have my money right here," the boy said impatiently. "Are you a lucky whore, too? Will you make me strong?"

I stood up, turning my back to Alma. Now I looked at the boy. What have I felt for my patrons? Apathy, mostly. Passion, sometimes. Affection rather less often. Now I was having my first taste of simple, blue-white hate. I had always been dispensing strength: to the doctors who had gone back rejuvenated to their jars of pickled organs; to the judges who had returned to the bench with the fortitude it takes to put a man to death or to grant him his life. Perhaps they had all been good men; perhaps they had all been bad. How could I know? They never asked me how the strength I gave them was to be used.

The soldier was waiting for his treat. I gave him a hard kick to the privates then scrambled towards the ladder, his screams—"Bitch! Bitch!"—in my ears. I was near the top rung when I felt the ladder tremble with the soldier's weight. I flung myself over the sandbags of the parapet, rolling onto the stone-sharp ground. I took out the last bomb. Evil is not moderate, I thought; how can I be? I yanked the pins out and lobbed the bomb into the pit.

After making my way back to Barcelona, I made the journey back home, leaving Franco's nightmare forever, or so I thought. For a time, impressions of Spain sank into the haze of a civilized life: daytrips on trains that ran to schedule; walks along the white brows of cliffs, through meadows where the breezes comb wildflowers into the grass. Sometimes and without warning, the faces of Alma and Gary would flicker and focus and the haze would lift. Then I would find myself driving my motorcar, careering down every street in London; driving in all weathers, at life-or-death speeds; trailblazing through alleyways to make a new shortcut; learning to read the city as if its streets were braille. Now, when the streetlamps dim to tiny embers and housewives draw the black shades down, when the city is as dark as a hillside in Spain, I steer an ambulance by the light of falling bombs.

THE LUCIFER OF BLUE
Sherry Coldsmith

This story is a confluence of fed-ups. Mainly, I was fed up with the way that prostitution is often represented in genre fiction. Before he was assassinated, Benigno Aquino said that whenever he wanted to take the measure of a city's economic health, he would visit its red-light district and count the prostitutes. Aquino's sensitivity to cost-benefit calculations is downplayed in much fiction, where romantic love is often seen as the cure for prostitution. By all indications money would be a far more reliable remedy. I was also fed up with Coach, the mass noun I give to the teachers I had back in high school. Coach taught only the Orwell of *Animal Farm*, suppressing the radical journalist who had fought against Franco.

Armed with my disgruntlements, and with a long-standing desire to set a story in the Barcelona of Orwell's *Homage to Catalonia*, I sat down to juxtapose mercenary soldiers of sex with idealistic soldiers of war. I felt sure that evil would declare its allegiances in the process. I hope I was right.

Born and raised in California, Scott Bradfield moved to London in 1985, where he published his first collection of stories, *The Secret Life of Houses*, in 1988. His novels include *The History of Luminous Motion, What's Wrong with America*, and *Animal Planet*. His collected stories were recently published in the U.S. under the title *Greetings from Earth*. His stories have appeared in *Omni, Conjunctions, the Los Angeles Times Magazine, Triquarterly, Interzone, The Pushcart Prize XVIII, The Year's Best Fantasy and Horror, Bad Sex*, and *The Vintage Book of Contemporary American Stories*. He's written both film and television adaptations of his work, and his books have been translated into more than a dozen languages.

Bradfield's short fiction occupies the same area of oddball mainstream in which the works of Jonathan Carroll and Steve Erickson often reside, all three occasionally breaking out into fantasy.

"The Queen of the Apocalypse" takes place today and is, simply, about a woman unhappy with her life.

THE QUEEN OF THE APOCALYPSE
SCOTT BRADFIELD

HARRIET OWEN SPENT HER YOUTH MAKING LOVE TO OTHER women's husbands. She spotted them in supermarkets and shopping plazas, and trapped them with her formidably blue eye-contact. While they solemnly pretended to inspect frozen food and sports equipment, Harriet provided them quick opportunities to introduce themselves, and redetermine who they were while their wives weren't around. Eventually there occurred brief lapses into soft words, too many margaritas and cigarettes, crying over telephones, sex in elevators. Then, as abruptly as recognition, the harried men went away again. Disconnected their office telephones and sent Harriet personal checks in the mail. For Harriet, affairs with married men were a sort of clock. Whirr, tock, tick. As a result, Harriet always knew what was happening in her life, and what would happen next.

Hardness was no stranger to Harriet, and neither was remorse. "You are not a good girl," her mother used to remind her. "You are not loving, or compassionate, or true. You never help with the housework, or care how I'm feeling. You never prepare meals for me unless I ask." Sometimes Harriet's mother would disappear for days and weeks at a time, returning with an ostentatious clatter of keys in the middle of the night, a bag of groceries under one arm, a six-pack of beer under the other. And it was always Harriet's turn to cook breakfast.

Harriet's mother liked to say that she had been an Abstract Expressionist long before being an Abstract Expressionist became popular. All day long she smoked marijuana out of a corncob pipe and wore a loose-fitting terry cloth bathrobe, gazing blurrily at her uncompleted canvases as if she couldn't tell them apart. Their large studio contained two mattresses, three splintering wooden benches, large enormous rolls of medium-grain canvas, knock-kneed stepladders, framing boards, and countless rusting splattered paint tins stacked everywhere in weird configurations—pyramids, crosses, triangles, and ellipses—as if someone, somewhere, secretly intended them to mean something.

Harriet left home when she was seventeen, moved to North Hollywood, and spent every night sitting on the floor of her unfurnished apartment gazing at the palms of her hands as if they were paintings on a wall. She wanted to know the things her mother never thought her capable of knowing, those things they hadn't taught her in school. She didn't want to be just plain old know-nothing Harriet anymore, because she wanted to be better, and wiser, and filled with more meaning than herself. "You can't see beyond the world you live in, which is why you will always be sad," her mother used to tell her. "Now stop crying and go to sleep."

Some nights Harriet clipped at the blue veins in her wrist with a pair of pale, dull scissors until the blood came. She did things to her toenails with matches and cauterized sewing needles. She gripped metal table knives and inserted them into the sudden frisson of bulbless lamps and open sockets. This, Harriet wanted to remind herself, was pain and attention. This was what happened when you were bad. A remote bright sensation of inflexibility and heat. A sort of visceral information. When Harriet felt pain, she didn't feel lost, she knew where she was. She realized there was a world outside, a world that wanted her, a world that would hold her in its arms.

Every night before she fell asleep, Harriet tried to imagine the total destruction of her own body. Flames would work, missiles or bombs. Stroke, angina, renal failure, poison in the bloodstream, plutonium in the water. Suns and planets might explode and take civilizations with them, or the dollar collapse so Americans couldn't buy bread. Comets might arrive just like prophecies, and then the entire world would know. Harriet tried to imagine herself shot in the head by hasty addicts, or run over by blundering buses in the street. When the body died, the mind went someplace else, escaped this embrace of skin and politics and metal. Continents grew infirm, galaxies milky, teeth loose, philosophies abstract. If you were lucky and didn't struggle, you might learn the pain that really mattered. You might even learn to be good. You might finally understand.

Sometimes the bleeding wouldn't stop and Harriet visited the doctor.

"Do you do this to yourself?" he asked. He stood over her during the examination, exerting force and profession. "Or was it some boyfriend? Is it something you ask them to do or do they just go ahead and do it anyway?"

"I'm clumsy," Harriet said, closing her eyes, seeing the white starry impact she saw whenever she contemplated herself. "It happens when I'm cooking at the stove, or chopping vegetables at the sink."

Sometimes the doctors sat behind their desks and watched her from far away. They stopped looking at her body. They tried to look into another part of her.

"Why do you do it?"

"*I* don't really *do* it."

"Is it because you don't like yourself?"

"I like myself fine."

"Have you ever been on medication? Have you ever visited a therapist?"

"I've consulted therapists," Harriet said. "But I've never taken any prescribed medication."

Then one day a man came along and tried to save her, a man Harriet consequently neither forgave nor forgot. Boyd Thomas left his wife and children, changed his job, and moved into Harriet's apartment on a Superbowl Sunday, setting up a sort of provisional base camp on the living room sofa. Every day he went out for groceries and supplies from the local market. He did the chores, washed the dishes, and emptied the trash. Every evening he prepared large, nutritious dinner salads and vegetarian pastas in Harriet's underequipped kitchen, and never even made a fuss when Harriet refused to eat. It was a type of cruelty Harriet had never known before. A man who wanted to take care of her. A man who wouldn't go away.

Boyd assembled his dense, secret ministry of affection in Harriet's life while Harriet wasn't looking: new dishes, silverware, appliances, furniture, vitamins, consolation, and advice. Some mornings Harriet awoke to discover new curtains in the kitchen, tools and workbench in the basement, roses in a vase beside the stove, Boyd's shoes under the sofa. "You need to get out more," Boyd told her, arranging the dull clatter of tea things on an aluminum tray. "You need to stop feeling so sorry for yourself. Reenroll in school for chrissakes. Career Management—that's what I was thinking. And *look* at me when I'm talking, why can't you ever *look* at me? All I ever do is give, give, give, and all you ever do is take."

Boyd could endure even more abuse than Harriet, and that's why she couldn't make him go away. He intercepted flying plates and glasses with ease, replacing them patiently on the shelves where Harriet could reach for them again. He entertained crude slurs about his manhood with an attitude of benign and sinister avowal. He took all the sharp objects from Harriet's apartment and destroyed all the matches, and refused to slap her whenever she slapped him. There didn't seem to be anything Harriet could do about it. Wherever she turned, there was Boyd trying to love her. Boyd with a cold washcloth to wipe her brow, and two strong arms to hold her.

In bed at night Boyd stroked her white back with his rasped, knuckly fingers. He whispered endearments at her as if he were pushing bulbs and garden implements into the dark earth. "I love you," he whispered, over and over again, a litany as inextricable as his embrace, his voice reaching into places even Harriet couldn't go. "You're a really great woman who deserves the best life has to offer. You shouldn't hate yourself so much; you shouldn't feel so insecure. You're a really strong, special, caring sort of person, and that's why I really, really love and respect you."

After a while Harriet would let Boyd make love to her, because it gave her distance and dimension back. Boyd and Harriet, him and her, man and woman, hammer and earth. She would close her eyes and go away into the wash of galaxies that wouldn't last, into the casual obliteration of planets that never mattered. The man would climb off her; he would insist on holding her in his arms. Then Harriet would fall asleep and dream of catastrophes. It was the only real submission she could make anymore.

He took her to meet his family—Wanda, Phil, Jane, and Eddy. Wanda and Phil were his parents, Jane and Eddy his father's children by a previous marriage. "You seem like a terrific young girl," Phil said, "and Boyd has told us so many wonderful things about you. He never gave us any idea, though, exactly how pretty you were." They sat on the splintery veranda, drinking sun tea spiced with licorice, watching the sunset expand over Hermosa Beach. Phil turned to Wanda. "But she really *is* pretty, don't you think? Especially her hair."

Boyd's family usually talked about Harriet in the third person.

"Not only that," Wanda said, "But just look at her teeth. I wish I had teeth like that. Then I could eat anything I wanted."

"And such a nice figure," Phil said, looking her up and down. Phil was a jeweler in Santa Monica. "Boyd must be the envy of all his friends at the office." Phil winked at Harriet and blushed, holding his bony knees together.

"We sure like her better than Marjorie," Jane and Eddy called out from the living room, where they basked in the pale, unearthly light of the RCA. "No matter how nice she pretended to be, Marjorie was always a big fat drag."

Wanda distributed more tea and packaged cookies. She leaned toward Harriet and stage-whispered: "Boyd's last wife was a very nice woman, and provided Boyd's children with a wonderful role model and all that. But she was never a very sexual sort of person. And Boyd, as you must know by now, likes to exchange a lot of good healthy pleasure with his women. Much like his father." Wanda showed Harriet lumpy sugar in a white ceramic bowl. "I forget already—do you take sugar?"

"No," Harriet said. "I never take sugar in my tea."

"She's watching her figure," Phil said. His flushed, vein-burst face winked inconstantly at Harriet, like a broken signal at a railway crossing. "She doesn't want to lose her gorgeous figure—and neither do we, hey, son? Neither do we."

Boyd married her and bought a house. That was the end, really. There was nowhere left for her to go.

"It's got a basement and an attic," Boyd said proudly. "Two bedrooms and a den. The kitchen needs work, but there's no problem with the heating. And the yard is enormous. Like ten normal-sized yards, really. A big, I mean a really *big* yard. We could have twelve kids running around in that yard and they wouldn't see each other for weeks."

The house was wide, complicated and dense, poured into the earth with concrete, hammered together with wood and nails. Harriet couldn't cry and couldn't sleep, lying in bed all day until Boyd returned home from his new subcontractor's job at the mall. She heard the power lines in the street, pigeons on the rooftop, the aluminum rustle of gas in the stove. Every morning cartons of fresh milk and butter appeared on the doorstep. Newspapers, shopping coupons, stray cats howling at the wind.

She bound her feet with twine in order to cut off the circulation. She plucked hairs from her face and secretly bit her tongue. She ate too many grapefruit, and rinsed the cold sores in her mouth with vinegar, salt, and lime concentrate. She explored those regions of her body where sewing needles didn't leave marks. It might be Boyd's house, but it was still her body. I, Harriet told herself, am completely *my* decision.

Boyd began exhibiting a strange and unhealthy concern for Harriet's menses, circling dates on the Val's Used Autos calendar with a black felt laundry marker. "Monday, Tuesday, Wednesday, *Thurs*day," Boyd told himself out loud, and circled the final date with a proud little flourish, as if he were endorsing a particularly generous check. Then he took the thermometer from the kitchen cabinet, swabbed it with alcohol, and called out Harriet's name.

There was something implacable about the way Boyd made love to her now, as if he were straining against the skin of a bubble, trying to tell her something language could not convey. "I've reinsulated the attic," Boyd told her in bed, rocking gently against her, as cautious as if he were caressing helium. "I've discussed the basement plumbing with a regional contractor. This spring, I'll paint the place. I'll put down new carpets and a new yard. Depreciation, baby. That's what finally buries you. By the way, did I tell you I love you, Harriet? Did I tell you you're the most beautiful woman I've ever seen in my life?"

There were books on the bureau beside the thermometer. *The Home Pregnancy Handbook, Fertility and Nutrition, Conception and the Stars.* Harriet, however, was wary of books. She was afraid they might not keep their words to themselves.

"I don't care if it's a boy or a girl," Boyd said later. "I just hope it's a Gemini."

By now, Harriet felt so estranged from her own body she couldn't believe any of it was happening to her. Nurses, obstetricians, waxed fluorescent corridors, hurrying orderlies, and drugged, dozing patients on gurneys. From the moment the doctor told her, Harriet pretended to play along.

"Get plenty of rest," the doctor told her. "And exercise. A nice long walk every morning should do it. Don't drink to excess, but a little wine in the evening won't hurt anything."

"Okay," Harriet said. She was looking at a dietary chart the doctor had presented her. The chart was printed on an embossed sheet of plastic and depicted colorful pie graphs, statistical charts, and a brief illustrated history of gestation. "I can do that."

"She looks like a madonna," Boyd's mother said. "She looks like the most beautiful mother-to-be in the entire world." Wanda and Phil arrived every Saturday afternoon bearing homemade soups, casseroles, Tupperware-clad fruit salads, and bright packaged gifts Harriet was expected to open. Blankets, diaper bags, Nerf toys, music boxes, Pooh books, illustrated nursery rhymes. Harriet would smile and try to look nonplussed.

"She seems so peaceful. So content with herself."

"Her body's generating this drug that helps her relax—I read about it once in a magazine."

"She used to be so edgy and insecure. Boyd's been really good for her. He knew all along she just needed someone to care for. It's a woman's biological role. Even when women aren't having babies, they dream about having them all the time."

"That's the full flush of motherhood, all right," Phil said wisely, and showed Boyd the roll of floral-patterned linoleum he had purchased for the family room. "And we know it'll be a beautiful baby, because *all* Boyd's women have beautiful babies."

Now at night it was Harriet who wanted to make love, and Harriet who wanted Boyd to hold her. Boyd was always reading now—*You and Your Baby, Dr. Spock's Guide to Infant Growth and Development, Owning Your Second Home, Building Your Own Bomb Shelter*. He ate Butterfinger candy bars, drank warm beer from aluminum cans, and watched war movies on late-night TV.

"Tell me," Harriet insisted, "tell me, tell me." Straining against Boyd's density, his steel and concrete and brick.

"We have to be careful," Boyd whispered, overturning his paperback on the end table, lowering himself under the blankets as if he were immersing himself in a cold tub. "Your condition. This trimester. For all concerned. You know I love you."

"Tell me," Harriet said, pushing, reaching, clenching his

callused hands against her breasts, demanding his skin, his impact, his intestinal flux and hiss.

"You're going to hurt yourself, honey. Now please, let me, let me . . ."

"Tell me, tell me, tell me," Harriet said, over and over again, trying to engage the secret harmony of it, trying to make her own words matter.

"Tell you what, Harriet? What do you need to know, honey? Tell me what it is you want me to say."

Boyd was always mending, reupholstering, abrading, polishing, trying to hide things from her. Nicks and imperfections, textures, conspiracies of pipe and cable. He painted things, and applied wallpaper, and hung new doors, working late into the night while Harriet slept. Sawing, hammering, painting. New bolts on the windows, new drapes in the living room. The scraping of metal against metal. The screak of vises. The shuddering of lathes.

"After we have the baby, Boyd, then what? What happens to us then?"

She lay beside him in bed. Boyd was sketching things on a clipboard.

"Hmm," Boyd said. He was consulting the latest issue of *Home Design Management* that lay open in his lap.

"You're not listening to me, Boyd."

"Of course I'm listening." He held a glimmering metric ruler up to the light. "Once we have the baby, we'll be happy. Then everything will be okay."

One night in early March Harriet awoke and discovered herself suddenly enormous. The sheets and blankets were soaking wet, wrapped around her sore, swollen thighs like the leaves of a cabbage. She felt surfeited and overindulged, washed up drunk on a beach somewhere, entangled with rubbery brown polyps and plankton. She reached for the bedside lamp and knocked aluminum cake tins onto the floor, ice-cream containers, extinguished cookie packets. She tried to sit up and failed. Then, again, on the count of three. She peeled the damp sheets from her legs. Suddenly, she was sitting up. She was sitting on the edge of the bed.

Silver shapes glided around the bedroom, as if the moon were riding a carousel. She looked through the gauzy drapes at the freeway, headlights skirling past, an entire universe filled with history and blind intention. She knew it before she heard it, like the shape of an extracted tooth, intimate and strange.

Somewhere deep inside the house the voice said:

This is it. Here we go. It's time.

"I know," Harriet said. "You don't have to tell me. I already know."

Boyd was getting out of bed. He was already wearing his Levi's and pulling on a blue T-shirt.

"Just relax and stay calm," Boyd said, guiding her down the front stairs, dispensing an aroma of Old Spice and Vaseline. Their car was idling in the driveway, a '55 Chevy Custom Chief with whitewall tires and padded dash. It was filled with animal patience, like something slumbering in a cave.

Then Harriet was in the car. Boyd adjusted her seat and pulled a small perforated wool blanket across her knees. She watched her fat, freckled hands in her lap.

The voice said, We'll be there in a few minutes, so try to relax. This is what you've been waiting for. Pretty soon, you'll have everything you've ever wanted. And then it'll all be yours.

"Is it really?" Harriet asked. Boyd was slamming the trunk and wiping the rear windshield with a soggy paper towel. "Is this what I've been waiting for? I knew I was waiting for something, but I guess I never knew what it was."

Boyd climbed into the driver's seat and slammed shut his door. The automobile was intact now, enclosing a perfect bubble of space and heat. The automobile started to move.

"I've been through this before," Boyd assured her. Mist thickened on the windshield and Boyd activated the wipers. "A piece of cake, really. It's all in the breathing. My first wife Betty, she panicked, couldn't breathe. Then they injected her with a sedative and bang. As soon as she stopped thinking, she breathed *per*fectly."

They were passing through streets lined with overturned garbage cans. City lights were everywhere. They just didn't seem to reveal anything.

"Why didn't you tell me before?" Harriet asked. "Why did I have to wait so long?"

"I'm sorry, babe." Boyd was gazing abstractly out the window, computing logistical distances, road conditions, those soft rear tires that needed replacing. "Why didn't I tell you what?"

"Can I ask questions?" Harriet asked the smooth white lights wheeling through the car. "Or am I just supposed to listen?"

The hospital was surrounded by brightly illuminated gray parking lots, like some neglected outdoor cinema. The doors to the emergency room opened automatically, and Boyd helped Harriet into a wheelchair. "I called ahead," Boyd told her, "and alerted Dr. Wilde. Don't be frightened. If you need anything, all you have to do is ask."

There was something in the silence behind Boyd's voice Harriet wanted to hear.

And then, with a long sustained gasp, Harriet felt her body start to breathe.

"Je-*sus*," Harriet said. "Je-*sus*."

Everything speeded up. Harriet was being conveyed down long corridors, and then transferred to a tissue-lined examination table. She reached out. She was holding someone. She pulled the hands closer, closer.

"Tell me," she said. "Tell me, tell me."

"It's okay, baby. They've gone for the doctor. Looks like you're not going to make anybody wait around, are you? I've told them to give you something for the pain—"

The entire room clenched around her, and she felt the deepness of her body exerting pressure back. "No," Harriet told him, "no, don't, no, no," without even listening, without trying to decipher what Boyd's words meant.

Then she felt two enormous hands come down, grip her by the waist and lift her up off the table.

"Je-*sus*," she said. "Je-*sus*."

Her body seemed very far away. She was connected to her own sensations by a long, microscopic filament of light.

"Tell me," she said. "Tell me, tell me, tell me, tell me."

"Tell you what, honey? You keep asking that. Tell you what? I'm listening, honey."

"Don't," Harriet told his hands. She was trying to reach into the light's white canvas, the pure white soundless texture that once filled her mother's apartment with everything Harriet couldn't be. She thought she saw Boyd, but it wasn't, wasn't him, because Boyd didn't matter, Boyd had never really *been*. Then she saw him, the man with the voice looking down at her, understanding how she felt and what she needed, loving her for all the right reasons. She could see him but she couldn't see him. He was there and he wasn't there.

It doesn't make things any easier, the voice told her. Even when you know, it doesn't make you happy.

"I understand," Harriet said, "it doesn't matter, I don't need to be happy, tell me, tell me, I really *will* understand." Harriet was crying. Exultation filled her with heat and oxygen and light. "This," Harriet cried, "is just *perfect*," and then the hands came swinging down again and struck iron through her stomach, her pelvis, and spine and lifted, lifted her off the table, up through the wide bright air and soft, impactless white glare of the ceiling. Nobody ever told her but now she knew, she knew. She was hurtling through the white air, the bellows of her lungs beating and swallowing at the rough pale atmosphere like an engine, and nobody had to tell her anything ever again because finally she knew, she knew, she knew, she knew.

―――――――――――――――――――――――――――――――――

QUEEN OF THE APOCALYPSE
Scott Bradfield

I don't appreciate the smugness of generic fiction. By "generic" (and I'm being deliberately nonacademic here), I mean just about anything you can *classify*. As soon as you find yourself wondering "Is this SF, or Fantasy, or Serious Literature?" you've stopped enjoying it, and listening to what it has to tell you. At this point, you might as well not bother.

I wrote "The Queen of the Apocalypse" while thinking a lot about the 1950s. Bomb shelters in the suburbs, bad marriages, too many places to shop, not enough things worth buying, and working forty hours a week surrounded by a universe of force. The end of the world, I've always thought, isn't an event which may or may not happen. It's an emotion most of us already know.

Richard Christian Matheson is a novelist, short story writer, and screenwriter/producer. He has written and produced more than five hundred episodes of television for over thirty prime-time series. A feature project tentatively called *The Glow* is in production. His short stories have been published in such diverse magazines as *Penthouse*, *Twilight Zone*, and *Omni*, and in anthologies including *Alien Sex*, *Millennium*, and *Dark Terrors*. His stories are collected in *Scars and Other Distinguishing Marks*. Matheson has published two novels, *Created By* and *Leading Man*. He lives in Southern California.

In "Oral," a man who has absented himself from the physical seeks alternative stimulation. Another of Matheson's short sharp little gems, this one demonstrates the eroticism of dialogue (as did *Vox*, Nicholson Baker's ode to phone sex).

ORAL

RICHARD CHRISTIAN MATHESON

"WHAT DO YOU WANT ME TO DO?"

"Seashells. Have you ever touched one?"

"Yes."

"In a detailed way?"

"What do you mean?"

"Describe it to me."

"The shell I touched was on a beach in Florida. It was a nautilus with a pearly spiral. Rough and sharp on the . . . skin of it."

"Analogy of touch. Good. Go on."

"It was heavy."

"How heavy?"

"A pound. Maybe a pound and a quarter."

"Tell me about the inside."

"There were . . . slender twists. Corkscrews. Glassy surfaces like . . ."

"... yes?"

"... feeling the interior of an ancient bottle."

"Did you put your hands into it?"

"... three fingers. I reached them in and they moved as if sliding on curved glass and they felt like they were gliding into a glove, they fit so perfectly. The walls were cool, and there were grains of sand that scraped my fingertips."

"Did your fingers get wet?"

"The interior was a little moist. I forgot that."

"Try to remember everything."

"I will. It felt . . . petrified. Is that the word?"

"Yes. Like rock. Hard and cold. Dead."

"But still alive. Able to sustain temperature and color. The contours were like a body. The textures seemed to be . . . feeling me."

A pleased stare.

"I made you feel something when I described the shell?"

"Yes."

"Like it was real?"

"Yes."

"Were you excited?"

"Yes."

"You could buy a shell."

"I don't come near what others have touched."

"People have touched everything. It's life."

"No. The opposite. Fingerprints signal oncoming death. Germs cling to surfaces. Waiting to cause illness, suffering. Disinfection is impossible."

Silence.

"But you miss touching things. You must."

Silence.

"Is that why I'm here?"

"Let's go on." Points. "The pencil."

"It's wooden. Painted to feel smooth. No heavier than a sugar cube. The name of the hotel is etched into the side like . . . inverted braille."

"What about the curves? How does the rubber feel on the eraser? Sticky? Firm? Angular? And the tip?"

"Well . . ."

"Frayed? Shredded? Or softly worn? Rounded? There's a

difference." Impatient. "How about the sharpness of the point? Somewhat blunted and oval-ended or almost pinpoint? And the lead. Soft? Chalky? Hard like bone? Cracked on one side? Does it bend between fingertips?" Almost angry. "You didn't describe the metal collar that anchors the eraser. Is it serrated? Grooved? Does it have a curved rise? Several rings? A sharp edge at the seam where it anchors the eraser. Could it draw blood if you ran skin over it? Is the pencil tubular, or seven-sided as is common design? Are the painted letters and numbers on the side more smooth than the painted section?"

"It's very . . ."

"Generalities. You have no feel for it."

"I'm sorry."

"I felt *nothing*."

Eyes downward. "Do you want me to go. You don't have to pay me anything."

A moment. A sigh. Gesturing. "The drinking glass."

She delicately picks it up.

"It's light, almost no weight at all. Cylindrical, warm from the hotel room heater. So smooth it seems to have no surface. So hard it has a brittle strength. A kind of tension like it could explode unexpectedly from the compacted frustration of the molecules."

"Interesting. Keep going."

"The edge where you touch it to your lips is rounded."

"Touch it to your lips."

"It rests on my mouth. Presses down my bottom lip. The upper edge of the glass touches my nose. It fits into my hand. Separates my thumb and index finger by two inches. It feels good to hold it. The weight and shape are comforting."

"Pour water into it. A little at a time."

"Alright." Pouring. "It's getting heavier, I can feel the weight in my wrist. My fingers have to grip more tightly."

"Can you feel the coolness of the water through the glass?"

"Yes."

"Describe it to me."

"It feels the way it feels when you take your glove off on an early winter day. The first seconds your skin can notice the cold."

"Vague. Give me another example."

"... the sensation of adding cold water to a hot bath and feeling chilly tendrils, struggling through the warm liquid to find you."

"Better."

"Can you remember that?"

"Yes."

"The water is climbing higher in the glass. A quarter inch at a time, splashing softly against the glass, spraying my hand with tiny, heatless droplets ... can you feel it?"

"Yes."

"... as it fills the glass, I feel the rising coolness, inside the glass, climb my palm...."

"... yes."

"... there's a dew forming on the outside of the glass. I can feel it with the sponge of my fingertips."

"Keep going."

"I feel the droplets from this moist film seep between my fingers. And I feel the weight of the glass shift, as the water tips from side to side."

"Drink it."

She leans the glass back, against full mouth, swallows; a voluptuous drain. Looks at him.

"I can feel it going down inside me like ..."

He breathes harder. Tightens; bends. Releases.

"Do you want me to describe it?"

"Later. I need to rest now."

Silence.

"We'll start again in a few minutes."

"Alright."

"Think about the lamps. The phone. The faucet handles. I want to hear about them." His voice shrinks; a whisper. "Before I forget."

He closes eyes. Leans back on the motel bed.

She watches him from her chair. Wants to gently touch him. To reassure, stroke his sad face. Calm his heart. She wonders what happened to him. What hurt had crept oddly inward; shaken his world.

As he rests with eyes shut, she moves to him and slowly reaches. Then, as her warm palm nearly touches his cheek, she looks at her hand.

All at once, she sees the small, healing cut on one knuckle that provides an unlocked door to the viral body within. The fingerprints that provide soft alleys and canyons for the poisons of mankind; infinite hiding places for illness, invisible beginnings of pain and plague. The immeasurable death affixed to the underside of her nails, barnacled in the deep creases of her palm.

She quietly withdraws her hand. Sits back down in her chair, waiting for him.

ORAL
Richard Christian Matheson

Need and fear.

The human gravities that make us seek another to listen. To deliver us. Priests, psychiatrists, family; our counselors and whores.

When lost, we need others to find us. To banish doubt. To hold what is too sharp for our hands. Too hurtful for mind or soul to host. Through the borrowed senses of another, transfusion occurs.

Mind nurturing mind. Heart nurturing heart.

And then your hour is up.

Simon Ings lives and writes in London. His third novel, *Hotwire*, was published in 1995. His current projects include *Headlong* (a sequel to *Hotwire*), and *Gloria*, a feature-length screenplay stuffed with sex and dead animals. Developed by the British Film Institute and the BBC, *Gloria* will be directed by Simon Pummell, for whom Ings wrote the short films *Rose Red* and *Butcher's Hook*. According to Ings, this brilliant career notwithstanding, he much prefers rock climbing and falling in love.

"Grand Prix" originally appeared in *Omni*, in a truncated form. It was one of those unfortunate (and—luckily—rare) times when a story has to be "cut to fit." I thought it deserved to be seen in its complete version because it's something relatively unusual in the field—an overtly political science fiction story that is nonetheless entertaining while critiquing relations between men and women.

GRAND PRIX

SIMON INGS

THE SEA IS OFF-WHITE, BANDED BY BLUE WAVE SHADOW. A line of clotted cloud lies between it and the cobalt sky of La Rochelle.

Angèle talks but I'm not listening. I'm building sand castles. First the foundation—a bay. (I wiggle my fingers over the smooth sand for waves.) Its sides make a natural amphitheater, rising to near alpine heights in a succession of tiers. (I have to dig for sand sticky enough to hold together, and still the gradients are too shallow.) For a while I look at it, reluctant to add more. Two hundred years ago, this place was as I've modelled it—a natural thing. Rock-strewn fields with a scattering of olive trees.

I sigh, add the Hotel de Paris, the Casino: all the anonymous infrastructure of the Principality. I lie down in front of the model and pick away the square and the Boulengrins with a fingernail. (Behind my eyes I fill the space with formal gardens, tropical trees, and cacti the size of oaks.) I press my little finger at a slant into the model to indicate the tunnel through to the harbor. The finishing touch: I trail sand between my fingers along the edge of the cliff to make the concrete wall Frasange demolished last year when his throttle jammed at 600 km/h.

I follow the route with eyes hijacked by memories; then I trace it with my fingers, plowing the damp sand—my sculptures tumble. For a moment I am a child again, a petulant little god. I ball my fist and obliterate the model. Only the route is left—a drunken O in the sand.

The Monaco Grand Prix is three days away.

Angèle peels off her shirt and heads for the water. Fifty years after Le Pen's death she's still the only Arab girl I've seen who will bare her tits on a French beach.

I want to join her in the water. The afternoon has steam-ironed my face and my shirt is dripping sweat. I want to dive into sea so cold it churns the gut, but I can't risk getting seawater in my jacks this close to a race.

It's sunset. The haze turns brown and rotten before Angèle reaches the diving tiers.

When she falls her silhouette is as sharp and black as the wave shadows, a black slash piercing a hyphenated surface. I think of trajectories, Gs and vectors, fire masks, halogens, wheel jacks and robots, flags like bunting and visors filled with drunken kanji.

The jack behind my anus is itching.

I turn my back to the sea. The twin towers guarding the harbor are peach, grey, black: the colors sharp and entwined like a fractal surface.

We walk back to town along the seawall. The houses have moldings above the door—sextants and galleys scoured to shadows by the salt air.

We try l'Ocean—maybe a room with a view across the harbor? It's hard to tell which they dislike most: my English or her color. We move on, through the arcades to the market. A man is hosing the forecourt with seawater. The gutters are full of tabloids and endive.

We get a room above a café with a view of the market roof. We fetch our luggage from the station. Angèle lays her PC at the foot of the bed, pulls out the IBCN lead and crawls about the floor cursing. We miss the first five minutes of *Danseuses Nouvelles.*

They came from Dijon a year ago and they're top of the TVP ratings. They dance to Salieri and Skinny Puppy, to De Machaut and The Crucial Bridging Group.

They are a women-only company and espouse the politics of the *Programme* Pour Femmes Fermes—the Agenda for Expressionless Women. Last year the French parliament, outraged by the atrocities of Août '34, placed a media ban on the *Programme*. The Amazons of the Sorbonne and the Academie Julienne are silenced now, but *Danseuses Nouvelles,* whose pieces grew out of their more sober semiotic researches, have never been more popular.

Few have forgotten or forgiven the sack of the Sacre Coeur, the onstage emasculation of *Bim Bam*'s lead guitarist or the siege of the Jeu de Paume.

And yet—

A glamour surrounds *Danseuses Nouvelles.* They weave space in strange, half-grasped rhythms. They convey strange messages, performing warped yet familiar roles with an inhuman grace. They are the *Programme*'s dream in its pure state—a glimpse of the end, uncompromised by violent means.

Their performances whisper of the world the *Programme* believes is to come: the world of strong women.

After the show Angèle and I make love.

I lay my head on her shoulder. She turns and strokes my hair. I lift her face up and kiss her lips. We sink back onto the bed. My fingers play with the buttons of her bodysuit. I slip a hand under the cloth and stroke her breast.

Angèle unbuckles my pants and pushes them down. She strokes the well of my erection through damp cotton. Her mouth is on my nipple—a wet, warm pulse over my heart.

I fumble the bodysuit down to her waist and stroke her legs apart. She shifts position on the bed. I slip a finger inside her, and stroke the firm dome of her cervix.

It is love with a fluid rhythm. There is a sweet, shared violence to it. Angèle gasps and clutches at me, the bed, anything; I gaze into her widening eyes. There, in the wet blankness of the pupil, I can see them. I gaze closer, closer—

Angèle's tongue flicks at my chin and I catch it in my lips, my teeth, suck at it like a baby put to the breast. *Danseuses Nouvelles*—missionaries from the land of strong women—are dancing in her eyes.

Catharine, I remember, used gestures as fluently as words. The first time I met her, she ordered Dublin Bay prawns. She broke their backs with casual, sadistic finesse. When her pointed red tongue scooped out the white pus inside them, she put me in mind of a cat, licking marrow from a rabbit bone.

It was six months ago, in Quimper. I don't know how she got my number. She told me quite openly who it was she worked for, and since the *Programme* had never to my knowledge worked with men, I was intrigued at her invitation. Perhaps it was naive of me.

"They say racing drivers talk more and do less about sex than men in any other sport." She held the orange carcass of her latest victim between finger and thumb and twirled it by its claw over her plate.

I treated her to a bitter smile. The playboy reputation, and its sarcastic flip side, is one we no longer deserve. There is no Baron von Trips on the circuit now, no Count Godin de Beaufort, no Inès Ireland, no Lance Reventlow. Everything has become too competitive and commercial. Indeed, by the nineties the playboy image had all but expired.

"Formula Zero has rekindled our infamy," I explained. "New cars. New regulations. They want to rekindle the old magic. It's plastic: packaged. Our sponsors twist incidents into publicity gimmicks. It helps the ratings."

"It doesn't anger you?"

I shrugged. "If it didn't, would I be here?"

The claw broke and the gutted corpse soft-landed in a pillow of saffron rice. It was her turn to smile.

She pushed aside her plate, lifted her PC onto the table, licked her fingers and typed. She read: "Cool, rational, seldom angered, seldom sulks when disappointed—" She gave me a cool glance. "Bisexual, last cruised in Groningen four years ago, in '42 had a short relationship with hypertext writer, male, in London, long-standing correspondence with lesbian activists in Seattle, New York, and with gays—ex-lovers—in Brisbane, Porto . . .''

She turned the screen round for me to see.

''Publish and be damned,'' I said.

Catharine tutted. ''I wouldn't dream of it. What would be the point? It says here your public image doesn't interest you.''

''It doesn't. It interests Havers, of course, and she has a way of buying off the right people before things go too far.''

''You must be quite a headache for her; a 'new man' at pole position.''

''Maureen Havers is *old*,'' I said. ''Because she's old, she's a legend. If a legend runs a company it has an interest in creating subsidiary legends—*appropriate* legends.''

''So she puts you in the closet.''

''I'm glad of the privacy. If I were Don Juan, she'd use it for a marketing gimmick: I wouldn't get any privacy at all.''

Catharine stroked her chin. ''Is she evil?''

''No,'' I said, ''she's sad. She lost her son to *Formula Libre* in Brazil. Her engineers built a car that cornered too well for him. The Interlagos circuit curves the wrong way round. He wasn't properly prepared for the G-strain.''

Catharine waved her hand dismissively. ''I'm not interested in technicalities.''

I looked at her a long time. I said, ''He was still burning when I pulled him out. His visor had melted into his face.''

She had the decency to blush: ''I'm sorry.''

''*Formula Libre* is just what it says''—I went on, ignoring her apology—''a free-for-all, a freak show for fast cars. But Formula One was outdated, and good new designers were turning to *Libre* rather than be straightjacketed. Havers built up Formula Zero to codify some of *Libre*'s better ideas. She made it, and dominated it; now, because she's old, it dominates her.''

''And she is hated, is she not?''

''Havers' constructors spend half their working lives stabbing each other in the back, but there's no real power to be had until she goes. But that's not what you meant, is it?''

A smile played about her lips. ''Touché.''

There's a lot of bad blood between the *Programme* Pour Femmes Fermes and Maureen Havers.

When she was young and cared nothing about cars, Maureen Havers revived *Psyche et Po,* Antoinette Fouque's 1972 outfit which dominated the French women's liberation movement into the eighties—all red jumpsuits and internecine foulness and right-wing religious overtones.

The *Programme* grew up at the same time Havers was wiring *Psyche et Po*'s corpse to the lightning conductor. Ensuing battles levelled the tactical gulf between the two movements till the main differences were intellectual ones. *Psyche et Po* read Lacan; the *Programme* read Lévi-Strauss. *Psyche et Po* were crypto-Capitalist; the *Programme* were retro-Structuralist. *Psyche et Po* played the system; the *Programme* deconstructed it.

The *Programme* won, but it was a Pyrrhic victory. Without intending it, they became not unlike *Psyche et Po*: an élite with no popular support.

Catharine drained her wineglass. "Ms. Havers is not our prime concern. I don't suppose she will like what we have in mind but—" She shrugged. "What do you know of the language of dance?"

The link between *Danseuses Nouvelles* and the *Programme* wasn't known then. I was thrown. I muttered something vague about semiotics and felt like an idiot.

She told me about *Danseuses.* I was privileged: some weeks passed before they leaked the news to *La Monde.*

"Are they the revolution?" I asked.

"A small part."

I toyed with my food. "Top ratings eight weeks running. Small?"

She was silent for some while, staring at me. I'd touched something important. "Since when did the man uninterested in publicity read ratings?"

"I don't. My manager does. *Danseuses* pushed my profile out of prime time last week. TVP wouldn't negotiate."

Catharine said: "*Danseuses*'s dancer/choreographer is Helene Ritenour. In '41 she had a curbside altercation with a heavy goods vehicle. Surgeons in São Paulo rebuilt her. Nanotech CNS upgrades saved her from spending the rest of her life in a wheelchair.''

I nodded. "And some." Helene was—and still is—a good dancer.

I thought about it.

Forty-one. In '42, Helene and *Danseuses* went on TV. "Quick work. *Programme* money?" I knew rushing the São Paulo technique cost a great deal.

"We look after our own," Catharine replied. "So does Havers. Doesn't she?"

The jack behind my arse itched.

We catch a train to Nice. It was twinned with Cape Town, once. It boasts a sand beach (imported) and no public telephones.

We eat at *Le Safari*. Angèle is pissed off and she won't tell me why. I'd show her the town, God knows I have sufficient plastic in my wallet, but hers is righteous anger, not to be bought off. She's sitting with her back to the window. Her face is in shadow. I can't see her eyes.

We haven't been together long. Catherine gave her to me— a contact and Woman Friday—not two months back. I find it hard to predict her moods.

Maybe it was Catharine's idea she sleeps with me; maybe she's got tired of playing the whore. It's not a thought I want to go to bed with so I try to get her talking.

Like an idiot I mention the *Programme*.

She screws up her face like she's swallowed something fatty. "I've no time for that," she snaps. "It's just play to them. Can't you just see them wanking off to the press reports after each sadistic little outing?"

"They're pointing up the language of repression," I say, wondering all the while at my own arrogance. Angèle doesn't know these kinds of words. She's an Arab street kid who was kicked once too often to stay lying down, not a semiotics graduate. "They're targeting metagrammatic nodes in the cultural ma-
      trix—"

Her look is enough to shut me up. Even against the light it's unmistakable.

"Don't talk to me about language!" She's the first woman I've met growls when she's angry. "What do I care that this word and this color and this dress mark the boundaries of chauvinism? What comfort is that to the mother with a drunk for a husband? Or the rape victim or the dyke or the pensioner? Go tell your good news to every lacerated clit in Africa then look me in the eye and say *this* is worth the money!"

She slams her hand down on the table, lifts it, and there's a tiny gold wafer winking up at me like the promise of El Dorado, from the marble tabletop.

I pick it up and weigh it gingerly in my hand. It's a ROM wafer—a packet of hardwired information. It slips into the port between my shoulders—the same kind of port they fitted to Helene Ritenour.

It's strange how Angèle can read me so well, even in anger. She leans over and strokes my hand with dark fingers. "Do you want to talk about it?"

I don't, but it's the only way I can thank her for tacitly forgiving me.

"It was bad," I say. "I slid off the track sideways—the near side of the monocoque took the impact. The whole thing failed in tension at the rear bulkhead. The engine and avionics went one way, the rear wheels the other. The heat exchanger was torn off. The steering column broke. The monocoque got crushed on the front offside. All the underbelly ceramics sheared—"

"I didn't mean the car."

"So—" Something misfires inside me and the old anger is back. "Tabloids have back numbers."

She starts back like I'd slapped her. "That wasn't fair. I'm not a ghoul. I didn't mean the accident, anyway. I meant the treatment. How you got better. What it did to you." She rubs her face with her hands. "I want to know you. What am I to you? A friend or a whore?"

Maybe this playboy bullshit is rubbing off on me because I really don't know. Sorry is the best answer I can come up with.

We sleep in the same bed but we don't touch.

I want to tell her what she wants to know. I want to tell her about São Paulo, and what they did to me. And why.

I want to tell her it hurt like hell.

She's asleep.

The Monaco Grand Prix is two days away.

Maureen Havers honestly believed she was doing me a favor. No one spends eight figures sterling on one man without *some* feeling behind it. She could have left me in a wheelchair. It wasn't her fault I was in that state, after all—I was the one who crashed.

Instead she saved me, after a fashion.

But she had other ideas too. I remember how flushed she became when Dr. Antonioni showed her the jack in my spine. I swear she made eyes at it. As far as she was concerned then, I was just the meat it plugged into.

Did I resent that? Not at the time. I was still in shock from the accident. I still couldn't quite get my head round the fact I could walk again—walk with a spine shot in five places.

Imagine you're lying there with a hospital bed your only future. Then they plug ROM cartridges into your back. On them are programs which teach your brain how to access and control a whole new nervous system. You can walk again, even shit when you want to. It's a miracle—and it takes a while to adjust.

Then, but too late for it to make a difference, it occurs to you—All that expensive tech, just to get you toilet trained again?

Of course not.

At least when the *Programme* paid for Helene they let her be her own boss—or so the popular science programs tell us. She uses an expert system, writing her prize-winning solo choreography direct to a ROM cartridge.

Me? I get fresh ROMs sent me every month from Achebi CyberPARC, where they analyze my race data. It helps me drive better. Only they went one stage further.

They built me a second jack, behind my arse. When I strap myself in, I hot-wire myself to the car. I don't drive it; I *become* it.

This has its consequences.

My body is a corporate concern. It has no solid boundaries. In short, it is a whore.

One of Formula Zero's damn few rules states: one car, one driver. Havers has got round that—they saved my spine and in return have turned me into a databus, a way of loading the aggregate wisdom of Achebi's Research Institute into a racing car; a smart messenger with a spine full of—what? Software? Wetware?

I have a name for it: *Slime.*

The Casino is fashioned in flamboyant style with towers at the corners and, sitting on the roof, great bronze angels, picked out by floodlighting which extends into the Boulengrins.

Angèle and I walk among the cacti. She is scared. Maybe it's the race. More likely it's being undercover, working for terrorists. I wonder how much they're paying her? She has no respect or liking for them. Her politics are much more homely. Maybe they agreed to fund some rape crisis centers.

"Do you think that wafer will kill you?"

"Maybe," I reply. Is this part of her job—to frighten me? Test my nerve? She may be right. To cause the world's best speed driver to die twirling in flames through the bijou houses of Monte Carlo—

No. Accidents themselves have their own phallic semiology. No sport on Earth so quickly forgets its widows. Grand Prix's finest take Death as their bride. Whisper their names in awe: *Depailler, Villeneuve, Willy Mairesse.*

I do not think the *Programme* will kill me. Perhaps I lack the cruelty to credit such deception. Perhaps, if I were a woman, I could be that cruel. Perhaps (I look at Angèle, the stoop of her shoulders, her tired eyes, the way she twitches her fingers through her hair)—perhaps I would have to be, to survive.

We return to the Hotel de Paris. We have a suite overlooking the Casino. Tomorrow Angèle will sit on our balcony; she will see the cars as they stream into the square and snake down the hill.

Perhaps she will think of me.

We watch *Danseuses Nouvelles*. There are only five dancers in the company, including Helene. If I didn't know better, I would say there were at least twenty. This is the heart of *Danseuses'* enduring novelty. The way they dance alters their appearance. They toy with the semiology of movement, with their audience's stereotypic racial and social expectations. They move in a way we expect certain kinds of people to move, and they become those people. The eye is tricked by the conditioned expectations of the brain. The government is outraged by the *Programme*'s violent acts. But I suspect they fear this quiet revolution far more. They can handle terrorism: but seduction?

The credits spool and I undress. I sit cross-legged on the bed. Angèle pushes the wafer into my back.

In a while the headache clears. Two green circles appear, one above the other, center-vision. In an eyeblink they are gone. They are the first and last I will see of the *Programme*'s system. It will perform its acts regardless. I will have no opportunity to intervene.

"It's all right now," I say.

Angèle turns on the light. She looks at me and she is afraid. Inside me, something flexes.

Formula Zero is a race for cars, not drivers. It is a vicious testing bed for crackpot ideas, the way Formula One used to be till the 1970s and the iron rule of Jean Marie Balestre.

Formula One's rule book ceased to reflect technical progress around that time. Formula Zero was conceived in the nineties as a way round the rule book and into the twenty-first century.

Anyway, crashes are good for business.

My eyes are full of lignocaine. Underlids count off the seconds. I tense my arse and spool the revcounter into the red, just out of my line of focus. I pop the clench plate into my mouth and bite down. The throttle glows green. I blink. The visor snaps down. It's made of kevlar. A projector micropored to my head beams eight external views onto the inner surface of the visor then settles for center-forward.

Eight seconds.

At -7.2 the car handshakes the processor behind my lumbar jack. Point nought nought one seconds into the race the handshake is complete and all this touch-and-blink gear takes second place to Achebi's direct-feed wizardry.

Four seconds.

I smile a special smile. Engine status icons mesh and flow behind my eyes.

Zero.

I'm in a different place. A green hillside. Rock-strewn fields and olive trees, the way it was. The track is a smooth black nothing under my wheels, swirling round the hill. I follow it with cybernetic eyes. Gentry in the Ferrari is a blue icon on my near side. He cuts me up on the first corner. I'll use him as a pacemaker. I'm so far ahead of the league table I'd be happy to let him win. But if I don't pass the post first, then Catharine's meme-bomb sits in me, waiting for the next victory. It only triggers if I'm race champion.

A sick fascination is driving me. That and a hope that the *Programme*'s attack on the machismo-oriented Grand Prix might dovetail with my own wish for vengeance on Maureen Havers.

My tires are the sort that go soft and adhesive in the heat of acceleration. I have five laps' advantage over the opposition, five laps glued to the road, before they lose their tack and I slip into something more hard-wearing.

There's the sea—a grey graphic nothing. My eyes spool white prediction curves and hazard warnings. I take Gentry on the skid in a maneuver that shortens my tire life by a lap. I feel the difference, the loss of traction. I'm picking up sensory information from every stressed member of the vehicle, directly, through my spine. I *am* the car—and the car is feeling queasy. At the pit robots tend me, probing and swapping and inflating the things that make up this surrogate body of mine. My wheels feel tight and warm again, hugged near to buckling by fresh, high-pressure tires.

I scream away from the pit. The Longines people send me a stop time and ETF. It flashes on my underlid for half a second and disappears. They're counting me down for the World Record—a special etherlink tells me how I'm doing.

The real danger now is the back-markers don't have the decency to pull in for me. They do not like me: Havers and Achebi have made me far too good. With me around, no one else can hope to get near the championship.

By next season, I reckon FISA will rule against my kind of

driving for the good of the sport. Then I'm back to clench plate and dataskin and honest dangerous driving. And in another twenty years Formula Zero will have accreted its own four-inch-thick Yellow Book and the whole process will start over again. A new breed of *Formula Libre*.

From São Paulo, maybe.

My shoulder blades itch. There's something strange in my nervous system.

I wonder what it does—

I'm tearing towards the tunnel (look no hands) when there's the most appalling jolt. The gearbox tears its guts out and my ribs try straining themselves through the crash-webbing. The strap across my visor slips. I round the bend along the harbor road and my neck isn't up to the G-strain.

I slide into the pit and nausea overtakes me. The car realizes I'm going to throw up. The helmet snaps open and the clench plate grows hot to make me spit it out. I throw up over the side of the car. A valet trolley wheels over and scrubs off the mess, revealing a smeared ELF decal.

My whole body burns green fire.

Every nerve sings with power.

Achebi's unmistakable Go signal. I scrabble under my seat for the clench plate. Its taste of sour saliva is nauseating and I wonder idly if I'm going to be sick again on the circuit. My helmet slams itself down and the graphics blink on.

It only takes a moment to become a car again.

But this time it's different. This time, I'm way down the field and will be lucky to be placed. This time—the first time this season—I will have to *race*.

I may not be able to live with what the *Programme* does through the medium of my flesh. But I *know* I cannot live with it buried in me—I cannot live in ignorance. I am compelled. What atrocity have they given me to perform?

Will I karate the neck of the president of FOCA? Will I tear Maureen's eyes out—or my own—in front of a billion couch potatoes?

Some of Angèle's special anger flows through my veins and into the car.

It feels good and dangerous, like the Grand Prix I remember. The différence is, back then I *knew* when I was stretching the car to its limits. Now I can *feel* it. I'm an athlete with a steel body, a middle distance runner doubling speed on the last five laps.

My arrogance is rewarded.

The car starts falling apart.

It's not anything you can see. Even though they're wired up my back, I nearly miss the signs—ticks and prickles and a hot metal taste in the back of my throat.

I don't have time for another pit stop. I hope to God they don't show me the black flag.

I'm an athlete, pushing my body and doing it damage and before long my knees are crumbling, my toes are burning away, my lungs are full of acid phlegm. I'm screaming cybernetic agony into my helmet as I come in sight of the prize pack. They are jockeying for position with all the cumbersome grace of whales. My scream becomes a roar. I think of the horror dozing fitfully in my spine, I think of the hurt behind Angèle's eyes, and every hurtful stupidity under the sun—and I hurl myself forward. Danger icons spill blood behind my lids.

Four and Three concede with grace and let me past. I run tandem with place Two—Ashid in the GM. I know from old he's no gentleman. We hug wheel-space through the square.

Odds-graphics blink on by my field of vision. Data chitters through me. I take hold of the wheel. I want to be ready. If this goes wrong it might crash my systems. The wheel recognizes my grip and unlocks, shaking me boisterously like an overfriendly scrum half.

I watch the odds-window, turn the car in, Ashid jerks sideways and back and already I'm wheeling past him. Our back wheels kiss and make up, then I'm running for pole.

Martineau leads and he is Havers' Number Two. If I can get within five lengths of him he'll slow down like a good boy and let me win.

All of a sudden I have a pacemaker to get me there.

I left Gentry behind at number three. Why Gentry—why not Ashid? The GM is still sound, my icons tell me—which is good because even a kiss can send an unlucky car tumbling—so maybe Ashid's nerve's gone, 'cause he's more than a match for this prick. I think Gentry must have popped a pill.

I let him come alongside. I know he rides with a clear visor so I let go the wheel and wave to piss him off.

Then I change gear.

This is easy. Achebi sussed this months ago. A simple algorithm—car on road. No obstacles, no other drivers, a full complement of feedback systems to make allowances for where the car is fucked.

Time for my 550 kph Sunday drive.

Longines sends regrets. The record is safe.

But my mind's on something else—

Martineau is tootling towards the line. I'd ride a dignified half length ahead of him only Gentry's been driving like a madman behind me for the past two minutes and I'm too hyped to slow down.

And as I pass the line I realize: I'm no different. I too am wedded to danger, which is a longer name for death. Achebi made me fast, yes, but they also made me safe. I don't hate Maureen Havers, or what she did to me. I hate Achebi for protecting me. I hate the doctors for repairing me. I'm like all the others. A life-hating thing—a phallus-cocoon finding new ways to die. Why else did

I let the *Programme* infect me? *What have I done to myself?*

Whisper their names. *Depailler, Villeneuve, Willy Mairesse.* Me.

My helmet snaps up on a view of a hundred thousand cheering would-be suicides. I smile and wave; the sun and the wind dry my tears.

I pull the jack out and adjust my flight pants and get out of the car.

Next stop the champagne.

Maureen Havers is up on the podium. Her grey hair sparks on the wind. She has a smile like death and I envy it. A nude girl hands me the champagne magnum. It's very hot here.

My hands are shaking.

It gets dark.

I look up at the sun, puzzled.

A blood spot on my retina, receding fast . . .

I wake up in my hotel room. Catharine is sitting by the bed. I look round. Angèle's not here.

"Is it over?"

Catharine smiles. "It's over."

"Did I do—what did I do?"

"Rest first."

"No!" I sit up in bed and it feels like I just shoved my head in a coffee grinder. I take a deep breath. "Show me now."

She lights up Angèle's PC.

Where is she?

We watch the rerun.

I see what a billion TV addicts have lived for all season. Me.

I don't believe it. There, on the podium, in front of them all—

I'm masturbating. I've got my hand inside my overalls and I'm . . .

It's terrible. I don't know whether to laugh or throw myself out the window. When it's over my voice is high with hysteria. "How did you—how could you—I didn't—I—" I force myself to stop. Tears of rage heat my cheeks.

"You didn't *do* anything. Look again."

My eyes are drawn to the screen.

She is right. I don't *do* anything, but by the end of it I'm shaking afresh with disgust and self-loathing and fascinated revulsion. It's worse than the act itself could ever be. The power of suggestion . . .

"I can't believe I did that—*didn't* do—" I'm babbling again. I turn to Catharine. Angèle must have told her I like Irish. She's pouring me a tumblerful.

"You didn't. Our ROM wafer did. It took you through a very special dance. Helene's been working on it for months."

"A dance."

"Yes." She hands me the tumbler.

I drink it down in one. "A repulsive dance."

When I calm down she sits beside me and says, "The Grand Prix. A phallocentric institution, wouldn't you say? But will men ever be able to draw that kind of strength from it, now its figurehead has lampooned it so ably—so *cleverly*?"

The truth clicks home. "You fucking bitch, I'll never race again."

She shrugs. She is prepared for my reaction.

I feel vivisected.

"There are other ways to drive," she says. "When Havers sacks you, as she surely must, we have other games for you to play. Networks. Security systems. Stock exchanges."

Through a veil of shock I sense the potential behind her words. I glimpse the power that is mine as a servant of the *Programme,* the riches my skills and my serviceable nervous system might yet yield—for me, and for the women of Brazil, Africa, the whole twisted world.

But. "How will I ever show my face again?"

"Which face?" She gets off the bed, and walks over to unplug the IBCN lead, and as she walks her legs grow stocky, her hair lengthens, her skin grows dark and when she turns to me, her mouth is more full, her forehead less pronounced, her cheeks have swollen a little—and Angèle smiles. It is beautiful.

"Everything has its place in the matrix of signification," Angèle says, in a voice I do not recognize. "You claim no prejudice, no chauvinism—yet a gesture, a turn of the head, a way of lowering the eyelids, all of that plays on your stereotypic view of things. See how the white bitch becomes the dusky whore."

"Oh no," I murmur. "Not now. Not anymore." I slip off the bed and walk clumsily toward Angèle and hold her in humility and run my hand over her back. I feel for the first time the ROM port between her shoulder blades. Her disguise hid that, too, till now. What a clever dance Helene has written for her!

My heart jolts up into my mouth. "Helene?"

"Hello." Her tongue is hot on my cheek.

She laughs, and her laughter is a promise: peace . . . riches . . . revolution . . .

GRAND PRIX
Simon Ings

When I wrote this, it was cool to be a "New Man"; why, I'll never know, but overnight this turned male fecklessness into some sort of political style statement. My decision to wire all this into semiotics and motor racing was entirely arbitrary: They were simply what I knew at the time.

My protagonist thinks he's very sophisticated, very postmodern: underneath he's just not that clever. We may imagine that for him, joining the *Programme* is only one in a long series of epiphanic episodes: sexual encounters; sexual-political conversions; motor racing, of course. He is without qualities: new ideas infect him continually. He will forever be repudiating one belief for another, one lover for another.

Brian Stableford was born in Shipley, Yorkshire, in 1948. He was a lecturer in sociology at the University of Reading until he became a full-time writer in 1988. He has published more than forty novels, including *The Empire of Fear* and *Young Blood*. He is also a prolific writer of nonfiction about the history of imaginative fiction; two collections of his essays were released by the Borgo Press during 1995.

Anna could well be a descendent of Miss Dade in "The Lucifer of Blue"—like her predecessor she's proud, or at least comfortable with her chosen profession. In the past, prostitutes and their johns were too often victims of incurable diseases such as syphillis and gonorrhea. In Stableford's future, the diseases are just as deadly and the attitudes of those outside the profession just as intolerant.

THE HOUSE OF MOURNING

BRIAN STABLEFORD

ANNA STARED AT HER THIN FACE IN THE MIRROR, WONDERING where the substance had gone and why the color had vanished from the little that remained. Her eyes had so little blue left in them that they were as grey as her hair. She understood enough to know that a disruption of the chemistry of the brain was bound to affect the body as profoundly as the mind, but the sight of her image in the soul-stealing glass reawakened more atavistic notions. It was as if her dangerous madness had wrought a magical corruption of her flesh.

Perhaps, she thought, it was hazardous for such as she to look into mirrors; the confrontation might be capable of pre-cipitating a crisis of confidence and a subsequent relapse into delirium. Facing up to the phantoms of the past was, however, the order of the day. With infinite patience she began to apply her makeup, determined that she would *look* alive, whatever her natural condition.

By the time she had finished, her hair was tinted gold, her

103

cheeks delicately pink, and her lips fulsomely red—but her eyes still had the dubious transparency of raindrops on a window pane.

Isabel was late, as usual. Anna was forced to pace up and down in the hallway, under the watchful eyes of the receptionist and the ward sister. Fortunately, she was in the habit of dressing in black for everyday purposes, so her outfit attracted no particular attention.

The ward sister was there because there was a ritual to be observed. Anna couldn't just walk out of the hospital, even though she was classed as a voluntary patient. She had to be handed over in a formal fashion, to signify that responsibility was being officially transferred from one sister to another. Not that Isabel really was her sister in a biological sense, any more than the ward sister was; she and Anna had simply been parts of the same arbitrarily-constructed foster family. They were not alike in any way at all.

When Isabel finally arrived, in a rush, with all her generous flesh and hectic color, the ceremony began.

"You must remember that this is Anna's first day out," the ward sister said to Isabel. "We don't anticipate any problems, but you must make sure that she takes her medication at the appointed times. If she shows signs of distress, you should bring her back here as soon as possible. This emergency number will connect you with a doctor immediately."

Isabel stared at the number scrawled on the card as though it were the track of some mysterious bird of ill omen.

To Anna, the sister said only: "Be good." Not "Have a nice time" or even "Take it easy," but simply "Be good." *It's better to be beautiful than to be good,* Anna thought, *but it's better to be good than to be ugly.* She had been beautiful once, and more than beautiful—so much more as to be far beyond the reach of Saint Oscar's ancient wisdom, but now there was nothing left to her except to be good, because her more-than-beauty had gone very, very bad.

Isabel, of course, had no idea that Anna was on her way to a funeral, and that her role was merely to provide a convenient avenue of escape. Anna waited until the car was a good two miles away from the hospital before she broached the subject. "Can you drop me at the nearest tube station," she said lightly, "and can you let me have some money."

"Don't be silly," Isabel said. "We're going home."

Isabel meant her own home, where she lived with a husband and two children, paying solemn lip service to the social ideal. Anna had seen Isabel's husband three or four times, but only in the distance. He was probably one of those visitors' partners whose supportive resolution failed at the threshold of Bedlam—many in-laws preferred to wait outside while their better halves attended to the moral duty of comforting their afflicted kin—but it was possible that Isabel had forbidden him to come in and be properly introduced. Few women relished the prospect of introducing their husbands to whores, even whores who happened to be their sisters—legalistically speaking—and whose sexual charms had been obliterated in no uncertain terms.

"No we're not," Anna said. "That's just something I had to tell the doctors, so they'd let me out. If I'd told them the truth, they'd have stopped me, one way or another."

"What truth?" Isabel wanted to know. "What on earth are you talking about? I'll have you know that I've gone to a lot of trouble over this. You heard what the nurse said. I'm responsible for you."

"You won't be doing anything illegal," Anna told her. "I'll get back on time, and nobody will be any the wiser. Even if I didn't go back, nobody would blame *you*. I'm the crazy one, remember. How much cash can you let me have?"

"I don't have any cash," Isabel told her, as she drove resolutely past Clapham South tube station without even hesitating. "I don't carry cash. Nobody does. It's not necessary anymore."

That was a half-truth, at best. At the Licensed House where Anna had worked, the clients had used their smartcards, and the transactions had been electronically laundered so that no dirty linen would be exposed to prying wives or the Inland Revenue. The streetwalkers who haunted the Euroterminal and the Bull Ring had smartcard processors too, but their laundering facilities were as dodgy as their augmentations and most of their clients paid in cash.

"You can still *get* cash, can't you?" Anna said, innocently. "Walls still have holes, just like spoiled whores. Don't worry about missing Clapham South. Vauxhall will be fine.''

"Just where the hell do you think you're going, Anna?" Isabel demanded, hotly. "Just what the hell do you think you're going to do?'' That was Isabel all over: repetition and resentment, with plenty of hell thrown in.

"There's something I need to do,'' Anna said, unhelpfully. She had no intention of spelling it out. Isabel would protest violently just as surely as the doctors would have done. Unlike the doctors, though, Isabel was easy to manipulate. Isabel had always been scared of Anna, even though she was two years older, two inches taller, and two stones heavier. Now that Anna was a shadow of her former self, of course, it was more like four stones—but that only increased Anna's advantage.

"I won't do it,'' Isabel said, although the hopelessness of her insistence was already evident.

"I can do anything I like,'' Anna said, reflectively. "It's one of the perks of being mad and bad—you can do anything you like, and nobody's surprised. I can't be punished, because there's nothing they can take away that I haven't already lost. I could do with a hundred pounds, but fifty might do in a pinch. I have to have cash, you see, because people with scrambled brain chemistry aren't allowed smartcards. Fortunately, there'll always be cash.'' As long as there were outposts of the black economy that weren't geared up for laundering, there'd be cash—and everybody in the world was engaged in the black economy in *some* fashion, even if it was only token tax-dodging.

"I don't like being used,'' Isabel said, frostily. "I agreed to take you out for the day because you asked me to, and because the doctors thought it would be a good idea—a significant step on the way to rehabilitation. I won't stand for it, Anna. It's not fair.''

Since she was six years old Isabel had been complaining that "it'' wasn't fair. She had never quite grasped the fact that there was no earthly reason for expecting that anything should be.

"There's bound to be a cash-dispenser at Vauxhall,'' Anna said. "Fifty would probably do it, if that's all you can spare. I've lost track of inflation since they put me in the loony bin, but money can't have lost that much value in three years.''

Isabel braked and pulled over to the side of the road. She was the kind of person who couldn't drive and have a fit at the same time. Anna could tell that her sister was upset because she'd stopped on a double yellow line; normally, she'd have looked for a proper parking place.

"What the hell is this about, Anna?" Isabel demanded. "Exactly what have you got me into? If you're using me as an alibi while you abscond from the hospital, I've a right to know."

"I'll be back on time," Anna assured her. "No one will ever know, except your husband and children. They'll probably be disappointed that they aren't going to meet your mad, bad, and dangerous-to-know foster sister, but they'll get over it. You can bring them in one day next week, to make up for it. I'll be as nice as pie, psychochemistry permitting."

"*What is this all about?*" Isabel repeated, pronouncing each word with leaden emphasis, as if to imply that Anna was only ignoring her because she was too stupid to know what the question was.

"There's something I have to do," Anna said, nobly refraining from adopting the same tone. "It won't take long. If you won't give me the fifty pounds, can you at least let me have enough for a Travelcard. I have to go all the way across town to zone four."

Anna knew as soon as she'd said it that it was a mistake. It gave Isabel a way out. She should have hammered on and on about the fifty until she got it. In the old days, she'd never have settled for a penny less than she'd actually wanted, whatever kind of client she was dealing with.

Isabel reached into her purse and pull a handful of coins out of its dusty depths. "Here," she said, as if to say, *It's all you're worth, you stupid, fouled-up slut.* "If you want to go, go—to hell if you want to—but if this goes wrong, just don't try to blame me. And take your medication." Long before she arrived at the last sentence she had reached across Anna to open the passenger door, so that she could mark her final full stop with one of those dismissive pushes that Anna remembered all too well.

Anna submitted to the push and got out of the car, even though she was only vaguely aware of where she was. She waited until Isabel had driven off before she asked for directions to Clapham Common. It was a long way, but not too far to walk even for someone in her debilitated condition. The value of the coins was just adequate to buy a Travelcard.

She wondered if things might have been different if she'd had a *real* sister, but she decided that they probably wouldn't have been.

It wasn't difficult to find the church from Pinner tube station. It was larger than she had expected. She was glad that the funeral announcement in the *Guardian* had given both time and place; so many didn't, because the people who placed them were afraid of being burgled while they were at the ceremony. She waited until everyone else was inside before she sidled in, but she didn't escape notice. Several people turned around, and whispers were exchanged.

When the service was over and the pallbearers carried the coffin out Anna moved behind a pillar, but the people who filed out behind the dead man knew perfectly well that she was there. She didn't go to the graveside; she stayed in the shadow of an old horse chestnut tree, watching from thirty yards away. She couldn't hear what the vicar was saying, but that didn't matter. She could have improvised her own service if she'd wanted to, complete with appropriate psalms. Every bedside locker on the ward had a Bible in the top drawer, and boredom had made her dip into hers more frequently than she liked to think. She knew that according to The Book of Ecclesiastes it was better to go to the House of Mourning than the House of Feasting, but she wasn't sure that Ecclesiastes had been in a position to make a scrupulous comparison, and he hadn't mentioned the House of the Rising Sun at all, although it would have made a better play on words if he had. Ecclesiastes had also offered the judgment that a good name was better than precious ointment, but Alan certainly wouldn't have agreed with him on that point.

Anna had no difficulty picking out Alan's wife, although she'd never seen a photograph. She was a good-looking woman, in a middle-class Home Counties sort of way. Her name was Christine, but Alan had usually referred to her as Kitty. Anna was mildly surprised that Kitty wasn't wearing a veil. Weren't widows supposed to wear veils, to hide their tears? Not that the woman was weeping; grim forbearance seemed to be more her style. Anna judged her—on the basis of an admittedly superficial inspection—to be a kind of up-market Isabel, who probably did believe, with all her heart, that a good name was infinitely to be preferred to any kind of balm that cunning cosmetic engineers could devise.

In the grip of a sudden surge of anguish, Anna wished that Isabel hadn't been so tight-fisted. If Isabel had given her a hundred pounds, or even fifty, she'd have been able to bring a wreath to add to the memorials heaped about the grave. So far as she could judge at this distance most of the mourners had gone for natural blooms, but she would have selected the most exotic products of genetic engineering she could afford, to symbolize herself and the crucial contribution she had made to Alan's life—and, presumably, his death.

Anna had no doubt that the accident hadn't been *entirely* accidental; even if it hadn't been a straightforward deceptive suicide, it must have been a case of gross and calculated negligence.

When the ceremony was over and done with, the crowd around the grave broke up, its members drifting away in all directions as though the emotion of the occasion had temporarily suppressed their sense of purpose. When the widow turned toward her, and shook off someone's restraining hand, Anna knew that the confrontation she had half feared and half craved was about to take place. She wasn't in the least tempted to turn and run, and she knew before the woman paused to look her up and down that *this* was what she had come for, and that all the sentimental rubbish about wanting to say good-bye was just an excuse.

"I know who you are," the widow said, in a cut glass voice which suggested that she took no pride in her perspicacity.

"I know who you are, too," Anna replied. The two of them were being watched, and Anna was conscious of the fact that the dissipating crowd had been reunited by a common urge to observe, even though no evident ripple of communication had passed through it.

"I thought you were in hospital, out of your mind." The widow's voice was carefully neutral, but had an edge to it which suggested that it might break out of confinement at any moment.

"I am," Anna told her. "But the doctors are beginning to figure things out, and they can keep me stable, most of the time. They're learning a lot about brain chemistry thanks to people like me." She didn't add *and people like Alan.*

"So you'll soon be back on the streets, will you?" the widow enquired, cuttingly.

"I haven't worked the streets since I was sixteen," Anna said, equably. "I was in a Licensed House when Alan met me. I can't go back there, of course—there's no way they'd let me have my license back after what happened, even if they could normalize my body chemistry. I suppose I might go back to the street, when I'm released. There are men who like spoiled girls, believe it or not."

"You ought to be quarantined," the widow said, her voice easing into a spiteful hiss. "You and all your rancid kind ought to be locked up forever."

"Maybe so," Anna admitted. "But it was the good trips that got Alan hooked, and it was the withdrawal symptoms that hurt him, not the mutant proteins."

A man had joined the widow now: the fascinated crowd's appointed mediator. He put a protective arm around the widow's shoulder. He was too old to be one of her sons and too dignified to be a suitor ambitious to step into the dead man's shoes; perhaps he was her brother—or even Alan's brother.

"Go back to the car now, Kitty," the man said. "Let me take care of this."

Kitty seemed to be glad of the opportunity to retreat. Whatever she'd hoped to get out of the confrontation, she hadn't found it. She turned away and went back to the black-clad flock which was waiting to gather her in.

Anna expected a more combative approach from the man, whoever he might be, but all he said was, "If you're who I think you are, you shouldn't have come here. It's not fair to the family."

Another Isabel, Anna thought. *You'd think someone like him would know better.* By "someone like him" she meant doctor, lawyer, or banker. Something *professional* in the nonironic sense of the word. Alan had been a stockbroker, careful overseer of a thousand personal equity plans. She'd often wondered if any of his clients had shares in the company which owned the House. Like everything else in today's complicated world, it had been part of some diverse conglomerate; the parent organization's share price was quoted every day in the *Guardian*'s financial pages, under the heading "Leisure and Entertainment."

"I'm not doing any harm," Anna said. "You could all have ignored me, if you'd wanted to."

"I believe that was the gist of the argument which prompted the legalization of prostitution," the other replied, mustering a sarcastic edge far sharper than Kitty's. "It does no harm, they said, and anyone who disapproves only has to ignore it. When the cosmetic engineers progressed from tinkering with shape and form to augmenting bodily fluids they said much the same thing. The new aphrodisiacs are perfectly safe, they said, it's all just for fun, they're definitely not addictive—and anyone who disapproves can simply stay away from the new generation of good-time girls, and let the fun-lovers get on with it. In the end, though, the rot crept in, the way it always does. It all went horribly wrong. Isn't it bad enough that we had to lose Alan, without having to suffer a personal appearance by his own particular angel of death?"

She felt something stirring in the depths of her consciousness, but the comfort blanket of her medication was weighing down upon it. It was easy to remain tame and self-possessed while the doctors' drugs were winning the battle against her own perverted psychochemistry. "I'm sorry," she said, effortlessly. "I didn't mean to cause distress." *Like hell I didn't,* she thought, by way of private compensation. *I came here to rub your turned-up noses in it, to force you to recognize how utterly and horribly unfair the world really is.*

"You have caused distress," the man said, accusatively. "I don't think you have the least idea how much distress you've caused—to Alan, to Kitty, to the boys, and to everyone who knew them. If you had, and if you had the least vestige of conscience, you'd have cut your throat rather than come here today. In fact, you'd have cut your throat, period."

He's a punter, Anna thought, derisively. *Not mine, and not the House's, but someone's. He fucks augmented girls, and*

*the juices really blow his mind, just like they're supposed to,
and he's afraid. He's afraid that one fine day he, too, might
find that he just can't stop, and that if and when his favorite
squeeze goes bad, it'll be cold turkey, forever and ever, amen.
Like every man alive his prayer has always been "Lord give
me chastity but please not yet!"*—and now it's too late.

"I'm sorry," she said, again. The words were the purified
essence of her medication, wrought by a transformation every
bit as miraculous as the one which had run its wayward course
within her flesh and her spirit. The real Anna wasn't sorry at
all. The real Anna wasn't sorry she had come, and wasn't sorry
she was alive, and wasn't sorry that this black-clad prick saw
her as some kind of ravenous *memento mori.*

"You're a degenerate," the black-clad prick informed her,
speaking not merely to her but to everything she stood for. "I
don't agree with those people who say that what's happened
to you is God's punishment for the sins you've committed,
and that every whore in the world will eventually go the same
way, but I understand how they feel. I think you should go
now, and never show your face here again. I don't want Kitty
thinking that she can't bring the boys to visit Alan's grave in
case she meets you. If you have a spark of decency in you,
you'll promise me that you'll never come here again."

The clichés begin to flow in full force, Anna thought—but
even the medication balked at sparks of decency. "I'm free to
go wherever I want to, whenever I wish," she asserted, un-
truthfully. "You have no right to stop me."

"You poisonous bitch," he said, in a level fashion which
suggested that he meant the adjective literally. "Wherever you
go, corruption goes with you. Stay away from Alan's family,
or you'll be sorry." She knew that he meant all of that quite
literally too—but he had to turn away when he'd said it, because he couldn't meet the unnaturally steady stare of her colorless eyes.

She stayed where she was until everyone else had left, and
then she walked over to the open grave and looked down at
the coffin, onto which someone had dribbled a handful of
brown loamy soil.

"Don't worry," she said to the dead man. "Nothing scares

me. Not anymore. I'll be back, and I'll get that wreath one way or another.''

She had no wristwatch but the church clock told her that she had five hours in hand before they'd be expecting her at the hospital.

Anna hadn't been to the Euroterminal meat-rack for seven years, but it didn't take long for her to find her way around. The establishment of Licensed Houses had been intended to take prostitution off the streets but it had only resulted in a more complicated stratification of the marketplace. It wasn't just the fact that there were so many different kinds of augmentation available, or the fact that more than three-quarters of them were illegal, or even the fact that there were so many girls whose augmentations had ultimately gone wrong or thrown up unexpected side effects; the oldest profession was one which, by its very nature, could never be moved out of the black economy into the gold. Sleaze, secrecy, and dark, dark shadows were marketable commodities, just like psychotropic bodily secretions.

She didn't bother to try for a managed stand; she'd spoken the truth when she'd told her dead lover that nothing scared her anymore, but she hadn't time to get into complicated negotiations with a pimp. She went down to the arches where the independents hung out. There was no one there she knew, but there was a sense in which she knew all of them—especially the ones who were marked like her. It didn't take long to find one who was a virtual mirror image in more overstated makeup.

"I'm not here to provide steady competition," she said, by way of introduction. "I'm still hospitalized. I'll be back on the ward tomorrow, but I need something to get me through today. Fifty'll do it—that's only one substitution, right?"

"Y'r arithmetic's fine," the mirror image said, "but y'got a lot of nerve. Demand's not strong, and I don't owe y'anything just 'cause we're two peas from the same glass pod. It's a cat-eat-cat world out here."

"We aren't two peas from any kind of pod," Anna informed her, softly. "Symptoms are all on the surface. They used to say that all of us were sisters under the skin, but we

were never *the same*. Even when they shot the virus vectors
into us, so that our busy little epithelial cells would mass-
produce their carefully designed mind expanders, it didn't
make us into so many mass-produced wanking machines. One
of my doctors explained to me that the reason it all began to
go wrong is that *everybody's different*. We're not just different
ghosts haunting production line machines; each and every one
of us has a subtly different brain chemistry. What makes you
you and me me isn't just the layout of the synaptic network
which forms in our brains as we accumulate memories and
habits; we tailor our chemistry to individual specifications as
well. You and I had exactly the same transformation, and our
transplanted genes mutated according to the same distortive
logic, but fucking you never felt exactly the same as fucking
me, and it still isn't. We're all unique, all different; we offered
subtly different good trips and now we offer subtly different
bad ones. That's why some of our clients became regulars,
and why some got hooked in defiance of all the ads which
promised hand-on-heart that what we secreted wasn't physically addictive. You don't owe me anything at all, either because of what we both were or because of what we both are,
but you could do me a favor, if you wanted to. You're free
to say no.''

The mirror image looked at her long and hard, and then
said: ''Jesus, kid, y'really are strung out—but y'd better lose
that accent if y're plannin' on workin' down here. It don't fit.
I was goin' for a cup of coffee anyway. Y'got half an hour—if
y'don't score by then, tough luck.''

''Thanks,'' said Anna. ''I appreciate it.'' She wasn't sure
that half an hour would be enough, but she knew she had to
settle for whatever she could get.

She'd been on the pitch for twenty-three minutes when the
car drew up. In a way, she was grateful it had taken so long.
Now, she wouldn't be able to go back afterward.

The punter tried to bargain her down to thirty, but the car
was a souped-up fleet model whose gloss shouted to the world
that he wasn't strapped for cash, and there was no one else on
the line with exactly her kind of spoliation.

The client was a wise guy; he knew enough about the chemistry of his own tastes to think he could show off. It probably

didn't occur to him that the doctors had taken pains to explain to Anna exactly what had happened to her, or that she'd been better able to follow their expert discourse than his fudged mess. Nor did it occur to him that she wouldn't be at all interested in the important lessons which he thought were there to be learned from the whole sorry affair. She didn't try to put him right; he was paying, after all, and the torrent of words provided a distraction of sorts from the various other fluxes generated by their brief and—for her—painful intercourse.

"That whole class of euphorics should never have been licensed, of course," he opined, after he'd stumbled through a few garbled technicalities. "It's all very well designing fancy proteins by computer, but just because something's stable in cyberspace doesn't mean it's going to behave itself under physiological conditions, and *physiological conditions* is a politer way of putting it, when we're referring to the kind of witch's cauldron you get up a whore's you-know-what. They say they have programs now that will spot likely mutation sites and track likely chains of mutational consequence, but I reckon they're about as much use as a wooden fort against a fire-breathing dragon. I mean, this thing is *out of control* and there's no way to lock the stable door now the nags have bolted. Personally, I'm not at all distressed—I mean, I've had all the common-or-garden stuff up to *here.* I never liked whores wired up for the kind of jollies you can get from a pill or a fizzy drink. I mean, it's just stupid to try to roll up all your hits into one. It's like praying mantises eating their mates while they fuck—no sense to it at all. Me, I like things spread around a bit. I like it sour *and* sweet, in all kinds of exotic combinations. People like me are the real citizens of the twenty-first century, you know. In a world like ours, it ain't enough not to be xenophobic—you have to go the other way. Xeno*philia* is what it takes to cope with today and tomorrow. Just hang on in there, darling, and you'll find yourself back in demand on a big scale. Be grateful that they can't cure you—in time, you'll *adapt,* just like me."

She knew that in her own way she *had* adapted, and not just by taking her medication regularly. She had adapted her mind and her soul, and knew that in doing that she had adapted her body chemistry, too, in subtle ways that no genetic engineer or ultrasmart expert system could ever have predicted. She knew that she was unique, and that what Alan had felt for her really did qualify as *love,* and was not to be dismissed as any mere addiction. If it had been mere addiction, there wouldn't have been any problem at all; he would simply have switched to another girl who'd been infected with the same virus vectors but had proved to be immune—so far—to the emergent mutations.

The punter wasn't a bad sort, all things considered. Unusual tastes weren't necessarily associated with perverted manners. He paid Anna in cash and he dropped her right outside the door of Lambeth North tube station. It was, he said, pretty much on his way home—which meant that he could conceivably have been Isabel's next-door neighbor. Anna didn't ask for further details, and he wouldn't have told her the truth if she had. There was an etiquette in these matters which had to be observed.

By the time Anna got back to the cemetery the grave had been filled in. The gravedigger had arranged the wreaths in a pretty pattern on the freshly turned earth, which was carefully mounded so that it wouldn't sink into a hollow as it settled beneath the spring rains. Anna studied the floral design very carefully before deciding exactly how to modify it to incorporate her own wreath.

She was a little surprised to note that her earlier impression had been mistaken; there *were* several wreaths made up of genetically engineered exotics. She quickly realized, however, that this was not a calculated expresson of xenophilia so much as an ostentatious gesture of conspicuous consumption. Those of Alan's friends and relatives who were slightly better-off than the rest had simply taken the opportunity to prove the point.

When she had rearranged the wreaths she stood back, looking down at her handiwork.

"I didn't want any of this to happen," she said. "In Paris, it might almost pass for romantic—man becomes infatuated with whore, recklessly smashes himself up in his car when she becomes infected with some almost-unprecedented kind of venereal disease—but in Pinner it's just absurd. You were a perfect fool, and I didn't even love you . . . but my mind got blown to hell and back by the side effects of my own mutated psychotropics, so maybe I would have if I could have. Who knows?''

I didn't want it to happen either, he said, struggling to get the words through the cloying blanket of her medication, which was deeply prejudiced against any and all hallucinations. *It really was an accident. I'd got over the worst of the withdrawal symptoms. I'd have been okay. Maybe I'd even have been okay with Kitty, once I'd got it all out of my system. Maybe I could have begun to be what everybody wanted and expected me to be.*

''Conformist bastard,'' she said. ''You make it sound like it was all pretense. Is that what you think? Just a phase you were going through, was it? Just a mad fling with a maddening whore who went completely mad?''

It was the real thing, he insisted, dutifully.

''It was a lot realer than the so-called real thing,'' she told him. ''Those expert systems are a hell of a lot cleverer than Old Mother Nature. Four billion years of natural selection produced spanish fly and rhino horn; forty years of computerized protein design produced me and a thousand alternatives you just have to dilute to taste. You couldn't expect Mother Nature to take that kind of assault lying down, of course, even if she always has been the hoariest whore of them all. Heaven only knows what a psychochemical wilderness the world will be when all the tailored pheromones and augmentary psychotropics have run the gamut of mutational variation. You and I were just caught in the evolutionary cross fire. Kitty and Isabel too, I guess. No man is an island, and all that crap.''

I don't think much of that as a eulogy, he said. *You could try to be a little more earnest, a little more sorrowful.*

He was right, but she didn't dare. She was afraid of earnestness, and doubly afraid of sorrow. There was no way in the world she was going to try to put it the way Ecclesiastes had—*in much wisdom is much grief, and he that increaseth knowledge increaseth sorrow* and all that kind of stuff. After all, she had to stay sane enough to get safely back to the hospital or they wouldn't let her out again for a *long* time.

''Good-bye, Alan,'' she said, quietly. ''I don't think I'll be able to drop in again for quite a while. You know how things are, even though you never once came to see me in the hospital.''

I know, he said. *You don't have any secrets from me. We're soul mates, you and I, now and forever.* It was a nicer way of putting it than saying he was addicted to her booby-trapped flesh, but it came to the same thing in the end.

She went away then: back to the tube station, across zones three, two, and one, and out again on the far side of the river. She wanted to be alone, although she knew that she never would be and never could be.

The receptionist demanded to know why Isabel hadn't brought her back in the car, so Anna said that she'd asked to be dropped at the end of the street. ''I wanted to walk a little way,'' she explained. ''It's such a nice evening.''

''No it isn't,'' the receptionist pointed out. ''It's cloudy and cold, and too windy by half.''

''You don't notice things like that when you're in my condition,'' Anna told her, loftily. ''I'm drugged up to the eyeballs on mutated euphorics manufactured by my own cells. If it weren't for the medication, I'd be right up there on cloud nine, out of my mind on sheer bliss.'' It was a lie, of course; the real effects were much nastier.

''If the way you're talking is any guide,'' the receptionist said, wryly, ''you're almost back to normal. We'll soon have to throw you back into the wide and wicked world.''

''It's not as wide or as wicked as all that,'' Anna said, with due kindness and consideration, ''and certainly not as worldly. One day, though, all the fallen angels will learn how to fly again, and how to soar to undiscovered heights—and *then* we'll begin to find out what the true bounds of experience are.''

''I take it back,'' the receptionist said. ''I hope you haven't been plaguing your poor sister's ears with that kind of talk—she won't want to take you out again if you have.''

''No,'' said Anna, ''I don't suppose she will. But then, she's not really my sister, and never was. I'm one of a kind.'' And for once, there was no inner or outer voice to say *Don't flatter yourself,* or *Better be grateful for what you've got,* or *We're all sisters under the skin,* or any of the other shallow and rough-hewn saws whose cutting edges she had always tried so very hard to resist.

THE HOUSE OF MOURNING
Brian Stableford

I suppose the seed of this story was sown in 1983, on the rainy day when I met Norman Macrae at Ascot to discuss some background material on possible developments in biotechnology that I was to provide for his futurology book *The 2024 Report.* He wondered whether the roads might become safer if we developed methods of getting high that didn't have the undesirable side effects of alcohol; I wondered whether sex might become more exciting once nature's ludicrously inefficient aphrodisiacs were replaced by all those which ingenious science could produce; Pusey Street won the big sprint at good odds by virtue of being drawn on the outside (Ascot drains toward the stands, so if it ever starts raining heavily when you're there, avoid horses drawn low on the straight course). *The 2024 Report* was an upbeat book—it suggested, among other things, that the Russians would simply give up Communism in disgust in the late 1980s—so my contribution to it concentrated on rewarding possibilities, but the time inevitably comes when one is tempted to turn such brightly minted coins over, just to see what might be lurking on the other side.

Martha Soukup is one of the dwindling number of writers who only writes short fiction. She has written stories for a number of science fiction magazines and anthologies, several of which have been finalists for the Hugo, Nebula, and World Fantasy Awards. Her story "In Defense of the Social Contracts" won the Nebula Award in 1995 and "Over the Long Haul" was adapted for Showtime. She waits for more Hollywood money to fall into her lap at her home in San Francisco.

"Fetish" is a surreal fantasy in which a masculine secondary characteristic takes on a symbolic power for the one who sports it. Think of "beard" as disguise, or in its other, related usage—the means of deflecting attention from one of the partners in an illicit relationship.

FETISH

MARTHA SOUKUP

IN THE AFTERMATH OF THE AFFAIR I DECIDE TO GROW A beard.

"Susan," my roommate Lelana says, warningly. Her skin is very dark and perfect; she would not risk its flawlessness. But she has seven tiny holes in her left ear. By day she wears seven small hoops of metal in them: copper, brass, bronze, pewter, silver, platinum, and gold. When she dresses to go out, seven gem studs spark her ear's rim: ruby, amber, topaz, emerald, sapphire, amethyst, and diamond. The diamond cost her two months' pay, and though she keeps it in a matchbox in the back of the tool drawer, she makes nervous remarks about burglars when she is not wearing it. A beard cannot be stolen.

I think about what it will look like. The tiny hairs I have plucked from under my chin are not light brown, but mahogany brown or translucent blond or light red. I wonder what they might combine to be.

• • •

There is a body-modification studio near my two favorite used-book stores. None of its signs ever attracted me: Tattoos. Piercing. Scarification. Branding. A new sign says Body Hair, and it did not at first attract me either. I thought of legs and chests and the busboy at the coffee shop who has grown his arm hair thick as an orangutan's, and dyed it orange-red. He wears a bloodred tank top to show it off. I always look in my coffee cup for orange hairs, which are never there.

I stand at the history shelf in the store next to the body studio and flip open a book on Egypt to a drawing of Cleopatra, her Pharaoh's beard, a proud ruler's beard. It is not real. Not like mine. Like mine will be.

I stroke my chin.

Inside the studio are displays of jewelry, steel rings, and chains, simple and in intricate combinations, stapled to framed swaths of black canvas. I don't know which parts of the body each piece is designed for. Perhaps a clever person can wear them anywhere. The woman behind the counter is talking to a young man. He is conservatively pierced, at least that I can see, two small silver hoops through one eyebrow. She has a pattern of scarification arching from the bridge of her nose across her temple, where it disappears in the wispy black hair over her left ear. I have lived in the city for six years now, and seen a thousand such alterations. It still looks odd to me.

"Yes?" she says, after the young man has written out a check and left.

"A beard," I say. When she opened her mouth I could see a silver stud in her tongue.

"Yes, what style are you interested in?" She lisps, just a little, enough to remind me not to look at her mouth. I look at her scar, a curlicue like an edge of paisley. If she didn't want me to look at it, she wouldn't have had it put there.

"What do you mean?"

"We'll stimulate the follicles wherever you want it," she says. Shtimulate. "You won't have to trim it like some man would, since you're starting out with nothing there at all. Where you don't have it added, nothing will grow." She gropes around under the counter and pulls out a small spiral-bound book, line drawings of strangely shaped sideburns, fringes of hair like necklaces, Dali moustaches: facial hair in patterns of tufts, in lines and curves, I have never imagined.

"I don't know. Just a beard."

"Think about it. You can call for an appointment." She gives me a brochure, "Hair Growth and You." "We haven't had too many women yet for this. I think you should do it."

"Would you?" I ask her.

"Oh no, that's not me," she says. She traces her forefinger in a curl down her right cheek and up to the corner of her mouth. "I'm going to mark myself here, as soon as I get the pattern drawn up exactly right. Hair would cover it up."

Myshelf.

At home I read from the brochure to Lelana. She frowns but stops telling me to shut up after the third time. " 'Within two days of topical Hirexiden application and regular intake of the supplemental hormones, most clients will find unstimulated fine body hairs falling out and new, thick hair taking its place.' "

"Who writes those things?" she asks. She's tried something new with her ear: four rings, three studs. I'm not used to seeing the diamond out of the bottom hole. She twists it, in its second position, between thumb and forefinger.

"It's fast," I say.

"It's a drug," she says. "Hormone. Thingie. Don't you need a doctor?"

"There's a doctor who prescribes it." His name is stamped in the blank space on the back of the brochure. "Then the person at the studio who applies it is a registered nurse. She does the branding and scarification, too. It's all very clean."

"Oh great," says Lelana. "Why are you doing this?"

The nurse has me sit back in a big old vinyl dentist's chair. Over its fake leather maroon it has been spray painted with gold and silver swirls.

She wears rubber gloves and holds a thin cloth patch. It has been traced already with the shape of my beard: larger than a goatee, but trim, with a moustache. When I told the receptionist I wanted a beard, not something abstract, she tried to talk me into leaving a blank design, my initials or a geometric space, in the middle. That's what the few fashionable bearded women are wearing, but I don't want that.

The nurse takes a scissors and cuts carefully on the thin red ink lines until it looks like a construction paper beard a child would put on with a string. Then she peels the adhesive from the patch. With her gloves, it takes her two false starts to peel it. I have washed my face thoroughly and wiped an astringent over it; my chin tingles. My breath feels tight in my chest as I wait for her to drape the patch over my face. Her movements are precise and careful. Where the patch clings to my skin I feel a heat, building slowly. I don't know if is the treatment or the excitement.

I have to wear the patch for twenty-four hours and go back to have things checked out. I have taken off work. I look at it in the mirror. It looks like a cheap Halloween costume. The patch is a light pink-tan color that looks like no one's skin ever did. It is darker than my own skin, so that, if I squint and blur my vision, it almost looks like a pale beard. Or like something is wrong with my skin.

It stings coming off. The nurse holds a moist strip of paper up against my twinging cheek. She looks at it. It is blue.

"Good," she says.

I have little white pills I'm supposed to take. In some way they direct testosterone to the follicles marked by the Hirexiden. They are so small they look like pills for a cat.

I swallow one with some orange juice and look in the mirror. My face looks the same as ever, but flushed, irritated, where the beard is supposed to come in. Makeup could smooth the color out, but the brochure says to clean the area gently and put no other products on it.

No one seems to look at me when I walk to the grocery store. I brush my fingers along the lower slopes of my cheeks. Has the peach fuzz fallen out, crowded out by more virile hairs? I can't tell. My fingertips seem too sensitive, they seem to have caught the tingling of my reddened cheeks. I pull at my chin, then stop, hoping I haven't disrupted anything.

I buy frozen burritos, pretzels, chocolate bars, and more orange juice. I think the checkout clerk is staring at me, too polite to say anything. I smile at him.

I wake Tuesday with a definite stubble on my chin. Lelana narrows her eyes at me when we pass in the bathroom hall. I put on mascara and a little more eyeshadow than I normally use and go to work.

Everyone in the office is pretty conservative in their grooming. They have seen facial hair in the high-fashion magazines and on MTV, but fancy, not like mine. Gaze after gaze glances off my chin without a word spoken. I spend most of the day on the phone trying to track down a lost report. The receiver pushes against the stubble. The people on the other end of the line don't know it. I eat lunch outside, in the courtyard by the downtown sidewalks, watching pedestrians watching me, men almost frowning, women looking carefully bored.

Between bites, I rub the stubble with the back of my hand. If I kissed a man now he would be the one scratched, his cheeks as reddened as the back of my hand is reddened. Which of these men passing by would I kiss? They lower their eyes toward the sidewalk as they pass. I finish the sandwich I brought, two bags of chips, an apple, a banana, and a bottle of beer, watching the men go by.

It's growing in thick and fast. I'm proud of it; I can hardly keep my hands off my face. The treatment, the hormones, they started it, but it's my follicles that have risen to the call, that are putting forth this rich growth, this life on my face.

Lelana's boyfriend comes over to pick her up Friday night and looks startled when I answer the door, the first open look of surprise I've seen. She must not have told him. She hurries past me and ushers him out of the apartment building. I sit through the afternoon watching arena football on cable. It's cute how they run around the small stadium wearing skintight uniforms bare up to the knee. After the game I watch two old black-and-white romance movies. I realize Lelana has come back in without my noticing, only when I hear a sullen rattle of pots and pans in the kitchen. Two commercial breaks later, the door to her room shuts firmly.

I wake with my fingers buried in the short thick growth of my beard, and, comfortable, sleep again.

It's beautiful, all the colors I thought it might be, an autumn beard of brown and red and sparkles of blond. I experiment with the best eye makeup to complement it. The sink is crowded with pencils and trays of powder and tiny tubs of cream in every color of brown, russet, charcoal. It is a month since I started growing the beard, and it is better than I ever hoped it would be. As I start to work on my face, I wonder idly where Lelana is. Around.

When I finish with my eyes I take a small scissors and carefully trim my beard until it is perfect.

I wear tight black pants and a clinging dark blue top, open in a small keyhole at the chest but with a turtleneck against which the beard glows. I shopped for the outfit for days. I brush my beard, I fluff it, I look at it from all angles in the mirror. I run my fingers quickly through my hair and go out the door.

Everyone looks at me at the club. Everyone.

I dance alone on the floor for an hour. For two hours. Then the men, tentatively at first, then in growing numbers, begin to crowd around me. I pick and choose from them. Too weedy, too loud, hair too limp. Finally I let one dance with me, slow, his breath warm and moist in my beard.

Lelana is not in the apartment when I take him home. I kiss the man and feel my beard catch on the angles of his smooth, naked cheeks, his lips. We do not need to talk. One hand tangled in my beard, the other on my breast, he lets me press him down against the bed. As he gasps, he pulls at my beard, pulls at my real and living beard.

When I send him home, I have not asked his name. I sleep with sweat and kisses in my beard and dream nothing at all.

• • •

In the morning, I shave.

FETISH
Martha Soukup

Sometimes you lie half-asleep and the first line of a story floats into your mind, like a dream that forgets you must be fully asleep before it can come into the room, and as enigmatic and self-evident as any dream.

It doesn't happen often enough.

This is a story about dealing with the pain from the alien by playacting the alien, incorporating the alien. It isn't a difficult concept. People have been doing it for as long as we've been human. Children do it when they put on their mothers' shoes. Adults do it, sometimes with less awareness. We take in change and survive. I think this is probably an optimistic story.

But I'm never sure about these things.

RED SONJA AND LESSINGHAM IN DREAMLAND

GWYNETH JONES

(WITH APOLOGIES TO E. R. EDDISON)

THE EARTH WALLS OF THE CARAVANSERAI ROSE STRANGELY
from the empty plain. She let the black stallion slow his pace.
The silence of deep dusk had a taste, like a rich dark fruit; the
air was keen. In the distance mountains etched a jagged margin
against an indigo sky; snow streaks glinting in the glimmer of
the dawning stars. She had never been here before, in life. But
as she led her horse through the gap in the high earthen banks
she knew what she would see. The camping booths around
the walls; the beaten ground stained black by the ashes of
countless cooking fires; the wattle-fenced enclosure where
travelers' riding beasts mingled indiscriminately with their
host's goats and chickens . . . the tumbledown gallery, where
sheaves of russet plains-grass sprouted from empty window-

spaces. Everything she looked on had the luminous intensity of a place often visited in dreams.

She was a tall woman, dressed for riding in a kilt and harness of supple leather over brief close-fitting linen: a costume that left her sheeny, muscular limbs bare and outlined the taut, proud curves of breast and haunches. Her red hair was bound in a braid as thick as a man's wrist. Her sword was slung on her back, the great brazen hilt standing above her shoulder. Other guests were gathered by an open-air kitchen, in the orange-red of firelight and the smoke of roasting meat. She returned their stares coolly: she was accustomed to attracting attention. But she didn't like what she saw. The host of the caravanserai came scuttling from the group by the fire. His manner was fawning. But his eyes measured, with a thief's sly expertise, the worth of the sword she bore and the quality of Lemiak's harness. Sonja tossed him a few coins and declined to join the company.

She had counted fifteen of them. They were poorly dressed and heavily armed. They were all friends together and their animals—both terror-birds and horses—were too good for any honest travelers' purposes. Sonja had been told that this caravanserai was a safe halt. She judged that this was no longer true. She considered riding out again onto the plain. But wolves and wild terror-birds roamed at night between here and the mountains, at the end of winter. And there were worse dangers; ghosts and demons. Sonja was neither credulous nor superstitious. But in this country no wayfarer willingly spent the black hours alone.

She unharnessed Lemiak and rubbed him down: taking sensual pleasure in the handling of his powerful limbs; in the heat of his glossy hide, and the vigor of his great body. There was firewood ready stacked in the roofless booth. Shouldering a cloth sling for corn and a hank of rope, she went to fetch her own fodder. The corralled beasts shifted in a mass to watch her. The great flightless birds, with their pitiless raptors' eyes, were especially attentive. She felt an equally rapacious attention from the company by the caravanserai kitchen, which amused her. The robbers—as she was sure they were—had all the luck. For her, there wasn't one of the fifteen who rated a second glance.

A man appeared, from the darkness under the ruined gallery. He was tall. The rippled muscle of his chest, left bare by an unlaced leather jerkin, shone red-brown. His black hair fell in glossy curls to his wide shoulders. He met her gaze and smiled, white teeth appearing in the darkness of his beard. *"My name is Ozymandias, king of kings . . . look on my works, ye mighty, and despair . . .* Do you know those lines?" He pointed to a lump of shapeless stone, one of several that lay about. It bore traces of carving, almost effaced by time. "There was a city here once, with marketplaces, fine buildings, throngs of proud people. Now they are dust, and only the caravanserai remains."

He stood before her, one tanned and sinewy hand resting lightly on the hilt of a dagger in his belt. Like Sonja, he carried his broadsword on his back. Sonja was tall. He topped her by a head: yet there was nothing brutish in his size. His brow was wide and serene, his eyes were vivid blue: his lips full and imperious; yet delicately modeled, in the rich nest of hair. Somewhere between eyes and lips there lurked a spirit of mockery, as if he found some secret amusement in the perfection of his own beauty and strength.

The man and the woman measured each other.

"You are a scholar," she said.

"Of some sort. And a traveler from an antique land—where the cities are still standing. It seems we are the only strangers here," he added, with a slight nod toward the convivial company. "We might be well advised to become friends for the night."

Sonja never wasted words. She considered his offer and nodded.

They made a fire in the booth Sonja had chosen. Lemiak and the scholar's terror-bird, left loose together in the back of the shelter, did not seem averse to each other's company. The woman and the man ate spiced sausage, skewered and broiled over the red embers, with bread and dried fruit. They drank water, each keeping to their own waterskin. They spoke little, after that first exchange—except to discuss briefly the tactics of their defense, should defense be necessary.

The attack came around midnight. At the first stir of covert movement, Sonja leapt up sword in hand. She grasped a brand from the dying fire. The man who had been crawling on his hands and knees toward her, bent on sly murder of a sleeping victim, scrabbled to his feet. "Defend yourself," yelled Sonja, who despised to strike an unarmed foe. Instantly he was rushing at her with a heavy sword. A great two-handed stroke would have cleft her to the waist. She parried the blow and caught him between neck and shoulder, almost severing the head from his body. The beasts plunged and screamed at the rush of blood scent. The scholar was grappling with another attacker, choking out the man's life with his bare hands . . . and the booth was full of bodies: their enemies rushing in on every side.

Sonja felt no fear. Stroke followed stroke, in a luxury of blood and effort and fire-shot darkness . . . until the attack was over, as suddenly as it had begun.

The brigands had vanished.

"We killed five," breathed the scholar, "by my count. Three to you, two to me."

She kicked together the remains of their fire and crouched to blow the embers to a blaze. By that light they found five corpses, dragged them and flung them into the open square. The scholar had a cut on his upper arm, which was bleeding freely. Sonja was bruised and battered, but otherwise unhurt. The worst loss was their woodstack, which had been trampled and blood-fouled. They would not be able to keep a watchfire burning.

"Perhaps they won't try again," said the warrior woman. "What can we have that's worth more than five lives?"

He laughed shortly. "I hope you're right."

"We'll take turns to watch."

Standing breathless, every sense alert, they smiled at each other in new-forged comradeship. There was no second attack. At dawn Sonja, rousing from a light doze, sat up and pushed back the heavy masses of her red hair.

"You are very beautiful," said the man, gazing at her.

"So are you," she answered.

The caravanserai was deserted, except for the dead. The brigands' riding animals were gone. The innkeeper and his family had vanished into some bolt-hole in the ruins.

"I am heading for the mountains," he said, as they packed up their gear. "For the pass into Zimiamvia."

"I too."

"Then our way lies together."

He was wearing the same leather jerkin, over knee-length loose breeches of heavy violet silk. Sonja looked at the strips of linen that bound the wound on his upper arm. "When did you tie up that cut?"

"You dressed it for me, for which I thank you."

"When did I do that?"

He shrugged. "Oh, sometime."

Sonja mounted Lemiak, a little frown between her brows. They rode together until dusk. She was not talkative and the man soon accepted her silence. But when night fell, and they camped without a fire on the houseless plain: then, as the demons stalked, they were glad of each other's company. Next dawn, the mountains seemed as distant as ever. Again, they met no living creature all day, spoke little to each other, and made the same comfortless camp. There was no moon. The stars were almost bright enough to cast shadow; the cold was intense. Sleep was impossible, but they were not tempted to ride on. Few travelers attempt the passage over the high plains to Zimiamvia. Of those few most turn back, defeated. Some wander among the ruins forever, tearing at their own flesh. Those who survive are the ones who do not defy the terrors of darkness. They crouched shoulder to shoulder, each wrapped in a single blanket, to endure. Evil emanations of the death-steeped plain rose from the soil and bred phantoms. The sweat of fear was cold as ice melt on Sonja's cheeks. Horrors made of nothingness prowled and muttered in her mind.

"How long," she whispered. "How long do we have to bear this?"

The man's shoulder lifted against hers. "Until we get well, I suppose."

The warrior-woman turned to face him, green eyes flashing in appalled outrage.

"Sonja" discussed this group member's felony with the therapist. Dr Hamilton—he wanted them to call him Jim, but

"Sonja" found this impossible—monitored everything that went on in the virtual environment. But he never appeared there. They only met him in the one-to-one consultations that virtual-therapy buffs called *the meat sessions*.

"He's not supposed to *do* that," she protested, from the foam couch in the doctor's office. He was sitting beside her, his notebook on his knee. "He damaged my experience."

Dr Hamilton nodded. "Okay. Let's take a step back. Leave aside the risk of disease or pregnancy: because we *can* leave those bogeys aside, forever if you like. Would you agree that sex is essentially an innocent and playful social behavior—something you'd offer to or take from a friend, in an ideal world, as easily as food or drink?"

"Sonja" recalled certain dreams—*meat* dreams, not the computer-assisted kind. She blushed. But the man was a doctor after all. "That's what I do feel," she agreed. "That's why I'm here. I want to get back to the pure pleasure, to get rid of the baggage."

"The sexual experience offered in virtuality therapy is readily available on the nets. You know that. And you could find an agency that would vet your partners for you. You chose to join this group because you need to feel that you're taking *medicine,* so you don't have to feel ashamed. And because you need to feel that you're interacting with people who, like yourself, perceive sex as a problem."

"Doesn't everyone?"

"You and another group member went off into your own private world. That's good. That's what's supposed to happen. Let me tell you, it doesn't always. The software gives you access to a vast multisensual library, all the sexual fantasy ever committed to media. But you and your partner, or partners, have to customize the information and use it to create and maintain what we call the *consensual perceptual plenum.* Success in holding a shared dreamland together is a knack. It depends on something in the neural makeup that no one has yet fully analyzed. Some have it, some don't. You two are really in sync."

"That's exactly what I'm complaining about—"

"You think he's damaging the pocket universe you two built up. But he isn't, not from his character's point of view.

It's part Lessingham's thing, to be conscious that he's in a fantasy world.''

She started, accusingly. ''I don't want to know his name.''

''Don't worry, I wouldn't tell you. ''Lessingham'' is the name of his virtuality persona. I'm surprised you don't recognize it. He's a character from a series of classic fantasy novels by E.R. Eddison. . . . *In Eddison's glorious cosmos ''Lessingham'' is a splendidly endowed English gentleman, who visits fantastic realms of ultra-masculine adventure as a lucid dreamer: though an actor in the drama, he is partly conscious of another existence, while the characters around him are more or less explicitly puppets of the dream . . .''*

He sounded as if he was quoting from a reference book. He probably was: reading from an autocue that had popped up in lenses of those doctorish horn-rims. She knew that the old-fashioned trappings were there to reassure her. She rather despised them: but it was like the virtuality itself. The buttons were pushed, the mechanism responded. She was reassured.

Of course she knew the Eddison stories. She recalled ''Lessingham'' perfectly: the tall, strong, handsome, cultured millionaire jock, who has magic journeys to another world, where he is a tall, strong, handsome, cultured jock in Elizabethan costume, with a big sword. The whole thing was an absolutely typical male power-fantasy, she thought—without rancor. *Fantasy means never having to say you're sorry.* The women in those books, she remembered, were drenched in sex, but they had no part in the action. They stayed at home being princesses, *occasionally* allowing the millionaire jocks to get them into bed. She could understand why ''Lessingham'' would be interested in ''Sonja'' . . . for a change.

''You think he goosed you, psychically. What do you expect? You can't dress the way 'Sonja' dresses, and hope to be treated like the Queen of the May.''

Dr. Hamilton was only doing his job. He was supposed to be provocative, so they could react against him. That was his excuse, anyway. . . . On the contrary, she thought. ''Sonja'' dresses the way she does because she can dress any way she likes. ''Sonja'' doesn't have to *hope* for respect, and she doesn't have to demand it. She just gets it. ''It's dominance display,'' she said, enjoying the theft of his jargon. ''Females do that too, you know. The way 'Sonja' dresses is not an invitation. It's a warning. Or a challenge, to anyone who can measure up.''

He laughed, but he sounded irritated. ''Frankly, I'm amazed that you two work together. I'd have expected 'Lessingham' to go for an ultrafeminine—''

''I am . . . 'Sonja' *is* ultrafeminine. Isn't a tigress feminine?''

''Well, okay. But I guess you've found out his little weakness. He likes to be a teeny bit in control, even when he's letting his hair down in dreamland.''

She remembered the secret mockery lurking in those blue eyes. ''That's the problem. That's exactly what I *don't* want. I don't want either of us to be in control.''

''I can't interfere with his persona. So, it's up to you. Do you want to carry on?''

''Something works,'' she muttered. She was unwilling to admit that there'd been no one else, in the text interface phase of the group, that she found remotely attractive. It was ''Lessingham,'' or drop out and start again. ''I just want him to stop *spoiling things.*''

''You can't expect your masturbation fantasies to mesh completely. This is about getting *beyond* solitary sex. Go with it: where's the harm? One day you'll want to face a sexual partner in the real, and then you'll be well. Meanwhile, you could be passing 'Lessingham' in reception—he comes to his meat sessions around your time—and not know it. That's *safety,* and you never have to breach it. You two have proved that you can sustain an imaginary world together: it's almost like being in love. I could argue that lucid dreaming, being *in* the fantasy world but not *of* it, is the next big step. Think about that.''

The clinic room had mirrored walls: more deliberate provocation. How much reality can you take? the reflections asked. But she felt only a vague distaste for the woman she saw, at once hollow-cheeked and bloated, lying in the doctor's foam couch. He was glancing over her records on his notebook screen: which meant the session was almost up.

''Still no overt sexual contact?''

"I'm not ready . . ." She stirred restlessly. "Is it a man or a woman?"

"Ah!" smiled Dr. Hamilton, waving a finger at her. "Naughty, naughty—"

He was the one who'd started taunting her, with his hints that the meat—"Lessingham"—might be near. She hated herself for asking a genuine question. It was her rule to give him no entry to her real thoughts. But Dr. Jim knew everything, without being told: every change in her brain chemistry, every effect on her body: sweaty palms, racing heart, damp underwear. . . . The telltales on his damned autocue left her precious little dignity. *Why do I subject myself to this?* she wondered, disgusted. But in the virtuality she forgot utterly about Dr. Jim. She didn't care who was watching. She had her brazen-hilted sword. She had the piercing intensity of dusk on the high plains, the snowlight on the mountains; the hard, warm silk of her own perfect limbs. She felt a brief complicity with "Lessingham." She had a conviction that Dr. Jim didn't play favorites. He despised all his patients equally. . . . *You get your kicks, doctor. But we have the freedom of dreamland.*

"Sonja" read cards stuck in phone booths and store windows, in the tired little streets outside the building that housed the clinic. *Relaxing massage by clean-shaven young man in Luxurious Surroundings* . . . You can't expect your fantasies to mesh exactly, the doctor said. But how can it work if two people disagree over something so vital as the difference between control and surrender? Her estranged husband used to say: "why don't you just *do it for me,* as a favor. It wouldn't hurt. Like making someone a cup of coffee . . ." *Offer the steaming cup, turn around and lift my skirts, pull down my underwear. I'm ready. He opens his pants and slides it in, while his thumb is round in front rubbing me. . . . I could enjoy that,* thought "Sonja," remembering the blithe abandon of her dreams. *That's the damned shame. If there were no nonsex consequences, I don't know that there's any limit to what I could enjoy. . . .* But all her husband had achieved was to make her feel she never wanted to make anyone, man, woman, or child, a cup of coffee ever again. . . . In luxurious surroundings. *That's what I want. Sex without engagement, pleasure without consequences. It's got to be possible.*

She gazed at the cards, feeling uneasily that she'd have to give up this habit. She used to glance at them sidelong, now she'd pause and linger. She was getting desperate. She was lucky there was medically supervised virtuality sex to be had. She would be helpless prey in the wild world of the nets, and she'd never, ever risk trying one of these meat-numbers. And she had no intention of returning to her husband. Let him make his own coffee. She wouldn't call that getting well. She turned, and caught the eye of a nicely dressed young woman standing next to her. They walked away quickly in opposite directions. *Everybody's having the same dreams . . .*

In the foothills of the mountains, the world became green and sweet. They followed the course of a little river, that sometimes plunged far below their path, tumbling in white flurries in a narrow gorge; and sometimes ran beside them, racing smooth and clear over colored pebbles. Flowers clustered on the banks, birds darted in the thickets of wild rose and honeysuckle. They lead their riding animals and walked at ease: not speaking much. Sometimes the warrior woman's flank would brush the man's side: or he would lean for a moment, as if by chance, his hand on her shoulder. Then they would move deliberately apart, but they would smile at each other. *Soon. Not yet. . . .*

They must be vigilant. The approaches to fortunate Zimiamvia were guarded. They could not expect to reach the pass unopposed. And the nights were haunted still. They made camp at a flat bend of the river, where the crags of the defile drew away, and they could see far up and down their valley. To the north, peaks of diamond and indigo reared above them. Their fire of aromatic wood burned brightly, as the white stars began to blossom.

"No one knows about the long-term effects," she said. "It can't be safe. At the least, we're risking irreversible addiction, they warn you about that. I don't want to spend the rest of my life as a cyberspace couch potato."

"Nobody claims it's safe. If it was safe, it wouldn't be so intense."

Their eyes met. "Sonja's" barbarian simplicity combined surprisingly well with the man's more elaborate furnishing. The *consensual perceptual plenum* was a flawless reality: the sound of the river, the clear silence of the mountain twilight ... their two perfect bodies. She turned from him to gaze into the sweet-scented flames. The warrior-woman's glorious vitality throbbed in her veins. The fire held worlds of its own, liquid furnaces: the sunward surface of Mercury.

"Have you ever been to a place like this in the real?"

He grimaced. "You're kidding. In the real, I'm *not* a magic-wielding millionaire."

Something howled. The bloodstopping cry was repeated. A taint of sickening foulness swept by them. They both shuddered, and drew closer together. "Sonja" knew the scientific explanation for the legendary virtuality-paranoia, the price you paid for the virtual world's superreal, dreamlike richness. It was all down to heightened neurotransmitter levels, a positive feedback effect, psychic overheating. But the horrors were still horrors.

"The doctor says if we can talk like this, it means we're getting well."

He shook his head. "I'm not sick. It's like you said. Virtuality's addictive and I'm an addict. I'm getting my drug of choice safely, on prescription. That's how I see it."

All this time "Sonja" was in her apartment, lying in a foam couch with a visor over her head. The visor delivered compressed bursts of stimuli to her visual cortex: the other sense perceptions riding piggyback on the visual, triggering a whole complex of neuronal groups; tricking her mind/brain into believing the world of the dream was *out there*. The brain works like a computer. You cannot "see" a hippopotamus, until your system has retrieved the "hippopotamus" template from memory, and checked it against the incoming. Where does the "real" exist? In a sense this world was as real as the other ... But the thought of "Lessingham's" unknown body disturbed her. If he was too poor to lease good equipment, he might be lying in the clinic now in a grungy public cubicle ... catheterized, and so forth: the sordid details.

She had never tried virtual sex. The solitary version had seemed a depressing idea. People said the partnered kind was the perfect *zipless fuck*. He sounded experienced; she was afraid he would be able to tell she was not. But it didn't matter. The virtual-therapy group wasn't like a dating agency. She would never meet him in the real, that was the whole idea. She didn't have to think about that stranger's body. She didn't have to worry about the real "Lessingham" 's opinion of her. She drew herself up in the firelight. It was right, she decided, that Sonja should be a virgin. When the moment came, her surrender would be the more absolute.

In their daytime he stayed in character. It was a tacit trade-off. She would acknowledge the other world at nightfall by the campfire, as long as he didn't mention it the rest of the time. So they traveled on together, Lessingham and Red Sonja, the courtly scholar-knight and the taciturn warrior-maiden, through an exquisite Maytime: exchanging lingering glances, "accidental" touches ... And still nothing happened. "Sonja" was aware that "Lessingham," as much as herself, was holding back from the brink. She felt piqued at this. But they were both, she guessed, waiting for the fantasy they had generated to throw up the perfect moment of itself. It ought to. There was no other reason for its existence.

Turning a shoulder of the hillside, they found a sheltered hollow. Two rowan trees in flower grew above the river. In the shadow of their blossom tumbled a little waterfall, so beautiful it was a wonder to behold. The water fell clear from the upper edge of a slab of stone twice a man's height, into a rocky basin. The water in the basin was clear and deep, a-churn with bubbles from the jet plunging from above. The riverbanks were lawns of velvet, over the rocks grew emerald mosses and tiny water flowers.

"I would live here," said Lessingham softly, his hand dropping from his riding bird's bridle. "I would build me a house in this fairy place, and rest my heart here forever."

Sonja loosed the black stallion's rein. The two beasts moved off, feeding each in its own way on the sweet grasses and springtime foliage.

"I would like to bathe in that pool," said the warrior-maiden.

"Why not?" He smiled. "I will stand guard."

She pulled off her leather harness and slowly unbound her

hair. It fell in a trembling mass of copper and russet lights, a cloud of glory around the richness of her barely clothed body. Gravely she gazed at her own perfection, mirrored in the homage of his eyes. Lessingham's breath was coming fast. She saw a pulse beat, in the strong beauty of his throat. The pure physical majesty of him caught her breath . . .

It was their moment. But it still needed something to break this strange spell of reluctance. *"Lady—"* he murmured—

Sonja gasped. "Back to back!" she cried. "Quickly, or it is too late!"

Six warriors surrounded them, covered from head to foot in red-and-black armor. They were human in the lower body, but the head of each appeared beaked and fanged, with monstrous faceted eyes, and each bore an extra pair of armored limbs between breastbone and belly. They fell on Sonja and Lessingham without pause or a challenge.

Sonja fought fiercely as always, her blade ringing against the monster armor. But something cogged her fabulous skill. Some power had drained the strength from her splendid limbs. She was disarmed. The clawed creatures held her, a monstrous head stooped over her, choking her with its fetid breath. . . .

When she woke again she was bound against a great boulder, by thongs around her wrists and ankles, tied to hoops of iron driven into the rock. She was naked but for her linen shift, it was in tatters. Lessingham was standing, leaning on his sword. "I drove them off," he said. "At last." He dropped the sword, and took his dagger to cut her down.

She lay in his arms. "You are very beautiful," he murmured. She thought he would kiss her. His mouth plunged instead to her breast, biting and sucking at the engorged nipple. She gasped in shock, a fierce pang leapt through her virgin flesh. What did they want with kisses? They were warriors. Sonja could not restrain a moan of pleasure. He had won her. How wonderful to be overwhelmed, to surrender to the raw lust of this godlike animal.

Lessingham set her on her feet.

"Tie me up."

He was proffering a handful of blood-slicked leather thongs. "What?"

"Tie me to the rock, mount me. It's what I want."

"The evil warriors tied you—?"

"And you come and rescue me." He made an impatient gesture. "Whatever. Trust me. It'll be good for you too." He tugged at his bloodstained silk breeches, releasing a huge, iron-hard erection. "See, they tore my clothes. When you see *that*, you go crazy, you can't resist . . . and I'm at your mercy. Tie me up!"

"Sonja" had heard that eighty percent of the submissive partners in sadomasochist sex are male. But it is still the man who dominates his "dominatrix": who says *tie me tighter, beat me harder, you can stop now. . . . Hey,* she thought. *Why all the stage directions, suddenly? What happened to my zipless fuck?* But what the hell. She wasn't going to back out now, having come so far. . . . There was a seamless shift, and Lessingham was bound to the rock. She straddled his cock. He groaned. *"Don't do this to me."* He thrust upward, into her, moaning. *"You savage, you utter savage, uuunnnh . . ."* Sonja grasped the man's wrists and rode him without mercy. He was right, it was as good this way. His eyes were half-closed. In the glimmer of blue under his lashes, a spirit of mockery trembled. . . . She heard a laugh, and found her hands were no longer gripping Lessingham's wrists. He had broken free from her bonds, he was laughing at her in triumph. He was wrestling her to the ground.

"No!" she cried, genuinely outraged. But he was the stronger.

It was night when he was done with her. He rolled away and slept, as far as she could tell, instantly. Her chief thought was that virtual sex didn't entirely *connect*. She remembered now, that was something else people told you, as well as the "zipless fuck." *It's like coming in your sleep,* they said. *It doesn't quite make it.* Maybe there was nothing virtuality could do to orgasm, to match the heightened richness of the rest of the experience. She wondered if he, too, had felt cheated.

She lay beside her hero, wondering, *where did I go wrong? Why did he have to treat me that way?* Beside her, "Lessingham" cuddled a fragment of violet silk, torn from his own breeches. He whimpered in his sleep, nuzzling the soft fabric, *"Mama . . ."*

• • •

She told Dr. Hamilton that "Lessingham" had raped her.

"And wasn't that what you wanted?"

She lay on the couch in the mirrored office. The doctor sat beside her with his smart notebook on his knee. The couch collected "Sonja's" physical responses as if she was an astronaut umbilicaled to ground control; and Dr. Jim read the telltales popping up in his reassuring horn-rims. She remembered the sneaking furtive thing that she had glimpsed in "Lessingham's" eyes, the moment before he took over their lust scene. How could she explain the difference? "He wasn't playing. In the fantasy, anything's allowed. But *he wasn't playing*. He was outside it, laughing at me."

"I warned you he would want to stay in control."

"But there was no need! I *wanted* him to be in control. Why did he have to steal what I wanted to give him anyway?"

"You have to understand, "Sonja," that to many men it's women who seem powerful. You women feel dominated and try to achieve 'equality.' But the men don't perceive the situation like that. They're mortally afraid of you: and anything, just about *anything* they do to keep the upper hand, seems like justified self-defense."

She could have wept with frustration. "I know all that! That's *exactly* what I was trying to get away from. I thought we were supposed to leave the damn baggage behind. I wanted something purely physical. . . . Something innocent."

"Sex is not innocent, 'Sonja.' I know you believe it is, or 'should be.' But it's time you faced the truth. Any interaction with another person involves some kind of jockeying for power, dickering over control. Sex is no exception. Now *that's* basic. You can't escape from it in direct-cortical fantasy. It's in our minds that relationships happen, and the mind, of course, is where virtuality happens too." He sighed, and made an entry in her notes. "I want you to look on this as another step toward coping with the real. You're not sick, 'Sonja.' You're unhappy. Not even unusually so. Most adults are unhappy, to some degree—"

"Or else they're in denial."

Her sarcasm fell flat. "Right. A good place to be, at least some of the time. What we're trying to achieve here—if we're trying to achieve anything at all—is to raise your pain threshold to somewhere near average. I want you to walk away from therapy with lowered expectations: I guess that would be success.''

"Great,'' she said, desolate. "That's just great.''

Suddenly he laughed. "Oh, you guys! You are so weird. It's always the same story. *Can't live with you, can't live without you. . . .* You can't go on this way, you know. Its getting ridiculous. You want some real advice, 'Sonja'? Go home. Change your attitudes, and start some hard peace talks with that husband of yours.''

"I don't want to change,'' she said coldly, staring with open distaste at his smooth profile, his soft effeminate hands. Who was he to call her abnormal? "I like my sexuality just the way it is.''

Dr. Hamilton returned her look, a glint of human malice breaking through his doctor act. "Listen. I'll tell you something for free.'' A weird sensation jumped in her crotch. For a moment she had a prick: a hand lifted and cradled the warm weight of her balls. She stifled a yelp of shock. He grinned. "I've been looking for a long time, and I know. *There is no tall, dark man . . .*''

He returned to her notes. "You say you were 'raped,' '' he continued, as if nothing had happened. "Yet you chose to continue the virtual session. Can you explain that?''

She thought of the haunted darkness, the cold air on her naked body; the soreness of her bruises; a rag of flesh used and tossed away. How it had felt to lie there: intensely alive, tasting the dregs, beaten back at the gates of the fortunate land. In dreamland, even betrayal had such rich depth and fascination. And she was free to enjoy, because *it didn't matter.*

"You wouldn't understand.''

Out in the lobby there were people coming and going. It was lunchtime, the lifts were busy. "Sonja'' noticed a round-shouldered geek of a little man making for the entrance to the clinic. She wondered idly if that could be "Lessingham.''

She would drop out of the group. The adventure with "Lessingham'' was over, and there was no one else for her. She needed to start again. The doctor knew he'd lost a customer, that was why he'd been so open with her today. He certainly guessed, too, that she'd lose no time in signing on somewhere else on the semimedical fringe. What a fraud all that therapy talk was! He'd never have dared to play the sex change trick on her, except that he knew she was an addict. She wasn't likely to go accusing him of unprofessional conduct. Oh, he knew it all. But his contempt didn't trouble her.

So, she had joined the inner circle. She could trust Dr. Hamilton's judgment. He had the telltales: he would know. She recognized with a feeling of mild surprise that she had become a statistic, an element in a fashionable social concern: *an epidemic flight into fantasy, inadequate personalities; unable to deal with the reality of normal human sexual relations. . . . But that's crazy,* she thought. *I don't hate men, and I don't believe "Lessingham" hates women. There's nothing psychotic about what we're doing. We're making a consumer choice. Virtual sex is* easier, *that's all. Okay, it's convenience food. It has too much sugar, and a certain blandness. But when a product comes along, that is cheaper, easier, and more fun than the original version, of course people are going to buy it.*

The lift was full. She stood, drab bodies packed around her, breathing the stale air. Every face was a mask of dull endurance. She closed her eyes. *The caravanserai walls rose strangely from the empty plain . . .*

RED SONJA AND LESSINGHAM IN DREAMLAND
Gwyneth Jones

Bondage probably isn't my ideal equal opportunities sport. I have poor circulation and a short temper. I'd never want to take my turn as the bondee. But this story isn't really about acting out control fantasies. It's about the invincible human vices (aka survival traits) of cowardice and laziness. Sexual negotiations are costly and dangerous, and as soon as there's a way to swipe the pleasure while avoiding the risks, nothing's going to stop people, of whatever gender, from opting for McDonald's.

I'm an unreliable witness on the subject of my stories and novels. I tend to give a different answer every time, as different aspects strike me as important. *Magna est veritas,* and there's no end to it. But this is certainly some of the thinking behind Sonja.

THE FUTURE OF BIRDS

MIKE O'DRISCOLL

WHILE DR. KLEINFELD CARRIES OUT HIS GYNECOLOGICAL EX-
plorations, I try to recall a life beyond the Sanctuary. It is an
old game, one whose necessity is greater than ever now that
the parameters of existence are closing in on me. The old
dream has become a sour and sterile reality; my new dreams
are of the disease.

Dr. Kleinfeld completes his probing and unhooks my legs
from the stirrups. He makes notes in silence, ignoring me; his
report is for Spengler's eyes, not mine. Seeking some reassurance, I ask him, "And how is my cunt, Doctor?"

He says, "Is it necessary to use such terminology?"

"That's what it is."

"No no," he protests. "Had you undergone reassignment
surgery in Brazil, then such a crude appellation would be appropriate." And then he's off into his spiel about the tech-

niques he developed to construct my labia, clitoris, and vagina, and the breakthrough he'd achieved in being able to lubricate the vagina from the seminal vesicles and Cowper's glands, on and on like some demented Frankenstein.

"I've been having dreams," I cut him off.

"Isn't that the purpose of dreamdust," he says, an attempt at sarcasm that doesn't become him. "Why do you need that stuff?"

"I've been dreaming about the disease."

I see the momentary panic in his eyes before it is replaced by a synthetic reassurance. "It can't harm you, my dear."

"It killed the woman who discovered it," I say.

He smiles and says, "A woman, Estela, which only confirms my point. What Dr. Komatsu found in her tests on precancerous cells from a patient's ovaries—the dysfunctional estrogen—merely served to illustrate what it was she would die from."

"She was an expert," I persist. "And she couldn't save herself."

Kleinfeld shakes his head, as if speaking to a capricious child. "It caught up with her too fast. By the time she discovered that luteinizing hormone was triggering an abnormal reaction in estrogen, and that symptoms were only manifesting in women, she was already at the hemorrhaging stage. She lived just long enough to establish the viral origins of the gonadotrophin mutation. It was left to others to prove that this Hormonal Dysfunction Virus caused the disease."

"But I carry the virus," I tell him, watching his reaction.

"Yes, as do eighty percent of males; but there are absolutely no cases of activation of the disease in men."

"How do you know it will stay that way?"

"Our knowledge of HDV is still growing, but the latest research indicates that the presence of male hormones may inhibit the viral activation. It's apparent that HDV is hereditary, and lies dormant in both male and female until the onset of a premature puberty. When the pituitary gonadotrophins are at a high enough level to stimulate production of the sex hormones, this process triggers the virus, which in turn causes the dysfunction of the estrogen in the ovaries. The indications are that when sex hormone production begins in males, the androgens produced somehow prevent the virus from becoming active.''

"I produce high levels of estrogen," I say.

"Yes," he agrees, "but you still produce androgens in sufficient quantities to counteract HDV." He pauses, as if to savor a triumph. "A feature of the surgery I performed on you six years ago; you carry the virus but it cannot interact with your production of female hormones. The triggering process cannot take place."

Despite the words, I sense his doubt. "Am I to be replaced?"

He frowns. "What have I just told you? There are no reported cases of Komatsu's Syndrome in transsexuals."

Soon afterward, Heinrich, my null, drives me back through the morning rain to my apartment overlooking the River Spree. As I undress I hear the phone hum, but I make no move to answer it. He picks it up, listens, then informs me that Spengler wishes to speak to me.

Spengler owns *The Birds of the Crystal Plumage*. He had me brought to Berlin; everything I have, has come from him—this apartment, the car, the clothes, the dust, and the body, most of all the body. Sometimes I feel I have as little free will as Heinrich. He is a eunuch in mind as well as in body, conditioned by hypnotics to respond only to my commands.

Reluctantly, I take the phone. "Estela," Spengler says, "some business associates are stopping in town tonight. I want to take them to the club. They're keen to see your act."

"They always are," I tell him. "I don't feel well."

Mock concern creeps into his voice. "What is it now, my dear?"

"Bad dreams."

Spengler laughs, a brittle, humorless sound. "Don't be stupid, you know they came for you." He goes on to tell me which costume to wear, which jewelry, which perfume. "I'll expect you at eight. Be in a good mood, Estela, don't disappoint them."

This life in paradise is my reward; it is the way I profit from the disease. I remember months of preparation, even after the surgery—instruction in oriental sexual techniques, as well more cerebral refinements, French, German, and English lan-

guages; literature; art—I can hold my own in the most refined
or debauched company. And I recall my first years in Berlin,
when the bars of my cage remained invisible.

I enter the bedroom, searching my body for signs of corruption. I lie on the bed as Heinrich comes in with a crystal
pipe on a tray. He loads the bowl with dreamdust. As he heats
it, my anticipation is tinged with the hope that I won't dream.

Late afternoon finds me stronger, vaguely pleased at some
dust-induced memory. This sense of well-being lasts only until
Rudy Thessinger calls. "What do you want?" I ask him.

Laughter flows down the line, poisoning my brain. Rudy
and I go back a long way, to Rio de Janeiro, more than six
years ago. Rudy brought me to Berlin. He's Spengler's talent
scout, my pimp.

As usual he inquires about my well-being, then says, "I
have some news about an old friend of yours."

"What friend?" I ask. I have no friends, only clients.

"Was Rio so bad you've forgotten who took you away from
giving head on the Rua Princesa Isabel?"

I recall a name from the dream. "Cledilce."

"She's been in Paris a month, undergoing reassignment surgery."

"You've seen her?"

"The word is she looks stunning," Rudy says, ignoring my
question. "You can imagine what—"

I hang up before his mindgames begin to sicken me. The
new image is fixed in my brain, the face from my other life.
Heinrich enters with a fix of dust and I surprise myself by
refusing it. I'm not certain what I feel, but it is something
strong.

Heinrich's skilled hands massage my dark flesh, forcing tension from my limbs. I sometimes wonder why he allowed—
why any null allows—himself to be surgically altered, his
brain adapted so that the production of endorphins is tied to
certain emotional states. Is it enough to have all feelings of
self-interest sublimated into a desire to serve? To enslave the
brain in return for the slow dripfeed of endorphins to its pleasure receptors? To be free forever of guilt and fear and stress?

Perhaps, in his rare moments of lucidity, he wonders about my alteration?

Images begin to clarify, take on meaning. I sift through the chaos of memories, seeking to impose on them a sense of order.

I was not always Estela de Brito. I see a young boy, nine or ten, living on the streets of Rochina, the stinking *favela* that sprawled up over the lure of the wealthy suburb of São Conrado. And a sister, a year older, a pretty girl who sold her body so that they might eat. But already the teeth marks of the disease were on her flesh; there were nights when the boy awoke in the corrugated iron shack that was home, to her cries of pain as blood poured from between her legs. There were no parents.

Gangsters ruled Rochina with machine guns and calculated terror; occasionally some city politician wanting to make a name for himself would send the police into the *favelas* to wipe out a few *marginals*—lowlife petty thieves; the politician's face would make the TV news and things would go on as before. Business-financed death squads would execute children; a cleansing process, ridding the city of future criminals, making Rio safe for gringo tourists. Their bullets spared the girl the worst ravages of the disease. The boy left Rochina and graduated to picking tourists' pockets on Copacabana, and from there to the docks at Maua, where he learned to give head for ten dollars a trick. Soon, he was working the streets off Rua Princesa Isabel, discovering that he could double his take if he dressed as a girl. Evenings, he'd work the cars parked along the seafront, blowing the men on their way home from work; in one car, suck suck, open the door, spit it out and move on to the next vehicle; for an hour or two each evening, a prolonged chorus of slamming car doors.

And all the while, the boy worked on his appearance, improving his makeup and clothes, avoiding the older hookers and pimps till one day he gave lip to a *marginal* who wanted his money. The man was going to cut him bad and would have too, if it hadn't been for the tall, raven-haired figure who buried a knife in the man's ribs. That was his first meeting with Cledilce Macedo. He was sixteen, street-smart, and was making more money than the boy had thought possible from giving head. Cledilce's johns—American and European tourists—were a long way up from the factory workers and dockers among whom the boy plied his trade. They had to be, because Cledilce was a Bird, a preoperative transsexual on a female hormone program, and like any other route out of the gutter, hormones cost big money. He took the boy home to a shabby apartment on the sixth floor of a block on Rua Toneleiros. He got him on to hormones, too, and told him he needed a new name.

For three years he . . . *I* learned, developing and refining my body, making contacts, saving money, and loving Cledilce. At first, I worried that I would no longer be able to perform sexually, that it would feel like nothing at all, but the strength of Cledilce's erection soon put my mind at rest. There would be no loss of libido he, or rather she, explained, not until after the operation. And even then, we wouldn't have to ejaculate to experience orgasm; sex, she said, was mainly in the head. As my breasts grew and I lost my facial hair, I began to worry about the operation itself. I had heard tales of the awful consequences of the gender reassignments carried out in the Centro clinics, even saw the evidence of their botched surgery with my own eyes. Till Cledilce had finally shared the dream with me, the dream of escaping to 'sanctuary,' where Parisian surgeons—not Centro butchers—would sculpt us anew, transforming us so that we would feel what women were meant to feel.

As Heinrich sits me up to arrange my jet black hair into a dazzling coiffure, one that, like my body, will impress Spengler's important friends, I think: they lied to us.

Heinrich guides the Mercedes through rain-slick streets, along Kanstrasse past shabby, smoke-filled *kneipen,* into Kurfürstendam, past sidewalk cafes with glassed-in terraces where unblemished middle-aged women sit alone with their drinks, past the Komödie theater till it pulls up outside the The Blue Angel. Young Babes—sexually precocious girls of nine or ten—flaunt themselves outside the entrance, some of them menstruating so profusely that, even through their heavy padding, blood streams down their stockinged legs. Images of Sally Bowles and Marlene Dietrich fill their minds, feeding the awful need that has drawn them here to plead with implacable doormen, seeking to gain entrance to the scene of their inspirations' former glories. One crumbling, anemic beauty falls to the pavement. The others start bickering over her as she crawls away to die. Then the doormen step out onto the pavement and form a cordon around Spengler, who comes out into the rain to greet me. The Babes try to grasp his arms and legs, but he strides through them, all lean arrogance and efficiency clothed in a black lounge suit. I get out of the car and he holds me at a slight distance, surveying my array of scarlet feathers and blue chiffon as if I were some prized possession. I move past him, into the club where a troupe of Birds reenact a Sapphic orgy on the main stage, while in the discreet alcoves an assortment of Birds and Babes provide a range of sexual favors for the rich clientele.

Backstage, I pop an Aktive 'poule against my neck, to blunt reality. A house null leads me down a blue corridor to Spengler's private suite, reserved for the entertainment of important friends. The null clips wires to my costume as Spengler introduces the queen of *The Birds of the Crystal Plumage,* and then a taped barrage of Brazilian drums heralds my entrance. There are twelve men in the room, seated on leather couches, their desires caged in refinement and respectability. I ruffle my feathers in time to the music as I strut across the marble stage, offering them glimpses into hidden dreams. Then Claudio swoops into view, suspended over the stage like a magnificent condor, the twelve-inch penis that Dr. Kleinfeld has crafted for him erect beneath the black plumage that adorns his laburnum flesh. He sweeps me up in his arms and lust thrums in the air like the sound of swarming insects, hot and feverish, no different from the lust of the dockworkers at Maua who came to be blown by a half-formed Bird. We glide over the stage, Claudio and I, borne on sensuous rhythms as we act out an improbable seduction. Until finally, in midair, he plucks my feathers with exaggerated care and then plunges his meat into me. Whatever perfunctory pleasures I once might have derived from these performances has been worn down by soulless repetition. We fuck like birds on the wing, Claudio's precision tool grinding against the template of my vagina. The only thing I feel is numb. He withdraws before he comes so that the audience may appreciate the bounty he showers over my breasts, a seemingly endless rain of semen; another of Kleinfeld's miracles.

The applause is thunderous as Claudio flies from view, while I wait without curiosity to see which of his guests Spengler has selected for participation in the second act of my performance. I feel no surprise as all twelve men begin to undress and crawl up onto the cool, white marble like hungry dogs, ravenous for a taste of game.

Backstage later on, as Heinrich bathes my bruised and battered body, I reflect on the bitterness I feel; it's not the taste of semen or any sense of degradation—I became inured to such things long ago on the docks at Maua—it's the realization of what I did to get here.

Spengler enters the room. "You pleased them, Estela," he says. "You may go now."

"Rudy called me," I tell him.

"You are looking forward to seeing him again?"

"He says Cledilce Macedo is coming to Berlin."

"So I hear. It's nothing for you to worry about."

"I don't feel well," I tell him. "I'm not sleeping."

He frowns. "Kleinfeld said you were in prime condition. It's the dust perhaps? You mentioned bad dreams."

"It helps me to remember," I say, wondering at his immunity to the poison in my words.

"There are things we can give you to help you forget."

"I *want* to remember."

Spengler sighs, a pained expression on his face. "You mustn't make things difficult," he says. "For either of us." Then he leaves and I tell Heinrich to fetch the car and drive me home.

Rudy is waiting, lounging on the bed, drinking my cognac. He smiles behind his wire-rim spectacles, then gets up and kisses me lightly on the cheek. I hate it when he does that, like a dog pissing against a tree, marking its territory. "It's late, Rudy, what do you want?"

In his white chinos and loose, Hawaiian shirt, he looks like a lost tourist, lacking only a camcorder. He runs a hand through his thick, brown hair and says, "You have been wondering about Cledilce?"

I ignore the question and pour myself a cognac.

He follows me to the drinks cabinet. "In two days she starts performing for the *Birds of Paradise*," he says.

"So soon?" I ask. "What about refinements?"

Rudy sips his drink. "They don't place the same emphasis on refinements anymore. She had one week with a Chinese courtesan. You're unique, Estela, a jeweled Bird. But these days, there isn't the same demand for cultured conversation; nobody wants to discuss Günter Grass or the poetry of Ernest Newboy, they just want to fuck you. This bothers you?"

It does, but I don't admit it, not to Rudy. "Spengler sent you?"

Rudy removes his glasses, holds them in front of him as if to magnify my features. "We talked. He's concerned about you, as an investment of course. I spoke with Kleinfeld; he mentioned you're worried about the disease."

"Shouldn't I be?"

Rudy shrugs his shoulders. "No, nor about Cledilce."

"I never wanted to leave her behind. That was you."

Rudy walks to the door, hesitates, and says, "There wasn't time, or have you forgotten what you did? By the time that mess was cleared up, our contract with her had lapsed." And then he is gone.

His parting words leave a fear stain on my mind. Faithful Heinrich brings the pipe. He heats the bowl and I hit on the dust, holding it down deep in my lungs, letting it flow into every dark corner of my mind, letting it illuminate the past. In the dream, I first see Cledilce, and then slowly, everything else begins to take shape around her.

Tall, copper-skinned, and haughty, seventeen-year-old Estela de Brito sipped Caipirinha outside a streetfront cafe and listened as the rhythms of the *batucadas* drifted up from Leblon beach. She was on a natural high. Beside her, Cledilce, half-drunk, slumped against her shoulder, her long, dark hair flowing over Estela's breasts. "Honey, rehearsal done me in," Cledilce said. She kissed Estela's cheek and yawned. Rehearsal was for the *Great Defile dos Escolas da Samba*, the parade of competing samba schools which form the climax to

Carnaval, and during which they would both dance at the head of the *Salgueiro* school. That was in two days time. Tomorrow, they would meet the German who had come to take them to Sanctuary in Berlin.

Night had fallen but the street still swarmed with participants of the local *banda,* a mass of two thousand swaying bodies moving in one continuous snakelike formation to a pounding samba beat, winding in and out of the bars and cafés, through streets and alleyways and across the avenue to the beach. Traffic had ground to a halt and many people had simply abandoned their cars and attached themselves to the *banda* for the duration.

Juan Griffiths ordered more drinks and spoke about the German, while groping Estela beneath the table. She felt like gouging his eyes out. Griffiths set up the deal. He was an asshole who drank cheap champagne and polluted the air with foul cigar smoke. Patagonian by birth, he went on about some place called Wales that Estela never heard of, and that she thought might not even exist. He was a freelancer who'd been drifting around the continent for five years, dabbling in arms, drugs, and organs, utilizing contacts he'd made in an eight-year stint in the Argentine secret service. He'd been coming to Carnaval for five years, recruiting whores for clients. A month ago he'd come down from Quito and met Cledilce. He told her he was looking for transsexuals who'd not yet had surgery, explaining how his European clients preferred to carry out their own alterations. When Cledilce had introduced him to Estela, he'd told them his partner would arrange for their client's representative to fly in for Carnaval. Estela tolerated him only because he had set the deal up, but she had taken a Carioca's instinctive dislike to his Argentine arrogance. He was no better than any other punk who'd used her body; a lot of them had paid good money for the privilege, whereas she'd blown Juan Griffiths three times without getting paid.

But her attitude toward Deborah Hernandez, the fourth member of the group, was more ambivalent. Unlike Griffiths, who was merely a slob with pretensions, Hernandez seemed imbued with a cool poise that reminded Estela of dead *Yanqui* actresses with names like Kelley or Michelle. She was a tall, elegant woman whose eyes were hidden behind dark sunglasses and whose ash-blond hair seemed too perfect. Her aloofness would have irritated Estela had it not been something that she herself aspired to. This, and the air of fragility that clung to her pale flesh, held an attraction for Estela that she was unable to explain. She wondered if Deborah had the disease, or if money had purchased her some sort of immunity. She had heard rumors of experimental drugs, illicit coagulants that stemmed—for a time at least—the flow of blood from those women who could afford black market prices.

With Cledilce only semiconscious and the Patagonian oblivious to anyone but himself, Estela felt the heat of Deborah's hidden gaze. It gave her an unexpected thrill, and she felt something more than just gratitude.

After midnight, when the streets had quietened, Griffiths hailed a taxi to take them all back to his hotel on Avenida Copacabana. As they approached the hotel, Deborah told the driver to pull over. "Walk with me," she said to Estela. Estela looked at the other two slumped against each other, then got out of the car.

They walked silently along the neon-lit promenade overlooking the beach, where a few hundred people cavorted naked on the imported sand.

Deborah said, "When do they ever stop?"

Estela recognized the faces of friends and neighbors. Laughing, she said, "These ones will fuck all night. They belong to the *Banda da Vergonha do Posto 6,* my neighborhood, you understand? Sex is all that matters at Carnaval."

After a while, Estela stopped and sat down on the edge of the promenade, feet dangling above the beach where a crowd of young Cariocas were playing soccer by neon light from the beachfront bars. "Sit down," she said, patting the ground beside her. "I used to play football. You?"

"No," Deborah said, sitting down. She removed her sunglasses and revealed her careworn eyes. "Can I tell you something?"

"Tell me what, Sugar?" Estela said.

Deborah lit two cigarettes, gave one to Estela. "I have the disease."

"I already guessed that, Honey," Estela said, curious as to

why Deborah felt the need to tell her now. "You don't show it."

"There are drugs that help."

Estela tried to picture Deborah naked; despite the fear of the disease, she found the image turned her on. She thought, does she *realize* what I am? Well she had to; she was Griffiths's partner.

Deborah said, "You don't have to be scared of me."

"What makes you think I'm scared?"

Deborah shrugged and went on, "Money I make from this deal, I can afford better treatments, maybe add a few years to my life."

"Yeah, well, I don't need to know about that," Estela said, wishing Deborah would talk about something else. Maybe Hollywood.

"You should know the things you profit by," Deborah said.

Estela smoked her cigarette, watching as one copper-skinned boy scored a goal. She felt an impulse to abandon Deborah and join in their game. What did Deborah expect? Guilt? Despite herself, she said, "What things, Sugar?"

Deborah spoke slowly and without bitterness, as if she were reciting the details of some half-remembered dream. "I'm thinking of girls of nine or ten having babies; twelve-year-olds whose periods go on so long they bleed to death; and of those few who survive the bleeding only to have their pussies dry out and shrivel so bad that nothing can get up there even though they still want it; they lose their hair then, Estela— you've seen that?—and get hair where they shouldn't." She paused to pull on her cigarette. "Their minds start to go— sure, you've seen that too—the way they still think of themselves as desirable right up to their God-awful, pathetic deaths, most of them by the time they're sixteen."

"Fuck it," Estela said, with a flash of temper. "Why you telling me this? It ain't my fault."

"I know that."

"Look at you—I don't see any of that shit happening to you?"

"Sometimes the virus doesn't start killing you till you reach adulthood. I guess that makes me lucky, huh?"

With an effort of will, Estela quelled her anger. She said, "How long have you got?"

Deborah stood up. "I'm twenty-four." Her voice was almost a whisper. "It doesn't matter."

Knowing Cledilce was with Griffiths at the hotel, they went to the apartment on Rua Toneleiros. Estela poured drinks and lit a *macohna* joint. Deborah took a glass and said, "They spent billions of dollars finding a vaccine for AIDS, took them twenty-five years. They haven't spent one-tenth of that on HDV. You know why?"

Estela shook her head and sat beside Deborah on the sofa.

"There's an institute in New York," Deborah continued, "where they're transplanting wombs into young boys. That's where the future is, not in women." She struggled to maintain her poise. "It's cheaper now to alter people like you, people with so few alternatives you allow yourselves to be reconstructed so you can service those who want a risk-free screw. These sanctuaries are for them, not you. You call yourself a Bird, as if it means freedom. But in Berlin they'll cage you like some damned nightingale."

Estela stubbed out the joint and said, "You feel that way, how come you got mixed up with Griffiths?"

Deborah leaned her head on Estela's shoulder. "I was a call girl in L.A. Guy I worked for ran an agency serving Hollywood big shots. I was doing well, enjoying the life. Then the symptoms started to show." She paused, to sip her *cachaca*. "First, it just blew me away—the heightened sex drive—God, screwing johns was suddenly something I enjoyed, some of them anyway. Then the bleeding started. Guys don't want to fuck a woman who's always on the rag, y'know what I'm saying? I knew as soon as Tony found out he'd dump me— bad for business. I also knew he'd been over to Europe a couple of times, where the clubs were recruiting transsexuals. Tony was an asshole but he had a good nose for business. He'd made some contacts there, where there was like forty guys to every woman. He planned to find them new flesh, send boys—preop transsexuals like you and Cledilce—to this gender reassignment clinic in Paris for surgery and hormonal treatments and contract them to the Sanctuaries. I took his list of contacts and flew down to Mexico City. I needed someone who knew their way around the continent, someone who'd know where to find what I needed. That's where I met Juan.''

Deborah stroked Estela's face. Estela was certain the *Yanqui* was attracted to her but she was confused as to whether these overtures were directed at the Bird or at the man. It had been a long time since she had fucked a woman and the vibes coming from Deborah were hard to ignore. She felt a moment of doubt, thinking of Cledilce, but the truth was, she was no longer sure what she felt for her. She said, "So this is more your deal than Juan's?''

"I don't give a shit who gets the credit," Deborah said. "All I care about is the money."

"You sure that's all?" Estela said, lightly kissing Deborah's lips. "You're still beautiful, Sugar."

Deborah's eyes searched her face. "Do you know what I want?"

Estela grinned, lasciviously. "Why don't you tell me?"

Deborah's voice was low and husky. "Maybe I can do that."

In the bedroom, when Estela pulled down her satin skirt and Deborah reached for her cock, she realized exactly what the *Yanqui* woman wanted.

When it stiffened in her grasp, Deborah said, "I wasn't sure you could still . . .''

"Get hard?" Estela said. "It still works, Sugar, at least till I get to Paris."

Deborah stood back then, and stripped slowly down to her panties. She saw Estela's gaze and said, "I'm bleeding. If you don't want to—"

"It's okay," Estela said, letting her gaze wander up from the wet padding, over the smooth stomach and the small, pale breasts, to the bruises lurking beneath the powdered flesh of her limbs. "Take them off."

Deborah removed the panties and the sodden towel. Blood oozed slowly down her legs. She did something to her hair then, and detached the ash-blond wig from her head. Her real hair was grey and cropped short on her skull. Somehow, this failed to detract from her beauty. "I've done many things, Estela," she said. "In many different ways. But it's been a long time since anyone touched me, any man. That's all I want. It's not so weird.''

Estela led her to the bed. She watched rivulets of blood trickle on to the sheets as Deborah stroked her cock. It was no longer a question of desiring this woman: she wanted to *be* her, to be a beautiful, elegant white woman, a product of Hollywood, instead of a young, black male *Carioca* with a good pair of tits and a fine round ass.

Lubricated by blood, she slid into Deborah and began to fuck her slowly. Deborah rolled and thrashed beneath her, as if she had come to the realization that this might be her final coupling. The strangeness of the act made it more precious for them both.

''Ah, Jesus,'' Deborah cried, grinding herself against Estela, who imagined that she was fucking a reconstructed image of herself, a white-skinned, blond-haired Estela, a Hollywood star that people might envy and wish that they could become.

Estela pounded against the fragile bones, gasping for breath. Deborah shuddered, then came in a frenzied rush, wrapping her brittle limbs about Estela's body in a wretched configuration of death.

Afterward, Estela listened to the *batucadas* that seemed more distant than they had all night, and found herself hoping that Deborah would somehow beat the disease. She imagined herself responding to sex the way Deborah had responded to her: in Berlin, cunt-equipped. Would she have the same strength of will? She wondered if she'd taken too much from the dying woman; maybe it was okay. Despite all the warnings about Berlin, she imagined that Deborah needed to feel that some small part of herself would live on in the Bird.

Griffiths picked the two Birds up from the apartment at eight that evening to take them to the *Flamengo* club. A thunderstorm had left the city steaming and tense. Estela wore a short, red satin skirt over a black leotard, and Cledilce was squeezed into a blue, Lycra one-piece that stretched from her neck to her ankles.

''How come Deborah ain't with you?'' Estela asked Griffiths.

"She's fucked up," he said. "Besides, I got things under control, so don't worry your ass."

After what Deborah had told her, Estela's loathing for Griffiths had intensified. "She was okay last time I seen her."

"Jeez, Estel," Cledilce said, annoyed. "Who fucking cares? Let Juan deal with it."

"Right," Griffiths said, patting Cledilce on the thigh. "Let's concentrate on Thessinger, put on a good show for him."

"Honey," Cledilce said, "I'll do whatever I have to."

The taxi slid through a crowded street where a wizened Babe in a red dress was reeling drunkenly in the road. She was balding and one strap of her dress had slipped from her shoulder, revealing a dry, shriveled breast. She glared at them as the taxi passed by.

Shortly afterward, they pulled up outside the *Flamengo* club, which was hosting the *Vermehlo & Preto Ball*. They forced their way through the crush of bodies on the stairwell, up to the second level balcony, where Griffiths had booked a table. On the dance floor below, more than two thousand people heaved and swayed to hectic samba rhythms. Birds and Babes draped themselves from the balconies, posing and taunting the men in the crowd down below.

A dark-haired man in jeans and a black, polo neck shirt sat waiting for them. He was wiping steam from his wire-rim glasses and beads of sweat stood out on his forehead.

"Rudy, my man," Griffiths called. The dark-haired man looked up and smiled as Griffiths clapped him on the back. "Ladies," Griffiths said, "say hi to Rudy Thessinger. Rudy, meet Cledilce and Estela."

Thessinger rose and kissed their hands. "I'm pleased to meet you both. The pictures Juan sent don't do you justice," he said.

"He got a habit of selling us short," Cledilce said, sitting down next to the German. Estela sat opposite him. Griffiths lit one of his awful cigars and pawed at her incessantly while he gave Rudy his Carnaval spiel, promising him a good time. First chance she got, Cledilce hauled Thessinger away to the dance floor.

Estela said, "Keep your fucking hands off me, Juan."

"Hey, you had a different attitude when I first came down here."

"Only 'cos you doing this thing for me and Cledilce."

Griffiths grabbed her arm and pulled her forward. "You were sweet on me then, remember?"

"I sucked your cock a coupla times—that doesn't mean I was sweet on you. Next time you pay like everyone else."

"You got a bad attitude. I can blow you right out of this deal."

"Maybe the deal's not all down to you."

"What you talking about?"

"Maybe Deborah's got something to say about this."

He released her arm and drained his glass. "What's that *Yanqui* bitch been saying? Giving you ideas? Don't cross me, Estela. I say when the deal goes through, not that cunt."

When Rudy and Cledilce returned, the German asked Estela to dance. The crush of seminaked bodies on the main dance floor pinned them together. When she saw him staring at her breasts beneath the leotard, she shouted in his ear, "You wanna feel?"

Thessinger laughed. "How real?"

She placed one of his hands across her breasts. "No silicone in there, Sugar," she said, smiling. "Hormones."

"You work hard on your bodies, you and your friend."

"She's more than a friend," Estela said.

"Yeah?" said Thessinger. "And Juan is your friend, too?"

Estela wondered what he meant, but for the moment she let it pass. He wasn't so bad, nice eyes, and he moved well, not slobbish like Griffiths. A drunken Cuban staggered into them and propositioned Estela. She shook her head but he groped clumsily at her crotch. Thessinger caught his arm and did something to it. The Cuban fell to the floor, howling.

"Jeez, Sugar," Estela said, surprised at what she considered an overreaction. "What you do to him?"

Thessinger smiled and guided her up the stairwell, where sweating couples made frenzied love. "You're a temptation, Estela, a beautiful one. Too much for a john like that."

"I thought you were gonna call me an investment."

Thessinger laughed and said, "Maybe that, too."

Later on, Griffiths told Thessinger about the parade of

samba schools, about how Cledilce and Estela would be dancing at the head of *Salgueiro*. The German winked at the two
Birds, told them he was looking forward to seeing it. Despite
giving the appearance of getting into the swing of things, Estela noticed that he drank little. She imagined what it would
be like to feel him inside her, and wondered if that would
happen in Berlin.

They left the ball after four, a taxi dropping the two Birds
at their apartment while Griffiths insisted on accompanying
Thessinger back to his hotel. Cledilce ran a bath while Estela
sat on the toilet bowl, skinning a joint. She remembered what
Deborah had said about the Sanctuaries, about being caged,
and tried to dismiss it as simply the envy of a dying woman.
She said, "What you think of Thessinger?"

"Why, Honey?" Cledilce said. "You wanna fuck him?"
She laughed and tested the water with her elbow.

"You know Deborah got the disease?"

"So," Cledilce said, losing her smile. "That ain't my problem."

"You don't feel sorry for her?"

"Sure, I feel sorry for all them bitches. But I'd feel a lot
more sorry if it didn't give us this chance to do something for
ourselves."

"You ain't worried 'bout the operation?"

"I explained that a dozen times, Estel, over there they do
it right. It ain't just cutting a gash between your legs."

Estela's fears were not placated. She said, "You think we'll
still feel the same way about each other?"

Cledilce smiled and hugged her. "Count on it, Honey."
Then she peeled the Lycra suit from her body, planted a kiss
on Estela's lips, and took the joint from her. She lit it and
stepped into the bath.

A sigh escaped Estela. Lately she had been wondering what
exactly it was she felt for Cledilce. Was it love? Or had she
simply mistaken gratitude and friendship for love? She said,
"I fucked Deborah."

Stretched out in the water with one hand held up to keep
the joint dry, Cledilce said, "Why?"

"Curiosity."

"That all?"

"You jealous?"

Cledilce shook her head. "Soon," she said, "you won't be able to do that."

"You didn't answer my question."

Cledilce reached out and squeezed Estela's cock through the satin skirt. "Remember, Honey, when this is gone, I'll still be with you."

Estela stood and undressed. She climbed into the bath and slid down between Cledilce's legs, leaning back against her breasts. She felt wet kisses on her shoulders and neck, and hard flesh prodding against her back. She turned round, kneeling in the water and took Cledilce's cock in her mouth. In her mind she was already dreaming of Berlin.

Deborah came by to help them prepare for the parade. They sat drinking bottles of *Pará* beer as they made alterations to their gowns of feathers and silk. Tonight, bedecked in these extravagant costumes, Estela and Cledilce would lead the *Salgueiro* school down to the asphalt at the *Sambódromo*.

Cledilce said, "Estela's worried 'bout the operation."

"It'll be okay," Deborah said. "They're investing a lot of money in you both."

"Will I be able to feel anything when I'm fucking?" Estela said.

"You should ask Thessinger."

"Would you do this, if you had the choice?" Estela asked her.

"She don't have that choice," Cledilce said, bluntly.

"Cledilce is right," Deborah said, draining her bottle. "I could never be a Bird like you."

Estela gave her a puzzled stare. She sensed a muted hostility and wondered if Deborah regretted sleeping with her. "I didn't mean—"

Cledilce cut her off. "You spent all this time fucking with your mouth; now you gonna have a chance to try the real thing."

"Well, I gotta go," Deborah said. "I told Griffiths I'd pick Thessinger up and get him something to eat before the parade." She stood up. "Now, lemme have a look at you." She draped the scarlet gown over Estela. Tall, black feathers sprouted from the back and shoulders, creating a panoply of star-flecked night. She helped Cledilce into a black gown adorned with scarlet feathers, then stood back, staring at them. "You're like two creatures from a dream."

Estela leaned forward self-consciously and embraced her. "I'll be watching for your face in the crowd, Sugar," she said.

"Sure," Deborah said, then she nodded to Cledilce and left.

Ninety thousand people had crowded into the seventeen-hundred-meter-long *Sambódromo* to watch the competition. The *Beija Flor* had already completed their routine, as had the pink and black of the *Mangueira* school. Now it was the turn of the *Salgueiro;* fueled by Aktives and amyl nitrate, they had worked themselves up into a state of feverish excitement and could hardly wait. When the signal came, the *baterias* began pounding out a relentless beat. Estela and Cledilce, leading a dozen or so magnificently arrayed performers, began to move slowly from the assembly area into the cauldron of the stadium itself. They were assaulted by a deafening roar and by waves of clammy heat; fireworks exploded in the sky overhead like a portent of some imagined apocalypse. Estela felt the blood begin to boil in her veins as the routines she had been practicing for the best part of a year took hold of her limbs and set her cutting a sinuous swath through the rainbowed night. Around her, Cledilce and the others flowed with liquid speed, intoxicated by complex rhythms as if they had freed themselves from invisible bonds. She, too, was aware of the sense of release, and as she danced she found it impossible to stick to the set routine. Alien maneuvers were imposed on her body and brain as she instinctively moved ahead of her companions and abandoned herself to a display of raucous sexuality, a primitive, vital, and threatening explosion of angry desire that exposed the sham hypocrisy of what Carnaval had become. Aktives exploded in her skull as heat consumed and transformed her into a creature of the air.

For an eternity there was only the music and the choreographed chaos of the dance as she lost all sense of place, time, and identity. She felt herself raised up above the noise and light that comprised her universe, and she understood for once what it was to fly.

Coming down in the *Sambódromo,* cradled in Cledilce's arms, Estela felt no elation when she learned that her school had been awarded first prize; she felt only a sense of loss. Despite the desire to escape, this was still her home, and those who had danced beside her were those she had called friends. It was also, she realized, her last dance at Carnaval.

It was eight-thirty in the morning by the time they had managed to fight their way from the stadium out into the crowded, steaming Centro streets. A thunderstorm broke overhead and cool but torrential rain battered their costumes and washed the heat from their limbs. A taxi slid to a halt beside them and Thessinger jumped out, opened the rear door, and ushered them in. "Cafe Tudo Ben," he told the driver as he slid into the front seat.

Despite her exhaustion, Estela watched Thessinger's face in the mirror, wondering what he had thought of her performance. She told herself she would fuck him when she became a proper Bird.

Griffiths was already high when they reached the café. He hastily filled glasses of champagne, then raised a glass toward them. "Hey, hey, hey," he said. "I seen you both on the TV; you were fantastic."

Estela said, "Where's Deborah?"

"Who cares?" Griffiths said. "Maybe she was fucked again, huh, Estela?"

"You asshole," Estela said. She caught hold of Thessinger's arm. "She was with you?"

"Earlier, yes," Thessinger explained. "She left before the end, said she would meet me here."

"Honey," Cledilce said, "don't worry 'bout it. Maybe she—"

"For Chrissakes," Griffiths snapped. "She knows where we're at. If she wants to come, then she will, right, Rudy?"

"Juan is right," Thessinger said. "She'll turn up."

But an hour passed without her showing. Fatigue and a sense of anticlimax conspired to depress Estela. She rose and told the others she was returning to the apartment to get some sleep.

"C'mon, Estel," Cledilce said. "Don't go yet."

Estela forced a weak smile. "I'm gone, Sugar."

"What the fuck's wrong with you, you stupid bitch?" Griffiths said, grabbing her arm. "What'll Rudy think?"

Estela pulled free of his grip and glared at Thessinger. "When the contract's done, you know where to find me."

"You faggot," Griffiths sneered.

Estela spit in his face and before Griffiths could respond, Thessinger restrained him with an arm across his chest. "Enough, Juan," he said. "My people don't want damaged merchandise."

Griffiths slumped back into his seat. "Fuck her," he said, "She needs a lesson to be taught."

"Jesus, Estela!" Cledilce said. "What the hell's up with you?"

Thessinger stood up. "I'll take her home."

He followed Estela out into the hot, morning light, where traffic moved slowly north toward Copacabana. He walked beside her and she felt her anger ebb. He seemed to understand her need to be treated with respect. She knew it was a game, of course; he was just another pimp. "I appreciate that," she said.

He shrugged and stopped a taxi. In the back, he said, "You don't like the señor." It wasn't a question.

"It was never part of the deal," Estela said, bitterly.

Thessinger wiped sweat from his forehead and nodded. "I have to see Ms. Hernandez before I take you home."

"What for?" Estela just wanted to sleep.

"About the deal." Thessinger watched her carefully before continuing. "What do you know about her?"

"She told me she set this up, not Juan."

"That's why I need to see her."

Estela felt relief that Deborah wasn't going to be cheated out of her cut. When the traffic slowed to a halt she grabbed Thessinger and pointed to a crazed old man stumbling in the middle of the road. In one hand he carried the skinned, decapitated corpse of a monkey.

"That's what I feel that fucking Argentine is doing to me," she said, nodding toward the dead animal.

Thessinger followed her gaze as the old man caught their

eyes and leered. He lurched over to the car and raised his other hand. It held a clear plastic bag containing the monkey's head. He swung it against Thessinger's window and laughed.

"He's gonna cheat her," Estela said. "But you already know that."

Thessinger said nothing as the car pulled slowly away.

In her room at the Luxor Copacabana they found Deborah lying on her back on the bed with two bullet holes showing neatly in her white, cotton vest; her head was turned sideways and her eyes stared sightlessly toward the open window.

"Oh shit, man," Estela moaned. Deborah's close-cropped hair and pale skin gave her the appearance of a delicate child. An empathy she didn't understand made her wonder what was the last thing Deborah saw.

Thessinger moved to the bed, checked for a pulse, then began to go through the room, turning out drawers and suitcases. "Quickly," he said, "we can't wait around."

Estela said, "That cocksucking bastard."

Thessinger said, "He left the parade about half an hour after her. Said he had to get things organized at the café."

Estela sat on the edge of the bed and stroked the dead woman's face. "Poor bitch deserved better than this."

"It's too bad."

"I told you he was gonna cheat her."

"There's nothing here to connect him with this," Thessinger said, as he moved around the room. "We better go."

"No," Estela said, bitterly. "He can't get away with it."

"Yes, he can," Thessinger said. "Just forget it. I have to get you to Berlin."

"I don't go before I see him," Estela said. "She was a friend."

Thessinger threw up his hands. "There's no time. You don't know where he'll be."

"With Cledilce. Listen, Rudy, there's a place I know up in Rochina. I wanna take him there."

"Okay," Thessinger said, wearily. "I'll bring Cledilce and meet you there." He took a small handgun from inside his shirt and held it toward her. "Take it."

She stared at it for a moment, confused. Was this really

what she wanted? Then she picked it up and stuck it in her bag.

She found Griffiths at the apartment, in bed with Cledilce. Both were unconscious from drink. "Hey Juan," she said, shaking him.

"Huh," he said, pawing at his eyes. "Estela? Where you been?"

"With Rudy. He straightened me out, said I owed you."

"What about the deal?"

"Later, at his hotel. First, I wanna do you a favor."

"What favor?" Griffiths slurred.

Estela got up and searched in a drawer. She came back to the bed and told him to sit up. She popped an Aktive 'poule against his fleshy neck. "Jeez," he said. He reached up and grabbed her breasts.

"Not here," Estela said, nodding toward Cledilce. "We'll go out, pick her up later."

She took him to the *Sayonara,* a club on the second floor of one of the high-rise blocks in Rochina. She led him up a dark flight of stairs to a dance hall. Paint peeled from the walls and the curtains at the side of the stage were dank and shabby. A band drowsed onstage and a few decrepit Babes sat perched on barstools, painting their nails. They climbed a second flight to where an old woman sat dozing at a dirt-stained desk. Griffiths gave her money and she pointed to a door. In the room a bed with a single sheet stood in the corner.

Griffiths sat on the bed and began to remove his clothes. She kept her back to him and removed the gun from her bag. "You owe it all to me," she heard him say. "I want you to suck me dry."

"You didn't have to do it, Juan," she said, turning with the gun in her hand.

"What's that?" Griffiths said. "You gone crazy or what?"

She saw the fear in his eyes. "You wanted it all for yourself."

"What are you fucking talking about?"

"Deborah, you cocksucker."

"Who gives a shit about that whore?"

"I did."

"She's nothing," Griffiths said. "She's the disease."

Her body shook with ferocious anger as she squeezed the trigger. The bullet hit him in the stomach and smashed him flat on the bed. He groaned and, with an effort, pushed himself up on one elbow. "You fucking bitch whore-cunt, you can't kill me," he said, his face a mask of incomprehensible rage as he pawed at the bloody hole. "I fucking own you. It's impossible for you to kill me. Fucking impossible."

"Yeah?" Estela said, then emptied the gun into his head. She ran downstairs and out into the street, where Thessinger was waiting in a taxi. He told the driver to take them out to Galeâo airport and it was only when they were aboard the shuttle waiting for takeoff to Paris that she remembered Cledilce.

"Where is she?" she asked him.

"The cops were there before I had a chance to get her out," Thessinger explained.

"What are you talking about? How the fuck did the cops find out?"

Thessinger sighed. "The Luxor is a big hotel, Estela, full of Americans and Europeans. If someone's shot dead in one of their rooms, then they have to be seen to be taking action if they don't want to lose business. So the cops make more of an effort than usual."

"But how did they get to Cledilce?"

"They must have found an address or something."

"Jesus," Estela said, seeing that that made sense. "They'll pin it all on her. We can't leave her to answer for this."

"Someone has to."

"They'll kill her." Which was probably true. But what could she do without Thessinger's help? "I owe her everything," she said, weakly.

"We'll protect her. Now think of yourself—you shot someone. I'm saving your ass. Remember that, remember in the future how much you owe to me." He talked continuously, trying to soothe her, holding her as the shuttle took off, telling her about all the wonderful things the future held. But Estela de Brito was no longer listening. Her thoughts had turned inward, searching for whatever it was that had motivated her to do what she had done. She needed that hatred now, that strength. For a long time she searched, but there was nothing there, only the sweet temptation of flight, and of Paradise.

Thessinger plays Satie's *Gymnopédies* on the piano as Heinrich enters the room to inform me that Cledilce Macedo will meet me for lunch at the Kopenhagen. Patterns of fear distort my perceptions, undermining the solidity of my bones. It's difficult to distinguish between the past and dreams. This morning I dreamed I awoke to find the sheets scarlet with blood and instructed Heinrich to burn them.

"You must go," Rudy tells me, but I ignore him because he does not know how the dream will turn out. "She can't harm you."

"Harm me?" The idea both attracts and repulses me. "I never dreamed that."

Rudy smiled. "I never took you for a dreamer, Estela, a sad romantic clinging bitterly to the wreckage of what never really was."

Is that what I am now? A broken fairy doll? "My dreams are all of the disease," I tell him.

"We've talked about that before. You have nothing to worry about."

"Why has she come?"

"I don't know," he lies, shrugging his shoulders; it's what gives him away. He's been lying to me for a long time.

"You knew she was alive all this time?"

"We were unable to maintain her contract at the time. It lapsed and someone else bought her option."

Over the years I've grown to despise Rudy. It's more than the fact that he and Spengler never sent for Cledilce, more even than hollowness of this life to which he brought me. I ask, "You think she knows what happened in Rio?"

"It hardly matters now, I'm sure she—"

"Shall I tell her this life is a lie?" I interrupt.

"Say what you like," Thessinger says. "She is owned." He leaves without another word.

Cledilce Macedo is waiting in a booth by the window at the Kopenhagen. She is resplendent in silver and black, her hair plaited and studded with jewels. I feel this meeting is part of the dream and that, in it, a solution will be revealed. I sense no threat.

"Cumo vai?" she says.

"I'm well," I say. "The police? They hurt you?"

She smiles and says, "They didn't kill me."

"I wanted to go back for you."

She waves her hand, dismissing the idea. "You look good."

"You shouldn't have come. They lied, it's not like our dream."

"I had no choice," Cledilce says. "He took you away from me."

"I had to go. I killed Griffiths."

"Juan was a fool. But why the Hernandez woman?"

Nausea hits me in the stomach. "What do you mean?"

Cledilce leans forward, touches my arm. "They were both killed by the same gun. It was in the reports; that's why they couldn't prove anything against me."

The truth infects and sickens me. I stumble to the bathroom, Cledilce close behind. She holds me while I vomit, uttering words of comfort, words I haven't heard since I left the other life. When there is nothing left to throw up I crouch on the floor, sobbing, searching for the words to beg forgiveness. But the words are dead on my tongue. Thoughts twist and reel in my skull and all I can do is sit and wait for the world to get back on an even keel.

In a room at the Kempinski Hotel, I watch the last of the daylight struggling through the blinds, falling on Cledilce's mahogany flesh. The surgeons have crafted a fine vagina for her and her fingers explore me to the full; even so I derive no pleasure from her touch. The truth is, the sex we shared was more like that between whore and client than between two lovers, except in this instance, neither of us feels the need to fake anything. She's silent and still but not sleeping. Neither of us has spoken for more than twenty minutes and the claustrophobic silence crushes any understanding we might have had. The gulf of the past yawns between us as I knew it would. I realize that what we'd once shared is now ashes.

I try to dream what is in her head. Once, we shared an intuition which was almost telepathic. I probe now but fail to penetrate the veil. Perhaps Cledilce has something to hide, doesn't want me inside her head. Anxiety gnaws my brain. Rudy has lied again, as he always does; she came to take my place. The disease wakens inside me as, one day, it will awaken in her.

I get up and pull on my clothes, aware of Cledilce's silent eyes following my movements. We stare at each other for a few seconds, knowing that we have nothing left to say, and sharing a fragile confusion as we acknowledge the death of the past. The moment slips by and I leave the room.

Heinrich returns with the purchase, unwraps it, and places it in my hand. The gun is dark, heavy, and silenced, filling me with a sense of power. I sit by the dressing table, searching my face in the mirror for the first signs, pondering the mess a bullet would make. I try to accept that it is Cledilce's turn to live the dream and that my part in it is drawing to a close. But it's not that easy, not when I picture the uncorrupted faith she still has in the charade, a faith that will allow her to usurp my role as the Queen of Berlin.

Light streams in the window, casting mottled patterns on the bed. Rudy will be here soon, to scour my flesh for warning signs, perhaps to gloat. Shame and fear crowd my skull, but I draw strength from hatred. The least I can do for Cledilce is spare her his attentions, the almost-obsessive concern he has shown me. In truth, ours has been a parasitic relationship: by allowing him to see himself as my protector, I give him strength and a sense of purpose; he, in turn, has organized my life in this city and, I realize now, protected me from certain unpalatable truths. It is time to rid myself of such false protection.

I put the gun inside my kimono and suck on the crystal pipe, just a little, enough to keep the dream alive. In the lounge, I drowse on the sofa, memories flitting back and forth through my mind; unedited and out of sequence, they provide a telling representation of my life. I wish I could unravel all the threads, but there is so little time.

Heinrich rouses me and announces Ms. Cledilce Macedo. A pang of guilt spears my heart as she enters the room. This is someone who I have both loved and betrayed; what has brought her to me at this moment? I feel delirious and immobilized. I think, has she come to witness my atonement, or simply to record my decay?

She kneels on the carpet at my feet and tells me that whatever I believe, she's never blamed me for what happened. She knows Rudy manipulated me. I listen, and realize this is true. I see the clear beauty shining out of her dark eyes, remember nights of cool ecstasy, and wonder how she intends to spring the trap. She says she still loves and needs me, and her eyes hold me tight, screaming that this too, is the truth, and all the pain and bitterness of old betrayals well up inside as Cledilce tells me it is still possible for us to be together. And it is at this precise moment that I finally realize how I can atone for having sinned against her. I pull the gun from my kimono and, allowing her illusions of sanctuary to remain intact, I quietly shoot Ms. Macedo dead.

A short time later, Rudy arrives and finds me sitting on the sofa, the gun in my hand, the body at my feet.

Spengler let me live, after a fashion. At first I was puzzled, but then I saw that I owe my preservation to that which made me unique. With what they know now of the virus, they no longer deem it worthwhile to bestow refinements on Birds.

I'm a different creature now, virus-sculpted, ever-changing. Kleinfeld's drugs have halted the hair loss and he treats me with synthetic Factor 8 to regulate the bleeding. Of course I no longer perform.

My new apartment looks out on the Siegessäule. I dream of climbing it soon to gaze down on the city from its magnificent perch; one day, when my strength returns. Then I shall swoop down on the Birds who stole my crown, to mock their preening beauty, perhaps to sing a lament for Cledilce.

Many months have passed since I last saw Rudy. I no longer wonder why I failed to exact revenge for Deborah by letting him live; perhaps, in those few minutes before he arrived at the apartment, the last vestiges of the dream tricked me into thinking that there was still a place for me in the future of Birds. Or maybe it was just that I was scared and, like so many times in the past, I knew he would take care of the mess. He took her body away and brought Kleinfeld to me. He left then, for the Far East, ostensibly to recruit new talent, but I was aware that he was running from the disease. Once, he sent me a pair of songbirds from Bangkok. But mostly he sends postcards, from places like Rangoon or Delhi, describing local customs and rituals as if he were some meticulous anthropologist charting the last days of a dying race. As time has passed, I've learned to read between the lines and have come to the conclusion that Rudy seeks redemption.

But even that is beyond me. Alone up here and caged, wings clipped like Rudy's songbirds, I hear no acolytes' prayers. The dream is my sustenance and my devourer; we two diminish, a little more each passing day.

THE FUTURE OF BIRDS
Mike O'Driscoll

I'd long been interested in the idea of a society where people found themselves forced to assume—for whatever reason—a sexuality that was alien to them, be they gay or straight. At the same time, I found that a recurrent theme in some of my stories has been an attempt to explore the politicization of AIDS and the scapegoating of its victims. I wondered what sort of consequences this would have on the future of human sexual behavior. The catalyst for bringing these ideas together was a TV documentary a couple of years ago about the transsexual scene in Rio de Janeiro. The program had an honesty that seemed rare for journalists looking at the subject, and the people themselves displayed an integrity and a normality that refused to conform to all the usual stereotypes.

In inventing a new disease that supersedes AIDS, I am perhaps being too optimistic about our ability to tackle HIV. But I needed a disease that gave the initial appearance of attacking a specific sector of society (in the same way that AIDS was initially perceived as a "gay plague"), in order to show how those who were unaffected dealt with, or exploited, those who were affected. However much factors such as greed or dreams or sexuality determine the choices made by Estela and Cledilce, they remain among the ranks of the used and abused. Maybe the one good thing about HIV is that it isn't gender selective.

Bruce McAllister has been publishing science fiction and fantasy since he was sixteen, when his first story, "The Faces Outside," was reprinted in Judith Merril's *Year's Best Science Fiction* series. Since then, his short stories have appeared in *Omni, Asimov's Science Fiction Magazine, Fantasy & Science Fiction,* "year's best" anthologies, and other anthologies and textbooks. His 1988 novel, *Dream Baby* (based on a Hugo- and Nebula-finalist novelette), was reissued in 1994 as a trade paperback. The Japanese edition appeared in 1995 and the Vietnamese edition has just been published in Vietnam and the United States. He is working on a novel, *Daughter of the Lions,* based on the general theme of the "Ark" stories which have appeared over the last decade in *Omni* and *Omni* books. McAllister teaches in the Creative Writing Program at the University of Redlands in Southern California, each summer at the Idyllwild School of Music and the Arts, and taught at Clarion West in 1995. He lives in Redlands, California, where his fiancée, choreographer Amelie Hunter, and his three children, Annie, Ben, and Liza also reside.

This is another stark look at the misuse of third world inhabitants. McAllister takes horrible but true events as a starting point for this horrific story—there have been and still *are* Laotian pirates roaming the seas, raping and pillaging and slaughtering refugees. There *are* women and children brought to the United States and sold into prostitution and slavery. Every once in a while one reads about such abuse in the newspaper and wonders at such ugliness and cruelty. "Captain China" is powerful and raw.

CAPTAIN CHINA

BRUCE MCALLISTER

NO ONE KNOWS CAPTAIN CHINA THE WAY I KNOW CAPTAIN China. No one sees him do what *I* see him do. I look down from my window on the hill and watch him walking the rooftops of Chinatown every night. I watch him climb the demon slides of the pagoda roof of the Ching Po Restaurant, where he looks out at the city lights, searching for someone, searching for me.

I see him look down at the round-eyed tourists, who are dressed so strangely and who never look up at him. I watch him save a kitten that has gotten lost on a roof. I watch him carry it in one hand as he leaps bravely from roof to roof, landing far below in the alley, which smells the way I imagine Chinatown smells—like the streets of My Tho when I was little, but different, because it is not My Tho. It is Chinatown, and the My Kong Delta is far away.

I watch him set the kitten free. I watch him watch it wander away happy.

I cannot see his face—so much like mine—from this window, but I see it in my dreams. I see his eyes, which are like mine. I see his skin which is paler than mine because my father's people left China so long ago that their skin darkened and their bodies grew smaller and thinner. I see the special suit he wears, his "cloak," which clings to his body like a woman's glove and sparkles in the night like the Phoenix Bird my father's brother told us of, how its magic was stronger than the Tiger's, though it never brought harm to a soul.

His suit sparkles in the night on the roofs of Chinatown but only *I* can see it. Because he wants it that way. He wants me to know he is looking, looking for *me*.

We have a secret, don't we, Chu—you and I? he tells me in my dream, as if we were in a comic book together.

The comic books that Mister Thupak brings for me to read (because he will not let me leave this room to get them for myself) are not in the language of my people or Mister Thupak's or even Chinese. But I have studied them and I *know* what those heroes do. We had comic books in My Tho— where I was born—and in the Thai camps, and in the bigger camp in Malaysia. Everywhere you go in the world, there are comic books, I know. That is how I know what the green man with the lamp is able to do, or the man who looks like a bat, or the man who is afraid of the green rock, or the man who climbs the sides of buildings. They are heroes because they want to *save* us. They want to save people who are about to be robbed. They want to save children who have no parents and kittens from rooftops. It is all the same for them. It is what they do. They do it sometimes without people knowing it, and they do it without asking for thanks. They spend their lives looking for ones to save—in cities, in rooms just like mine. That is why they are our heroes, why there are comic books in every country about them, and why so many of them have names like the one I have given my friend: *Captain China*.

Captain China has come from a world far far away, he tells me, in my dreams. He, too, is looking for someone to save—Someone like *me*.

The most famous story in my country is not a comic book. It is the story of *Kim Van Kieu,* a girl who does what she must because it is right. She gives up the young man she loves to take care of her father. She gives up a free life, out of duty. She gives up everything, because she must so that she will know, at the end of the her life, that she has lived her life correctly, and, most importantly, so that she will not have to return to this world and live again.

If I could believe that my own life is like hers, I would be happy. But it is difficult to do. I have lost everything—but for what? For the men who come to me in this room?

Captain China knows I am *somewhere,* but not where. Mister Thupak, the villain, has hidden me very well. If I try to escape, Mister Thupak will catch me and beat me. If I try to shout through the window (to let Captain China know where I am, of course), Mister Thupak will catch me and beat me. The window is never open. My shout cannot get out. The walls are thick, not like those of the house of my childhood. With the windows closed and the walls so thick Captain China cannot find me, except in dreams. This is the way of his kind, he tells me. *If you cannot find the one you love in the real world, there are always dreams. . . .*

In my dreams he smiles, to let me know he is looking, and that he will not stop.

The men that Mister Thupak brings to my room are of many kinds. Some wear expensive clothes—suits like the ones I see on the tourists down the hill, or suits made in Hong Kong, or suits I have never seen before. Some are dressed no better than Mister Thupak himself, smelling like him. Are they his cousins or brothers? I must wonder. Some of the men who come to my room speak languages I have heard before, though I do not understand them. Some do not. If they speak the language of my own people, I do not hear it. I do not want to. Some want me to face them when I do what they want me to do, or when they do to me what they want to do. A few ask only that I stand by the window, so that they can see me in the sunlight. That is all. They look at me and touch themselves and then leave. Most ask me to get down on my hands and knees, tell me not to look at them. This is what I prefer. This way I cannot see them. I can close my eyes and see Captain China jumping from roof to roof, his dark cape flying behind him. *This* is what I would rather see.

The touch of skin is the touch of skin, but people—no matter who they are—are more than this. They are what they *feel*. I know what the men feel who come to my room. I know what Captain China feels.

I would rather see Captain China, and by seeing him, feel what *he* must feel.

They do not hit me, or if they do, it is only once or twice. Mister Thupak has his rules. Mr. Thupak may hit me—if I am standing by the window when he comes in with *nuoc mam* or *pho* soup from the restaurant, or if one of the men complains that I have not been worth the money and tells Mister Thupak, with words or gestures of the hand, what I did wrong. But the men, they cannot—unless they have paid for it—and even then, only once or twice.

Captain China knows about all of this, and it makes him angry. He believes that no one should hit a boy like me. He says this in my dreams. He says it with tears in his eyes, so I know that he is feeling it.

This room is on the highest hill in Chinatown, but Chinatown isn't Chinatown any longer. There was a part of Saigon called Cholon, I remember. A part where the people spoke Chinese. Maybe it is still there, maybe not. After the war many people left Cholon to come across the ocean, just as I did, to the Chinatown in this city, and by coming they have changed it.

They speak Chinese but are not Chinese. They are from my country, yet we do not speak the same language. They have money. My father's people do not. I can see them on the streets in my dreams. I can hear them speaking Chinese, though I do not know that language. Were it not for my dreams—and the *nuoc mam* and *pho* that Mister Thupak brings from a restaurant down the hill—I would not know any of this. I would sit in my room without anyone to talk to and not know how Chinatown has changed.

When, in my dreams, I hear the Cholonese of this Chinatown speak my language (because they know both languages, because they had to) I am sad. I wake up crying. *How could hearing your father's language not make you sad?* I ask myself.

When people lose what is most important to them, they are always sad. That is how people are. No matter where they go, or what they do, or what is done to them afterward, they are sad.

Could he speak my father's language, Mister Thupak—who is darker than my people, whose eyes are rounder than mine, whose hair is coarse and very dark—would call me *moi*. That is our word for *animal*—and it is the word we use for the simple people who live in the mountain jungles of our country and live like animals.

That is how I live—like an animal, on my hands and my knees in a little room full of the sounds each night that animals make. That is how Mister Thupak has kept me since he bought me four years ago.

That would be the word he would use.

I can hear children playing in the apartments across the alley. I do not need dreams for this. They have found a metal hoop and nailed it to the wall above the automobiles that are parked there. They try to make a ball go through the hoop. They laugh when it does. They laugh when it does not. I remember *phung thy* and *muong,* but not this game. It is a game they have learned here. They have families. Their aunts and uncles and brothers and sisters came with them, were not left behind, did not die when the boats sank or the Thai pirates came. They did not have to say good-bye to each other in camps. Perhaps (I tell myself) they did not have to come in *boats* at all—perhaps they came another way—and that is why they are still together. *Can cha hoa.* The luck of the lucky.

I saw (in a dream last night) Captain China walking on the roof of their apartment building, so close. He does not know roofs like these. In his world, there are only buildings of glass reaching like hands toward the sky. I saw him looking down at their hoop and wondering to himself: *Why do they wish to put a ball through a hoop when there is a boy—alone in a room somewhere in Chinatown—who is unhappy, who is so much more important than any ball?*

He was so close, yet he could not hear me.

I was crying.

In the dream.

I do not know the man who comes to my room today. He has never visited before. His skin is as dark as Mister Thupak's, but there are freckles on it, something I have never seen on someone so dark. He grabs me by the hair (which I must keep long, Mister Thupak says, because most men like it this way) and hits me in the face. He is the kind of man who will hit me once—I know this—but whether he wants me to cry or be silent, I do not know. I do not know what kind of man he is except that he will hit me *once.* I am silent. I do not cry, and I know this is right. He does not get angry. He grabs me and turns me so that I am facing the wall. He says something in his language. It is rough, yes, but it is only a sound.

He wants me to *hurt,* but he does not want me to cry. He is *that* kind of man, I see now.

He pushes me down, so that I am on my hands and knees. He gets behind me. I hear the animal—the one I always hear. A tiger, a dragon whose breath is like rotting cloth. The animal begins to chase me through the great shadows of the U Minh Forest, where my family lived for a year, past the Hoa Binh rebels in their dirty camps, through the great bomb craters that filled with rainwater (catching the light of every sunset), through the paddy water where dead bodies floated like dolls. The animal growls. It grunts, wanting to kill me and eat me. It chases me on to the sands of the South China Sea, into the water, into the beautiful sea, where the boat sank and my uncle—

I close my eyes. I see *him*. I see Captain China. I see his head turn to listen. He hears it, the hideous sound. It makes him angry, but what can he do? He does not know where I am. He knows only what I am *feeling,* as I know what he is feeling.

Please, I say.

The animal snarls.

People do not understand. There are no orphans in my country. There never have been. I remember an Englishman talking about this to my father in My Tho, one day when I went with him. The Englishman knew French, as my father did, and so they spoke in French. When we returned home, my father told me what they had talked about. "You have no *orphans,*" the Englishman had said to him. My father did not understand at first, but no one in my country would have. In my country, there is only *family.* "*Mu cheng ni chuong ma,*" we say. "The world ends at the hedgerow," we say. We have said this for a thousand years. We mean there are no loyalties, no duties, as strong as those of *family* . . . nothing that calls to us beyond the thorny hedge around our village. If a child's parents die, there are aunts and uncles and cousins to take care of him. There is always *someone.* After all, an "orphan" is but a boy or a girl *without family* . . . and in my country this is not possible.

But I am not in my country. I am in the Chinatown of a country far far away, across a sea. Mister Thupak is the one person I know, and he is *not* family.

Unless a family sells its children for the pleasure of others.

Captain China understands this. He is far from home, too, and he understands. He cannot return until he has done what he must do here—

Which is *save* someone—someone who needs saving.

Because, he says, *of what I did long ago and must be forgiven for* . . .

I do not understand this, but it is true.

Because of what he did long ago and must be forgiven for.

• • •

I lie on my bed—which smells of skin and bad dreams—and I dream of the camp in Thailand, where Mai and Cam got sick and were taken away. I see Captain China. I see him going through the camp looking for us, when there are so many others, too. Shouldn't he save the little boy with one eye from Phankek, the teenage girl so beautiful that even filth cannot make her ugly, the old woman who cries every night for her husband (though he died thirty years ago)?

There are so many here who need saving, and only one Captain China.

When he finds us at last, he is too late. We are in the water, our heads are bobbing, the waves are swallowing us, spitting us out again. The pirates are drifting closer, trying to decide which of us they will leave to drown and which they will pull from the water, dry off, and sell.

He sees us—Mangh and Li and Phue and me—floating in the water, but which will he save *first?* He is late. There is time only for one. A hero, but only one.

He is crying because he knows he can save but one.

Mangh drowns. I watch his head disappear in the waves and I shout: *Save* **him**, *Captain China. Save* **him**. Mangh is gone, taken by the water. Li tries to grab the pirate boat, its wooden side, but the pirates aim their rifles and shoot him. I shout: *Save Li, Captain China. Save Li!* But Li is gone, the water as red as flame trees. Captain China can only watch, his face in pain, his eyes full of sadness as the pirates pull Phue and me from the water because we are young and handsome.

And then Captain China comes for me.

He covers me with his cape, so that I will be invisible—so that the pirates will not see me and I can escape—but I shout: *No! Go back to My Tho. Save my mother, Captain China. Go back to the camp. Save my father and uncle. Put the cape around Li or Phue—not* **me**. *Without them, I tell him, I am* **nothing**. *Do you understand?*

I can see this in Mister Thupak's eyes: *You do not exist. You eat* **nuoc mam**, *you eat* **pho** *soup, you read comic books I give you, but you do not exist. You are* **nothing**.

"You have no orphans," the Englishman says.

In my dream.

* * *

In other dreams I do—I let him save me. I let him come to my room. I let him take me in his arms, and hold me. I feel his skin against mine, my cheek against his chest. I touch his arm with my fingers. He wants nothing from me. I let his cape surround me, so that I will be invisible to the men who visit my room.

This is the dream I love best. The dream I dream to feel happy.

The room smells of the salt and rotten fish of *nuoc mam*. I have gotten *nuoc mam* on the comic books. I have been careless. I turn off the light and look out the window into the night. I do not see him on the pagoda roofs of the tourist streets. I do not see him by the statue of the Chinese men who long ago helped build a train track in this country, or in the dark alleys to the west, where you can watch the sun set. For a moment, in the darkness of this room, I am afraid he is gone, he has given up because he is tired of looking. After all, he is only one man.

But then I see him, and it is *not* a dream. I am not asleep. I see him from the window. He is walking in an alley, one where I have never seen him before.

He keeps his eyes on the pavement, as if looking for something—a footprint, something I might have dropped.

I have never called out to him—because of what Mister Thupak would do to me—but I do it now.

I slide the window open—the one too high for me ever to jump from—and before he can disappear, the way he does in dreams, I shout at him. I shout in my father's language:

"*Chin lo cang! Chin lo cang!*"

I am here! I am here!

He turns.

"*Muong ki,* Captain China!" I shout. "*Muong ki!*"

The children playing at the hoop look up. They hear me. They shout back, laughing: "*Muong chi ki tip! Muong chi ki tip!*"

I blink my eyes, looking for him in the shadows of the alley. He was there. I know he was. He turned—I saw him turn. He heard me and he turned—

As the children shout and laugh I see him again, his body

still, his eyes looking up at me at last. And then my face hits the window. I cry out. I am jerked back into the room.

I do not know what happens next. I am on the floor. My head is under the bed. Mister Thupak is beating me. He beats the parts of my body that are not under the bed. He beats them with his piece of wood.

I wake up in the morning with my head under my bed. My lips are hurting. My face feels like fire. I cannot move my arm.

I do not *want* to move. I want to lie here forever. I want to be *nothing*.

I have tried to keep it from Mister Thupak—these marks on my skin, this cough. I hide my arms from him. I scratch my face and arms so that he will think it is only scratches—ones left by some man—and he will shout at me for that. If I am ill, the men will not want me, I know, and what would happen then? What would Mister Thupak do then?

I have not looked out the window for many days. I have not dreamed of him.

When I go to the window I shake. It is as if Mister Thupak were standing behind me, waiting.

I am weak. I have been weak for thirteen days.

I do not see him when I close my eyes. I see nothing because I am nothing.

I dream of the lepers on the beach at Can Tho, the ones I saw with my mother and my aunt. I dream of the camps where the skin peeled from our feet like white rubber, hurting us.

I dream of skin.

Why would Captain China want to see me this way, my skin like this?

Mister Thupak points to the scratches on my face and asks questions. I do not understand the words, but I know what he asks. He grabs at me. I step back. He grabs at me again, catches my arm and holds it, looking at the scratches. He looks at my face. I am thinner. He can see this. The marks, the thinness, and my cough—which he has heard through the door. He is thinking:

The men will not want him now.

When he leaves, I lie down. I am breathing hard and I cannot stop.

Please, I say. *Please.*

Mister Thupak comes to my room and puts a cream the color of my skin on my face and arms, where the marks and scratches are. He makes a coughing sound and shakes his head. *If you cough, I will beat you.* He will. He changes the sheets on my bed. He opens the window to let in air, to let out the smell of *nuoc mam* and illness. He points a little can in the air and sprays it. It smells like familiar flowers.

A man comes to me two days later. He is thin like a wire and his eyes are like empty jars. But when he looks at me, his eyes fill with happiness. He is thinking of death—my death—how he will do it—and it makes him happy. I tell myself I am mistaken, but when I look at those eyes again, I know I am not. I have not seen eyes like his since the South China Sea, but I argue with myself. I say: *He will only* **dream** *it while he is with you. Chu—he will not really do it. Mister Thupak will not let him. Mister Thupak can hide your illness with cream and still make money from you.*

I say this to myself, but I am weak. I cannot think clearly. I cannot stand up without shaking. I am afraid.

He gestures to me, like the others. He knows I do not speak his language. I take the position he wishes me to and no longer have to see his eyes. I feel him against me and then something cold against my neck.

I jerk away. He swears, angry, but the cold metal—I have never felt this before—makes me jerk. I cannot help myself.

I know what it is.

It is a gun. He likes to do this, I tell myself. He likes to *scare* his young men. He likes to *imagine* things when he is with them—like that man two years ago who paid Mister Thupak to have me cut myself, so that he could see my blood; that man a year ago who wore a special shirt with buttons to hurt me; that man six months ago who wanted me to believe he was going to blind me with his knife . . . so that he could feel my fear.

No. I am wrong.

This is the last man, I realize now.

He has paid Mister Thupak more money than I can imagine to kill me—to be inside me when I die.

Because Mister Thupak no longer wants me. Because I am sick and no one will want me now. If he can get this money—so much—before people hear how sick I am, he has not lost everything.

This man will grow ill and die. He doesn't know it, though I do. But it doesn't matter. I will die now, instead of later—that is all.

I close my eyes. He has begun to move against me. I feel his bones. It is difficult for him to stay still. A cough slips between my teeth. He should sound like an animal to me, but he does not. He sounds like a man, that is all. A man hurting me a little but not as much as some.

The metal wobbles. Can he do it? Can he hold the gun long enough?

He makes his sounds. The cold metal presses harder on my ear and I know it will be soon. It will be sooner than he imagined, because he is so excited. He wants his moment to be the same as mine, and my moment, the bullet from his gun.

I see Captain China. He is standing in front of me, so close that I could touch him, or him, me. I try to see his face clearly and cannot. He *has* no face. No eyes, no lips—

I do not understand this.

And I do not understand what happens next.

A window breaks, the screen tears, something slips in. The room fills with a wind. It is a dream, I tell myself, something I am dreaming from the illness. The cold metal at my neck jerks away, the body against me jerks away, the man is screaming. The door into the room opens, slamming. I hear Mister Thupak's voice. Then he is screaming too. The room explodes with the bullet. I hear nothing else. The screams are gone. The voices are gone. I am deaf. I feel only the wind rushing through the room.

Something grabs me, lifts me into the air, and puts me back down again.

I know what is happening.

He has found me through dreams. He has found me at last.
I start to cough and cannot stop.

I am standing. I am weak but I am standing. It is as if the illness were only a waiting, and the waiting is over. I start to look down at the floor, to see what is lying there, when I have not been hurt, but a voice—one I can hear even in the deafness—tells me: No. It is the voice from my dreams. *His* voice. There is indeed something on the floor—a body, two—and he would prefer that I not look at them.

If you do, Chu, the voice tells me, you will be afraid.
I will never be afraid of you, I tell him.

I look at him instead, standing beside me—the way I have always dreamed he would—and as I do, I start to scream.

His head is the color of red wine, old blood in a glass. Things move under its skin, folding against each other.

I look at his face, but it is not a face—and I go on screaming.

The smile is not a smile. It is a wound at the top of the head, a mouth that never closes, never eats. The eyes—all six of them, not shaped like mine at all—are not eyes, but gills like a shark's at the fish market in Can Tho.

I cannot look anymore. He says: *You must. It is time.*

My heart moves in my chest like the engine of an old boat. My eyes want to find his face—the one from dreams.

Look at me, he says. I do.

The cape is not a cape. It is even darker than his skin. It moves like an animal, one that lives and eats and will do *anything* for him—even kill.

He says: Touch it. And I do.

The cape shifts like fog. It makes a sound like teeth on glass. It moves away from me, unsure.

He speaks to it. He tells it to be still, to let me touch it.

I touch it again and see a *dog.* I see a *monkey,* because it wishes me to, because he has told it to. I see a man—one with a cape and a smile just like mine, eyes like mine. It will show me whatever I need to see, to stop screaming.

And I would be screaming if it weren't for the *monkey* and the smile.

Instead, I am crying.

I thought, I tell him, *that you were a* **man.**

The cape moves. I smell the jasmine of My Tho. I see the flame trees of Hue and the sands of Vung Tau, where my mother and father met, and the blue waters of the South China Sea. I see my mother and my father by the hedgerow of our village, my uncles and aunts, my brothers and sisters and cousins. I see myself standing with them, my family. I am with them again.

Without the people you love, you are nothing.

For you, the voice says, *I am.*

He is taking me away, he tells me now. He is taking me *home*—not to my parents' country, no, but to his world, where there are no beaches, though water laps at the roots of trees, where the trees grow down instead of up, toward water, where buildings grow like crystals toward the light, and two suns set like eyes at evening, like flowers, and when these suns have set, the winds begin to roar. Where children that do not look like children laugh and play with their own dark capes, which are not really capes, but living things, until these things learn what the children wish them to do . . . carrying them into the sky on those winds, hiding them from what might hurt them, playing with them if they are bored.

Why? I ask him.

I killed a creature long ago, he tells me again. *I should not have. There was no reason except anger. It wasn't even my world, so the anger was only vanity. I must save another, if I am to save myself. . . .*

That is what his kind believes.

This is what it has been like for them on their world, and on the worlds they have known.

Without forgivenness, we have only our own darkness, he says.

We will go the way I came, he says.

How? I ask. *On a boat? A plane?*

Yes, he says. *On a thing like a* **boat.** *But there is no way for you to really understand,* he says.

I can take you away, he says, his eyes again like mine, his hand—like my father's, bony and wrinkled—reaching out as if to touch me. *But that is all I can do, Chu.*

What does he mean?

I can take you away, the voice says. *I can heal your sickness, but I cannot touch you.*

I understand.

He cannot hold me. He cannot hold me naked in his arms the way I have dreamed he would.

I understand, I say.

I try to.

I do.

And then he is taking his cape, unwinding it from his back, and putting it on my shoulders. I do not understand why. I do not understand why he would do this, for when it touches me, it enfolds me like someone else's skin, someone else's blood, water I cannot breathe in, and I can barely scream. I barely have enough air to scream.

And then it passes.

I breathe again.

I feel what *he* has always felt. What his kind has always felt:

To be held forever by someone—or something—that will always be yours. . . .

I'll get another one on the boat, he says brightly.

It is Captain China saying this, grinning, ready for our adventure.

The room begins to spin like another dream, and I go with him where this story, this comic book that is ours and ours alone, wants us to go.

CAPTAIN CHINA
Bruce McAllister

We should not be afraid of anything in life except the *absence* of love, and in turn, love's "touch." Women—it is women—tell me this is a story about *love,* not "skin" at all; that it is about a child's need to be held, about a father and a son separated (as they sometimes are) by light-years, by species, by the journeys that take them into the "differences" they are. That it is in the face of such impossible distance (light-years, biology, "difference") that their need to love and be loved, to hold and be held—even if "skin" will not allow it—becomes the miracle it is. This is true; and so we should not fear this story.

Lisa Tuttle was born and raised in Houston, Texas, and began writing as a child. She sold her first short stories while a student at Syracuse University (New York) in the early 1970s. After five years working as a journalist on a daily newspaper in Austin she became a full-time freelance writer, and moved to Britain in 1980. Besides the novels *Familiar Spirit, Gabriel,* and *Lost Futures,* she has had three collections of short stories published, *A Nest of Nightmares, A Spaceship Built of Stone,* and *Memories of the Body.* She is the author of nonfiction works, including *Encyclopedia of Feminism and Heroines: Women Inspired by Women.* She has edited *Skin of the Soul,* an anthology of original horror stories by women. Her most recent novel, *Panther in Argyll,* was written for young adults and has just been published in the U.K. She lives in rural Scotland with her family.

In contrast to the last two stories, this one is relatively lighthearted—focusing on a part of the human anatomy that seems to hold great fascination for both sexes.

BACKGROUND: THE DREAM

LISA TUTTLE

YOU'VE ASKED ME TO TELL YOU ABOUT MYSELF.

I'll begin with the dream.

First, the precipitating cause: One night I noticed a small excrescence on my inner thigh. It wasn't painful or disfiguring, but once having noticed it I became increasingly aware and self-conscious whenever dressing or undressing brought it to my attention, and I wondered how long it had been there, and what it was. You know how it is, especially getting older, when every minor bodily change or malfunction makes you think in terms of Early Warning Signs rather than simple mutability. One day, sitting naked on the edge of the bed, I began to prod and then to pinch it until eventually I pressed it between my thumbs and squeezed it like a pimple. And I guess it was a pimple, or something similar, because when I squeezed, out shot a long, thin yellow stream. I was mildly shocked, squeamishly excited, a child again in my response to a bodily emission. The little bump or lump was gone. There was a slight redness at the site for the next day or two, then nothing.

I didn't forget. For a long time I examined the skin of my inner thighs compulsively, but I never again found a similar blemish.

Phallic symbolism? Call it what you like, but it really happened, and seems to me to be an (if not the) obvious source for the dream that followed, some months later.

In the dream I'd had a small, fleshy growth on my inner thigh for some time without doing anything about it. I was vaguely aware that it was growing larger, but when I finally examined it closely I was shocked to see an excrescence as long and thick as one of my fingers. I felt squeamish about handling it, and knew at once that I would not be able to rid myself of it by squeezing it. The excrescence was enormously, seemingly abnormally, sensitive to the slightest pressure. And even after I'd dressed myself I was morbidly aware of it chafing between my thighs. I had the horrible feeling it was growing larger and didn't dare look at it again, fearful that it had been my own examination of the thing which had made it suddenly so much worse. Terrified, I wondered what it was. It was too much to hope that such a thing could vanish as suddenly as it appeared; I'd have to see a doctor about getting it removed.

With a tremendous sense of relief that there was something I could do, I woke, and for a few moments, swimming hazily in the aftermath of sleep, I could think of nothing but calling my doctor, wondering how soon he'd be able to see me, and how simple or difficult the subsequent operation would prove to be.

Then I woke a little more and realized I'd been dreaming. The relief was that much greater: there was no peculiar growth on my inner thigh; the whole thing had been a dream. To prove it to myself I passed my hand across, over, down and up my bare thighs beneath the sheet. Bare, smooth flesh made me smile until I felt it.

So much bigger, fatter, grosser than it had been in the dream—full of pus, I thought in helpless horror—and attached to me, undeniably growing out of my body, sprouting not from one of my legs as in the dream, but in reality from my trunk, rooted in my pubis and dangling—this was no mere phallic symbol but the thing itself.

Nauseous with shock, I struggled to cling to the idea that this, too, was a dream and in a moment I would wake.

But I was as wide-awake then as I am now. I am what I have always been, and I have always had this thing, this normal, fleshy excrescence. I've been told that my memories of a different sort of body are delusions. I can't argue with the records, pictures, doctors, facts, authorities, you—but neither can I argue with my feelings. I don't want this fat, swelling thing. It's not me. I've tried and tried to get rid of it, but now they've tied my hands. Please, won't you help me? Please, just squeeze it for me.

BACKGROUND: THE DREAM
Lisa Tuttle

This is one of only two stories I've ever written based on a dream. It's all true, except the ending.

AYE, AND GOMORRAH...

SAMUEL R. DELANY

AND CAME DOWN IN PARIS:

Where we raced along the Rue de Médicis with Bo and Lou and Muse inside the fence, Kelly and me outside, making faces through the bars, making noise, making the Luxembourg Gardens roar at two in the morning. Then climbed out, and down to the square in front of St. Sulpice where Bo tried to knock me into the fountain.

At which point Kelly noticed what was going on around us, got an ashcan cover, and ran into the pissoir, banging the walls. Five guys scooted out; even a big pissoir only holds four.

A very blond young man put his hand on my arm and smiled. "Don't you think, Spacer, that you ... people should leave?"

I looked at his hand on my blue uniform. *"Est-ce que tu es un frelk?"*

His eyebrows rose, then he shook his head. "Une *frelk*," he corrected. "No. I am not. Sadly for me. You look as though you may once have been a man. But now..." He smiled. "You have nothing for me now. The police." He nodded across the street where I noticed the gendarmerie for the first time. "They don't bother us. You are strangers, though..."

But Muse was already yelling, "Hey, come on! Let's get out of here, huh?" And left.

And went up again.

And came down in Houston:

"God damn!" Muse said. "Gemini Flight Control—you mean this is where it all started? Let's get *out* of here, *please!*"

So took a bus out through Pasadena, then the monoline to Galveston, and were going to take it down the Gulf, but Lou found a couple with a pickup truck—

"Glad to give you a ride, Spacers. You people up there on them planets and things, doing all that good work for the government."

—who were going south, them and the baby, so we rode in the back for two hundred and fifty miles of sun and wind.

"You think they're frelks?" Lou asked, elbowing me. "I bet they're frelks. They're just waiting for us give 'em the come-on."

"Cut it out. They're a nice, stupid pair of country kids."

"That don't mean they ain't frelks!"

"You don't trust anybody, do you?"

"No."

And finally a bus again that rattled us through Brownsville and across the border into Matamoros where we staggered down the steps into the dust and the scorched evening with a lot of Mexicans and chickens and Texas Gulf shrimp fishermen—who smelled worst—and *we* shouted the loudest. Forty-three whores—I counted—had turned out for the shrimp fishermen, and by the time we had broken two of the windows in the bus station they were all laughing. The shrimp fishermen said they wouldn't buy us no food but would get us drunk if we wanted, 'cause that was the custom with shrimp fishermen. But we yelled, broke another window; then, while I was lying on my back on the telegraph office steps, singing, a woman with dark lips bent over and put her hands on my cheeks. "You are very sweet." Her rough hair fell forward. "But the men, they are standing around and watching *you*. And that is taking up *time*. Sadly, their time is our money. Spacer, do you not think you . . . people should leave?"

I grabbed her wrist. "*¡Usted!*" I whispered. "*¿Usted es una frelka?*"

"*Frelko in español.*" She smiled and patted the sunburst that hung from my belt buckle. "Sorry. But you have nothing that . . . would be useful to me. It is too bad, for you look like you were once a woman, no? And I like women, too . . ."

I rolled off the porch.

"Is this a drag, or is this a drag!" Muse was shouting. "Come *on!* Let's *go!*"

We managed to get back to Houston before dawn, somehow.

And went up.

And came down in Istanbul:

That morning it rained in Istanbul.

At the commissary we drank our tea from pear-shaped glasses, looking out across the Bosphorus. The Princess Islands lay like trash heaps before the prickly city.

"Who knows their way in this town?" Kelly asked.

"Aren't we going around together?" Muse demanded. "I thought we were going around together."

"They held up my check at the purser's office," Kelly explained. "I'm flat broke. I think the purser's got it in for me," and shrugged. "Don't want to, but I'm going to have to hunt up a rich frelk and come on friendly," went back to the tea; *then* noticed how heavy the silence had become. "Aw, come *on*, now! You gape at me like that and I'll bust every bone in that carefully-conditioned-from-puberty body of yours. Hey you!" meaning me. "Don't give me that holier-than-thou gawk like you never went with no frelk!"

It was starting.

"I'm not gawking," I said and got quietly mad.

The longing, the old longing.

Bo laughed to break tensions. "Say, last time I was in Istanbul—about a year before I joined up with this platoon—I

remember we were coming out of Taksim Square down Istiqlal. Just past all the cheap movies we found a little passage
lined with flowers. Ahead of us were two other spacers. It's a
market in there, and farther down they got fish, and then a
courtyard with oranges and candy and sea urchins and cabbage. But flowers in front. Anyway, we noticed something
funny about the spacers. It wasn't their uniforms: they were
perfect. The haircuts: fine. It wasn't till we heard them talking—They were a man and woman dressed up like spacers,
trying *to pick up frelks!* Imagine, queer for frelks!''

"Yeah," Lou said. "I seen that before. There were a lot of
them in Rio."

"We beat hell out of them two," Bo concluded. "We got
them in a side street and went to *town!*''

Muse's tea glass clicked on the counter. "From Taksim
down Istiqlal till you get to the flowers? Now why didn't you
say that's where the frelks were, huh?'' A smile on Kelly's
face would have made that okay. There was no smile.

"Hell," Lou said, "nobody ever had to tell me where to
look. I go out in the street and frelks smell me coming. I can
spot 'em halfway along Piccadilly. Don't they have nothing
but tea in this place? Where can you get a drink?''

Bo grinned. "Moslem country, remember? But down at the
end of the Flower Passage there're a lot of little bars with
green doors and marble counters where you can get a liter of
beer for about fifteen cents in lira. And there're all these stands
selling deep-fat-fried bugs and pig's gut sandwiches—''

"You ever notice how frelks can put it away? I mean liquor,
not . . . pig's guts.''

And launched off into a lot of appeasing stories. We ended
with the one about the frelk some spacer tried to roll who
announced: "There are two things I go for. One is spacers;
the other is a good fight . . .''

But they only allay. They cure nothing. Even Muse knew
we would spend the day apart, now.

The rain had stopped, so we took the ferry up the Golden
Horn. Kelly straight off asked for Taksim Square and Istiqlal
and was directed to a dolmush, which we discovered was a
taxicab, only it just goes one place and picks up lots and lots
of people on the way. And it's cheap.

Lou headed off over Ataturk Bridge to see the sights of New City. Bo decided to find out what the Dolma Boche really was; and when Muse discovered you could go to Asia for fifteen cents—one lira and fifty krush—well, Muse decided to go to Asia.

I turned through the confusion of traffic at the head of the bridge and up past the gray, dripping walls of Old City, beneath the trolley wires. There are times when yelling and helling won't fill the lack. There are times when you must walk by yourself because it hurts so much to be alone.

I walked up a lot of little streets with wet donkeys and wet camels and women in veils; and down a lot of big streets with buses and trash baskets and men in business suits.

Some people stare at spacers; some people don't. Some people stare or don't stare in a way a spacer gets to recognize within a week after coming out of training school at sixteen. I was walking in the park when I caught her watching. She saw me see and looked away.

I ambled down the wet asphalt. She was standing under the arch of a small, empty mosque shell. As I passed she walked out into the courtyard among the cannons.

"Excuse me."

I stopped.

"Do you know whether or not this is the shrine of St. Irene?" Her English was charmingly accented. "I've left my guidebook home."

"Sorry. I'm a tourist too."

"Oh." She smiled. "I am Greek. I thought you might be Turkish because you are so dark."

"American red Indian." I nodded. Her turn to curtsy.

"I see. I have just started at the university here in Istanbul. Your uniform, it tells me that you are"—and in the pause, all speculations resolved—"a spacer."

I was uncomfortable. "Yeah." I put my hands in my pockets, moved my feet around on the soles of my boots, licked my third from the rear left molar—did all the things you do when you're uncomfortable. *You're so* exciting *when you look like that,* a frelk told me once. "Yeah, I am." I said it too sharply, too loudly, and she jumped a little.

So now she knew I knew she knew I knew, and I wondered how we would play out the Proust bit.

"I'm Turkish," she said. "I'm not Greek. I'm not just starting. I'm a graduate in art history here at the university. These little lies one makes for strangers to protect one's ego . . . why? Sometimes I think my ego is very small."

That's one strategy.

"How far away do you live?" I asked. "And what's the going rate in Turkish lira?" That's another.

"I can't pay you." She pulled her raincoat around her hips. She was very pretty. "I would like to." She shrugged and smiled. "But I am . . . a poor student. Not a rich one. If you want to turn around and walk away, there will be no hard feelings. I shall only be sad."

I stayed on the path. I thought she'd suggest a price after a little while. She didn't.

And that's another.

I was asking myself, *What do you want the damn money for anyway?* when a breeze upset water from one of the park's great cypresses.

"I think the whole business is unhappy." She wiped drops from her face. There had been a break in her voice and for a moment I looked too closely at the water streaks. "I think it's unhappy that they have to alter you to make you a spacer. If they hadn't, then *we* . . . If spacers had never been, then we could not be . . . the way we are. Did you start out male or female?"

Another shower. I was looking at the ground and droplets went down my collar.

"Male," I said. "It doesn't matter."

"How old are you? Twenty-three, twenty-four?"

"Twenty-three," I lied. It's reflex. I'm twenty-five, but the younger they think you are, the more they pay you. But I didn't *want* her damn money—

"I guessed right then." She nodded. "Most of us are experts on spacers. Do you find that? I suppose we have to be." She looked at me with wide black eyes. At the end of the stare, she blinked rapidly. "You would have been a fine man. But now you are a spacer, building water-conservation units on Mars, programing mining computers on Ganymede, serv-

icing communication relay towers on the moon. The alteration . . .'' Frelks are the only people I've ever heard say ''the
alteration'' with so much fascination and regret. ''You'd think
they'd have found some other solution. They could have found
another way than neutering you, turning you into creatures not
even androgynous; things that are—''

I put my hand on her shoulder, and she stopped like I'd hit
her. She looked to see if anyone was near. Lightly, so lightly
then, she raised her hand to mine.

I pulled my hand away. ''That are what?''

''They could have found another way.'' Both hands in her
pockets now.

''They could have. Yes. Up beyond the ionosphere, baby,
there's too much radiation for those precious gonads to work
right anywhere you might want to do something that would
keep you there over twenty-four hours, like the moon, or Mars,
or the satellites of Jupiter—''

''They could have made protective shields. They could have
done more research into biological adjustment—''

''Population Explosion time,'' I said. ''No, they were hunting for any excuse to cut down kids back then—especially
deformed ones.''

''Ah yes.'' She nodded. ''We're still fighting our way up
from the neo-puritan reaction to the sex freedom of the twen-
tieth century.''

''It was a fine solution.'' I grinned and put my hand over
my crotch. ''I'm happy with it.'' And scratched. I've never
known why that's so much more obscene when a spacer does
it.

''Stop it,'' she snapped, moving away.

''What's the matter?''

''Stop it,'' she repeated. ''Don't do that! You're a child.''

''But they choose us from children whose sexual responses
are hopelessly retarded at puberty.''

''And your childish, violent substitutes for love? I suppose
that's one of the things that's attractive. Yes, I know you're a
child.''

''Yeah? What about frelks?''

She thought awhile. ''I think they are the sexually retarded ones they miss. Perhaps it was the right solution. You really don't regret you have no sex?''

''We've got you,'' I said.

''Yes.'' She looked down. I glanced to see the expression she was hiding. It was a smile. ''You have your glorious, soaring life—*and* you have us.'' Her face came up. She glowed. ''You spin in the sky, the world spins under you, and you step from land to land, while we . . .'' She turned her head right, left, and her black hair curled and uncurled on the shoulder of her coat. ''We have our dull, circled lives, bound in gravity, *worshipping* you!''

She looked back at me. ''Perverted, yes? In love with a bunch of corpses in free fall!'' She suddenly hunched her shoulders. ''I don't like having a free-fall-sexual-displacement complex.''

''That always sounded like too much to say.''

She looked away. ''I don't like being a frelk. Better?''

''I wouldn't like it either. Be something else.''

''You don't choose your perversions. *You* have no perversions at all. *You*'re free of the whole business. I love you for that, Spacer. My love starts with the fear of love. Isn't that beautiful? A pervert substitutes something unattainable for 'normal' love: the homosexual, a mirror, the fetishist, a shoe or a watch or a girdle. Those with free-fall-sexual-dis—''

''Frelks.''

''Frelks substitute''—she looked at me sharply again—''loose, swinging meat.''

''That doesn't offend me.''

''I wanted it to.''

''Why?''

''You don't have desires. You wouldn't understand.''

''Go on.''

''I want you because you can't want me. That's the pleasure. If someone really had a sexual reaction to . . . us, we'd be scared away. I wonder how many people there were before there were you, waiting for your creation. We're necrophiles. I'm sure grave robbing has fallen off since you started going up. But you don't understand . . .'' She paused. ''If you did, then I wouldn't be scuffing leaves now and trying to think from whom I could borrow sixty lira.'' She stepped over the knuckles of a root that had cracked the pavement. "And that, incidentally, is the going rate in Istanbul."

I calculated. "Things still get cheaper as you go east."

"You know," and she let her raincoat fall open, "you're different from the others. You at least *want* to know—"

I said, "If I spat on you for every time you'd said that to a spacer, you'd drown."

"Go back to the moon, loose meat." She closed her eyes. "Swing on up to Mars. There are satellites around Jupiter where you might do some good. Go up and come down in some other city."

"Where do you live?"

"You want to come with me?"

"Give me something," I said. "Give me something—it doesn't have to be worth sixty lira. Give me something that you like, anything of yours that means something to you."

"No!"

"Why not?"

"Because I—"

"—don't want to give up part of that ego. None of you frelks do!"

"You really don't understand I just don't want to buy you?"

"You have nothing to buy me with."

"You are a child," she said. "I love you."

We reached the gate of the park. She stopped, and we stood time enough for a breeze to rise and die in the grass. "I . . ." she offered tentatively, pointing without taking her hand from her coat pocket. "I live right down there."

"All right," I said. "Let's go."

A gas main had once exploded along this street, she explained to me, a gushing road of fire as far as the docks, overhot and over-quick. It had been put out within minutes, no building had fallen, but the charred facias glittered. "This is sort of an artist and student quarter." We crossed the cobbles. "Yuri Pasha, number fourteen. In case you're ever in Istanbul again." Her door was covered with black scales, the gutter was thick with garbage.

"A lot of artists and professional people are frelks," I said, trying to be inane.

"So are lots of other people." She walked inside and held the door. "We're just more flamboyant about it."

On the landing there was a portrait of Ataturk. Her room was on the second floor. "Just a moment while I get my key—"

Marsscapes! Moonscapes! On her easel was a six-foot canvas showing the sunrise flaring on a crater's rim! There were copies of the original Observer pictures of the moon pinned to the wall, and pictures of every smooth-faced general in the International Spacer Corps.

On one corner of her desk was a pile of those photo magazines about spacers that you can find in most kiosks all over the world: I've seriously heard people say they were printed for adventurous-minded high school children. They've never seen the Danish ones. She had a few of those too. There was a shelf of art books, art history texts. Above them were six feet of cheap paper-covered space operas: *Sin on Space Station #12*, *Rocket Rake*, *Savage Orbit*.

"Arrack?" she asked. "Ouzo, or pernod? You've got your choice. But I may pour them all from the same bottle." She set out glasses on the desk, then opened a waist-high cabinet that turned out to be an icebox. She stood up with a tray of lovelies: fruit puddings, Turkish delight, braised meats.

"What's this?"

"Dolmades. Grape leaves filled with rice and pignolias."

"Say it again?"

"Dolmades. Comes from the same Turkish word as 'dolmush.' They both mean 'stuffed.' " She put the tray beside the glasses. "Sit down."

I sat on the studio-couch-that-becomes-bed. Under the brocade I felt the deep, fluid resilience of a glycogel mattress. They've got the idea that it approximates the feeling of free fall. "Comfortable? Would you excuse me for a moment? I have some friends down the hall. I want to see them for a moment." She winked. "They like spacers."

"Are you going to take up a collection for me?" I asked. "Or do you want them to line up outside the door and wait their turn?"

She sucked a breath. "Actually I was going to suggest both." Suddenly she shook her head. "Oh, what do you want!"

"What will you give me? I want something," I said. "That's why I came. I'm lonely. Maybe I want to find out how far it goes. I don't know yet."

"It goes as far as you will. Me? I study, I read, paint, talk with my friends"—she came over to the bed, sat down on the floor—"go to the theater, look at spacers who pass me on the street, till one looks back; I am lonely too." She put her head on my knee. "I want something. But," and after a minute neither of us had moved, "you are not the one who will give it to me."

"You're not going to pay me for it," I countered. "You're not, are you?"

On my knee her head shook. After a while she said, all breath and no voice, "Don't you think you . . . should leave?"

"Okay," I said, and stood up.

She sat back on the hem of her coat. She hadn't taken it off yet.

I went to the door.

"Incidentally." She folded her hands in her lap. "There is a place in New City you might find what you're looking for, called the Flower Passage—"

I turned toward her, angry. "The frelk hangout? Look, I don't *need* money! I said *anything* would do! I don't want—"

She had begun to shake her head, laughing quietly. Now she lay her cheek on the wrinkled place where I had sat. "Do you persist in misunderstanding? It is a *spacer* hangout. When you leave, I am going to visit my friends and talk about . . . ah, yes, the beautiful one that got away. I thought you might find . . . perhaps someone you know."

With anger, it ended.

"Oh," I said. "Oh, it's a spacer hangout. Yeah. Well, thanks."

And went out.

And found the Flower Passage, and Kelly and Lou and Bo and Muse. Kelly was buying beer so we all got drunk, and ate fried fish and fried clams and fried sausage, and Kelly was waving the money around, saying, "You should have seen him! The changes I put that frelk through, you should have *seen* him! Eighty lira is the going rate here, and he gave me a hundred and fifty!" and drank more beer.

And went up.

—Milford
September 1966

AYE, AND GOMORRAH ...
Samuel R. Delany

Afterword: 1994.

This story was written in September of 1966—three years before Stonewall and half a dozen years before anyone was aware there might even be a disease *like* AIDS. Had you asked me what it was about when I wrote it, I'd have said it was my try at taking two characters—one, the narrator, whom most readers would relate to as male, and another who was objectively female—and, through science fictional distortion of the world around them, making this disturbingly "normal" couple stand in for the range of the perversions.

I'm not sure how the change in the social status of homosexuality, sadomasochism, and the like have changed the way we read the story today. Ask me what the story is about now, however, and I'll probably say it's somehow about the desire for desire.

But what direction is this account—of a woman who wants sex and a man who, finally, says no—casting its irony in? Is it a satirically serious version of Peg and Al Bundy? Is it a role reversal of a young female prostitute and the older male john? Is it some sort of analogue of the straight hustler and the older gay john, but with some of the parts switched along other axes?

I don't know. But I suspect that only by asking such questions does the story become even vaguely interesting—to those readers who might want to reanimate it with whatever traces of life it once might have held at the longer and longer-ago time of its writing.

Kathe Koja is the author of *The Cipher, Bad Brains, Skin, Strange Angels*, and *Kink*. She was cowinner (with Melanie Tem) of the Horror Writers Association's Bram Stoker Award for *The Cipher* (Superior Achievement in a first novel) which also won the *Locus* poll in the same category. She is the author of many short stories, several of which have appeared in best of the year anthologies. She lives with her husband, artist Rick Lieder, and her son, Aaron, in the suburbs of Detroit.

Barry N. Malzberg is the author of over seventy novels, among them *Herovit's World, Beyond Apollo* (winner of the John W. Campbell Memorial Award), *Underlay, The Men Inside, The Remaking of Sigmund Freud;* the essential essay collection *Engines of the Night* and numerous fiction collections, including *The Man Who Loved the Midnight Lady, The Many Worlds of Barry N. Malzberg*, and *The Passage of the Light: The Recursive Science Fiction of Barry N. Malzberg.*

Kathe Koja and Barry N. Malzberg have been collaborating since 1992; their work includes a novel and thirty short stories which have appeared in Omni magazine, *Alternate Outlaws, Dinosaur Fantastic, Little Deaths,* and other anthologies.

"Ursus Triad, Later" is a difficult piece both stylistically and in content. The reader is thrust into the middle of an endless nightmare inspired by the innocent classic fairy tale, "Goldilocks and the Three Bears."

URSUS TRIAD, LATER

KATHE KOJA AND
BARRY N. MALZBERG

NOW THE DOOR, THE KNOB ON THE DOOR, THE SMALL SLIVER of light dense, concentrated, aiming from the room behind: where the bears nested. The splinters of the floor, the brutal surfaces upon which she had rolled, scrambled, been pawed and lumbered over, half-suffocated between fur and ragged blanket and fear of the splinters, pointed always but always somehow missing puncture: of her eyes, the worn but tender skin beneath; her suffering lips.

Once her perspective had been larger, once—she thought, or believed she had thought—she had seen the house entire, light everywhere: the gleam of glass and porcelain, the glimpse of cages through transparent walls, but that must have been a long time ago or perhaps some trick of perspective, some dull accident of sensibility, for now she could see only that door, that knob, the light, the floor from the position to which she had sunk: the dainty ordnance of paws, the heavy intake of the bears' breath somehow framing conditions without providing illumination. The cages had come open some time ago, were never closed now; the keeper—if there had been a keeper, a jailer, some master who had schooled them (and if so for what extravagant enjoyment, who under God's sun could train animals to purposes like these?)—now fled, the house the bears' alone, she the intruder, she the peeping, curious, external force crushed now to this sullen, sunken wood and the creaking sound of their inhalations as one by one, solemnly, they played with her: over and over, opening her up like a wound, their paws and fur the ancient sutures drawn by that wound, bleached and stanched and then somehow magnified by their withdrawal as one by one, each by each they left her on the floor: to gather her own breath and breathing wounds together before another one returned to rend her now anew.

Somewhere through all of this she must have eaten, drunk, found a way to eliminate; slid into coma and emerged; there must have been some kind of passage in which the common tasks of consciousness were conducted but she knew—and it was all that she knew—that she had no knowledge of those times, could remember it as little as her initial swim in the womb: it was literally some other life because now everything was the bears, the tumbling conjoinment, the snaffle from their muzzles and the cascading, indifferent light which at odd angles swooped over, swooped through her; the dazed and cavernous surfaces of her sensibility sometimes roused briefly by that light, only to plunge again in the tumble and harsh necessity of their breath. She had become emptiness, and they filled her again and again.

Bach, Beethoven, and Brahms: her names for them, her three assailants, masters and dumb slaves as she herself was a slave. Dumb and sullen, beneath or beyond language, but she had to try to assign some meaning to the situation, had given them names to suit what she took to be their personalities in that time before this time when she must have come here, must have had reasons—what were they?—to enter this strange and damaged cloister, this space beyond redemption, to emerge as if from death or fever into the circling stare of the bears: eyes dull and compliant, slow struggle of limbs as they balanced on hind legs, ready to begin the dance anew; and she their silent partner, pink and breathing on the wood.

There was no real communication amongst them; they seemed to her to work within circumscription, intersecting only to bump as one left, another came to snort and root around her stricken body. She had known from the first that appeals, cries, struggles, resistance of any kind would only have attenuated her situation; the animals were beyond command, beyond whatever powers of humanity she had then been still able to summon and so: the splinters: the fur: the paws and the breathy stink. Her agony. Their arabesques. Submitting to them, over and over, submitting to Bach now, the largest of them and the most regular, the most rhythmic, the most metronomic: Bach because this B seemed to believe in order, in a kind of regulation of movement which rattled and thrust in clearly identifiable rhythms, rhythms as solid and inescapable as Bach, Beethoven, and Brahms, as the distorted perspective of this floor, this light, this distance inside and out.

Now Bach yawed and steamed against her, the smell of the beast in her head, on her lips like some dry unguent, his huge body seeking, seeking, humped and breathing, gigue and largo and then subsiding, guiding himself away from her, the turgid genitals of the metronomic bear refracted in the shadows, those shadows already diminishing as Bach moved slowly from her in an odd, abbreviated limp, humping his way into the darkness. The shadows seemed lifeless even in motion, even as she seemed lifeless there on the wood of the floor.

In this silence, in this momentary partition, she thought she might be spared for a while, that Bach had now had his ceremonial fill and that Beethoven and Brahms were in the upper room, casting circles of darkness, silent beyond bearish grunts and small explosions of fathomless feeling, but even as she turned in this moment's relief, moved to gather the ragged blankets, to press that sleeve of insubstantial protection against herself, she felt them eased from her grasp and then Brahms, a huge, sordid mass was settling himself against her. Brahms: the autumnal bear, the bear of sneezes and sighs and small, absent groans, passion expended, fallen desire and she, too, groaned with the futility, the hopelessness of the bear's attributed despair as on her stomach he cast circles with a paw, then clumsy in wintry desire straddled her at last. Sinking slightly beneath the bear, resigned to assist as much as possible; unlike the others Brahms seemed to her to appreciate some kind of gesture, to have a sense of her presence and collaboration whereas the others, so locked into their own spasms and black rhythms, gave no sense of recognition or response at all. Snorts, sighs, the press of fur against her as she raised her hands, grasped the bear to draw him to a kind of crooning concentration as deep underneath the fur the small shudders, foreshadowed expenditure and then the bear's yelp, a human sound, a high, girlish shriek as he rolled away from her to lie, streaked by light, a wheezing heap: damp fur, sweat, soot, and for her again that dim shudder within her thighs, sensibility risen and draining from her just as she had drained from this house that which she had found before her.

She must have found something before her, must have been outside this house at one time, brought into it by accident of desire or curiosity now denied recollection: there was a past beyond and before this house, that smell, those shudders creeping like insects up and down her helpless legs, thighs, spread and spraddled, and she would have wept, great groaning tears against the wood, wood pressed to her lips, splinters like the wafer of God himself between her teeth, but here there was if not godlessness then the orbit of no salvation, here was the constellation, the great cross of heat, sour stink, black upon black upon fur upon flesh; nothing and everything, here in this room. Reeking, aseptic cavern, drawn and enthralled and diminished like the vessel that drains but is not emptied, there must have been *something* prior to this but it was closed to her now, closed forever like the doors of nascence, slammed like the gates of death on the yearning faces of the living: there is no going forward nor back, there is nothing. This is what is: this floor, these animals, the faint metallic scent of her own fluid, her body pinned in rags and speckled with old blood; and the door; and the light.

Brahms sobbed in a corner, again she reached for the blankets but the great sounds of imminence flooded the room and she knew before the collision that Beethoven, the most jolting and demoniac of the three, had come to seek in her his own fulfillment; Beethoven of the sudden, shuddering strokes, the silences, the storms, the great uneven swings of the body: the one she feared most in those broken unleashings of spine and heat grabbing her, grabbing her, the alternating cycles of some unknowable need seizing the hammer and tongs of the bear's body as it rammed against her and this, now, was the present, the animal against her, great in its need but curiously empty and tentative for all that; at the core the same uncertainty and brokenheartedness of Brahms but the shell was hard, hard, and she felt Beethoven pass through, over, above her like a storm, his hoarse grunts of emission, and she thought, eyes closed, *no more, no more* as she sank beneath fur, paws, breath, spasm, eaves, and darkness of the house collapsing around her and all around the darkening trot of the beasts as at some time later or perhaps this was earlier—smashed chronology, chronology smashed—they gathered to confer.

It was the feast she remembered, if memory gave her any gifts at all: some telescoping of circumstance found her seated high in the room, a table of fruits and desserts before her, all of the spices and jellied treats and cakes smeared lascivious with icing spread on a table the size of an altar, a table larger than any she had ever seen and she leaned toward that feast, thinking *I want this,* the food enormous in her hand, her hand spreading to encompass the feast entire: and in the moment before enjoyment, before even its possibility she heard them: there at the far side of the room, their small, luminescent eyes fixed upon her, the shaggy blackness of their fur not harbinger but frankest truth: and the seizure of breath, the cakes toppled, the fruit rolling and smashing as she rolled and smashed, pulped and tore, juices everywhere as in that new posture of dreadful and fixed attention they came, one by one, upon her, for the first of an endlessness of times.

Reaching for Brahms' tail as he rooted and muttered around her, lifting herself to some less strenuous accommodation, she felt that she in some way was sinking toward some kind of new, ursine splendor, had somehow—by pain, by terror, by the pink pity of her ravaged limbs—dissolved the barrier between herself and the beast atop her. Picking and poking at the secret heart of the great animal she found herself served as well as serving, become more than sheer receptacle: it was a kind of way out, perhaps: it was the method of escape that sinks one more fully into the pit, and as the bear commenced its familiar, groaning adumbration of expenditure she shouted something, hoarse and guttural, *caw* like the bark of an animal, something before language which was itself language and gripping that fur tried to come *up* with Brahms even in the bear's descent: and the long, pivoting drop which in its suspension and calamitous nature seemed in some way to mimic her confused ideas of escape, to *be* escape: go farther in: become: belong. Sunk into slivers, vaulted into light, she felt herself as one with Brahms even as the seizure squirted to the expected silence and the bear shambled away as if she did not exist at all.

The dream of the feast: their waiting eyes.
She waited, too.
All feasts are one.

In the rapid metronomic shudderings of Bach, she now found—earlier or later, but *now*—that some deepened surge of her own entrails, her own wordless wants was smoothed, engaged to rhythmic response by the motions of the bear and so it was no surprise at all when, yielding in sudden spasm, Bach broke from that complex rhythm and, balancing perilously on one paw, began a fragmented, syncopated movement which she first accommodated and then seemed to pass through, as light passes through a window, as semen passes through the tubing flesh and in that passing she ascended, risen as Bach, like Brahms, fell to snuffling and somehow troubled silence beside her, before himself rising to shamble away in unaccustomed ursine muttering.

And now she, beyond language but not gesture, beckoned

from the floor to Beethoven, beckoned in the light: *Come on,* she said to the beast, *come on then, you too* and again the clasp, the enclosure, the idea bursting in her mind: becoming one with them, grunting and heaving as Beethoven grunted and heaved, her own fur rising in small shreds and hackles as she rotated her knees, her long scarred open legs against the spiteful silence of the bear against her, the gigantic hammer of the bear against her, and this time she took it without a cry, without sound at all until Beethoven's own grunt of sudden and arrhythmic expenditure from which he fell as the others had fallen, shambled as they had shambled, sat now as they sat: staring at her, clumps of soot and sweat, muzzles uplifted as if to scent on the air the smell of her change and she watched them back, watched those brooding and immobile shapes as if she were in control of this situation, which in no real sense could ever be the case. She had abdicated all control in her greed for the feast: very well. Let greed be her master, then; let escape be entrance; let in be furthest in of all.

She had entered in curiosity and hunger, bedazzled by that unexpected house in the shattered woods, untroubled by the warnings of those with whom she had traveled before she had embarked, alone, on this more rigorous journey; and in what measure had they cared, to allow her the journey at all? And so the door, the house, the feast on the table one soaring poem of satiation: *this: here: take: eat:* and reaching beyond the sweetmeats, reaching toward some gorging fulmination which would have been, she knew, as close to ecstasy as she would ever come in the lonely and desperate life which was all that had been granted her, in that reach and grasp she had heard only the marveling thunder of her heart, that aching engine of greed in the presence of fulfillment: but she had not gone far enough, it seemed, had wanted but not fully, had reached but not taken, grasped, eaten, become: had only raised her eyes to see their eyes, little and bright, empty and full, to hear above the bewildered crooning of her own empty breath their breath murmurous, the sour and tangible entry into the world of the door, the floor, the light, the slivers, the odd varying rhythms of the beasts. You wanted to be filled? their postures asked her as they came upon her. Then *be* filled. To bursting.

But that was the secret, was it not? After all? The floor,

yes, the slivers and the pains, yes, but yes, too, her own new knowledge, sieved from degradation, obtained from going all the way in: take the bears, receive them, *be* a bear, the Queen of the Bears, the queen of the magic forest and the empty house, daughter of the night born to gambol in stricken and ecstatic pleasure with those three refracted selves restored to her through pain: the autumn, the pedant, and the hammer, all three dense with need, her own need, her own greed as she raised herself on her elbows, there on the floor, there at the feast, and she bared her stained and filthy teeth to say *Come: come to me now,* and as if in their first true moment of attention came the hawking groans, the motions of the bears: turning, first toward one another, then to form a circle, a unit, one lumbering and dreadful mass as all three, as one, advanced upon her: to receive her benediction: to pour and fill and to become.

URSUS TRIAD, LATER
Kathe Koja and Barry N. Malzberg

Fiction grants us monsters, constructs, masks—to explain, to deflect, to deny those actions, those thoughts and longings we feel but feel to be intolerable—as sex grants us roles to play, positions to assume: but in both arenas need is the only gospel: *feed me,* says the beast, and so we do.

We are Pound's pallid leash-men, and all the beasts are one.

Joe Haldeman is the author of the novels *Worlds, Worlds Apart,* and *Worlds Enough and Time.* He also wrote the award-winning novel, *The Forever War* and the recently published *1968.* His short fiction is collected in *Infinite Dreams, Dealing in Futures,* and *Feedback.* He has recently finished the novels *The Coming* and *Forever Peace.* His short fiction has appeared in various science fiction magazines and in *Omni* and *Playboy* and his poetry has appeared in *Harper's Magazine* and in *Omni.* He has won the Hugo Award, the Nebula Award, the World Fantasy Award, the Ditmar Award (Australian), and the Rhysling Award for his novels, short fiction, and poetry. He lives in Florida and Massachusetts.

Jane Yolen is the author of more than 100 books for children, teenagers, and adults, including *Sister Light, Sister Dark, White Jenna, Cards of Grief, Tales of Wonder, Briar Rose,* and *Touch Magic: Essays on Fantasy and Fairy Tales.* Her most recent works are (for children) *Here There Be Dragons, Good Grizelle, The Girl in the Golden Bower,* and *The Wild Hunt.* Her short fiction has appeared in *The Year's Best Horror* and in *The Year's Best Fantasy and Horror.* Yolen is also editor of her own imprint with the book publisher Harcourt, Brace, and has edited anthologies, including most recently, *Xanadu 3.* She and her husband have homes in Massachusetts and Scotland and travel between them often.

SEXTRATERRESTRIALS

JOE HALDEMAN AND
JANE YOLEN

THIS STRANGE LITERARY ARTIFACT IS THE BASTARD CHILD OF cyberspace and formal poetry. Jane Yolen and Joe Haldeman both talk to their readers and other writers via the GEnie Science Fiction Bulletin Board. Both of them are novelists who write a bit of poetry on the side—or poets who write novels because, as Willy Sutton noted, "that's where they keep the money."

The electronic conversation got around to "challenge" poems, where one poet gives the other one a subject and a set of constraints. Then, to be fair, the challenging poet does one herself.

It started this way:

Okay, Joe: let's see.... Interspecial marriage love poem, at least three of the following words need to be used (and one of them in an unusual way): centerfold, pouch, larder, ruby, increment, sacrament, moon, engorge. A specific time period. The poem to be in a rhymed, traditional format (sonnet, villanelle, etc.) and not more than twenty-five lines or less than eight.

Want to play?

Haldeman's response was this:

To the marriage of two kinds

On either of our worlds our love would be
obscene. But on free Ariel the hymns
of marriage play in any key.
              Your three
breasts, the changing number of your limbs,
the slippery centerfold that is the nexus
of our love—my human sacraments
never could apply. Your many sexes
would confuse the law; our love incense
the natives.
         But on Ariel our marriage can
have no impediments. For the space
of one moon's wax and wane, we are man
and something. Let us move apace.

Let them tut, and mutter "Apples, oranges"—
I measure time by how a body changes.

Jane Yolen came back with this:

Intermarriage

As I slid down the aisle, he woke
To stretch inside my wedding pouch

Like an odalisque upon a couch
Posed for the artist's final stroke.
Lardered there since birth,
My husband, child, and final meal
Engorges on my blood, my weal.
He is my dowry, goods, and worth.

Who could have guessed the embryo
Found in the egg beyond the stars
Would give us back a world once ours
Near lost when birthrates fell so low.
The midwife by the altar now does wait
To help me bear the meal that is my mate.

Then Jane whacked Joe with another gauntlet—

If you are up for it, another poetic challenge to go along with
the first. This time a human involved (somehow) in another
species' sexual activity—observer or commentator or involved
in the act but not the actual other partner. Use at least two
color words, one word from nature, and a set amount of time.
Again the poem needs to be in a traditional rhymed pattern,
but NOT a sonnet. Oh yes—there should be a pun somewhere
in the poem, though it can be quite disguised and may be a
second language pun.

—so he wrote this one:

Sex on the Planet of the Trees

At first I didn't realize
that they were having sex at all!
It rather took me by surprise,

in that treetop shopping mall . . .
no one less well trained could see
that they were having sex at all

(hard to tell the "she" from "he").
She turned pink and held his hand—
no one less well trained could see

that both appendages were glands!
He turned blue and sighed because
she turned pink and touched his hand;

in a moment's pregnant pause
she'd made a father out of him.
He turned blue and sighed because

she'd knocked him up. They looked so prim,
at first I didn't realize
she'd made a father out of him . . .
it rather took me by surprise.

Jane responded to that terzanelle with a villanelle—

First Contact/Second Coming

I came upon the mating pair in pain,
As, ravenous, they fucked themselves apart.
I called an SOS, but all in vain.

Their golden blood was salty, like their rain,
A potpourri of sex, now sweet, now tart.
They seemed to be a mating pair in pain.

Yet neither one was by that mating slain.
They fought, they fucked through skin and bone and heart.
I called an SOS, but all in vain.

Still watching, I twice filled, and then was drained.
In alien engagements that I chart
I come, with all such mating pairs, in pain.

What sings through red blood, courses to the brain
When watching partners cannot take a part.
I called an SOS, but all in vain.

Such voyeuristic voyages make plain
The moment when first contact can first start.
I came upon that mating pair in pain
And called my SOS, but through a vein.

Finally, Joe moved to even up the score—

Okay; I guess it's time for me to issue a challenge. A rhymed poem with nine stanzas, describing an alien sex act that is not being performed for procreation or (primarily) pleasure. The first and last stanzas are introduction and summation; each of the middle (presumably short) stanzas concerns one of these seven senses: sight, hearing, taste, touch, smell, interoceptivity (thirst, hunger, pain, nausea, suffocation), and proprioceptivity (equilibrium or kinesthesia), in any order. Alien POV.

This was Jane's—

SEX AMONG THE ABOS

*Sex among the Abo creatures
On this planet has strange features.
There are seven in each act;
Sex in bed is tightly packed.*

*Creature one is there to glom,
Aboriginal Peeping Tom.*

*Creature two can hear them come,
Like the sanding of a drum.*

*Creature three licks up the mess.
Can't have cum upon a dress.*

*Creature four does all the stroking,
Rubbing, tapping, touching, poking.*

*Creature five sits at the head,
Sniffing pheromones in bed.*

*Creature six can't catch its breath,
Fainting at each little death.*

*Creature seven feels them all,
With its back against the wall.*

We, of course, deplore the notion
Sex is heat and light and motion.

Sex is done inside the head
With a solemn five in bed!

—and Joe replied with this:

Come, talk

It's time you see:
I have to get this thing across to you:
those weird "human" creatures sometimes do
make sense. But look: the twitching they call sex
has no familiar causes or effects!
Attend to me:

I slide out into position.
You flex and choose a posture
that prepares you for coition;

selecting (from six) the one aperture,
that carries the sweet reek of power,
that almost-rotting allure,

and open it wanton wide. Your flower
of wet flesh puckers and throbs. A drop
spatters me. I tongue it and taste the sour

invitation and hunger to fill up
your hunger. Now give me that small sign
for us to merge and meet. The very top

of your eyestalk grows rigid. I align
tentacle to flower, concentrate, struck
with your hungry beauty. Then intertwine
six and six, and hear you start the long suck
from deep inside me to deep inside you.
If humans only knew the one true fuck

we could talk to them. But what humans do
is feel each other's bodies and excrete
dumb juices. Not like the way I flow to you.

Hard to say
if they can know each other well at all
without this flow. They stand and call
out noises based on patterns in their minds.
Hardly ever taste or smell. And just plain blind
to DNA.

Joyce Carol Oates is the author, most recently, of the collection, *Haunted: Tales of the Grotesque*, the Pen/Faulkner Award–nominated novel, *What I Lived For*, and *Zombie*. Her short work has appeared in *Omni*, *Playboy*, *The New Yorker*, *Harper's Magazine*, *The Atlantic*, as well as in literary magazines and in anthologies such as *Architecture of Fear*, *Dark Forces*, *Metahorror*, *Little Deaths*, *Ruby Slippers*, *Golden Tears*, and *The Year's Best Fantasy and Horror*.

We all possess male and female sides to our nature whether we like it or not, and repressing either side can cause harm to the self and to others. Oates has written several stories about women whose subconscious desires burst into consciousness through dreaming. "The Dream-Catcher" is about confronting the alien in oneself.

THE DREAM-CATCHER

JOYCE CAROL OATES

AS SOON AS SHE SAW IT, SHE KNEW SHE HAD TO HAVE IT.

There amid the finely wrought silver and turquoise jewelry, the hand-tooled leather goods, glazed earthenware pottery and baskets and coarse-woven fabrics in the Paiute Indian Reservation gift shop at Pyramid Lake, Nevada, the curious item seemed to leap out at Eunice's eye: no more than four inches in diameter, an imperfect circle made of tightly woven dried vines or branches threaded with small filmy feathers. An artifact of some kind, exquisitely fashioned, its colors, like most of the colors of the handmade items in the shop, predominantly brown, beige, black. Eunice found herself staring at it, and there, suddenly, it lay in the palm of her hand—virtually weightless. Remarkable! *Dream-Catcher* the printed label explained. It was so dry Eunice feared it might crack in her fingers. When she lifted it to examine it more closely, noting how the interior of the woven branches was a net, or web, braided with leather thread, in the center of which a tiny agate-like stone dully gleamed, the filmy feathers came alive, stirred by her breath. The feathers, too, were beautiful, finely marked, streaks and speckles of dark brown like strokes of a water-colorist's brush on a fawn-colored background.

Seeing Eunice's interest in the *dream-catcher,* the Indian proprietor of the store explained to Eunice that it was a gift given only to those who were "much loved"—especially to be hung over a cradle or a crib. "The spiderweb inside catches the good dreams, but the bad dreams—no. Guaranteed!" He called out affably to Eunice, as if speaking to a child. Presumably a Paiute Indian, he was a man of vigorous, muscular middle age, who wore a faded black T-shirt, faded jeans, and a hand-tooled leather belt with a brass eagle buckle; his graying black thinning hair was caught in a loose, careless ponytail that gave him a disheveled yet playful look. His forehead was veined and knobby—scarred?—as if vexed with thought and the voice of exaggerated good cheer in which he spoke to Eunice, as to other customers, verged on mockery. From an exchange Eunice had overheard between him and a previous customer she gathered he was a Vietnam veteran. Yet he managed to smile at most of his customers as he rang up their purchases; he certainly smiled at Eunice.

"Yes ma'am!—the good dreams are caught for you," the Indian said, handing over Eunice's fragile *dream-catcher* in a paper bag, "—and the bad dreams go away. You hang it over your bed, O.K.?—even if you don't believe, something will happen."

"Thank you," Eunice said. "I'll do that."

Eunice was not so young as she appeared, but with her pale, faded-gold hair and her smooth, fair skin and large, intelligent gray eyes she was an attractive woman, and she was alone. She smiled at the Indian proprietor though seeing that his smile held no warmth. His lips were drawn back tightly from discolored, uneven teeth, and his eyes, agate-shiny, recessed beneath his blemished forehead, were fixed upon her insolently. As if to say *I know you. Even if you don't know me.* Eunice, who was not accustomed to being treated impolitely, still less rudely, maintained her poise, and her forced smile; leaving the store, she felt the man's gaze drop to her ankles and rise rapidly, assessingly up her slender figure. She did not glance back when he called after her, "Come back again soon, lady, eh?" with exaggerated good cheer.

Even if you don't believe. Something will happen.

When Eunice returned to Philadelphia, to her Delancey Street brownstone, she impulsively fastened the *dream-catcher* to the foot of her bed, and lay down to sleep. Exhausted from the plane flight, her brain assailed by images, impressions. Her twelve-day visit to the Southwest, to Nevada and Arizona, was the first extended vacation she'd taken in years. How vivid, many of its moments!—the ceramic blue sky, the extraordinary complex, ravaged-looking beauty of the mountains, the dun colors, shimmering salt flats, whitish silence of Death Valley . . . Yet, travel itself fatigued her, and bored her. There was no personal identity to it. No sense of mission.

Eunice was thirty-seven years old, unmarried, vice provost at the Philadelphia Academy of Fine Arts. Her Ph.D. was from Harvard; her dissertation, subsequently published as a book, was titled *Aesthetics and Ethics: A Postmodernist Debate.* Early on, as a girl, Eunice had hoped for a life that would be a public life and not a domestic life, involved in some way with the arts. She had been the only child of older parents, her father a popular philosophy professor at the University of Pennsylvania, and she had a memory of herself as a shy, precociously intelligent child, pale hair hanging heavily about her narrow face. The odd mixture of vanity and insecurity of the "special" child. Yet, disconcertingly mature as a young girl, Eunice seemed hardly to have grown much older in adulthood—a common phenomenon among the precocious. Now in young middle age, she still retained a slender, lithe girlishness; her attractive face unlined, her manner cheerful; she possessed an air of innocent authority that suited her as a professor at Swarthmore, and subsequently as an administrator there, and elsewhere. Her reputation among her professional colleagues was for exceptionally fine, detailed work; she was prized, if perhaps sometimes exploited, for her generous, uncomplaining good nature. It was said of her, not unkindly, that Eunice Pemberton lived for her work, through her work, in her work. If she had a personal life, it was kept very private. If she'd had lovers, she never spoke of them.

Nor was she a religious, certainly not a superstitious, woman. She'd become moderately interested in the culture of the Native Americans indigenous to the area of the Southwest she'd visited, but it was no more than a moderate interest, an intellectual's speculation. Since early adolescence, Eunice had been incapable of believing in anyone or anything "supernatural": she'd inherited from her mild-mannered, skeptical father a distrust of faith, which is to say the objectification of mankind's wish fantasies into codified religions, institutions. What was skepticism but simple common sense?—sanity? An island of sanity in a seething fathomless ocean of irrationality, and often madness. The contemporary world of militant, fanatic nationalism, fundamentalist religions, intolerance.

Something will happen. Even if you don't believe.

Eunice had affixed the feathered *dream-catcher* to the foot of her bed in the hope that it might stimulate her to dream, for she rarely dreamed; her nights were deep, silent pools of water, featureless, rippleless. Yet, so far as she knew, she did not dream that night, either. Her sleep was unnaturally heavy, like a weight pressing against her chest and threatening her with suffocation. Her breasts ached; she woke several times, her nightgown damp with perspiration. In the early morning, before sunrise, she woke abruptly, eager to get up. Her eyes were sore as if she'd been staring into the desert sun and her mouth was badly parched. And there was an odor in her bedroom as of something humid, overripe, like rotted fruit—a faint odor, not entirely disagreeable. *And so—did I dream? Is this what a dream is?*

Eunice quickly showered, and dressed, and would have forgotten the *dream-catcher* except, as she made her bed, the shimmering feathers drew her attention. How like a bird's nest it looked—she hadn't quite seen that, before. She touched the cobweb of leather twine at its center, and the glass gem which was like an eye. No dream, good or bad, had been caught in it. Still, the *dream-catcher* was an exquisite thing, and Eunice was glad she'd bought it.

In the kitchen, Eunice heard a strange sound, like mewing, or whimpering, from the rear of the house, and went uneasily to investigate. (Eunice had inherited the four-story Delancey Street brownstone from her widowed mother; it was in an old, prestigious Philadelphia neighborhood within walking distance of the Penn campus, and only a ten-minute drive to Eunice's office at the Philadelphia Academy of Fine Arts. A handsome property, coveted by many, though bordering on an area with an ever-increasing crime rate.) In the winterized porch, on an antiquated sofa-swing, partly hidden beneath an old blanket, was what appeared to be a living creature—at first Eunice thought it must be a dog; then, panicked, she thought it must a child. "What?—what is it?" Eunice stammered, transfixed in the doorway. The rear porch was shut off from the house, rarely used. A smell as of decayed leaves, overripe peaches was so strong here, Eunice gagged.

The creature, neither an animal nor fully human, was about two feet long, and curled convulsively upon itself. Its head was overlarge for its spindly body, and covered in long thin damp black hairs. Its skin was olive-dark, yet pallid, like curdled milk; its face was wizened, the eyes shut tight, sunken. How hoarsely it breathed, as if struggling for oxygen!—there was a rattling sound in its throat, as of loose phlegm. Eunice thought, *It's feverish, it's dying.* Her breasts ached, the nipples especially, as if she were a nursing mother in the presence of her infant.

Eunice tried to think: should she run outside, get help from one of her neighbors? Should she call an ambulance?—the police? There were friends and colleagues she might call, a married cousin in Bryn Mawr . . . *But what would I say? What is this—visitation?* She felt a stab of pity for the creature, struggling so desperately to live; she understood that it was starving, and that there was no one else in all the world, except her, to feed it.

Now its eyes opened, and Eunice saw that they were beautiful eyes, whether animal or human: large, dark, tremulous with tears, with an agate sheen, recessed beneath the oddly bony forehead.

Aloud Eunice murmured, "Poor thing—!"

Knowing then that she had no choice: she had to nourish the helpless creature that had fallen into her care, however she could. She could not allow it to die. So she hurried to bring it water, at first in a glass, which was impractical; then soaked in a sponge, which worked fairly well, as if the creature (toothless, with tender, pink gums) knew by instinct how to suck a sponge. Then she soaked the sponge in milk, which was even better. "Don't be afraid, you won't die," Eunice murmured, "—I won't let you die." Nursing frantically, the creature mewed and whimpered, its thin hands, very like forepaws, kneading against Eunice's arms. Eunice felt again, with painful sharpness, that sensation in her breasts as if they were swollen with milk.

So an hour passed, swiftly. By the time the creature had drunk its full and dropped off to sleep, Eunice had soaked the sponge in milk nearly a dozen times. Her breath was coming quickly and her skin was as damp and feverish as the creature's own; she heard herself laugh, excited, frightened. *Yet I've done the right thing: I know it.*

This, then, was Eunice's strategy on that first day: she left the slumbering creature on the porch swing, the door to the backyard ajar and the inner door locked, and drove, as usual, to work at 8:20 A.M. *It will leave, the way it came.* The day was mild for mid-March, snow melting on pavement; an air of reprieve after one of the most severe Philadelphia winters in memory. The poor thing would not suffer from cold, Eunice reasoned. She was certain it would be gone when she came home.

What was wholly unexpected then, as it was to be during the course of subsequent weeks, was how adroitly Eunice shifted her attention to her duties as vice provost. As if there had not been an astonishing visitation at her home!—an inexplicable intrusion into her life! At the most, during her long, busy day at the Academy of Fine Arts, it might have been observed that Eunice Pemberton was uncharacteristically distracted; several times, during a meeting with the provost and other administrators, she'd had to ask politely, "Yes?—what did you say?" When colleagues inquired after her vacation she said, "It was fine, very—fine. Picturesque." And her voice trailed off, her eyes vague, blinking. Eunice was thinking of the enormous desert sky, of Pyramid Lake and the shabby dwellings of the Paiute Reservation and the handicraft store where she'd bought the *dream-catcher.* She was thinking of the ponytailed Indian with the insolent eyes. *Come back again soon, eh!*

In fact, Eunice was grateful that the day was so long, and so complicated. At 4:30 P.M. there was a visiting art historian from Yale who lectured on the iconography of Hieronymus Bosch, and following the lecture there was a reception in his honor; that evening, there was a dinner at the home of the president of the Academy, for selected administrators, faculty, and donors, from which Eunice could not slip away until 10: 30 P.M. When she returned to Delancey Street it was to hurry trembling to the rear porch, where she saw—now was it with relief, or disappointment?—that the swing was empty, the soiled blanket lay on the floor, the strange creature was gone. As Eunice had anticipated, it had left by the back door, as it had arrived.

Quickly Eunice shut the rear door, and made certain it was firmly locked.

What had the creature been?—a raccoon, perhaps? Suffering some sort of mange, hairless. Prematurely wakened from its winter hibernation. Desperate for food. Lucky for Eunice, it had not been rabid.

And so for the second night Eunice slept with the *dream-catcher* at the foot of her bed. Somehow she'd forgotten it was there, and as she drifted off to sleep, remembering it, with a pang of apprehension, she was incapable of getting up to remove it, her limbs paralyzed in sleep.

Even if you don't believe. Something will happen.

Again her sleep was heavy, ponderous. Her head ached, her heart beat erratically and painfully. Yet this was not dreaming—was it? Someone, or something, was in the bed with her, beneath the bedclothes where no one had ever been. A short, stunted creature, with a veined, knobby forehead, jagged teeth. A bat, clambering upon her. Yes, it had wings, leathery webbed wings, and not arms—it was a bat, yet also a man. Eunice shook her head violently from side to side—*No! no!*— but she could not cast off the loathsome creature. It—he— was pressing his mouth against hers, slick with saliva. And rubbing himself against her breasts, belly, thighs. A rubbery rod, a penis, sprouting from his groin—as soon as Eunice became aware of it, to her horror and revulsion it rapidly hardened, like a plastic hose into which water began to flow. *No!— leave me alone!* In disbelief, her eyes open and blind, Eunice felt the creature prodding between her thighs, forcing her thighs apart; felt the penis like a living thing, blind, groping, seeking an opening into her body. Eunice screamed but it was too late—a sudden sexual sensation rose swift and needlelike in her loins. She grunted, and shuddered, and threw the creature off—except, as she woke, it vanished. It was gone. Alone, panting, Eunice sat up in bed, knuckles pressed against her mouth. Her heart was beating so violently she feared it would burst.

About her, in the handsome old mahogany four-poster bed Eunice had inherited from her parents, the sheets were damp and rumpled. A sharp odor as of decaying peaches lifted from them.

Now you know you've had a dream, now you know what a dream is—yet, early in the morning, waking again before dawn from a thin, wretched sleep, Eunice understood that the hideous bat-creature in her bed had not been a dream.

She heard him, downstairs: an intermittent whining, murmurous singsong. He was in the rear porch, or possibly in the kitchen.

Quietly, slipping on her robe, Eunice made her way downstairs. Her hair was sticky against her forehead and the nape of her neck; her body was covered in an acrid film of perspiration; the tender skin of the insides of her thighs chafed. Yes, he was in the kitchen: the strange sound was coming from there. Eunice hesitated a moment before pushing open the door, boldly entering. *This is my house, my life. He's come to me. Why should I be fearful!*

This time, Eunice saw clearly that the creature was human: batlike about the head, with a monkey's long spindly arms, but obviously human. And male.

Obviously, male.

Eunice had surprised him in the act of pawing open a box of uncooked macaroni. He'd climbed up onto the kitchen counter and had managed to open one of the cupboard doors.

They stared at each other. The creature was crouched, but

Eunice could see he had grown to about the size of a ten- or eleven-year-old boy. He was starkly naked, his ribs showed, his chest rapidly rising and falling as he panted. His head was disproportionately large for his shoulders; his legs were stunted, bowed as if from malnutrition; his skin was olive-dark, with that pallor beneath, and covered in fine, near-invisible black hairs like iron filings. His shrunken genitalia hung shyly between his thighs like skinned fruit. His eyes were fierce, shining, frightened, defiant.

Eunice said, in a voice of surprising calm, "Poor thing!— you're starving."

Never in her life had Eunice felt such a sensation of pity, compassion, urgency. As the naked creature, crouched on her counter, made a bleating, pleading sound, she felt her breasts ache, throbbing with the need to nurse.

But it was solids Eunice fed the creature, for he had teeth now, however rudimentary, set sparely and unevenly in his tender gums. Eunice wrapped him in a quilt, found an old pair of furry slippers for his knobby-toed feet, sat him in the break-fast nook (which alarmed him initially—his instinct was to resist being cornered, trapped) and spoon-fed him three soft-boiled eggs, most of a pint container of cottage cheese, a tangerine. How hungry he was!—and what pleasure in sating that hunger! His eyes brimmed with tears, like Eunice's own, as rapidly he chewed and swallowed, chewed and swallowed. Eunice said, "Don't ever be frightened again! Nothing bad will happen to you. I promise. I promise with my life."

Eunice's voice fairly vibrated with excitement yet she spoke practicably, calmly. Her years of authority as professor and administrator stood her well in such an emergency.

As before, Eunice left the creature sleeping on the old sofa-swing in the porch, for he was resistant to coming farther into the house, even into the living room where it was warm. Groggy after his feeding, he seemed virtually to collapse, to become boneless, very like a human infant as Eunice half carried him out onto the porch and laid him gently on the sofa-swing. How astonished she would have been, as a girl growing up in this house, sitting on this swing years ago and reading one of her innumerable books, to imagine what the future held: what fellow creature would one day lie on this very piece of furniture! Beneath the quilt the creature curled up at once, knees to chest, face pushed against knees, sinking into the deep, pulsating sleep of an infant. For many minutes Eunice crouched beside him, her hand against his bony forehead, which seemed to her overwarm, feverish. Unless it was she who was feverish.

I promise. With my life.

Frequently he was gone when Eunice returned from the Academy and forlornly she walked through the empty house calling, "Where are you? Are you hiding?"—her manner stern, to disguise the abject sound of worry. To disguise her helplessness—so female. There was no name for the creature she could utter save *you*; to herself, she thought of him as *he, him.*

In the kitchen, she might find the remains of his feeding, for by degrees he'd become capable of feeding himself, though messily: a gnawed rind of cheddar cheese might be lying on the floor, part of a banana (he had not yet learned to peel bananas, though Eunice had tried to instruct him—he bit into both fruit and peel, and chewed as best he could), an emptied container of raw hamburger. Though Eunice had not yet succeeded in coaxing him into a bathtub, for the sound of running water, perhaps the very smell of water, as well as the confinement of a bathroom, threw him into a panic, it seemed to her that his odor was less defined now. At any rate, she had ceased to notice it.

(Though one day, at the Academy, a colleague who had entered Eunice's office quite visibly glanced around, sniffing, puzzled—did *she* notice the elusive scent? Without breaking their train of conversation, Eunice unobtrusively rose from her desk and opened a window and the offensive odor vanished. Or so Eunice thought.)

By night he might suddenly reappear. One moment the brownstone was empty of all inhabitants save Eunice, the next—the creature was waiting in the shadows on the stairway landing, his eyes gleaming agate-bright and sly as she ascended into their beam; or he was gliding noiselessly, barefoot along the carpeted hall outside her bedroom. He'd learned to laugh, somehow—a low, guttural, thrilling chuckle. Thick black hairs now sprouted on his head, on his chest and beneath his arms; Eunice would never have looked, but knew that his pubic region bristled with such hairs. He was growing, maturing rapidly, nourished by her care. His shining eyes glanced level with hers. He could speak, not words exactly but sounds—"Eeee?—eeee? Eeeeeyah?" which Eunice believed she could interpret.

"Downstairs," Eunice would say. Pointing with her forefinger, so there could be no misunderstanding. "You're not to be *up here*. But *down there*."

Always at such times Eunice spoke sternly to the creature. He might choose to disobey her but he could not choose to misunderstand her, and Eunice knew that that was crucial.

Sometimes, ducking his head, he murmured, "Eeeee?—eeee—" and turned to rapidly descend the stairs, like a scolded dog. At other times, a rebellious dog, he threw back his head defiantly, stared at Eunice from beneath his bristling eyebrows, and drew his lips taut across his uneven teeth. Maintaining her poise Eunice said, "You hear me! You know perfectly well what I'm saying—*you!*"

With dignity then Eunice would brush past the creature, who stood long-armed and resistant, in shirt, slacks, sneakers Eunice had bought for him which he'd already outgrown: brushed past him coolly, and entered her bedroom, and shut the door firmly against him. It was a door with an old-fashioned bolt lock.

So long as Eunice was awake, there was no danger.

Often, she sat up in bed, reading, or working on reports and memos in longhand for her secretary at the Academy to type out on a word processor the next morning. She did not think of herself as an obsessive person, one driven by her work. There was a true pleasure in such nighttime concentration; the sense, at such times, of the world radically narrowed, shrunken to the size of the light that illuminated her bed. *I love and respect my work and that's why I'm good at it*—Eunice's father once surprised her with these words, and so it seemed to Eunice the same might be said of her as well, though she was not one for such pronouncements. *I love and respect my work and that's why I'm good at it.* Yet how ironic—a thorn in her heart—that the creature who shared her home with her, whose life she had saved, and continued to save, knew nothing of her outer, public, professional self. *And cares nothing. For why should he?*

At about 1:00 A.M., and inevitably by 2:00 A.M., Eunice's eyelids began to grow heavy. The room dissolved to shifting, eerily oscillating planes of light and shadow. There was a muffled *Eeeeee* sound somewhere close by, a faint scratching at the door. Eunice knew she was losing consciousness, and thus control; knew this was dangerous; yet could not forestall the process though she shook her head, slapped her cheeks, forced her eyes open wide. A tarry-dark tide rose about her, and in her.

The *dream-catcher* at the foot of her bed! During the day, she never thought of it—never thought to remove it; at night, it was too late.

So she sank into sleep. Helpless. And *he* took immediate advantage.

Brashly entering her bedroom, pushing the door open as if— there was no door, at all.

The creature was physically mature now. Of that there could be no question. However he presented himself by day, his *Eeeee? eeee? eeeyah?* bleating and pleading, by night he was far different. The size of an adult man, with compact, muscled arms, shoulders, thighs. Covered in coarse black hairs. His eyes glaring, he yanked the bedclothes off Eunice, despite her protests; he gripped her so tightly, she thought he would break her ribs. In the morning, her body would be covered in bruises. In oddly lovely patterns. He mouthed her breasts, which had grown abnormally tender, her nipples sensitive to the slightest touch as they had never before been in Eunice's life, her belly which was slick with perspiration, the secret flesh between her legs at which, at the age of thirty-seven, Eunice never once glanced, and rarely touched except to cleanse, and dry. *No. Stop. I hate this. This is not me!* Yet she found herself desperately embracing the creature, even as he penetrated her body, as a drowning person might embrace anyone, anything— Eunice's arms, her trembling legs, her ankles locked together, gripping his legs between hers. Sometimes, a scream awoke her—a woman's scream, high-pitched, helpless. Horrible to hear.

• • •

Eunice pushed at the bedclothes that were suffocating her, forced herself free. The bedside lamp was still burning. It might be only 1:35 A.M., it might be 4:00 A.M., the dead of night. The liquid silence of night. Utter unspeakable loneliness of night. The door to Eunice's bedroom was shut again, of course—locked.

Yet the bedclothes, and Eunice herself, smelled of *him*. Damp, disgusting. Vile. That overripe peachy odor. Eunice must shower to remove it from her, every pore, every hair follicle.

At the foot of the bed, attached to the rail, was the *dream-catcher*. Delicate as a bird's nest. Filmy feathers stirred by Eunice's agitated breath, it seemed to float upon darkness.

"Oh God. If there is a God. Help me."

There came the day in early May, at an Academy luncheon, the conversation paused, like a withheld breath, and, after a moment, Eunice became uneasily aware of everyone at the table, including the provost, looking at her. Had she been asked a question?—if so, by whom? Had she been daydreaming, distractedly stroking the underside of her jaw, which felt sore? The provost, a balding, kindly gentleman known to be grooming Eunice Pemberton to take his place when he retired, thereby to become the first female provost in the 170-year history of the Philadelphia Academy of Fine Arts, smiled, with pained solicitude, and, as if to spare Eunice further embarrassment, turned to another guest, and said, "And what do *you* think—?" and so, in a dreamlike blur and buzz, the moment passed.

Eunice, conscious of a terrible blunder, made a belated effort to listen; to be brightly attentive; to appear to be, in her colleagues' eyes, entirely normal—entirely herself. Yet: *not a one of you can guess what my life is! my secret life!* And in a rest room afterward she saw to her horror that there was an ugly bruise on the underside of her jaw—a lurid purplish orange, the hue of rotted fruit. How in God's name had she left the house that morning without noticing it?—had she not dared to glance into a mirror? She might have disguised the bruise somehow, might have tied a cheery bright scarf around her neck. Except now it was too late. Of course her colleagues had been staring at her.

They know.

But what is it they know?

It was in the early evening of that day, a mild, fragrant day in spring, that, on her way home from the Academy, Eunice stopped by a sporting goods store to purchase a hunting knife, with a stainless steel twelve-inch blade.

The shopkeeper smiled, asking Eunice if the knife was for her, if she was a hunter?—expecting her to say no, it's a gift, it's for my nephew, my sister's son, for certainly a woman like Eunice would not want, or need, a hunting knife—would she? But Eunice smiled in return, and said, quietly, "Yes, in fact, it *is* for me. I'm a hunter, too. I've been learning."

When Eunice let herself into the brownstone, it was to an empty house. You would think so. No sound, no murmurous muffled laughter—no creaking floorboards in the rear porch. Or on the stairs. Only the faintest smell of *him*—which might be mistaken for any slightly rotted, rancid kitchen smell.

You would think so.

He had been with her the night before, rudely and selfishly with her. Though she'd told *him* to remain downstairs—she'd been stern, and she'd been forthright. She was not a woman like so many women, even professional women, whose disapproval means approval; whose *no* means *yes*. But he'd paid no attention to her pleas, her words. From the start, he had not.

Yet perhaps the house *was* empty? Eunice no longer turned on the alarm system, for *he* had several times triggered it with his comings and goings. Instead she left lights burning in several rooms, and her radio on continuously. This, police recommended as a way of discouraging break-ins. So far, the simple strategy had worked.

Eunice walked slowly through the first floor of her house. If *he* was anywhere, it was likely to be the porch—but, no, the porch was empty this evening. The old sofa-swing, its floral canvas badly faded. The quilt Eunice had given him, now soiled, lying on the floor. And the smell of *him,* unmistakable.

The kitchen, too, was empty. The counters were clean and bare, as Eunice had left them; the sink was gleaming, as she'd left it. One of her outlets for nervous energy was cleaning, scouring her kitchen; her mother had always hired a maid for such work, but Eunice preferred to do it herself. Why invite a stranger into her life?—it was enough, that a stranger had come into her life unbidden.

The Formica top of the kitchen nook was clean, too. When *he* fed in the kitchen, *he* avoided that corner; only when Eunice was feeding him did he consent to sit there, Eunice close beside him.

Eunice was about to leave the kitchen when she noticed something gleaming on the floor—a small pile of gnawed chicken bones. And, kicked back alongside the refrigerator, part of an orange, which someone had bitten into, peeling and all. It was *his* way of eating, and Eunice shook her head in bemused dismay.

Animal. From the start. Hopeless.

Such shame!—she caressed her bruised jaw, ruefully.

Upstairs, Eunice entered her bedroom, sensing, in the split moment before the assault, that something was wrong, the very air into which she stepped seemed agitated; yet she wasn't quite prepared for the violence with which she was seized from behind, an unseen man's arms thrown about her torso, shaking her as if in fury—"Don't fight me, bitch!" Eunice dropped her handbag, her briefcase, the bag containing the hunting knife—she was on the floor herself, on her hands and knees, too astonished to be terrified. For it was not like *him* to attack her so roughly, with such evident hatred: it was not like *him* to wish to injure her. Kill her?

Eunice drew breath to scream. She was struck on the side of the head by a man's fist. She fell, half-conscious, lay on the carpet dazed and struggling to breathe and half-seeing a man's figure, a shadowy hulking figure, at her bureau, yanking open drawers, throwing things onto the floor and muttering furiously to himself, an inexplicable violence in his very presence and Eunice understood. *He will kill me, he will stomp me to death with no more conscience than he might stomp an insect to death,* she crawled to retrieve the paper bag that lay close by, she had the knife in her hand and pushed herself to her feet and rushed at him, this man she believed she knew yet had never seen before, taller than she by several inches, heavy in the shoulders, dark-skinned, turning to her astonished as with a manic strength she brought the knife blade down hard against the back of his neck. There was an immediate eruption of blood, the man screamed, a high womanish shriek, he tried in his desperation to shield himself with his outspread fingers from the plunging blade, but Eunice did not weaken, Eunice brought the knife down against him again, and again, his throat, his face, his upper torso, as he threw himself from her, turning in agony from her she stabbed into the nape of his neck, the top of his spine—sobbing, panting, ''You! you! you!'' not knowing what she did, still less where the super-human strength came from welling in her veins and muscles that allowed her to do it, except she must do it, it was time.

Hours later Eunice lifted her head, which throbbed with pain. There was something clotted in her vision. She smelled him, smelled it—Death?—that sweetish-sour, rotted odor—before she saw him. The body. The body he'd become.

She was in her bedroom. A man, a stranger, lay on the floor a few yards away. He was dead: clearly dead: the carpet was soaked with his blood, and there was a trail of blood, like an open artery, on an edge of the hardwood floor beside the wall. The man was a black man in his mid-thirties perhaps. He was wearing a dark nylon jacket, badly stained trousers, scuffed boots. He lay on the carpet on his side, in an attitude of child-like peace, or trust, his head lolling awkwardly on his shoulder, his bloodied mouth slack; he was looking away from Eunice through droopy, hooded eyes but she could see the curve of his thick nose, jaw, his wounded cheek—a stranger. It seemed clear that he'd been struck down in the act of yanking a drawer from her bureau; other drawers had been yanked out, and lay in a violent tumble of jewelry, lingerie, sweaters on the floor. The knife with its bloodied blade and handle lay on the carpet close by the body. You would think, seeing it there, that it belonged to the body.

Whose knife?—Eunice did not remember.

Except in a dream how she'd wielded it!—with what desperation, and passion.

There was a stillness here in this room that was the stillness of night. For now it *was* night. A dark tide rising about Eunice and the dead man both, gathering them in it, buoying them aloft. She would telephone the police, she would explain what she knew. *I had to do it, I had no choice.* She would not tell them what she knew also—that her life was over, her deepest life. Hers, and his.

On her feet now, swaying, unsteady, she went to her bed and took into her shaking hands the delicate, finely wrought thing fastened to the railing. The bird's nest, the Indian souvenir, whatever it was, with its woven branches, its intricate interior web, its filmy speckled feathers that stirred with her breath as if stirring with their own mysterious life.

The *dream-catcher.* Grown so dry and brittle, it broke suddenly in her fingers. And fell in pieces to the floor.

THE DREAM-CATCHER
Joyce Carol Oates

As I sit here, the dream-catcher is on a windowsill about two feet from me, smaller than the dream-catcher of my story, but as intricately fashioned, and quite exquisite. It was given to me by a stranger—an attractive, androgynous, *very* exotic stranger—when I was signing books in a bookstore in Washington, D.C. in the fall of 1993. People sometimes give me presents at such occasions, or mail things to me, but this object seems to have made an unusual impression on me, or on my psyche. I'm sure that, that night, in my hotel room, it caused me to dream unusually vivid dreams, since I remember walking in the middle of the night, and rapidly writing down ideas for stories; of these, two or three have found their way into actual stories, including "The Dream-Catcher," though it must be said that dream-originated stories are, for me, the most difficult of all to render into prose. The dream-suggestion seems truly to come from a stranger, a source not inside me, and often I have no clue what it might mean; nor any coherent plot; I'm left with a powerful sense of *emotion*—but it's abstract, mysterious.

I believe that the mysterious—the not-to-be-explained—is a key to our inner lives; to that part of our inner selves that has no sense of time past or time present or time future. We can contemplate and we can try to write about it, but we can never comprehend it. Always elusive, and tantalizing, it recedes before us like a desert mirage, and perhaps this very elusiveness is the subject about which we write, given finite dimensions.

Out of an actual *dream-catcher*, and a night, or nights, of dream fragments, the story "The Dream-Catcher" gradually emerged. I did not write the story for some time after the dreams, needing time to imagine a coherent structure for them, and an ostensible "theme." The story bears a glancing resemblance, at least in my eyes, to a story of mine called, "The Doll," written almost twenty years ago . . . a discovery I made some time after I'd written it.

What this might mean, I don't know. And I assume I'm better off not knowing.

Roberta Lannes lives in Los Angeles, where she works as a teacher, freelance
designer, and graphic artist. Her first published story appeared in the 1986 an-
thology *Cutting Edge.* Since then she has had stories published in the magazines
Iniquities, Fantasy Tales, and *Pulphouse* and in the anthologies *Lord John Ten,
Splatterpunks, Alien Sex, Still Dead, Ruby Slippers, Golden Tears, Best New
Horror,* and *The Year's Best Fantasy and Horror.* She is working on a novel called
The Hallowed Bed.

   On the surface of "His Angel," a really bad guy meets the perfect mate, repents
his evil ways, and is redeemed by a force greater than himself. Or, a misunderstood creep only wants nonjudgmental love—a mother figure—but can't really
hack it. Or, it's all just a case of faulty communication between two beings alien
to one another. . . .

HIS ANGEL

ROBERTA LANNES

FRANK GARLAND KNELT BY A MOUND OF SOIL, SCOOPED A
handful, and held it beneath his nose. He loved the smell of
fresh, moist earth. It recalled a youth of camping trips with
his father, playing in the mud with his older brother, and burying secret things. He chuckled. He hadn't grown up much in
thirty years. Here he was, still burying things that he didn't
want found. Before it was broken toys, uneaten food, and
pieces of his mother's jewelry. Now it was broken women.

   Standing, he let the dirt fall into the depression, nearly full.
He shoveled in the remaining loam and patted it down. There.

   As he reached up to pluck a leafy bough for scrabbling the
earth, he was distracted by a glint in the pearly gray sky. He
broke off the limb and stepped into a small clearing.

   Across the ravine, over the next ridge, a hang glider was
falling. He knew the thermals off the granite quarry below
often popped a glider up too fast for even the best aviator to

recover. Light bounced off the white wings as they crumpled like origami. The pilot tumbled and the wings came open a moment. Frank saw that it wasn't a guy wrapped in a polyester cocoon, but a woman dressed in flowing white. He blinked, then rubbed his eyes with his jacket sleeve. "Oh, Lord," he whispered, "it's an angel."

She fell into the forest, swallowed by a thicket of trees. Frank closed his eyes, in his mind marking the spot where she landed as just beyond the boundary of the quarry works. The road up the mountainside from where he stood would take him to the bridge a few miles down, then across to the gravel strip leading into the quarry works. He knew the patch of land where she touched down. He'd get there before anyone else. This angel was going to be *his*.

A cassette tape of Roy Buchanan, his guitar screaming "Country Boogie," filled the car. Frank drove in haste, warily watching the Sunday roads for errant traffic. He reached the gravel road quickly, sped up, his compact car shifting over the stones like a skier on icy snow. Past the quarry to a dirt road, into the forest, he turned his headlights on. The canopy of fir and evergreen blotted out the sun. His beams found a twisting path which slowed him down.

When he found the way blocked by fallen trees, he pulled over, his heart working like a jackhammer. He got out of the car to stand in the lush, still shade. His mind's eye was on the area where the angel had landed, and he would let that image guide him as he wended his way through the dense growth of the forest floor. He was feeling what his father had called the "feral hunting mechanism." Allowing himself to be led by pure sensation. A sensation of hunger, not for food but for something else: prey, love, release. It drove him forward, blinding him with an appetite he didn't understand.

After a while, Frank began to spin in the shadowy light. Sweat poured through his scalp, down his neck, into his shirt. She was there, not far, but his sense of direction had begun to elude him. The ground had flattened out. He was no longer near the ridgeline. He was lost. Frustration grew until he howled out loud. The sound came from a cavern of sheer anger, rising up with the power of a child's fear.

The sounds of animals scurrying away yanked him from his

rage. He told himself to breathe. Relax. Turning to his left, he headed toward a shaft of light a couple of hundred feet away. The ground began to slope and he knew he had found his direction again. As he neared the light, he felt the frustration pass into irritation then disappear as elation filled him.

"There you are," he whispered. He found her, resplendent on the mossy loam amidst ferns at the edge of an opening in the trees.

Frank slowed until he was just out of view, behind a tree. The shaft of light seemed focused on her. For a moment, Frank could swear he heard a choir of angels in the far distance. He stood there, watching, searching for signs she was alive. God was watching, too, he thought. Cautiously, he moved near.

Her wings were wrapped about her like a gossamer chrysalis. Up close, he saw that her wings weren't made of feathers, but long thin flaps of pearlescent white skin. The angel's face was turned toward the earth, her pale golden hair splayed against the ferns. Bare feet curled out from the bottom of her wings; the toes long, tapering to pink points.

He wiped his dirty hands on his jeans and reached out to touch her. As his fingertips alighted upon her wing, she quaked. Frank recoiled, then suddenly, without a warning of sorrow, fell to his knees weeping.

"Oh . . . my angel. God, please, don't let her die." A deep, barbed pain ripped forth from him, wrenching his body with spasms of anguish. He blubbered over her, a ten-year-old boy once again, mourning his father. Seeing him at the bottom of the cliff, his body twisted in ways for which it was not built. An accident. An act of God. He hadn't cried since. Or perhaps it was at his brother's funeral. He felt as weak and flimsy as a new leaf. His father would have told him to get a hold of himself. He had an angel to save.

All business, Frank began untangling the angel's hair from the foliage. He put his hand under her neck and turned her face up. Her skin was so pale, he thought she was dead. He put his dirty hand against her cheek, full of hope. She felt warm!

"Come on, angel, I'm just going to lift you up and carry you to my car. I won't hurt you." He worked his hands under her and swept her into his arms. Incredibly, she was almost weightless. When he'd carried Sharon down from his car just a couple of hours ago, she'd felt like a two-hundred-pound sack of flour. The angel was as light as a loaf of bread.

With her life in his hands, Frank moved stealthily toward his car. The angel made cooing noises, occasionally forming her lips around a word. He thought she whispered "Lord" a few times, though he could swear everything he heard was like a thought in his own head.

Effortlessly, his car came into view, as if every frantic and false move he'd made before in trying to find her had been amended. He looked up, thinking God had the life of this angel in His interest as well.

Frank attempted to lay her down in the backseat, but she was a foot too long. Scrunching her feet, bending her knees, he got the door shut, cramming her in. He went into the trunk and got out the blanket he'd used with Sharon. It was littered with leaves and detritus. The bloodstains had turned nearly black. It disturbed him, having to put it over the angel, but there was no way he could risk anyone seeing her before he got her home.

"It'll be all right, angel. I'll just take you to my place and fix you up. Okay?" He cranked the car on, turned it around, and raced back into the city, to the privacy of his apartment.

Frank set her on his bed. He clasped his hands in reverence, staring down at her. She was like a huge, beautiful waxen doll.

He poured warm water and bath oil into a bowl, retrieved a towel from his linen rack, then commenced ablutions. Her wings clung to her until he began wiping them with the warm water. As they fell away, he eyed her body, draped in a diaphanous fabric. Her breasts were high and small, her mons hairless. She had no navel, nor did her rib cage extend below her breasts. Her torso was long, hipless; her legs also lengthy and thin. Her ankles were crossed, much to Frank's annoyance. He wanted to see her precious honeypot. He thought even God would understand his curiosity. How often did a mortal see an angel this close up?

Lifting the material of her gown, he washed her body. He felt the spreading heat in his groin, hoping God wouldn't think he was a pervert. He spread her legs, staring at the seamless flesh there.

"Sheesh! She's a fucking *Barbie* doll." Maybe if he pried the skin apart . . .

She moaned, her arms rising up from her wings, self-consciously pulling down her gown. Frank grumbled. He wiped down her feet, then brushed her hair. It was thick and felt fake, like thin nylon filament. Not the silky stuff he expected. Nevertheless, running his fingers through it was keeping him hot.

Just then, he remembered God, His ever-present love . . . and judgment. Frank swam in a torrent of guilt. "I'll just leave you here and let you rest. Call out if you need me. I'm Frank Garland. Frank."

He leaned over her, staring at her mouth, his cock still throbbing in his jeans. She had no discernible lips, but he could imagine her mouth opening, closing around his . . . Shit, he thought, he *was* acting like a pervert. As God was his witness, this was an angel, not some self-serving bitch!

Just the same, he didn't want her flying off on him. He tied her up with clean nylon rope, then left her there while he took a cold shower.

Frank turned down the Charger game when he thought he heard her calling. Her voice had the quality of a wind chime tinkling in his head. When he hurried into the bedroom, she was wrestling with the ropes, her wings strained against the constriction. Her mouth worked, but no sound came. Instead, Frank heard her entreaty—frenzied, fearful—in his mind.

"Hey, hey. Don't be frightened. I just tied you up so you wouldn't try to walk or anything. I couldn't tell how hurt you were in that fall. Here . . . let me untie you." He noticed the angel's eyes were black, like onyx marbles. She seemed to be looking at him with marked incredulity.

Once untied, the angel crawled off the bed and stood in the corner of the room. He could feel her wonder, *where am I?*, her eyes wide.

"You're in my apartment. I found you in the woods when you crashed. You fell from the sky." He put his hands behind him, full of humility. "I saved you."

She searched the room until she saw the doorway, then moved toward it. Her movements were awkward, as if she was trying to stay on the ground. He watched her go down the hall, into the living room, and followed. She was staring at the television.

"It's a football game. Don't you have those in heaven?"

She shook her head, turning toward the kitchen.

"That's my kitchen. Food? Are you hungry?"

She nodded, moving buoyantly in that direction.

Frank opened his cupboards. There were two cans of SpaghettiOs, an open bag of chips, a nearly empty jar of coffee, and an unopened box of animal crackers. Trying the fridge, he found a six-pack minus two cans, the doggie bag from the restaurant he'd taken Sharon to, and an apple so wizened, it looked like a large walnut.

He grabbed the doggie bag and set it on the counter. "I don't have much. You can have the leftovers."

Suddenly, he was aware she needed water. He poured her a glass. She drank voraciously, the sound of her gullet like a cricket chirping. She shivered as she swallowed, her wings trembling behind her. He held up the barbecue chicken from the bag. She turned away. With that, he started on the leftovers himself.

After she'd consumed two quarts of water, Frank watched her glide over to the sofa. Her hand went over the nubby fabric, pressing, testing, before she sat down.

"Hey, you want to talk or something?" Frank sat across from her in the vinyl recliner he'd inherited from his stepfather.

Her voice twittered and tinkled in his mind. *Where on earth am I? Where is she, my other, who I am to meet?*

Frank grinned. "You're in Denton. It's a suburb of Henderson. The city's about a twenty-mile ride northeast of here. I work in the city. At a big hotel." Frank paused. "You're supposed to meet somebody?"

She nodded. An image of a pale, stiff-looking, professor-type woman flashed in his mind. She wasn't familiar to Frank. He didn't travel in intellectual circles, he thought, chuckling.

"You must be her guardian angel, huh? Sorry you ended

up with me, but I'm sure I need you more than she ever could.''

A question slid into Frank's mind. He snorted. "How do I need you? As God is my witness, I'm having one serious shortage of faith. Started way back when I lost my dad. I'm a fucking spiritual nightmare, right now. That's how I just know God sent you to me. That woman you're supposed to meet? She has to be a mistake.''

The angel glanced around the room, disinterested in Frank's banter. She put her hands to her nose, sniffed them. The angel wanted to know what she sensed on her.

"Oh, that. I bought some nice-smelling bath stuff for my last girlfriend and it was in the water I used to clean you up. Hope you don't mind. It smells pretty good, huh?''

The angel cocked her head. He felt something searching under his clothes, over his skin, like a feather brushing lightly on the surface, from his feet up to his chin. The effect made him horny again. His erection did not go unnoticed. The feather touch seemed to concentrate there, lapping over the taut skin, then traveled up his body, and away.

"Jesus.'' Frank felt as if he was about to come. He looked into and away from her obsidian eyes, sensing her curiosity with his prick, and displeasure with his scent.

"Oh, sorry. I took a cold shower. No soap. I forget shit like that. Go to the store and buy everything but . . .'' His erection shrank. "I'll pick some up later, really.''

The phone trilled, making Frank jump. He was suddenly wary, the boundary of his apartment walls dissolving into full exposure. Everyone will know. He grabbed the receiver.

"Yeah?''

"Is that how you answer the phone now?''

He slumped against the bar that divided the kitchen and living room. "Ma. What *is* it?''

She sighed audibly. Frank steeled himself.

"We missed you at church today. That makes three Sundays in a row. I wanted to know what in the devil you've been up to?'' Her tone went from benign concern to grand suspicion in a few seconds.

Frank gritted his teeth. "Ma, I've got a life, you know. I

went to *another* church. Across town. With my friend Andrea.''

"Oh?'' It was her incredulous 'oh,' not her resigned 'oh.' "Which church was that?''

"Grace Baptist. I know it isn't our church, but God was still there.''

"God, and apparently this Andrea.''

"I told you about Andrea six months ago, Ma. She's the woman from the shoe store.'' He'd buried her two months ago, September. It had been a Sunday then, too.

"Oh, yes. Well, bring her over to dinner one night. Your stepfather and I really enjoyed that girl you brought over last month. What was her name... Susan. No, Shelly. No, Sharon.''

"I don't know, Ma. Sharon didn't work out for me, and Andrea isn't anything to me anymore.''

"Frank, you're my only boy, now. Will you ever settle down and get married? Have grandchildren for me?''

"Ma, don't start.'' Frank glanced over at his angel. She sat still, her eyes on the football game. He turned his back to her.

"Lord, you're just too picky. What was wrong with Sharon?''

Everything, he thought. She wanted what she wanted, when she wanted it, and when she couldn't get it, she cut him off. Trying to control him. Regularly. Just like all the others. "She was looking for someone more ambitious. I'm happy doing what I do.''

"Well, then good riddance. You're a baker. That's an honorable profession. If that's not good enough for her, then you're better off. God...''

"Ma, do you believe in angels?''

"Of course, Frankie, why?''

"Do you think they ever fall from heaven down here, to earth?'' Frank glanced back at his angel. When she began to look at him, he turned away.

"Why don't you ask Reverend Dooley? He'd know.''

"But, do *you* think so?''

Her silence told him she was either going to make up an outrageous fabrication or admit she didn't know.

"I believe they can fall to earth, but only after they've committed some form of blasphemy in heaven. Then they're cast down to hell, but might hit earth accidentally." She didn't know. "So, why do you want to know?"

Telling his mother would ruin it. "The sermon this morning. Baptist stuff. I wondered was all."

"Baptists. Hmph. Oh. I see your stepfather's finished his beer and supper's ready, so I'll say good-bye. And I hope to see you next Sunday."

"Next Sunday." If he had ever doubted God's existence, the angel had changed him forever. He'd go to church. He'd never miss it again.

He felt a light touch on the back of his head. He spun around to find the angel there, her fingertip drawing back from him, her face unreadable. He smiled at her.

"That was my mother. Nosy lady. I didn't want to tell her about you. You don't mind, do you?"

She shook her head. She sent him the thought that she wanted to rest, that she needed to be ready to meet her *other* in the place where Frank had found her. Tomorrow.

"Uh, well, I was hoping you'd want to stay with me. I know I don't have a luxurious place or anything, and I'm not much of a host yet, but I think we could get along. Besides, I really need you."

She looked at him the way his fourth grade teacher had, the time he'd come back from when his father died. Then, the look felt like sympathy. Now he saw it as pity.

"Look, I don't know what you want, but I'll do anything. Anything."

She projected the image of herself on the forest floor, crumpled and alone, then standing with the nameless woman, embracing her. Somehow, Frank sensed how terribly important the meeting was. Maybe, he thought, he would take her, let them meet, then take the angel back with him. Cooperate. Gain their trust. Let them both know he wanted to care for the angel.

She frowned. He felt the tug of her distress. Like Denise. Andrea. Sharon.

"All right, I'll take you back. But I just want one thing."

She floated around him, wings shuddering, her delight conveyed in the phosphorescence of her skin. Anything, she told him, anything he wished.

The image slid into his mind as easily as muffins off a greased tin. She and him, in bed, making love, him giving her something so good, she'd never leave him. Marking her with his semen. Truly making her *his* angel.

"Maybe God wouldn't want it, though." He was shy. Awkward. "I mean, I'm not pure like you. Maybe I'd pollute you. You know, make you unclean."

She cocked her head, her eyes becoming black holes, drawing him in. With every cell in her being, she was letting him know it was all right, that he would be made clean by her. He felt himself losing his peripheral vision, then saw stars, as if he was fainting. Then there was nothing.

He regained consciousness slowly, swimming up from a syrupy deep sleep. He was naked on his bed. By the glowing numbers on his clock radio, he saw it was the middle of the night. He reached over for the lamp, his panic palpable, certain she was gone.

There, in the amber light, she was asleep beside him. He reached down and felt his flaccid cock. It was puckered with dried jism. His mouth tasted strange. As if he'd been sucking on roses. He remembered her lack of orifices, save one, and leaned over her. His fingers deftly probed the surface of her mons. Nothing.

He closed his eyes. In flashes, it came to him. Her floating ahead of him into the bedroom. Her bathing him, pampering him with her hands, her mouth. His wanting to ravage her, but her insistence on passivity, and his inability to refuse her. His paralysis. How she seemed to make all the parts of his body feel like his cock, erect with an unrelenting trapped heat that demanded release. And her providing it. Even his hair follicles knew orgasmic pleasure.

And then he recalled something stranger, more unsettling. Her taking his hand and putting it to her lips, then sucking it in, first fingers, then hand, to wrist, his arm up past his elbow. Then, there he somehow knew to strum a place inside her, flesh stretched like catgut, smooth as velvet, vibrating like the strings of a harp. The sound she made was like a choir, singing up to the Lord. As she reached her crescendo, a place inside her wept. When she released him, his arm slid slowly from inside her. He knew to lick off all the moisture that remained—moisture with the scent of roses.

Why he'd been put into some kind of coma to experience it, he didn't know, but he felt different now. Redeemed. She *had* cleansed him. Forgiven him the horrible results of his temper, his intolerance, over the years. The little deaths, and the important ones.

"I love you." He spoke to her sleeping form. He'd never said those words before and meant them. From the bottom of his miraculously rescued heart, he meant it now.

He slid off the bed to his knees and, for the first time in twenty years, prayed.

The hotel where Frank worked was not happy to learn that he needed the day off to show an out-of-town guest around, but Frank's assistant could easily handle the Monday baking demands.

Frank showered and dressed as if for church. His angel watched. His mind was silent, empty of her thoughts. What the hell was going on with her? He resigned himself to the fact that women mystified him. What went on inside them seemed more trouble than it was worth to learn. Hell, he thought, he had enough to say for both of them. He talked to her of how he wanted to care for her, what kind of a life they could have together. She gave him no sign she was listening.

The angel drank an enormous amount of water, but otherwise ate nothing. Frank was so hungry he almost ate the gnarled apple. Instead he devoured the animal crackers, gone hard as wood. He wanted a beer, but a wonderful feeling infused him, giving him a deep feeling of satisfaction. As if he'd already had the beer. Quite a few of them.

"Let's go." He took the angel, wrapped in his raincoat, to his car. He saw Mrs. Levin peeking out her window, as usual. If he ran into her in the laundromat, she'd ask him who the girl was. Where she'd come from, as she had with all the others. The woman was nosier than his mother. Only more dangerous.

The highway was busy with Monday traffic and the road out to the quarry full of double trailer trucks hauling granite.

"We'll have to drive through the quarry works. You have

to hunker down then, or I'll have to explain about you.''

The angel seemed to shrink until she was a lumpy pile of raincoat on the floor of the car. Frank turned up his tape of Buchanan's ''When a Guitar Plays the Blues,'' as the sound of gravel under his wheels began to make him nervous.

No one paid him any mind until he reached the far end of the quarry works and the dirt path began. A truck blocked his way and he had to get out and ask that it be moved.

A man in a business suit stood nearby, talking with a worker.

''Hey, you the driver?'' Frank asked the worker.

The suit turned. ''Can I help you?''

''I need that truck moved.''

''You can't go down that path, man. It's quarry property. A dirt road. We don't want to be liable for what could happen if . . .''

''I was here yesterday.'' He thought fast. ''Hang gliding. I left some of my gear there. Too heavy to walk it all out with me. I'll be in and out. Promise.'' He smiled reassuringly.

The suit checked his watch. He frowned, looked up to the sky, then down at his watch again.

''In and out. You have ten minutes.''

''Thanks. That's all I need.''

The suit instructed the worker to move the truck and Frank was off.

''Boy, that was close. We almost got stopped.'' She oozed back up onto the seat, her hair covering her face.

For the first time all day, he sensed her apprehension, anxiety. He felt her growing distress.

''Don't you worry. We'll get there. I lied to the guy, but I don't think they'll come in and get us. He's probably too busy worrying about some granite problem.''

She looked at him plaintively. He patted her knee. Her wings fluttered a tiny bit under the raincoat.

He stopped the car at the end of the road at the felled trees. Another car, a huge sedan, was parked just off the road. Maybe that was her. The stiff, professor-looking woman, he thought.

''Let me scout ahead. I don't want anybody to hurt you.''

She sent him her feelings of trepidation, then acquiesced.

He sauntered down the mountainside, slipping in his Sunday shoes. He could see someone in the small clearing where he'd found his angel. A tall woman, dressed soberly, her pale hair tied into a severe bun. She began to turn toward him, so he hid behind a tree.

Just then, he felt a subtle vibration, a quaking of the air. His skin itched ever so slightly. While he was still staring at the woman, she looked up. Frank's eyes followed hers.

The gray sky became strangely pixilated, as if all its atoms had expanded to an inch in diameter and were randomly dancing and jittering over him. The clouds thickened like marshmallow puffs, then grew skittery, too. The vibration in the air became more palpable. Frank looked back down.

His angel was standing beside the woman. They weren't speaking with their mouths, but it was clear they were deep in conversation. The woman began disrobing. Frank felt himself go ramrod hard watching. When the woman was naked, he saw she was built just like his angel, and that she had deep long scars where her wings had been removed. The two of them embraced, their hands slowly tracing over the other's body. Frank shuddered, ejaculating in his Sunday slacks.

After regaining his composure, Frank got angry. He'd made it clear to his angel that she was going back with him, but since witnessing this relationship, his doubts grew.

He'd just be patient. Yes, that was it. Once the meeting was over, he'd go in, introduce himself, and they'd leave. He might even have to be a bit forceful. Females required a firm hand, he thought.

The itching worsened, reminding Frank of how his nose felt when he brushed his teeth. The sky grew darker, gradually, until it was as dark above the trees as it was below. When he looked at his angel and the woman, they were staring at him. His angel gestured for Frank to come closer. She reached out to him, but it was as though his head was stuffed with cotton. What she wanted wasn't clear.

Sluggishly, Frank walked toward them. His angel's wings were beating a waltz rhythm in the air behind her. She was absolutely beaming with happiness, her body aglow like neon in the night.

He could almost hear his angel as he stood at the edge of

the clearing. He thought he heard her call to him, "Come stand here." He stepped closer, into the ferns.

He yelled to the other woman, "She's my angel! I'm taking her back with me when you're done."

The woman shook her head, pointing to her back. Then she put her hands together, touched them to her lips, then to his angel's, as if to pray.

Frank understood. God. God was coming to take this woman up to heaven to return her wings. It was as his mother had said, after all. The woman was an angel—a fallen angel. And *his* angel was her guide back. It would be up to him to wait for his angel to return. God would smile favorably on that. On his patience. Not one of Frank's virtues before. But a virtue God wanted for all His children.

The faint sound of a choir filled Frank's ears. The two angels seemed to hear it too, and gazed up. His angel reached out and took the other in her arms as a beam of white light thrust through the darkness like a fist. The light engulfed them. A corona of orange light cascaded down around the white.

Frank looked up, his hands together, his eyes full of tears, his heart full of reverence. The light was so intense he couldn't see God. Still, he spoke to Him.

"Lord, I've been reborn. I never believed in you before. Not really. It was just to please my mother, and because my father told me to always listen to her. But, you've sent me proof. I've been saved. All the bad stuff I've done? Never again.

"I know maybe I should tell the truth, and go to jail. Do my penance. But, wouldn't it be better if I just go forward and do your good work now? I hope so.

"Me and my angel. For you. Anything."

Frank glanced over to the fallen angel, now wrapped in his angel's arms in the center of the white light. His angel's wings built speed until she lifted them both off the ground. The orange light seemed to pulsate around them. His angel scanned him, her black eyes glinting in the light. He heard her say loudly and clearly, in his mind, "Good-bye."

"NO!" He screamed, racing toward the light. "I want to be with you! With God!"

252 · HIS ANGEL

He fell to the ground on his knees, arms outstretched, weeping.

"Please, God, please."

His angel disappeared up into the light. Frank felt a deep sorrow. He didn't know if it was his sorrow or hers, or both.

The very next feeling he had was of warmth. Radiant, soul-soothing warmth. It's God's hand, he thought. God, I'm ready.

The orange light swallowed the white, then intensified, focusing on Frank. He knew then that God had chosen to call him. Knew it in his very bones. Knew it, even as the light turned every molecule in his body to dust.

HIS ANGEL
Roberta Lannes

Often I don't know the origin and inspiration for a story until after it is done and sent off to an editor. "His Angel," on the surface, is a tale of a madman who seeks a twisted redemption in the saving of an angel, and finds his just reward. The more I thought about the story, I realized it's about the power of faith, hope, and a belief in God, about the sexual component and profoundly sick compulsion in the serial killer's act, and lastly about the question of whether we are visited and studied by aliens or guarded by angels. Each of these things on its own fascinates me, and as happens during the magical process of creation, an interesting mix that became "His Angel," was born.

Neil Gaiman is a transplanted Briton who now lives in the American Midwest. He is the author of the award-winning *Sandman* series of graphic novels and coauthor (with Terry Pratchett) of the novel *Good Omens*. He also collaborated with artist Dave McKean on the brilliant book *Mr. Punch*. Gaiman is also a talented poet and short story writer whose work has been published in *Snow White, Blood Red, Ruby Slippers, Golden Tears, Midnight Graffiti*, and *Touch Wood: Narrow Houses 2*. Several of his stories have been reprinted in *The Year's Best Fantasy and Horror*. His collection *Angels and Visitations* reprints much of his shorter work.

"Eaten" is a poem in iambic pentameter, one of several pieces in this book inspired by dreams. It is generally more raw than most of Gaiman's work.

EATEN (SCENES FROM A MOVING PICTURE)

NEIL GAIMAN

INT. WEBSTER'S OFFICE. DAY
As WEBSTER sits
reading the LA Times, MCBRIDE walks in
and tells in

FLASHBACK
how his SISTER came
to Hollywood eleven months ago
to make her fortune, and to meet the stars.
Of how he'd heard from friends that she'd "gone strange."
Imagining the needle, or far worse,
he travels out to Hollywood himself
and finds her standing underneath a bridge.
Her skin is pale. She screams at him "Get lost!"
and sobs and runs. A TALL MAN DRESSED IN BLACK

253

grabs hold his sleeve, tells him to let it drop
"Forget your sister," but of course he can't . . .

(IN SEPIA
we see the two as teens,
a YOUNG MCBRIDE and SISTER way back when,
giggles beneath the porch, "I'll show you mine,"
closer perhaps than siblings ought to be . . .
PAN UP
to watch a passing butterfly.
We hear them breathe and fumble in the dark:
IN CLOSE-UP now he spurts into her hand,
she licks her palm: first makes a face, then smiles . . .
HOLD on her lips and teeth and on her tongue).

END FLASHBACK
WEBSTER says he'll take the case,
says something flip and hard about LA,
like how it eats young girls and spits them out,
and takes a hundred dollars on account.

CUT TO
THE PURPLE PUSSY. INT. A DIVE,
THREE NAKED WOMEN dance for dollar bills.
WEBSTER comes in, and talks to one of them,
slips her a twenty, shows a photograph,
the stripper—standing close enough that he
could touch her (but they've bouncers on patrol,
weird steroid cases who will break your wrists)—
admits she thinks she knows the girl he means.
Then WEBSTER leaves.

INT. WEBSTER'S CONDO. NIGHT.
A video awaits him at his home.
It shows A WOMAN lovelier than life
Shot from the rib cage up (her breasts exposed)
Advising him to "let this whole thing drop,
forget it," promising she'll see him soon . . .

DISSOLVE TO
INT. MCBRIDE'S HOTEL ROOM. NIGHT.
MCBRIDE'S alone and lying on the bed,
He's watching soft-core porn on pay-per-view.
Naked. He rubs his cock with vaseline,
lazy and slow, he doesn't want to come.
A BANG upon the window. He sits up,
flaccid and scared (he's on the second floor)
and opens up the window of his room.
HIS SISTER enters, looking almost dead,
implores him to forget her. He says no.
THE SISTER shambles over to the door.
A WOMAN DRESSED IN BLACK waits in the hall.
Brunette in leather, kinky as all hell,
who steps over the threshold with a smile.
And they have sex.

        THE SISTER stands alone.
She watches as THE BRUNETTE takes MCBRIDE
(her skin's necrotic blue. She's fully dressed).
THE BRUNETTE gestures curtly with her hand,
off come THE SISTER'S clothes. She looks a mess.
Her skin's all scarred and scored; one nipple's gone.
She takes her gloves off and we see her hands:
Her fingers look like ribs, or chicken wings,
well chewed, and rescued from a garbage can—
dry bones with scraps of flesh and cartilage.
She puts her fingers in THE BRUNETTE'S mouth . . .
AND FADE TO BLACK.

INT. WEBSTER'S OFFICE. DAY.
THE PHONE RINGS. It's MCBRIDE. "Just drop the case.
I've found my sister, and I'm going home.
You've got five hundred dollars, and my thanks."
PULL BACK on WEBSTER, puzzled and confused.

MONTAGE of WEBSTER here. A week goes by,
we see him eating, pissing, drinking, drunk.
We watch him throw HIS GIRLFRIEND out of bed.
We see him play the video again . . .

The VIDEO GIRL stares at him and says
she'll see him soon. "I promise, Webster, soon."

CUT TO
THE PLACE OF EATERS, UNDERGROUND.
Pale people stand like cattle in a pen.
We see MCBRIDE. The flesh is off his chest.
White meat is good. We're looking through his ribs:
his heart is still. His lungs, however, breathe,
inflate, deflate. And tears of pus run down
his sunken cheeks. He pisses in the muck.
It doesn't steam. He wishes he were dead.

A DREAM:
As WEBSTER tosses in his bed
He sees MCBRIDE, a corpse beneath a bridge,
all INTERCUT with lots of shots of food,
to make our theme explicit: this is art.

EXT. LA. DAY.
WEBSTER's become obsessed.
He has to find the woman from the screen.
He beats somebody up, fucks someone else,
fixated on "I'll see you, Webster, soon."

He's thrown in prison. And they come for him,
THE MAN IN BLACK attending THE BRUNETTE.
Open his cell with keys, escort him out,
and leave the prison building. Through a door.
They walk him to the car park. They go down,
below the car park, deep beneath the town,
past shadowed writhing things that suck and hiss
and glossy things that laugh, and things that scream.
Now other feeder-folk are walking past . . .
They handcuff WEBSTER to A TINY MAN
who's covered with vaginas and with teeth,
and escorts WEBSTER to

THE QUEEN'S SALON.

(An interjection here: my wife awoke,
scared by an evil dream. "You hated me.
You brought these women home I didn't know,
but they knew me, and then we had a fight,
and after we had shouted you stormed out.
You said you'd find a girl to fuck and eat."

This scares me just a little. As we write
we summon little demons. So I shrug.)

The handcuffs are removed. He's left alone.
The hangings are red velvet, then they lift,
reveal THE QUEEN. We recognize her face,
the woman we saw on the VCR.
"The world divides so sweetly, neatly up
into the feeder-folk, into their prey."
That's what she says. Her voice is soft and sweet.
Imagine honey ants: the tiny head,
the chest, the tiny arms, the tiny hands,
and after that the bloat of honey-swell,
the abdomen enormous as it hangs
translucent, made of honey, sweet as lust.

THE QUEEN has quite a perfect little face,
her breasts are pale, blue-veined; her nipples pink;
her hands are white. But then, below her breasts
the whole swells like a whale or like a shrine,
a human honey ant, she's huge as rooms,
as elephants, as dinosaurs, as love.
Her flesh is opalescent, and she calls
poor WEBSTER to her. And he nods and comes.
(She must be over twenty-five feet long.)
She orders him to take off all his clothes.
His cock is hard. He shivers. He looks lost.
He moans "I'm harder than I've ever been."
Then, with her mouth, she licks and tongues his cock . . .

We linger here. The language of the eye
becomes a bland, unflinching, blowjob porn,
(her lips are glossy, and her tongue is red)

HOLD on her face. We hear him gasping "Oh.
Oh, baby. Yes. Oh. Take it in your mouth."
And then she opens up her mouth, and grins,
and bites his cock off.

                                  Spurting blood pumps out
into her mouth. She hardly spills a drop.
We never do pan up to see his face,
just her. It's what they call the money shot.

Then, when his cock's gone down, and blood's congealed,
we see his face. He looks all dazed and healed.
Some feeders come and take him out of there.
Down in the pens he's chained beside MCBRIDE.
Deep in the mud lie carcasses picked clean
who grin at them and dream of being soup.

Poor things.

We're almost done.

We'll leave them there.

CUT to some lonely doorway, where A TRAMP
has three cold fingers up ANOTHER TRAMP,
they're starving but they fingerfuck like hell,
and underneath the layers of old clothes
beneath the cardboard, newspaper and cloth,
their genders are impossible to tell.

PAN UP

to watch a butterfly go past.

(ENDS)

Eaten (Scenes from a Moving Picture)
Neil Gaiman

This began, somewhere in my head, in May 1993, as a musing on the way people treat other people; and on film, and on the limits and language of film; on pornography and the low standards of pornography; on the language of film treatments and scripts; and on the relationship between food and sex. Or it began one night in 1984, when I had a nightmare in which I was being eaten alive by an elderly witch-woman; I was being kept for food, a zombie, following her around. My left arm and hand were just bone and clinging morsels of chewed flesh. I turned the dream into a story back then, but fragments of it still lingered and began, slowly, to wrap another story around themselves, layers of nacreous image accreting, layering themselves around something I would still rather not have in my head.

When I read scripts, and when I write them, I always pronounce, in my head, 'Int' and 'Ext' as just that, not 'Interior' or 'Exterior.' I was surprised to discover, on showing a few early readers this poem, that other people do not do this. "Eaten" is a very literal poem, however, and pronounces these words just like I do.

IN THE MONTH OF ATHYR

ELIZABETH HAND

In the month of Athyr Leucis fell asleep.
—C.P. CAVAFY, "IN THE MONTH OF ATHYR"

THE ARGALA CAME TO LIVE WITH THEM ON THE LAST DAY OF Mestris, when Paul was fifteen. High summer, it would have been by the old Solar calendar; but in the HORUS station it was dusk, as it always was. The older boys were poring over an illustrated manual of sexual positions by the sputtering light of a lumiere filched from Father Dorothy's cache behind the galley refrigerator. Since Paul was the youngest he had been appointed to act as guard. He crouched beside the refrigerator, shivering in his pajamas, and cursed under his breath. He had always been the youngest, always would be the youngest. There had been no children born on the station since Father

Dorothy arrived to be the new tutor. In a few months, Father Dorothy had converted Teichman Station's few remaining women to the Mysteries of Lysis. Father Dorothy was a *galli,* a eunuch who had made the ultimate sacrifice to the Great Mother during one of the high holy days Below. The Mysteries of Lysis was a relatively new cult. Its adherents believed that only by reversing traditional gender roles could the sexes make peace after their long centuries of open hostility. These reversals were enacted literally, often to the consternation of non-believing children and parents.

On the stations, it was easier for such unusual sects and controversial ideas to gain a toehold. The current ruling Ascendancy embraced a cult of rather recent vintage, a form of religious fundamentalism that was a cunning synthesis of the more extreme elements of several popular and ancient faiths. For instance, the Ascendants encouraged female infanticide among certain populations, including the easily monitored network of facilities that comprised the Human Orbital Research Units in Space, or HORUS. Because of recent advances in bioengineering, the Ascendants believed that women, long known to be psychologically mutable and physically unstable, might also soon be unnecessary. Thus were the heavily reviled feminist visionaries of earlier centuries unhappily vindicated. Thus the absence of girl children on Teichman, as well as the rift between the few remaining women and their husbands.

To the five young boys who were his students, Father Dorothy's devotion to the Mysteries was inspiring in its intensity. Their parents were also affected; Father Dorothy believed in encouraging discussions of certain controversial gender policies. Since his arrival, relations between men and women had grown even more strained. Paul's mother was now a man, and his father had taken to spending most of his days in the station's neural sauna, letting its wash of endorphins slowly erode his once-fine intellect to a soft soppy blur. The argala was to change all that.

"Pathori," hissed Claude Illo, tossing an empty salt-pod at Paul's head. "Pathori, come here!"

Paul rubbed his nose and squinted. A few feet away Claude and the others, the twins Reuben and Romulus and the beautiful Ira Claire, crouched over the box of exotic poses.

"Pathori, come *here!*"

Claude's voice cracked. Ira giggled; a moment later Paul winced as he heard Claude smack him.

"I *mean* it," Claude warned. Paul sighed, flicked the salt-pod in Ira's direction and scuttled after it.

"Look at this," Claude whispered. He grabbed Paul by the neck and forced his head down until his nose was a scant inch away from the hologravures. The top image was of a woman, strictly forbidden. She was naked, which made it doubly forbidden; and with a man, and smiling. It was that smile that made the picture particularly damning; according to Father Dorothy, a woman in such a posture would never enjoy being there. The woman in the gravure turned her face, tossing back hair that was long and impossibly blonde. For an instant Paul glimpsed the man sitting next to her. He was smiling too, but wearing the crimson leathers of an Ascendant Aviator. Like the woman, he had the ruddy cheeks and even teeth Paul associated with antique photographs or tapes. The figures began to move suggestively. Paul's head really *should* explode, now, just like Father Dorothy had warned. He started to look away, embarrassed and aroused, when behind him Claude swore—

"—move, damn it, it's Dorothy!—"

But it was too late.

"Boys . . ."

Father Dorothy's voice rang out, a hoarse tenor. Paul looked up and saw him, clad as always in salt-and-pepper tweeds, his long grey hair pulled back through a copper loop. "It's late, you shouldn't be here."

They were safe: their tutor was distracted. Paul looked beyond him, past the long sweep of the galley's gleaming equipment to where a tall figure stood in the shadows. Claude swept the box of hologravures beneath a stove and stood, kicking Paul and Ira and gesturing for the twins to follow him.

"Sorry, Father," he grunted, gazing at his feet. Beside him Paul tried not to stare at whoever it was that stood at the end of the narrow corridor.

"Go along, then," said Father Dorothy, waving his hands in the direction of the boys' dormitory. As they hurried past him, Paul could smell the sandalwood soap Father Dorothy had specially imported from his home Below, the only luxury he allowed himself. And Paul smelled something else, something strange. The scent made him stop. He looked over his shoulder and saw the figure still standing at the end of the galley, as though afraid to enter while the boys were there. Now that they seemed to be gone the figure began to walk towards Father Dorothy, picking its feet up with exaggerated delicacy. Paul stared, entranced.

"Move it, Pathori," Claude called to him; but Paul shook his head and stayed where he was. Father Dorothy had his back to them. One hand was outstretched to the figure. Despite its size—it was taller than Paul, taller than Father Dorothy— there was something fragile and childlike about it. Thin and slightly stooped, with wispy yellow hair like feathers falling onto curved thin shoulders, frail arms crossed across its chest and legs that were so long and frail that he could see why it walked in that awkward tippy-toe manner: if it fell its legs would snap like chopsticks. It smelled like nothing else on Teichman Station, sweet and powdery and warm. Once, Paul thought, his mother had smelled like that, before she went to stay in the women's quarters. But this thing looked nothing like his mother. As he stared, it slowly lifted its face, until he could see its enormous eyes fixed on him: caramel-colored eyes threaded with gold and black, staring at him with a gaze that was utterly adoring and absolutely witless.

"Paul, come *on!*"

Ira tugged at him until he turned away and stumbled after the others to the dormitory. For a long time afterwards he lay awake, trying to ignore the laughter and muffled sounds coming from the other beds; recalling the creature's golden eyes, its walk, its smell.

At tutorial the next day Father Dorothy said nothing of finding the boys in the galley, nor did he mention his strange companion. Paul yawned behind the time-softened covers of an ancient linguistics text, waiting for Romulus to finish with the monitor so he could begin his lesson. In the front of the room, beneath flickering lamps that cast grey shadows on the dusty floor, Father Dorothy patiently went over a hermeneutics lesson with Ira, who was too stupid to follow his father into the bioengineering corps, but whose beauty and placid nature guaranteed him a place in the Izakowa priesthood on Miyako

Station. Paul stared over his textbook at Ira with his corkscrew curls and dusky skin. He thought of the creature in the galley—its awkwardness, its pallor; the way it had stared at him. But mostly he tried to remember how it smelled. Because on Teichman Station—where they had been breathing the same air for seventeen years, and where even the most common herbs and spices, cinnamon, garlic, pepper, were no longer imported because of the expense to the station's dwindling group of researchers—on Teichman Station everything smelled the same. Everything smelled of despair.

"Father Dorothy."

Paul looked up. A server, one of the few that remained in working order, lurched into the little room, its wheels scraping against the door. Claude snickered and glanced sideways at Paul: the server belonged to Paul's mother, although after her conversion she had declared it shared property amongst all the station women. "Father Dorothy, KlausMaria Dalven asks that her son be sent to her quarters. She wishes to speak with him."

Father Dorothy looked up from the monitor cradled in his hand. He smiled wryly at the ancient server and looked back at Paul.

"Go ahead," he said. Ira gazed enviously as Paul shut his book and slid it into his desk, then followed the server to the women's quarters.

His mother and the other women lived at the far end of the Solar Walk, the only part of Teichman where one could see outside into space and realize that they were, indeed, orbiting the moon and not stuck in some cramped Airbus outside of New Delhi or one of the other quarantined areas Below. The server rolled along a few feet ahead of him, murmuring to itself in an earnest monotone. Paul followed, staring at his feet as a woman passed him. When he heard her leave the Walk he lifted his head and looked outside. A pale glowing smear above one end of the Walk was possibly the moon, more likely one of the station's malfunctioning satellite beacons. The windows were so streaked with dirt that for all Paul knew he might be looking at Earth, or some dingy canister of waste deployed from the galley. He paused to step over to one of the windows. A year before Claude had drawn an obscene figure in the dust along the edge, facing the men's side of the

Walk. Paul grinned to himself: it was still there.

"Paul, KlausMaria Dalven asks that you come to her quarters. She wishes to speak with you," the server repeated in its droning voice. Paul sighed and turned from the window. A minute later he crossed the invisible line that separated the rest of Teichman from the women's quarters.

The air was much fresher here—his mother said that came from thinking peaceful thoughts—and the walls were painted a very deep green, which seemed an odd choice of colors but had a soothing effect nonetheless. Someone had painted stars and a crescent moon upon the arched ceiling. Paul had never seen the moon look like that, or stars. His mother explained they were images of power and not meant to resemble the dull shapes one saw on the navgrids.

"Hello, Paul," a woman called softly. Marija Kerényi, who had briefly consorted with his father after Paul's mother had left him. Then, she had been small and pretty, soft-spoken but laughing easily. Just the sort of pliant woman Fritz Pathori liked. But in the space of a few years she had had two children, both girls. This was during an earlier phase of his father's work on the parthogenetic breeders, when human reproductive tissue was too costly to import from Below. Marija never forgave Paul's father for what happened to her daughters. She was still small and pretty, but her expression had sharpened almost to the point of cunning, her hair had grown very long and was pulled back in the same manner as Father Dorothy's. "Your mother is in the Attis Arcade."

"Um, thanks," Paul mumbled. He had half-turned to leave when his mother's throaty voice echoed down the hallway. "Marija, is that him? Send him back—"

"Go ahead, Paul," Marija urged. She laughed as he hurried past her. For an instant her hand touched the top of his thigh, and he nearly stumbled as she stroked him. Her fingers flicked at his trousers and she turned away disdainfully.

His mother stood in a doorway. "Paul, darling. Are you thirsty? Would you like some tea?"

Her voice was deeper than it had been before, *when she was really my mother,* he thought; before the hormonal injections and implants; before Father Dorothy. He still could not help but think of her as *she,* despite her masculine appearance, her throaty voice. "Or—you don't like tea, how about betel?"

"No, thanks."

She looked down at him. Her face was sharper than it had been. Her chin seemed too strong, with its blue shadows fading into her unshaven jaw. She still looked like a woman, but a distinctly mannish one. Seeing her Paul wanted to cry.

"Nothing?" she said, then shrugged and walked inside. He followed her into the arcade.

She didn't look out of place here, as she so often had back in the family chambers. The arcade was a circular room, with a very high ceiling; his mother was very tall. Below, her family had been descended from aristocratic North Africans whose women prided themselves on their exaggerated height and the purity of their yellow eyes and ebony skin. Paul took after his father, small and fair-skinned, but with his mother's long-fingered hands and a shyness that in KlausMaria was often mistaken for *hauteur*. In their family chambers she had had to stoop, so as not to seem taller than her husband. Here she flopped back comfortably on the sand-covered floor, motioning for Paul to join her.

"Well, *I'm* having some tea. Mawu—"

That was the name she'd given the server after they'd moved to the women's quarters. While he was growing up, Paul had called it Bunny. The robot rolled into the arcade, grinding against the wall and sending up a little puff of rust. "Tea for me and my boy. Sweetened, please."

Paul stood awkwardly, looking around in vain for a chair. Finally he sat down on the floor near his mother, stretching out his legs and brushing sand from his trousers.

"So," he said, clearing his throat. "Hi."

KlausMaria smiled. *"Hi."*

They said nothing else for several minutes. Paul squirmed, trying to keep sand from seeping into his clothes. His mother sat calmly, smiling, until the server returned with tea in small soggy cups already starting to disintegrate. It hadn't been properly mixed. Sipping his, bits of powder got stuck between Paul's teeth.

"Your father has brought an argala here," KlausMaria announced. Her voice was so loud that Paul started, choking on a mouthful of tea and coughing until his eyes watered. His mother only stared at him coolly. "Yesterday. There wasn't supposed to be a drop until Athyr, god knows how he arranged it. Father Dorothy told me. They had him escort it on board, afraid of what would happen if one of the men got hold of it. A sex slave. Absolutely disgusting."

She leaned forward, her long beautiful fingers drumming on the floor. Specks of sand flew in all directions, stinging Paul's cheeks. "Oh," he said, trying to give the sound a rounded adult tone, regretful or disapproving. *So that's what it was,* he thought, and his heart beat faster.

"I wish to god I'd never come here," KlausMaria whispered. "I wish—"

She stopped, her voice rasping into the breathy drone of the air filters. Paul nodded, staring at the floor, letting sand run between his fingers. They sat again in silence. Finally he mumbled, "I didn't know."

His mother let her breath out in a long wheeze; it smelled of betel and bergamot-scented tea powder. "I know." She leaned close to him, her hand on his knee. For a moment it was like when he was younger, before his father had begun working on the Breeders, before Father Dorothy came. "That's why I wanted to tell you, before you heard from— well, from anyone else. Because—well, shit."

She gave a sharp laugh—a real laugh—and Paul smiled, relieved. "It's pathetic, really," she said. Her hand dropped from his knee to the floor and scooped up fistfuls of fine powder. "Here he was, this brilliant beautiful man. It's destroyed him, the work he's done. I wish you could have known him before, Below—"

She sighed again and reached for her tea, sipped it silently. "But that was before the last Ascension. Those bastards. Too late now. For your father, at least. But Paul," and she leaned forward again and took his hand. "I've made arrangements for you to go to school Below. In Tangier. My mother will pay for it, it's all taken care of. In a few months. It'll be fall then, in Tangier, it will be exciting for you . . ."

Her voice drifted off, as though she spoke to herself or a server. "An argala. I will go mad."

She sighed and seemed to lose interest in her son, instead staring fixedly at the sand running between her fingers. Paul waited for several more minutes, to see if anything else was forthcoming, but his mother said nothing more. Finally the boy stood, inclined his head to kiss her cheek, and turned to go.

"Paul," his mother called as he hesitated in the doorway.

He turned back: she made the gesture of blessing that the followers of Lysis affected, drawing an exaggerated *S* in the air and blinking rapidly. "Promise me you won't go near it. If he wants you to. Promise."

Paul shrugged. "Sure."

She stared at him, tight-lipped. Then, "Goodbye," she said, and returned to her meditations in the Arcade.

That night in the dormitory he crept to Claude's bunk while the older boy was asleep and carefully felt beneath his mattress, until he found the stack of pamphlets hidden there. The second one he pulled out was the one he wanted. He shoved the others back and fled to his bunk.

He had a nearly new lumiere hidden under his pillow. He withdrew it and shook it until watery yellow light spilled across the pages in front of him. Poor-quality color images, but definitely taken from life. They showed creatures much like the one he had seen the night before. Some were no bigger than children, with tiny pointed breasts and enormous eyes and brilliant red mouths. Others were as tall and slender as the one he had glimpsed. In one of the pictures an argala actually coupled with a naked man, but the rest showed them posing provocatively. They all had the same feathery yellow hair, the same wide mindless eyes and air of utter passivity. In some of the pictures Paul could see their wings, bedraggled and straw-colored. There was nothing even remotely sexually exciting about them.

Paul could only assume this was something he might feel differently about, someday. After all, his father had been happy with his mother once, although that of course was before Paul was born, before his father began his work on the Breeders Project. The first generations of geneslaves had been developed a century earlier on Earth. Originally they had been designed to toil in the lunar colonies and on Earth's vast hydrofarms. But the reactionary gender policies of the current

Ascendant administration suggested that there were other uses to which the geneslaves might be put.

Fritz Pathori had been a brilliant geneticist, with impressive ties to the present administration. Below, he had developed the prototype for the argala, a gormless creature that the Ascendants hoped would make human prostitution obsolete—though it was not the act itself the Ascendants objected to, so much as the active involvement of women. And at first the women had welcomed the argal3/4. But that was before the femicides; before the success of the argalæ led Fritz Pathori to develop the first Breeders.

He had been an ethical man, once. Even now, Paul knew that it was the pressures of conscience that drove his father to the neural sauna. Because now, of course, his father could not stop the course of his research. He had tried, years before. That was how they had ended up exiled to Teichman Station, where Pathori and his staff had for many years lived in a state of house arrest, part of the dismal constellation of space stations drifting through the heavens and falling wearily and irretrievably into madness and decay.

A shaft of light flicked through the dormitory and settled upon Paul's head. The boy dove beneath the covers, shoving the pamphlet into the crack between bedstand and mattress.

"Paul." Father Dorothy's whispered voice was surprised, shaming without being angry. The boy let his breath out and peered up at his tutor, clad in an elegant grey kimono, his long iron-colored hair unbound and falling to his shoulders. "What are you doing? What do you have there—"

His hand went unerringly to where Paul had hidden the pamphlet. The shaft of light danced across the yellowed pages, and the pamphlet disappeared into a kimono pocket.

"Mmm." His tutor sounded upset. "Tomorrow I want to see you before class. Don't forget."

His face burning, Paul listened as the man's footsteps padded away again. A minute later he gave a muffled cry as someone jumped on top of him.

"You idiot! Now he *knows*—"

And much of the rest of the night was given over to the plebeian torments of Claude.

•　　•　　•

He knew he looked terrible the next morning, when, still rubbing his eyes, he shuffled into Father Dorothy's chamber.

"Oh dear." The tutor shook his head and smiled ruefully. "Not much sleep, I would imagine. Claude?"

Paul nodded.

"Would you like some coffee?"

Paul started to refuse politely, then saw that Father Dorothy had what looked like real coffee, in a small metal tin stamped with Arabic letters in gold and brown. "Yes, please," he nodded, and watched entranced as the tutor scooped it into a silver salver and poured boiling water over it.

"Now then," Father Dorothy said a few minutes later. He indicated a chair, its cushions ballooning over its metal arms, and Paul sank gratefully into it, cupping his bowl of coffee. "This is all about the argala, isn't it?"

Paul sighed. "Yes."

"I thought so." Father Dorothy sipped his coffee and glanced at the gravure of Father Sofia, founder of the Mysteries, staring myopically from the curved wall. "I imagine your mother is rather distressed—?"

"I guess so. I mean, she seems angry, but she always seems angry."

Father Dorothy sighed. "This exile is particularly difficult for a person as brilliant as your mother. And this—" he pointed delicately at the pamphlet, sitting like an uninvited guest on a chair of its own. "This argala must be very hard for KlausMaria to take. I find it disturbing and rather sad, but considering your father's part in developing these—things—my guess would be that your mother finds it, um, *repellent*—?"

Paul was still staring at the pamphlet; it lay open at one of the pages he hadn't yet gotten to the night before. "Uh—um, oh yes, yes, she's pretty mad," he mumbled hastily, when he saw Father Dorothy staring at him.

The tutor swallowed the rest of his coffee. Then he stood and paced to the chair where the pamphlet lay, picked it up and thumbed through it dismissively, though not without a certain curiosity.

"You know it's not a real woman, right? That's part of what's *wrong* with it, Paul—not what's wrong with the thing itself, but with the act, with—well, *everything*. It's a genes-lave, it can't enter into any sort of—relations—with anyone of its own free will. It's a—well, it's like a machine, except of course it's *alive*. But it has no thoughts of its own. They're like children, you see, only incapable of thought, or language. Although of course we have no idea what other things they *can* do—strangle us in our sleep or drive us mad. They're incapable of ever learning, or loving. They can't suffer or feel pain or, well, *anything*—"

Father Dorothy's face had grown red, not from embarrassment, as Paul first thought, but from anger—real fury, the boy saw, and he sank back into his chair, a little afraid himself now.

"—institutionalized rape, it's exactly what Sofia said would happen, why she said we should start to protect ourselves—"

Paul shook his head. "But—wouldn't it, I mean wouldn't it be easier? For women: if they used the geneslaves, then they'd leave the women alone . . ."

Father Dorothy held the pamphlet open, to a picture showing an argala with its head thrown back. His face as he turned to Paul was still angry, but disappointed now as well. And Paul realized there was something he had missed, some lesson he had failed to learn during all these years of Father Dorothy's tutelage.

"That's right," his tutor said softly. He looked down at the pamphlet between his fingers, the slightly soiled image with its gasping mouth and huge, empty eyes. He looked sad, and Paul's eyes flickered down from Father Dorothy's face to that of the argala in the picture. It looked very little like the one he had seen, really; but suddenly he was flooded with yearning, an overwhelming desire to see it again, to touch it and breathe again that warm scent, that smell of blue water and real sand and warm flesh pressed against cool cotton. The thought of seeing it excited him, and even though he knew Father Dorothy couldn't see anything (Paul was wearing one of his father's old robes, much too too big for him), Father Dorothy must have understood, because in the next instant the pamphlet was out of sight, squirreled into a cubbyhole of his ancient steel desk.

"That's enough, then," he said roughly. And gazing at his

tormented face Paul thought of what the man had done, to become an initiate into the Mysteries; and he knew then that he would never be able to understand anything his tutor wanted him to learn.

"It's in there now, with your father! I saw it go in—"

Ira's face was flushed, his hair tangled from running. Claude and Paul sat together on Claude's bunk poring over another pamphlet, a temporary truce having been effected by this new shared interest.

"My father?" Paul said stupidly. He felt flushed, and cross at Ira for interrupting his reverie.

"The argala! It's in there with him now. If we go we can listen at the door—everyone else is still at dinner."

Claude closed the pamphlet and slipped it beneath his pillow. He nodded, slowly, then reached out and touched Ira's curls. "Let's go, then," he said.

Fritz Pathori's quarters were on the research deck. The boys reached them by climbing the spiral stairs leading up to the second level, speaking in whispers even though there was little chance of anyone seeing them there, or caring if they did. Midway up the steps Paul could see his father's chambers, across the open area that had once held several anaglyphic sculptures. The sculptures had long since been destroyed, in one of the nearly ritualized bouts of violence that periodically swept through the station. Now his father's balcony commanded a view of a narrow concrete space, swept clean of rubble but nonetheless hung about with a vague odor of neglect and disrepair.

When they reached the hallway leading to the chief geneticist's room the boys grew quiet.

"You never come up here?" Claude asked. For once there was no mockery in his voice.

Paul shrugged. "Sometimes. Not in a while, though."

"I'd be here all the time," Ira whispered. He looked the most impressed, stooping to rub the worn but still lush carpeting and then tilting his head to flash a quick smile at himself in the polished metal walls.

"My father is always busy," said Paul. He stopped in front of the door to his father's chambers, smooth and polished as the walls, marked only by the small onyx inlay with his father's name engraved upon it. He tried to remember the last time he'd been here—early autime, or perhaps it had been as long ago as last Mestris.

"Can you hear anything?" Claude pushed Ira aside and pressed close to the door. Paul felt a dart of alarm.

"I do," whispered Ira excitedly. "I hear them—listen—"

They crouched at the door, Paul in the middle. He *could* hear something, very faintly. Voices: his father's, and something like an echo of it, soft and soothing. His father was groaning—Paul's heart clenched in his chest but he felt no embarrassment, nothing but a kind of icy disdain—and the other voice was cooing, an almost perfect echo of the deeper tone, but two octaves higher. Paul pressed closer to the wall, feeling the cool metal against his cheek.

For several more minutes they listened, Paul silent and impassive, Claude snickering and making jerking motions with his hands, Ira with pale blue eyes growing wide. Then suddenly it was quiet behind the door. Paul looked up, startled: there had been no terminal cries, none of the effusive sounds he had heard were associated with this sort of thing. Only a silence that was oddly furtive and sad, falling as it did upon three pairs of disappointed ears.

"What happened?" Ira looked distressed. "Are they all right?"

"Of course they're all right," Claude hissed. He started to his feet, tugging Ira after him. "They're finished, is all—come on, let's get out of here—"

Claude ran down the hall with Ira behind him. Paul remained crouched beside the door, ignoring the other boys as they waved for him to follow.

And then before he could move the door opened. He looked up and through it and saw his father at the far end of the room, standing with his back to the door. From the spiral stairs Claude's voice echoed furiously.

Paul staggered to his feet. He was just turning to flee when something moved from the room into the hall, cutting off his view of his father; something that stood teetering on absurdly long legs, a confused expression on its face. The door slid closed behind it, and he was alone with the argala.

"Oh," he whispered, and shrank against the wall.

"*O,*" the argala murmured.

Its voice was like its scent, warm yet somehow diffuse. If the hallway had been dark, it would have been difficult to tell where the sound came from. But it was not dark, and Paul couldn't take his eyes from it.

"It's all right," he whispered. Tentatively he reached for it. The argala stepped towards him, its frail arms raised in an embrace. He started, then slowly let it enfold him. Its voice echoed his own, childlike and trusting.

It was irresistible, the smell and shape of it, the touch of its wispy hair upon his cheeks. He opened his eyes and for the first time got a good look at its face, so close to his that he drew back a little to see it better. A face that was somehow, indefinably, female. Like a child's drawing of a woman: enormous eyes surrounded by lashes that were spare but thick and straight. A round mouth, tangerine-colored, like something one would want to eat. Hair that was more like feathers curled about its face. Paul took a tendril between his fingers, pulled it to his cheek and stroked his chin with agonizing slowness.

His mother had told him once that the argalæ were engineered from human women and birds, storks or cranes the boy thought, or maybe some kind of white duck. Paul had thought this absurd, but now it seemed it could be true—the creature's hair looked and felt more like long downy filaments than human hair, or fur. And there was something birdlike about the way it felt in his arms: fragile but at the same time tensile, and strong, as though its bones were lighter than human bones, filled with air or even some other element. Paul had never seen a real bird. He knew they were supposed to be lovely, avatars of physical beauty of a certain type, and that their power of flight imbued them with a kind of miraculous appeal, at least to people Below. His mother said people thought that way about women once. Perhaps some of them still did.

He could not imagine any bird, anything at all, more beautiful or miraculous than this geneslave.

Even as he held it to his breast, its presence woke in him a terrible longing, a yearning for something he could scarcely fathom—open skies, the feel of running water beneath his bare feet. Images flooded his mind, things he had only ever seen in files of old movies. Small houses made of wood, clouds skidding across a sky the color of Ira Claire's eyes, cream-colored flowers climbing a trellis beside a green field. As the pictures fled across his mind's eye his heart pounded: *where did they come from?* Sensations spilled into him, as though they had been contained in too shallow a vessel and had no-where else to pour but into whomever the thing touched. And then those first images slid away, the white porch and cracked concrete and saline taste—bitter yet comforting—of tears running into his mouth. Instead he felt dizzy. He reached out and his hands struck at the air feebly. Something seemed to move at his feet. He looked down and saw ripples like water, and something tiny and bright moving there. A feeling stabbed at him, a hunger so sharp it was like love; and suddenly he saw clearly what the thing was—a tiny creature like a scarlet sal-amander, creeping across a mossy bank. But before he could stoop to savage it with his beak (*his beak?*), with a sickening rush the floor beneath him dropped, and there was only sky, white and grey, and wind raking at his face; and above all else that smell, filling his nostrils like pollen: the smell of water, of freedom.

Then it was gone. He fell back against the wall, gasping. When he opened his eyes he felt nauseated, but that passed almost immediately. He focused on the argala staring at him, its eyes wide and golden and with the same adoring gaze it had fixed on him before. Behind it his father stood in the open doorway to his room.

"Paul," he exclaimed brightly. He skinned a hand across his forehead and smiled, showing where he'd lost a tooth since the last time they'd met. "You found it—I wondered where it went. Come on, you!—"

He reached for the argala and it went to him, easily. "Turned around and it was gone!" His father shook his head, still grinning, and hugged the argala to his side. He was naked, not even a towel draped around him. Paul looked away. From his father's even, somewhat muffled, tone he could tell that he'd recently come from the neural sauna. "They told me not to let it out of my sight, said it would go sniffing after anyone, and they were right. . . ."

As suddenly as he'd appeared he was gone, the metal door

flowing shut behind him. For one last instant Paul could see the argala, turning its glowing eyes from his father to himself and back again, lovely and gormless as one of those simulacrums that directed travellers in the HORUS by-ports. Then it was only his own reflection that he stared at, and Claude's voice that he heard calling softly but insistently from the foot of the spiral stairs.

He had planned to wait after class the following morning, to ask Father Dorothy what he knew about it, how a mindless creature could project such a powerful and seemingly effortless torrent of images and sensations; but he could tell from his tutor's cool smile that somehow he had gotten word of their spying. Ira, probably. He was well-meaning but tactless, and Father Dorothy's favorite. Some whispered conference during their private session; and now Father Dorothy's usual expression, of perpetual disappointment tempered with ennui, was shaded with a sharper anger.

So *that* was pointless. Paul could scarcely keep still during class, fidgeting behind his desiccated textbooks, hardly glancing at the monitor's ruby scroll of words and numerals when his turn came to use it. He did take a few minutes to sneak to the back of the room. There a huge and indescribably ancient wooden bookcase held a very few, mostly useless volumes— *Reader's Digest Complete Do-It-Yourself Manual, Robert's Rules of Order, The Ascent of Woman.* He pulled out a natural history text so old that its contents had long since acquired the status of myth.

Argala, Paul read, after flipping past *Apteryx, Aquilegia, Archer, Areca,* each page releasing its whiff of Earth, mildew and silverfish and trees turned to dust. *Adjutant bird: Giant Indian Stork, living primarily in wetlands and feeding upon crustaceans and small amphibians. Status, endangered; perhaps extinct.* There was no illustration.

"Hey, Pathori." Claude bent over his shoulder, pretending to ask a question. Paul ignored him and turned the pages, skipping *Boreal Squid* and *(Bruijn's) Echidna,* pausing to glance at the garishly colored Nebalia Shrimp and the shining damp skin of the Newt, *Amphibian: A kind of eft (Juvenile salamander).* Finally he found the Stork, a simple illustration beside it.

> Tall stately wading bird of family *Ciconiidae,* the best-known species pure white except for black wing tips, long reddish bill, and red feet, and in the nursery the pretended bringer of babies and good fortune.

". . . you hear me?" Claude whispered hoarsely, pinching his ear. Paul closed the book and pushed it away. Without a word he returned to his desk, Claude following him. Father Dorothy raised his head, then went back to explaining the subtleties of written poetry to Ira Claire. Paul settled into his seat. Behind him Claude stood and waited for their tutor to resume his recitation. In a moment Father Dorothy's boyish voice echoed back to them—

> ". . . I make out a few words—   . . . "SORROW,"
> then again "TEARS,"   and "WE HIS FRIENDS MOURN."
> It seems to me that Leucis   must have been dearly beloved . . ."

Paul started as Claude shook him, and the older boy repeated, "I have an idea—I bet he just leaves it alone, when he's not in the room. We could get in there, maybe, and sneak it out . . ."

Paul shrugged. He had been thinking the same thing himself; thinking how he would never have the nerve to do it alone. He glanced up at Father Dorothy.

If he looks at me now, he thought, *I won't do it; I'll talk to him later and figure out something else. . . .*

Behind him Claude hissed and elbowed him sharply. Paul waited, willing their tutor to look up; but the man's head pressed closer to his lovely student as he recited yet another elegiac fragment, wasted on the hopeless Ira—

> "A poet said, 'That music is beloved
> that cannot be sounded.'
> And I think that the choicest life
> is the life that cannot be lived."

"Paul!"

Paul turned and looked at Claude. "We could go when the rest are at dinner again," the older boy said. He too gazed at Ira and Father Dorothy, but with loathing. "All right?"

"All right," Paul agreed miserably, and lowered his head when Father Dorothy cast him a disapproving stare.

Trudging up the steps behind Claude, Paul looked back at the narrow plaza where the sculptures had been. They had passed three people on their way here, a man and two women; the women striding in that defiant way they had, almost swaggering, Paul thought. It was not until they turned the corner that he realized the man had been his mother, and she had not acknowledged him, had not seen him at all.

He sighed and looked down into the abandoned courtyard. Something glittered there, like a fleck of bright dust swimming across his vision. He paused, his hand sliding along the cool brass banister.

On the concrete floor he thought he saw something red, like a discarded blossom. But there were no flowers on Teichman. He felt again that rush of emotion that had come when he embraced the argala, a desire somehow tangled with the smell of brackish water and the sight of a tiny salamander squirming on a mossy bank. But when he leaned over the banister there was nothing there. It must have been a trick of the light, or perhaps a scrap of paper or other debris blow by the air filters. He straightened and started back up the stairs.

That was when he saw the argala. Framed on the open balcony in his father's room, looking down upon the little courtyard. It looked strange from this distance and this angle: less like a woman and more like the sombre figure that had illustrated the Stork in the natural history book. Its foot rested on the edge of the balcony, so it seemed that it had only one leg, and the way its head was tilted he saw only the narrow raised crown, nearly bald because its wispy hair had been pulled back. From here it looked too bony, hardly female at all. A small flood of nausea raced through him. For the first time it struck him that this really *was* an alien creature. Another of the Ascendants' monstrous toys, like the mouthless hydrapithecenes that tended the Pacific hydrofarms, or the pallid bloated forms floating in vats on the research deck of Teichman Station, countless fetuses tethered to them by transparent umbilical cords. And now he had seen and touched one of those monsters. He shuddered and turned away, hurrying after Claude.

But once he stood in the hallway his nausea and anger faded. There was that scent again, lulling him into seeing calm blue water and myriad shapes, garnet salamanders and frogs like candied fruit drifting across the floor. He stumbled into Claude, the older boy swearing and drawing a hand across his face.

"Shit! What's that smell?—" But the older boy's tone was not unpleasant, only befuddled and slightly dreamy.

"The thing," said Paul. They stood before the door to his father's room. "The argala . . ."

Claude nodded, swaying a little, his dark hair hiding his face. Paul had an awful flash of his father opening the door and Claude seeing him as Paul had, naked and doped, with that idiot smile and a tooth missing. But then surely the argala would not have been out on the balcony by itself? He reached for the door and very gently pushed it.

"Here we go," Claude announced as the door slid open. In a moment they stood safely inside.

"God, this is a mess." Claude looked around admiringly. He flicked at a stack of 'files teetering on the edge of a table, grimaced at the puff of dust that rose around his finger. "Ugh. Doesn't he have a server?"

"I guess not." Paul stepped gingerly around heaps of clothes, clean and filthy piled separately, and eyed with distaste a clutter of empty morpha tubes and wine jellies in a corner. A monitor flickered on a table, rows of numerals and gravid shapes tracing the progress of the Breeders Project.

"Not," a voice trilled. On the balcony the argala did not turn, but its bright tone, the way its vestigial wings shivered, seemed to indicate some kind of greeting.

"All right. Let's see it—"

Claude shoved past him, grinning. Paul looked over and for a second the argala's expression was not so much idiotic as tranquil; as though instead of a gritty balcony overlooking shattered concrete, it saw what he had imagined before, water and wriggling live things.

"*Unh.*"

Claude's tone abruptly changed. Paul couldn't help but look: the tenor of the other boy's lust was so intense it sounded like pain. He had his arms around the argala and was thrusting at it, his trousers askew. In his embrace the creature stood with its head thrown back, its cries so rhapsodic that Paul groaned himself and turned away.

In a minute it was over. Claude staggered back, pulling at his clothes and looking around almost frantically for Paul.

"God, that was incredible, that was the *best—*"

Like what could you compare it to, you idiot? Paul leaned against the table with the monitor and tapped a few keys angrily, hoping he'd screw up something; but the scroll continued uninterrupted. Claude walked, dazed, to a chair and slouched into it, scooped up a half-full wine jelly from the floor and sucked at it hungrily.

"Go on, Pathori, you don't want to miss *that!*" Claude laughed delightedly, and looked at the argala. "God, it's amazing, isn't it? What a beauty." His eyes were dewy as he shook his head. "What a fucking thing."

Without answering Paul crossed the room to the balcony. The argala seemed to have forgotten all about them. It stood with one leg drawn up, staring down at the empty courtyard, its topaz eyes glittering. As he drew near to it its smell overwhelmed him, a muskier scent now, almost fetid, like water that had stood too long in an open storage vessel. He felt infuriated by its utter passivity, but somehow excited, too. Before he knew what he was doing he had grabbed it, just as Claude had, and pulled it to him so that its bland child's face looked up at him rapturously.

Afterwards he wept, and beside him the argala crooned, mimicking his sobs. He could dimly hear Claude saying something about leaving, then his friend's voice rising and finally the snick of the door sliding open and shut. He grit his teeth and willed his tears to stop. The argala nestled against him, silent now. His fingers drifted through its thin hair, ran down its back to feel its wings, the bones like metal struts beneath the breath of down. What could a bird possibly know about what he was feeling? he thought fiercely. Let alone a monster like this. A real woman would talk to you, afterwards.

To *complain,* he imagined his father saying.

. . . *never enjoyed it, ever,* his mother's voice echoed back, and Father Dorothy's intoned, *That's what's wrong with it, it's like a machine.*

He pulled the argala closer to him and shut his eyes, inhaling deeply. A wash of yellow that he knew must be sunlight: then he saw that ghostly image of a house again, heard faint cries of laughter. Because it was a woman, too, of course; otherwise how could it recall a house, and children? but then the house broke up into motes of light without color, and he felt the touch of that other, alien mind, delicate and keen as a bird's long bill, probing at his own.

"Well! Good afternoon, good afternoon . . ."

He jumped. His father swayed in the doorway, grinning. "Found my little friend again. Well, come in, come in."

Paul let go of the argala and took a few unsteady steps. "Dad—I'm sorry, I—"

"God, no. Stop." His father waved, knocking a bottle to the floor. "Stay, why don't you. A minute."

But Paul had a horrible flash, saw the argala taken again, the third time in what, half an hour? He shook his head and hurried to the door, face down.

"I can't, Dad. I'm sorry—I was just going by, that's all—"

"Sure, Sure." His father beamed. Without looking he pulled a wine jelly from a shelf and squeezed it into his mouth. "Come by when you have more time, Paul. Glad to see you."

He started to cross to where the argala gazed at him, its huge eyes glowing. Paul ran from the room, the door closing behind him with a muted sigh.

At breakfast the next morning he was surprised to find his mother and Father Dorothy sitting in the twins' usual seats.

"We were talking about your going to school in Tangier," his mother announced, her deep voice a little too loud for the cramped dining hall as she turned back to Father Dorothy. "We could never meet the quotas, of course, but Mother pulled some strings, and—"

Paul sat next to her. Across the table, Claude and Ira and the twins were gulping down the rest of their breakfast. Claude mumbled a goodbye and stood to leave, Ira behind him.

"See you later, Father," Ira said, smiling. Father Dorothy waved.

"When?" said Paul.

"In a few weeks. It's nearly Athyr now"—that was what they called this cycle—". . . which means it's July down there. The next drop is on the Fortieth."

He didn't pay much attention to the rest of it. There was no point: his mother and Father Dorothy had already decided everything, as they always did. He wondered how his father had ever been able to get the argala here at all.

A hand clamped his shoulder and Paul looked up.

"—must go now," Father Dorothy was saying as he motioned for a server to clean up. "Class starts in a few minutes. Walk with me, Paul?"

He shook his mother's hand and left her nodding politely as the next shift of diners filed into the little room.

"You've been with it," the tutor said after a few minutes. They took the long way to the classroom, past the cylinders where vats of nutriment were stored and wastewater recycled, past the spiral stairs that led to his father's chamber. Where the hallway forked Father Dorothy hesitated, then went to the left, towards the women's quarters. "I could tell, you know—it has a—"

He inhaled, then made a delicate grimace. "It has a smell."

They turned and entered the Solar Walk. Paul remained at his side, biting his lip and feeling an unexpected anger churning inside him.

"I like the way it smells," he said, and waited for Father Dorothy to look grim. Instead his tutor paused in front of the window. "I love it."

He thought Father Dorothy would retort sharply; but instead he only raised his hands and pressed them against the window. Outside two of the HORUS repair units floated past, on their interminable and futile rounds. When it seemed the silence would go on forever, his tutor said, "It can't love you. You know that. It's an abomination—an animal—"

"Not really," Paul replied, but weakly.

Father Dorothy flexed his hands dismissively. "It can't love you. It's a geneslave. How could it love anything?"

His tone was not angry but questioning, as though he really thought Paul might have an answer. And for a moment Paul thought of explaining to him: about how it felt, how it seemed like it was showing him things—the sky, the house, the little creatures crawling in the moss—things that perhaps it *did* feel something for. But before he could say anything Father Dorothy turned and began striding back in the direction they'd come. Paul hurried after him in silence.

As they turned down the last hallway, Father Dorothy said, "It's an ethical matter, really. Like having intercourse with a child, or someone who's mentally deficient. It can't respond, it's incapable of anything—"

"But I love it," Paul repeated stubbornly.

"Aren't you listening to me?" Father Dorothy did sound angry, now. "*It* can't love *you*." His voice rose shrilly. "How could something like *that* tell you that it *loved* you!? And *you* can't love it—god, how could you love *anything*, you're only a boy!" He stopped in the doorway and looked down at him, then shook his head, in pity or disgust Paul couldn't tell. "Get in there," Father Dorothy said at last, and gently pushed him through the door.

He waited until the others were asleep before slipping from his bunk and heading back to his father's quarters. The lights had dimmed to simulate night; other than that there was no difference, in the way anything looked or smelled or sounded. He walked through the violet corridors with one hand on the cool metal wall, as though he was afraid of falling.

They were leaving just as he reached the top of the spiral stairs. He saw his father first, then two others, other researchers from the Breeders Project. They were laughing softly, and his father threw his arms around one man's shoulders and murmured something that made the other man shake his head and grin. They wore loose robes open in the front and headed in the opposite direction, towards the neural sauna. They didn't see the boy pressed against the wall, watching as they turned the corner and disappeared.

He waited for a long time. He wanted to cry, tried to make

himself cry; but he couldn't. Beneath his anger and shame and sadness there was still too much of that other feeling, the anticipation and arousal and inchoate tenderness that he only knew one word for, and Father Dorothy thought that was absurd. So he waited until he couldn't stand it anymore, and went inside.

His father had made some feeble attempt to clean the place up. The clothing had been put away, and table tops and chairs cleared of papers. Fine white ash sifted across the floor, and there was a musty smell of tobacco beneath the stronger odors of semen and wine jelly. The argala's scent ran through all of it like a fresh wind.

He left the door open behind him, no longer caring if someone found him there or not. He ran his hands across his eyes and looked around for the argala.

It was standing where it usually did, poised on the balcony with its back to him. He took a step, stopped. He thought he could hear something, a very faint sound like humming; but then it was gone. He craned his neck to see what it was the creature looked at but saw nothing; only that phantom flicker of red in the corner of his eye, like a mote of ruby dust. He began walking again, softly, when the argala turned to look at him.

Its eyes were wide and fervent as ever, its tangerine mouth spun into that same adoring smile; but even as he started for it, his arms reaching to embrace it, it turned from him and jumped.

For an instant it hung in the air and he could imagine it flying, could almost imagine that perhaps it thought its wings would carry it across the courtyard or safely to the ground. But in that instant he caught sight of its eyes, and they were not a bird's eyes but a woman's; and she was not flying but falling.

He must have cried out, screamed for help. Then he just hung over the balcony, staring down at where it lay motionless. He kept hoping that maybe it would move again but it did not, only lay there twisted and still.

But as he stared at it it changed. It had been a pale creature to begin with. Now what little color it had was leached away, as though it were bleeding into the concrete; but really there was hardly any blood. Its feathers grew limp, like fronds plucked from the water, their gold fading to a grey that was all but colorless. Its head was turned sideways, its great wide eye open and staring up. As he watched the golden orb slowly dulled to yellow and then a dirty white. When someone finally came to drag it away its feathers trailed behind it in the dust. Then nothing remained of it at all except for the faintest breath of ancient summers hanging in the stale air.

For several days he wouldn't speak to anyone, not even responding to Claude's cruelties or his father's ineffectual attempts at kindness. His mother made a few calls to Tangier and, somehow, the drop was changed to an earlier date in Athyr. On the afternoon he was to leave they all gathered, awkwardly, in the dormitory. Father Dorothy seemed sad that he was going, but also relieved. The twins tried to get him to promise to write, and Ira cried. But, still without speaking, Paul left the room and walked down to the courtyard.

No one had even bothered to clean it. A tiny curl of blood stained the concrete a rusty color, and he found a feather, more like a furry yellowish thread than anything else, stuck to the wall. He took the feather and stared at it, brought it to his face and inhaled. There was nothing.

He turned to leave, then halted. At the corner of his eye something moved. He looked back and saw a spot on the ground directly beneath his father's balcony. Shoving the feather into his pocket he walked slowly to investigate.

In the dust something tiny wriggled, a fluid arabesque as long as his finger. Crouching on his heels, he bent over and cupped it in his palm. A shape like an elongated tear of blood, only with two bright black dots that were its eyes and, beside each of those, two perfect flecks of gold.

An eft, he thought, recognizing it from the natural history book and from the argala's vision. A juvenile salamander.

Giant Indian stork, feeding upon crustaceans and small amphibians.

He raised it to his face, feeling it like a drop of water slithering through his fingers. When he sniffed it it smelled, very faintly, of mud.

There was no way it could have gotten here. Animals never

got through by-port customs, and besides, were there even things like this still alive, Below? He didn't know.

But then how did it get here?

A miracle, he thought, and heard Father Dorothy's derisive voice—*How could something like that tell you that it loved you?* For the first time since the argala's death, the rage and despair that had clenched inside him uncoiled. He moved his hand, to see it better, and with one finger stroked its back. Beneath its skin, scarlet and translucent, its ribs moved rapidly in and out, in and out, so fine and frail they might have been drawn with a hair.

An eft.

He knew it would not live for very long—what could he feed it, how could he keep it?—but somehow the argala had survived, for a little while at least, and even then the manner of its dying had been a miracle of sorts. Paul stood, his hands folding over the tiny creature, and with his head bowed— though none of them would really see, or understand, what it was he carried—he walked up the stairs and through the hall-way and back into the dormitory where his bags waited, past the other boys, past his mother and father and Father Dorothy, not saying anything, not even looking at them; holding close against his chest a secret, a miracle, a salamander.

IN THE MONTH OF ATHYR
Elizabeth Hand

I wrote this amidst my first three novels and wanted to use their milieu as a backdrop. Connie Willis's "All My Darling Daughters" has a nice space station setting, which also seemed like a good idea: I liked the notion of an insular culture giving birth to its own sexual depravities, which over time would come to be considered normal. The rest was just spun out of the fictional history of my novels' Ascendants and their geneslaves.

Cavafy's work has seen me through four novels, now, and innumerable stories; the title of this one was taken from his poem of the same name. In the ancient Egyptian calendar, Athyr is the month which corresponds roughly to our October, the traditional time to honor the dead.